UNCHARTED WATERS

Printed in Australia
First Printing: September 2022
Shawline Publishing Group Pty Ltd
www.shawlinepublishing.com.au

Paperback ISBN 978-1-9228-5018-8
eBook ISBN 978-1-9228-5025-6

A catalogue record for this work is available from the National Library of Australia

UNCHARTED WATERS

PETER CRUSKALL

Dedication

Throughout my early teenage years every evening my mother would invariably be juggling a myriad of household chores while striving to have dinner on the table at five thirty. Somehow amidst the daily grind of cleaning, washing, cooking, shopping, dog feeding and organising activities for my three younger siblings she still managed to find the time, energy and enthusiasm to supervise and critique my homework.

Mum was proud of her verbal and written English language skills and her interest piqued even more whenever I brought out my English book. She used to particularly delight in reminding me of her spelling prowess, and justifiably so. She was extremely good. Whilst I passed seven of my eight subjects in my final year's school examination it must have been a huge disappointment to her when I failed English, of all subjects.

Little did I know that decades later I would have the capacity to put pen to paper and write a novel.

This is for you, Mum.

Contents

Australian Federal Police Headquarters　　1
Oceanic Hotel Darling Harbour　　10
Australian Federal Police Headquarters　　16
Coral Sea Queensland　　18
Luxe Gym Newtown　　24
Chinatown Sydney　　27
Coral Sea Queensland　　31
Oceanic Hotel Darling Harbour　　36
Unnamed Bay　　39
Bondi Beach　　44
Coral Sea Queensland　　48
AMSA Control Room Canberra　　51
East of Hydrographers Passage　　54
Macquarie Suite – Oceanic Hotel　　57
Bennelong Room Treasury　　61
AMSA Control Room Canberra　　66
Balmain Inner West Sydney　　69
Sydney Daily News Surry Hills　　72
Milk and Honey Café　　75
Macquarie Suite　　80
Oceanic Hotel Corporate Offices　　83
Desk of Julie-Anne　　85
Jimmy Chan's Café Burwood　　88
Chinatown Sydney　　92
Bayside Café Pyrmont　　97
Maritime Border Command Canberra　　100
Bayside Café Pyrmont　　106
Desk of Julie-Anne　　110
Alegrias Spanish Tapas Restaurant　　113

Bondi Junction 118

Tip of My Tongue 121

Port of Brisbane 125

Macquarie Suite 129

ABF Offices Brisbane Airport 137

Sydney Daily News 145

AFP Headquarters 150

AFP Headquarters 155

Oceanic Hotel Darling Harbour 158

Sydney Daily News 161

Bennelong Room 166

Bennelong Room 172

Macquarie Suite 177

AFP Headquarters 179

Maritime Border Command Brisbane 183

Consulate General Cocktail Reception 190

Consulate General Cocktail Reception 196

The QV Wine Bar 203

Unnamed Bay 209

Seafarer's Mission Brisbane Port 215

Golden Phoenix Restaurant 218

Bayside Café Pyrmont 225

Macquarie Suite 232

Balmain Inner West Sydney 237

ABF Offices Brisbane Airport 244

Milk and Honey Cafe 248

AFP Headquarters 251

MBC / AFP Conference Call 257

Melissa's Townhouse 262

Melissa's Townhouse 270

Julie-Anne's Desk 275

Rogue Café Surry Hills 282

Macquarie Suite 288

Julie-Anne's Apartment Newtown 293

Sydney Daily News 301

Oceanic Security Control 305

Chinese Consulate General 308

North Bondi Fish 316

Dolphins Point 324

Oceanic Security Control   333
Jack and Danielle Sappho Cafe   338
Oceanic Security Control   343
Macquarie Suite   346
Treasury Department   351
AFP Headquarters   355
RPA Emergency Ward   360
Macquarie Suite   366
Central Station Sydney   369
Randwick Safe House   375
AFP Headquarters   382
Oceanic Security Control   386
AFP Headquarters   390
Tong-Li – Wujiang District China   398
Danielle's Apartment   401
Randwick Safe House   405
Macquarie Suite   408
Oceanic Security Operations Room   412
Treasury Department   417
Oceanic Security Operations Room   423
Danielle's Apartment   429
AFP Headquarters   431
AFP HQ Conference Room   437
AFP Headquarters   442
AFP Headquarters   447
362 Sussex Street Sydney   455
AFP Headquarters   461
AFP Headquarters   468
Chinese Consulate General   475
AFP Headquarters   478
AFP Headquarters   483
AFP Headquarters   485
The Boathouse   494
Balmain Inner West Sydney   505
Epilogue. AMSA Control Room Canberra   513
About the Author   516

Australian Federal Police Headquarters
January 2020

The MBC's Security Operation Centre in Canberra had identified a suspect foreign vessel and tracked its movements as it headed into Australian territorial waters. Now the unnamed vessel was only sixty nautical miles north-east of Newcastle and thirty nautical miles offshore from picturesque Nelson Bay. What was of particular concern to the MBC, was an Australian commercial fishing vessel, the Wayfarer, which had now rendezvoused with the foreign vessel.

Alistair Nicholson, the captain of the Cape Byron, one of the Australian Border Force's new Cape Class patrol boats, had been alerted to the potential for an at-sea transfer of illegal contraband. As a result, the Byron had departed Newcastle at dusk and was now heading in an east-north-easterly direction at a steady twenty-five knots towards the vessels. Tonight, there was a full moon, but fortunately for Nicholson, there was a thick covering of cloud that would aid their stealthy approach. He had also switched off the Byron's Automatic Identification Signal transponder. If either suspect vessel was monitoring marine traffic websites, there would be no sign of the Cape Byron on their monitors.

Detective Jack Wagner from the Australian Federal Police was part of a joint task force with Detective Michael Sanderson from the New South Wales Police and Agent Charlie Romano from MBC. The men stood on the bridge, looking out into the darkness.

'How long until we reach the target vessels, Captain?'

'We should reach the rendezvous point in thirty minutes, give or take a minute or two, Jack.' The captain turned to face the assembled law enforcement officers. 'Okay, here's the plan,. gents. Jack, you and Sanderson will take two of my men with you in one of the RHIB's and board the Wayfarer. Agent Romano knows what we're looking for, so he will have four of my guys with him in the second RHIB and board and search the foreign vessel. Charlie, your crew will wear tactical gas masks as a failsafe.'

'Is that really necessary, Captain?'

'We have no intelligence on the contents or conditions aboard the foreign vessel, so I'm taking no chances. These masks are the ultimate in military-grade technology and provide comprehensive protection against the full spectrum of chemical, biological and radiological agents. Your safety is my priority. Now, I assume you're all armed.'

'Yes,' they replied in unison.

'Captain,' Jack heard the Executive Officer call out fifteen minutes later. 'What is it, XO?'

'The two vessels have separated. The foreign vessel is heading due east and the local fishing vessel appears to be heading directly for Nelson Bay.'

'Thank you, XO.'

The ABF captain had a decision to make: pursue the foreign fishing vessel or chase down and board the Australian commercial fishing vessel.

Jack looked across to Nicholson. 'I guess it's decision time, captain.'

The captain looked down his prominent nose at Jack. 'Thank you for that timely reminder, detective,' he said with intended sarcasm. 'With millions of square kilometres of predominantly empty ocean to the east and twenty-five million Australian citizens to the west, it's a no-brainer.'

Jack knew full-well about Australia's Exclusive Economic Zone, extending into the Pacific Ocean to a distance of two hundred nautical miles. No doubt the foreign vessel would be hightailing it eastwards at full throttle back into international waters. Nicholson made the appropriate decision.

'XO, set a course for 32.65 degrees South and 152.41 degrees East.' 'Yes, Captain.'

'Change of plans, gentlemen. The suspect fishing vessel appears to be heading for Nelson Bay, so based on our speed and that of the Wayfarer, I've set a course to intersect them well before they reach the marina. Wagner, you, Sanderson, and Romano should be able to handle this, but I'm sending Able Seaman Docherty with you to navigate just in case. For safety reasons, when we arrive at our rendezvous point, I'm going to keep the Byron one hundred metres off from the Wayfarer and stand watch.'

'Captain, we are now five hundred metres from the target vessel,' the XO called out across the bridge fifteen minutes later.

'Thank you, XO. Okay gents, your RHIB will be lowered by now and you need to be aboard asap.' As the team left the bridge, the captain turned on the Byron's powerful spotlight.

Five minutes later, their Rigid Hulled Inflatable Boat was skimming across the placid waters at a comfortable twenty-five knots towards the Wayfarer. As the boarding party drew closer, they were momentarily stunned as the sky ahead of them lit up like daylight. The captain had turned on the Byron's powerful spotlight and his voice now boomed out from behind them.

'Wayfarer, this is the Australian Border Force vessel, Cape Byron, switch off your engines immediately. I repeat, switch off your engines immediately.' Whomever was at the helm of the pursued vessel ignored the order and continued on their course towards the distant coastline. Captain Nicholson repeated the message.

Jack heard a burst of short, sharp, shots in reply. It sounded to him like an AK47 assault rifle. 'Get down,' he shouted as he grabbed Sanderson's arm. The men, all except the Able Seaman, at the helm dived for the floor of the boat. 'Jesus Christ, they're actually firing upon an Australian naval vessel.'

Sanderson hit the deck next to him. 'Yeah, and unfortunately for us it's ours, Jack,' he replied as the AK's rounds whistled overhead. Able Seaman Docherty at the helm of the RHIB, now crouching behind the console, wrenched the steering wheel hard to his left to avoid the incoming fire. The men heaved sighs of relief as the RHIB retreated into the darkness and out of the shadows of the Byron's spotlight.

'Well, I guess the Captain got his answer,' Jack replied.

Romano inclined his head. 'And knowing Captain Nicholson, he won't take kindly to that.'

'Well, whatever they're smuggling, it must be worth a fortune,' offered Sanderson.

Captain Nicholson watched on as two spotlighted men opened up on the RHIB. 'XO, have the gunners man the 50 Cals and be ready to fire upon the Wayfarer.' Using live munitions in Australian waters without approval was a no-no, but other than retreating, Nicholson knew of no other means to stop the incoming fire. He had the safety of the men in the RHIB to consider. He thought of one of his favourite cliches. *It's better to ask for forgiveness than seek permission.* Damn right.

'XO, contact the RHIB and confirm their status and position.'

'Yes, sir, right away.'

The Byron maintained its course and the captain switched off the spotlight while the machine guns were being readied.

'Captain, the RHIB is four hundred metres west-south-west of our position. It is three hundred metres off of the Wayfarer and travelling further south-west to avoid the attack. All on board are safe.'

The pinging of rounds off the aluminium hull interrupted the conversation. The Wayfarer's crew, having lost sight of the RHIB in the night's darkness, turned their attention to the Cape Byron.

They had to know that firing upon a heavily armed navy patrol boat was an enormous risk, so whatever illicit cargo the Wayfarer was transporting, it had to be worth it.

'Okay, XO, let's keep it that way. Initiate fire, but the gunners are to aim above the vessel. I want to avoid any casualties at all costs, and we need whatever intel those guys can provide us with. Just warning shots for now.'

'Roger that, Captain.'

'Detective Wagner, this is the Captain,' the RHIB crew heard over the radio. Jack depressed the push-to-talk button on his headset. 'Go for Wagner.'

'Wagner, we are going to fire off a few warning shots and see if that deters them. Maintain your position for now and await further instructions. Is that clear?'

'Roger that, Captain.'

Jack looked left towards the Wayfarer and then swivelled to the right and drew an imaginary line in his head between the two. 'Able Seaman, the Byron is about to open up with the 50 Cals. Are you certain we're out of the line of the fire?' Jack asked.

'Yes. We're about two hundred metres to the south of the Wayfarer. We should be fine.'

'Okay, let's stay down just in case.'

Brat-a-tat-tat, brat-a-tat-tat, they heard, as the Byron's powerful .50 calibre machine guns opened up on the Wayfarer. 'Jesus, when I joined the police force, I never thought the day would come when I would be involved in a gun battle on the high seas,' Sanderson said.

'Expect the unexpected comes to mind, Michael.'

Moments later, there was a deathly silence. Both the Byron and Wayfarer's crews had ceased firing. Able Seaman Docherty rose from his crouch and risked a look across to the Wayfarer. 'Shit,' Jack heard him say as he became unbalanced and rolled across the floor as the RHIB veered sharply to the right and quickly accelerated.

'What's going on?' Jack asked as he righted himself.

'The Wayfarer's on fire.'

'So much for warning shots.' Jack rose to his feet and looked towards the burning fishing vessel. The wheelhouse was ablaze, and he could see two shadowy figures standing at the stern silhouetted in the glow. One of the 50 Cal's projectiles had obviously hit metal and the resultant spark had ignited the fire. 'I assume you have fire extinguishers on board?' Jack asked.

'There's two A2s below the console.'

As the muzzle flashes from the Wayfarer ceased, the captain turned on the spotlight again. The fire onboard the Wayfarer was providing sufficient light that she was easily detectable, but he needed visibility of the RHIB as well. 'Okay, let's go check this out, XO. Steady as she goes.'

Across the calm waters, Jack saw that the Cape Byron was on the move again, but still about four hundred metres from the burning fishing vessel. 'Able Seaman, can you manouevre in close to the stern?' Jack yelled, trying to be heard above the powerful diesel engine.

'Sure, but what are you proposing?'

'We need to secure the assailants first then we can think about suppressing the fire. I need you to drop me off.'

'Shouldn't we wait for the Byron, detective?'

'There's no time. If that fishing vessel blows, we'll lose whatever contraband they're protecting and also any potential intel from those on board.'

'Okay,' the Able Seaman replied.

'Look, I'm pretty sure that there are only two of them. I should be fine. Wait until I have them under control, then you take Sanderson and Romano around to the port side.' Jack handed them both a fire extinguisher, and then, wiping the salt water spray from his face, he retrieved his Glock 22 from its holster. 'Okay, let's do this.' The Able Seaman pushed forward on the throttle and the bow of their RHIB lifted sharply as it raced towards the burning vessel.

'Jack, did you see that?' Sanderson said, stunned, as he looked back to see Jack checking the slide on his Glock.

'No, what?'

'Two guys just jumped overboard.'

Jack wiped spray from his face again and looked towards the Wayfarer. 'Can you see them?' he asked.

'Detective, what do you want to do now? Shouldn't we rescue them?' The young Able Seaman asked.

'No,' was Jack's firm reply. 'We don't know who or what is onboard, and we need to secure whatever evidence we can. But first we need to extinguish that fire.' Jack looked towards the fishing vessel as they neared. The wheelhouse was alight, but to his untrained eye it didn't look out of control. Yet. 'Get as close as the heat will allow and then we'll let the guys do their thing with the extinguishers.' As they approached, he looked past the stern of the Wayfarer, but couldn't see any sign of the boat's former occupants. Turning back to the fire, Jack watched on as Sanderson and Romano squeezed their extinguisher's handles together to discharge the foaming agent. The RHIB was now about five metres off the Wayfarer and the foam from the extinguishers was only just reaching the flames.

'This is not working. Take us around to the stern. The guys need to be on board to get to the seat of the flames,' Jack called out to Docherty.

Thirty seconds later, the RHIB pulled up to the stern and Jack legged Sanderson and Romano on board before passing them the extinguishers. He watched on as they swept the nozzles from side to side directing the foam at the base of the flames. Within a minute, the flames began to subside, and the smoke started to dissipate.

'Okay, let's go find what was so important to these guys. Charlie, bring that extinguisher. Able Seaman Docherty, can you start a grid search for the two missing assailants?'

'On it, detective.'

With the wheelhouse still smoldering, the three men began their search of the vessel, Sanderson to the bow, Romano at the stern and

Jack went down the stairs to the hold. Sanderson spotted what looked like a square shaped box covered with an olive-coloured tarpaulin. *Here we go.* He pulled back the tarp, only to be disappointed. It was covering a large vegetable crate containing cane fishing pots. 'Bugger.' He walked along the starboard side of the boat to the stern. 'Anything, Charlie?'

'Nada. Not a thing.'

'Down here,' they heard Jack call out. One by one, they climbed down the ladder to the cargo hold. Jack was holding a steel ring that was attached to a sheet of flooring and pointing down into the dark hole in the floor. 'Here you go gents. Now we know why they risked firing upon an armed ABF vessel. What do you reckon the street value of this is, Michael?'

Sanderson grabbed a torch from a workbench, depressed a button and pointed it down into the hole. He counted five rows across, ten down and eight layers deep. 'If my math's are any good, that's about four hundred kilos there. A street value of something over a hundred million.'

'Jesus, Michael.' Jack wiped sweat from his forehead with the back of his hand. 'Charlie, you better call this in to Nicholson asap.'

'Jack to Able Seaman Docherty.'

'Go for Docherty,' he replied, backing off the throttle.

'Any sign of our drug smugglers out there?'

'Unfortunately, no. I reckon I've covered an area of a couple of square kilometres and there's no sign of them. It's pretty dark out here, so we may need the Byron's spotlight if we're going to be any chance of finding them.

'Jack, this is the Byron. We need to find those guys asap. Are you guys okay on board for a while?'

'Roger that Captain.'

Two hours later, after an unsuccessful search for the missing drug smugglers, the captain had advised Marine Rescue NSW and the Nelson Bay Police of their last known location. It would be up to them now to resume the search at first light. The Wayfarer was tied off to the Byron and was now being towed in a west-south-west direction at twenty knots to the Port of Newcastle.

The clouds had drifted further out into the Pacific Ocean, and Jack and Michael Sanderson were lying on the decking of the Wayfarer, looking up at the maze of constellations.

'There's the Southern Cross, Jack.'

'I see it, but I bet you don't know what that cluster is to its left?' Jack replied as he pointed to the sky off the port side of the vessel. He handed Sanderson the binoculars he had found in the wheelhouse.

'Oh, yeah, I've got it now. What's it called?'

'The Jewel Box. Apparently, the astronomer who discovered the cluster thought the stars resembled pieces of jewellery.'

'That makes sense. I imagine this is what the hordes of tourists do at night on those cruises, Jack.'

'Yeah, but the difference being they're not sitting on four hundred kilos of coke, Michael.'

'Now wouldn't that make for some sort of cruise.'

$$\textbf{2}$$

Oceanic Hotel Darling Harbour
Six Weeks Later Sunday 1st March 2020

Li Qiang released a muted sigh as he leant back on the plush, red velvet sofa of the Oceanic Hotel and Casino's thirty eighth floor penthouse suite overlooking Darling Harbour. Whenever he visited this beautiful city, he was feted by the casino's executives and always afforded the use of the Macquarie Suite, named after one of the colony's early governors. As a valued client of both the hotel and casino, Li wouldn't have accepted anything less. He often wondered what the erstwhile former governor would have made of something so luxurious, perched four hundred feet above the fledgling colony he oversaw nearly two hundred years ago.

Li had arrived at Mascot Airport mid-afternoon following a tiresome overnight fourteen-hour flight from Shanghai. Normally he handled the flight's duration with considerable ease, and thanks to his flatbed, managed to avoid being overcome by jetlag. On this particular occasion, the Qantas Dreamliner had been forced to divert around a cyclone hovering above Papua New Guinea, adding two hours to his journey. The turbulence had unnerved him, so he was looking forward to a calming release prior his dinner engagement. He had arrived late, and she would be tired of waiting for him, but that was of little concern to him.

He kept her waiting even longer while he indulged himself with a long, hot shower. Now he was dressed only in a Frette Milano bathrobe, his favourite, and held a tumbler of Glenlivet fifteen-year-old in his left hand and a Monte Christo in his right. Standing in front of him was this woman of impeccable appearance. She called herself Sophie Zhao, but Li preferred her traditional name of Kaili Wang, which meant 'beautiful' in his native language. Standing at just under six foot, she was statuesque, yet a tad curvaceous in the right places, exuded the exotic looks he favoured, had a rich olive complexion, lustrous black locks and intelligent dark eyes. Li had made use of her services numerous times when visiting Sydney, and this woman was suitably accustomed to his needs.

As usual, she accessed the suite using her swipe card. Shrouded with dread at the task ahead, she had waited for an inordinate length of time in the suite for Li's impending arrival. As was his want, she was dressed only in the matching women's bathrobe and a pair of fire engine red Jimmy Choo Aveline 100s.

After removing her heels and as seductively as she could muster, disrobing, Sophie went to work just as she had done so obediently on many occasions prior. She promised herself that one day she would find a way to extricate herself from the hold he had over her. For now, though, she had little choice but to give in to his demands. She closed her eyes and thought only of the promise she had made to herself. Li Qiang meant strong in Chinese, but she thought him anything but, and for one brief instant she held unwanted power over him. Although not one for astrology, Sophie thanked her lucky stars that she was acutely aware that a male orgasm releases a cocktail of chemicals from the brain that made men drowsy afterwards. And this was always the case with Li, allowing her to make a quick exit.

'I have another little task for you today, Kaili Wang.'

God, she hated that name. She mistakenly thought that he had drifted off on the sofa and was disappointed when he called her name, just as she was dressing. All she wanted to do was head for the door and go home for a long, hot shower of her own.

'I have someone else for you to entertain on my behalf this afternoon, Kaili Wang.'

Sophie was surprised as Li handed her an envelope which, judging by its thickness, contained a generous wad of cash, more than she was accustomed to. She wasn't in the right headspace for another client, but given the sizeable amount of money he had just given her, she was obliged to be accommodating.

'I have to go out to a meeting, so make yourself at home while I shower and dress,' he said.

Li returned to the vast living room dressed in his favourite charcoal grey Armani suit, watermelon coloured Hermes tie, matching pocket square and Louis Vuitton Minister Derby shoes. He was ready for business. 'I think you'll enjoy your second task much more than your first,' Li chortled as he was closing the suite door behind him. Li knew Kaili Wang despised every minute she spent with him, but he couldn't care less. After all, she was well-rewarded for her services.

Sophie went to the bathroom and freshened up for her next appointment. Li had never arranged another assignment for her previously, so she wondered what his reasoning was, because, as she well aware, he didn't do anything without an ulterior motive. She was strictly an escort and masseur, and it was only Li's hold over her that necessitated her providing him with other less honourable services.

A short while later Sophie heard the doorbell chime. She looked through the security peephole and was surprised to see a smartly dressed man in business attire standing outside the door. She thought she recognised him from somewhere, so opened the door and introduced herself.

'Wow,' the man said, clearly astonished by the appearance. 'Hi, I'm Tony,' he said, having regained his composure.

This makes a nice change, she thought to herself. He was a tall, athletic, handsome man with blonde hair and deep blue eyes. 'I'm Sophie, come in, Tony.'

They sat on the expansive sofa sipping Li's Glenlivet and making stilted conversation. It was apparent to Sophie that neither of them knew exactly what was supposed to occur. Tony was being a gentleman and Li hadn't told her what was expected of her. She had no intention of being there when Li returned, so she thought she had better expedite things. She leaned across, placed her neatly manicured hand on the man's thigh and said, 'shall we start.'

He leaned close, cupping Sophie's cheek with his hand and kissed her. Sophie hated kissing clients, but at least this guy was handsome, and appealingly, quite bashful, so she allowed him to get away with a cheeky kiss. *Bashful didn't last long.*

His hand moved from her cheek, to behind her head and he held her in place as he kissed her passionately. Sophie felt his other hand massaging her breasts. 'They are magnificent,' he whispered.

She had read this completely wrong. The gentleman had disappeared quickly; she needed to slow him down before he got too far ahead of himself, and she lost more control over his behaviour. Maybe she had been momentarily charmed by his good looks and shy demeanour. She slapped his errant hand. 'I was referring to the massage, nothing else, Tony,' she said. 'Would you like a massage or not?' She asked, pulling back and sliding sideways on the sofa and out of his reach. She didn't know who this man was to Li or what had been promised to this presumptuous man, but anything more than a massage wasn't on the menu.

'Yeah, why not.'

'Okay, why don't you get undressed and lay on the rug while I gather my massage oils.' When she returned to the living room, his muscular, naked body was face down on the plush carpet with his head resting on one of the sofa cushions. Sophie pulled her dress up over her head and draped it over the arm of the sofa. She knelt alongside him and massaged his back, shoulders, thighs, and lower legs.

'Aaahh, that's just wonderful, Soph,' he groaned.

Ugh, first Kaili Wang and now Soph. 'Stay there and I'll massage your neck and relieve some stress.' She clasped her index finger and thumb on either side of his neck and began pulsing as she moved up and down.

'That's just fabulous; I can feel the stress pouring out of me.'

She hated the next part of the massage, but she was a professional. 'Okay, roll over please.'

As he obeyed, he noticed she was naked except for her lacy French underwear. 'Have I told you your breasts are magnificent?'

'You might have mentioned it once or twice,' she chuckled, endeavouring to keep this transaction cordial. *Okay, things are back on track,* she thought. Then, as he completed the roll onto his back, she noticed he was rock hard. If it had been a boyfriend's, she might have been impressed.

'Look what I've got for you, Sophie,' he boasted, the intent being obvious.

'That belongs to you, so you keep that to yourself, Tony,' she said, her tone calm but assertive. Just as she finished speaking, he swiftly reached up, placed his hand behind her head once more and pulled her down towards him.

'No, that's all yours, Sophie.'

She reflexively twisted her body, fixed her arm in a ninety-degree arc and brought her elbow joint crashing heavily into his stomach.

'Oh, fuck, what did you do that for, you bitch?' he bellowed, gasping for air.

'Get your clothes on and get out now,' she yelled. Sophie rose to her feet and took a step backwards, readying herself for any further aggressive behaviour.

'You'll pay for this when Li finds out, you bitch.'

'Do you want me to hit you again?'

'Fuck off, I'm out of here,' he snarled.

Sophie picked up his clothes and threw them at him, his belt buckle hitting him in the face. *Who does this guy think he is?* She would find out soon enough.

She was embarrassed. For such an experienced escort, how had she allowed herself to get into such a compromising position? She had only permitted him a cheeky kiss to break the awkward impasse on the sofa. A rookie mistake. It would never happen again.

Since she was last in Li's suite, Sophie had been racking her brain, seeking a way to extricate herself from this situation. She knew she didn't have enough tangible evidence of any of the illicit activities that Li was involved in. And his subtle threats of intimidation against her family in China would only be her word against his, so she couldn't go to the police for help. Besides, she was an escort, so what sympathy or cooperation would she receive anyway.

There was one avenue that she had been considering, now even more so since the distasteful episode with Tony. It was time to make the call. The person she would contact had a reputation as a fierce investigator, and as a woman, she may be more empathetic to Sophie's situation. Or so Sophie hoped.

$$\left(\begin{array}{c}3\end{array}\right)$$

Australian Federal Police Headquarters
Sunday 1st March

'What are you doing here, boss?'

'I could ask you the same thing,' John Robertson replied, pulling up a chair to Jack's desk. The Deputy Commissioner of the Australian Federal Police was wearing a light blue polo shirt, denim jeans, and tan loafers. This was the first time Jack had seen his boss in casual clothes. He seemed to be in a relaxed mood for a change as well.

'I'm just closing out the file on the Nelson Bay coke seizure.' The AFP, in a joint operation with the New South Wales Police, Australian Border Force and Maritime Border Command, had seized four hundred kilos of cocaine with a street value of over one hundred million dollars from a fishing vessel off the coast of Sydney.

'That's very diligent of you, but shouldn't you be spending the day with your girlfriend?'

Jack felt a shiver up his spine at his boss' use of the word girlfriend. 'JA's gone shopping for the day, so I thought I may as well use the time to catch up on some paperwork.'

'Listen, Jack, I can tell you from experience that a man can score some serious brownie points by accompanying his wife or girlfriend on a shopping excursion.'

'I can't think of anything more boring, especially in bohemian Newtown.'

'You've got to give a little, but I promise you'll receive a lot in return.'

'It's okay, JA is coming to dinner at my place tonight.'

'That's good. Well, since you're here, let's talk business.'

Jack leaned back in his chair and crossed his legs. 'Sure boss.'

'That seizure will seriously impact the supply to cartels, triads and gangs across the state—probably the whole country. They can't afford to let that occur again. They'll be seeking out new and innovative ways to avoid a repeat. Supply will be severely depleted for some time and the bad guys have dealers and customers to please. We need to stay vigilant. Hit the streets and talk to your informants.

'I wonder what happened to the guys from the Wayfarer. I doubt they could have swum to the shore. Maybe they drowned or were taken by sharks.' He grimaced as another possibility was considered. 'Or maybe they were picked up by their drug running compatriots.'

'We'll never know, so let's just focus on what's in front of us, Jack.'

'I'm meeting with one of my informants tomorrow. He's usually pretty clued in, so we'll see what he has to say.'

'Okay, that's a start. Now, I'll be off to the club for a couple of schooners then.'

Jack gave his boss a sideways glance. 'Whatever happened to brownie points?'

'Oh, I've earned my stripes over the years. Don't you worry about that.'

Coral Sea Queensland

The Chinese Horizon, a Hong Kong registered dry cargo ship of twenty-one thousand gross tonnage, was making its way south from Dalian on the southern tip of the Liaodong Peninsula in northeast China to Brisbane, and then onto Sydney and Melbourne. As always, Captain Hsin Han was careful to adhere to the GBRMPA mandated General Use Zone or Designated Shipping Areas when navigating through the notoriously shallow, shoal riddled waters of the Great Barrier Reef Marine Park. He knew all too well that many freighters had previously run aground on the shoals within the park causing outrage and condemnation among the local, national and international environmental organisations and maritime authorities.

Subsequent AMSA investigations had led to ships being confiscated, captains being arrested, and large fines imposed on the ship's owners. Although the Chinese Horizon was registered in Hong Kong, the vessel was owned by a well-known captain of the appliance industry in China with close ties to the Chinese Communist Party. CAC, or the Chinese Appliance Company had become one of the world's largest home appliance manufacturers and distributors. Three years ago, in an endeavour to reduce its freight costs, it had branched out into shipping, forming the not-so imaginatively named China Shipping

Company. Captain Han was aware of the ramifications that would befall him and CSC should he fall foul of the Australian Maritime Safety Authority. The political and financial fallout back in China would be considerable, but of greater concern to Captain Han, however, would be the immediate repercussions on himself, and most likely also to his family back home in China.

Whilst being a ship's captain was well regarded in image conscious China, the annual salary wasn't commensurate with the stature of the position. Then in 2018, Han and his wife Le had taken advantage of China's relaxed policy on childbirth, further diluting his income. He needed to be more resourceful and find ways to supplement his modest salary. And this was how he became acutely aware of the Designated Shipping Areas within the Great Barrier Reef Marine Park and now found himself cautiously navigating the reefs and shoals to the east of the world-famous Whitsunday Island Group.

Captain Han was on the bridge of the Chinese Horizon as it gently navigated its way through the entry to Hydrographers Passage. The passage was the designated waterway through the Great Barrier Reef for ocean-going vessels to access the commercial port of Mackay and various mining company terminals dotted along the coastline. The sun was dropping below the horizon, but the surrounding shoals still radiated a subtle pink glow which aided his visual navigation. The wonderous sights, sounds, and smells of the Great Barrier Reef Marine Park constantly amazed Han.

He caught a glimpse of a dolphin's fin breaking the calm surface below and that brought a smile to his face. Dolphins were a good luck charm for seamen and he now knew everything would be alright tonight. On his many voyages south, he had seen giant ocean-going turtles, manta rays nearly as big as his modest house, the occasional whale shark, migrating turtles and hundreds of Humpback whales during their annual north-south-north pilgrimages. He wondered if he would ever be fortunate enough to bring his family here and live in this country with its abundance of natural beauty.

All vessels seventy metres or more in length and any tankers carrying chemicals, oil or gas regardless of their length are required to use the services of a licensed pilot when traversing Hydrographers Passage. This was well known to Han, but it wasn't his intention to navigate through the entire passage, and he would never entertain the notion of calling for pilot assistance. He had also checked the Marine Traffic website and was relieved that the nearest ocean-going vessel was more than one hundred nautical miles away, to the north of his current position. And just as important, his position was a similar distance from the Port of Mackay, where the maritime authorities lurked. If all the information was correct, then there was no vessel within four hours of his position. He would be back out into the Coral Sea and heading south again well within that timeframe.

As required by the SOLAS international convention for long–range identification and tracking, Han transmitted their identity, position and the time and date while twenty-five nautical miles east of the Passage. Under the convention, he had six hours until he was required to transmit the information again; more than enough time to undertake his required task. Then he would return to the open sea, transmit the required data again, and continue the voyage south.

Before he entered the passage proper, Han turned off the ship's AIS transponder. He wasn't about to let the Australian maritime authorities know of the Chinese Horizon's precise location, even if they did happen to be diligently checking their screens. After consulting his depth chart and using his most experienced able seaman as his lookout, Han cautiously navigated the Chinese Horizon into a sheltered cove adjacent to Wackett Reef. The cove was three kilometres in width, provided shelter to windward, and afforded him an expedient exit back out into the Coral Sea if circumstances called for it. He certainly hoped not.

Angel Reyes was Han's most experienced seaman and had been with him and the Chinese Horizon since the ship's purchase by CSC. Like many international seamen, he was Filipino and as such was renowned as a hard worker. He was also well respected by Han for his loyalty. His years of travelling the world had hardened both his skin and his soul and he doubted if Angel could ever live on dry land again. Angel was well aware of the reasons for dropping anchor in the cove. He had no problem with his involvement and was well rewarded by Han's masters for his role and more importantly, his discretion. He was now alone with his captain on the bridge of the ship, with the remaining eight crew members having been sent on a timely break. They didn't need to know what was about to go down.

'Angel, go below and start bringing up the packages.'

'Aye, aye, Capitan.' Han chuckled whenever Angel responded in that way. There were twenty packages each weighing five kilograms, and such was the condition of his lean, muscular body, Angel had no trouble completing the task in three trips. The packages were placed in a small steel cage attached by a wire cable to a hydraulic derrick located on the foredeck. He covered the cage with a tarpaulin of a military green colour.

'Now we wait. How many times have we been here?'

'Labing dalawa,' he replied in his native Tagalog. 'I think twelve, Capitan.'

'My friend, we have been truly fortunate to escape detection so far and we owe many thanks to Mazu, the Chinese Goddess of the Sea for our safety.'

'Capitan, I also give thanks for my protection, but to Haik, the ancient Filipino God of the Sea. Same blessings, different God.'

'I will have to find a way to eliminate this part of our journey in the future. Every time we make this stopover, I always think we're one step closer to getting caught. I don't want there to be an unlucky thirteen. Surely one of the many authorities that oversee this precious place in the world will one day notice our detour.' Han stared out into the still, dark waters and Angel knew what he was thinking. 'That will be the end of our lives as we know it. All good things must come to an end and I think we are getting close to the end now, Angel.

I will miss the extra money, but I will miss my family more if we are caught.'

Han with his trained ear, then Angel, heard the hum of twin diesel engines becoming louder by the minute. An added bonus of dropping anchor in the tranquil waters of the cove was their ability to detect all noise that might waft across the calm waters of the passage.

The sound was familiar to them, so they leaned on the bow railing, lit a cigarette and waited.

As the Viking 48 Cruiser drew near, Han chuckled at the name of the boat. 'A boat called Midnight Express carrying drugs.' He was well aware of the cruiser's name, although the scarred hull was a reminder of the crew's amateurish attempt to remove it. She rounded the bow of the Chinese Horizon and pulled alongside the larger vessel on the sheltered port side. The cruiser wouldn't be there any longer than necessary and given the calmness of the water and ease of the transfer, there was no need to tie up to the larger vessel.

There was no documentation to complete, no identity papers to check, and no sampling of the goods necessary. Both Han and Angel instantly recognised the two men on board the cruiser and acknowledged them with a nod. The two men ignored the greeting, with the taller of the men waving his arms, 'jiàngdī bāozhuāng.' Lower the package, he was demanding.

Han didn't like the demeanour of the two men who looked to him more like criminal enforcers than couriers, but as long as they kept their distance, it was no business of his.

'Angel, swing the derrick to the port side and lower the cage, por favor.' Once the cage was unloaded, Angel raised it back to deck level and swung the derrick back to its default position. He looked down and saw that the cruiser had already rounded the bow and was motoring across the passage and into the darkness of the night towards a destination unknown. The operation had taken less than five minutes.

'Go down to the staff quarters and advise the crew that we are about to get underway and have them return to their stations. I will weigh the anchor and start the engines in readiness to continue our voyage south to Brisbane.'

'Aye, aye, Capitan.'

5

Luxe Gym Newtown

It was still a balmy twenty-five degrees as Julie-Anne walked along King Street to the gym in her eclectic neighbourhood of Newtown. She lived five minutes' walk away from the bustling shopping strip. She loved the funky and retro fashion boutiques where she occasionally scored a bargain, the book shops including her favourite, *Better Read Than Dead*, the antique shops, the mix of hip cafes and of course, the pubs and bars.

On occasion, Julie-Anne would have breakfast at the western end of the strip and then walk the entire length of the southern side of the street before returning along the northern side. By the time she had completed the two kilometre loop of browsing, foraging, window shopping, hair and nail appointments and people watching, she was ready for lunch. Invariably she would stop at *The Bank*, her favourite pub, and have a Roasted Cauliflower Salad and a schooner of lager.

Julie-Anne had been so busy making the final changes to her latest feature article these past few days that she had neglected her health and fitness. She needed a blowout, and it was time to get back on track. Walking into the Luxe Gym in Newtown, she placed her gym bag in her locker, walked across to the cardio area and looped her towel over the treadmill's handrail and placed her water bottle in the holder. She was wearing a navy sports bra with light blue trim and matching mini yoga shorts. A twenty something guy on the adjacent treadmill gave her the once over.

'Nice to know I've still got it,' she said, winking at him. His face flushed and he turned back to watching the television.

She liked to keep her mind and body active and she was intent on achieving both today. She would use the time to conduct research on a topic that she had pigeon holed until now. With her employer, *Sydney Daily News*, trying to maintain relevancy in the new digital media age, the pressure was always on her as one of the senior investigative journalists to unearth the next big story. All things China, good and bad, were omnipresent in the news in recent times and in particular tales of Chinese interference were becoming increasingly common. She unlocked her mobile phone, clicked on the Podcast app, then typed Chinese Interference into the search bar.

Julie-Anne was fascinated by the subject, but was intent on finding a different angle to delve into for her next investigation. Finally discovering a podcast that sounded intriguing, she plugged in the hands-free device and inserted the buds into her ears. She stepped up onto the treadmill and set the speed at ten kilometres per hour. As the treadmill gained speed she stretched her legs out and after ten or fifteen seconds she got into a comfortable rhythm. Now she focused on the podcast. It was investigating the lengths the Chinese Communist Party was going to, to influence Australia's politicians. One of those politicians mentioned was a former Labor Party Senator.

She thought back a couple of years. The senator had quit the Australian parliament amid allegations that he had deceptively contradicted his own party's policy on the South China Sea at the request of the Chinese Communist Party in return for financial favours. Earlier in 2016, he had resigned from the party's frontbench after it was revealed that he may have broken rules on political donations. Evidently, the senator had been encouraging Chinese donors to make payments on his behalf to cover his travel and legal bills. *Nice work.*

None of this was news to Julie-Anne, but she was thinking about approaching the political interference issue from a different angle. A subject that surprisingly hadn't been discussed; where do they get the money from to fund their campaign? She knew it wasn't possible to conduct sizeable international money transfers into Australia without expecting some level of scrutiny from the Australian Transaction Reports and Analysis Centre. And in the current environment, surely Austrac would be extraordinarily vigilant when it came to monies being transferred into the country, especially from China. *Follow the money.* That would be the focus of her next investigation and she was fairly certain that her Editor-In-Chief would endorse her decision.

Julie-Anne was inspired now, so she raised the speed on the treadmill to twelve and a half kilometres per hour and her long legs went to work. Ten minutes later, she checked the time. Six o'clock. *Sheesh.* She had been so invested in the podcast that time had gotten away from her and she was due at Jack's at seven o'clock for dinner. *Time to go, Julie-Anne.*

(**6**)

Chinatown Sydney

As was usually the case, Li had multiple reasons for his visit to the harbour city and with his hectic schedule, it was important to be on time for his first appointment. He had rung the hotel's VIP Client Services number and ordered a limousine to take him to his dinner meeting. On the drive around Darling Harbour he wondered how Wang Li was making out with her unscheduled appointment. He chuckled to himself. Shortly thereafter, he arrived at Chinatown's Golden Phoenix Restaurant in Sussex Street. Whenever conducting business in Sydney, Li always preferred to do so over lunch or dinner at his favourite restaurant. The Golden Phoenix wasn't elegant like many highly regarded restaurants with their precious hats and stars, but it was comfortable, and he always felt at ease there in the heart of Chinatown. And the signature dish of Pipis in XO Sauce was the best outside of his native Shanghai. He stood at the entrance and marvelled at the fish tanks full of live lobster, prawns, mud crabs, coral trout, parrot fish and of course, his beloved Pipis.

'Welcome, Mr Li. It is good to see you again. How are you?'

'Thank you, Huang, I am well and very much looking forward to this evening.'

'Shall I take your briefcase for you?' Li was carrying a navy Louis Vuitton soft leather briefcase.

'No, that won't be necessary. Is my guest here, Huang?'

'Yes. I took the liberty of seating him at your usual table. I trust that was in order. I will show you to your table.' Li always sat at the rear corner table adjacent to the waiter's station, so he could see the comings and goings of the restaurant.

His dinner guest was standing with an outstretched arm as he approached the table and they warmly shook hands. Li had known Wie Ping Lie for more than a decade now and they had a business venture from which they both benefited handsomely. No sooner had they sat down when a steaming bowl of his favoured Pipis was delivered to the table. Li consumed them like Australians ate Chilli Mussels and he duly excused himself to his guest as he enthusiastically tucked in. In accordance with Chinese custom, he then invited Wie to enjoy the dish too.

'Now that I have sated my appetite for these delicious little creatures, we should discuss our business venture, Wie.' As he opened the discussion, using his foot he subtly nudged the navy blue briefcase across the floor to Wie's side of the table.

'What would you like to discuss?'

'Not one individual thing specifically, Wie. One mustn't take things for granted in life, so I just want to assure myself that we are not at risk through our business transactions. Call it my regular check-up if you like.'

'Lucie is conducting the final deliveries from our last shipment, and we eagerly await the arrival of the next one. As far as the process went, the Chinese Panorama was where it was intended to be at the appointed date and time. The transfer on the water went smoothly, as did the transportation down to Sydney. And another shipment is being handed over off the coast as we speak. A seamless process, as always.'

'That is good to hear my friend, but what I would like to discuss is whether we are becoming complacent as a result of our success. I have a fondness for the western saying, "if it seems too good to be true, then it probably is." Managing risk is a key component in any successful company and business models need constant review and updating.'

'That was the very reason I moved into the eastern suburbs, and it has proven to be very profitable.'

'Yes, it has, but I'm sure it will only be a matter of time before the incumbents in the area retaliate. They won't take kindly to you infiltrating their territory.'

'It's not infiltration; we have completely different products and client bases. There is room for us, and anyway, the clients are delighted with the new product.'

'I know. All I am saying is that we will complete another transaction in the near future, and this seems an opportune time to review our business.'

'Li, with great respect, I prefer another western saying, "if it isn't broken, then don't fix it." We have the ideal ports of origin in Dailan and Qingdao, convenient and continued access to suitable ships, well rewarded and loyal captains, a sheltered transfer location, discreet coastal access, easy road transport, a timely process, and loyal distributors. Which of these successful functions would you like to review?'

'All of them,' said Li as he gazed earnestly at his business partner. 'The Australian authorities aren't stupid, Wie. They generally have excellent intelligence gathering and investigative resources. Just in our supply chain alone, we could encounter the navy along the top end, AMSA and the Maritime Border Command on the voyage down the coast, any number of suspicious local port authorities and both state and federal police. And the Australian Border Force are everywhere these days. Surely you heard about that large coke seizure by the AFP and Border Force a few weeks ago. You must have seen them all in their dress uniforms at the news conference salivating at their success.'

Wi leaned across the table. 'Yes, of course I did. And that's the very reason we changed our business model a few years back. Our current supply chain and operating model is more secure now.'

'I agree, but after many successful shipments we would be wise to consider the possibility that somewhere within that supply chain our activities have been noticed. I'm sure the increased accessibility of our higher purity product will have not escaped the attention of the local and federal police. With government agencies expanding their intelligence gathering and sharing information they will join the dots eventually.' Li was thirsty following his little speech and sipped his wine.

Wie was becoming bored with his business partner's conservative notions, but for now he would play nice. 'The fact that we have successfully completed many shipments undetected, and with another about to arrive in the country, tells me we should be searching for a way to increase the frequency of shipments. It seems to me that with everything progressing seamlessly, we have an opportunity to increase the supply of our product. And hence increase our profits.' With that, Wie carefully nudged his matching briefcase across the floor and rested it up against Li's leg. It contained a gentle reminder as to the reason they were in business together.

Li smiled wryly. 'That wasn't very subtle, my friend, but I accept your point. We should take the time to respectfully consider each other's point of view and meet again in a day or so, if you agree.'

'I am pleased that you have not forgotten *Sīxiǎng kāimíng de* from your roots Li; it is a necessary characteristic for conducting business.'

'I always have an open mind when it comes to making money, Wie.'

(**7**)

Coral Sea Queensland

The transfer had gone smoothly as usual and Ling Jun was navigating the Midnight Express in a south-westerly direction while his offsider, Wang Wei, was checking the quality of their product and stowing the cargo in the galley. Their ultimate destination was immediately to his west, but to minimise zigzagging through the shoals of the outer reef, he would stay in the open water for as long as possible. Once clear of Square Reef, he would navigate to the northwest, steer around the dark outlines of the Whitsunday Islands and then make his way due west to their destination in the hidden bay. On his first excursion out to Wackett Reef, he had done his homework and carefully studied the marine charts for the immediate area. The first fifteen nautical miles of open water didn't present any unknown dangers, so he was able to make good time, especially in these calm waters. Ling sat in the captain's chair of the cockpit, lit a cigarette, and contemplated the next stage of his land journey down to Sydney. Moments later, he was jolted out of his thoughts by a booming voice racing across the water from behind him.

'This is the Australian naval vessel, Cape York. Turn off your engines immediately,' blared a voice from some sort of loudspeaker system.

'La shi,' he blurted out as a blazing beam of light suddenly illuminated his vessel.' He had been warned to be careful by his boss, Wie Ping Lie, many times, but even he couldn't have anticipated this. 'Wang, up here now!' he roared. With the pursuing vessel concealed behind its dazzling light he couldn't be certain what type it was. Before he had undertaken his first transaction three years ago, he had researched what vessels were used by the various Australian maritime agencies. The most sophisticated were the relatively new Cape-class patrol boats that were operated by the Border Force and Royal Australian Navy. He guessed that this was a Cape- class, and if so, that might just work in his favour.

'This is the Australian naval vessel, Cape York. Turn off your engines immediately,' the booming voice repeated.

Given his illicit cargo, that wasn't an option. Ling quickly checked his navigational chart, which he had previously marked with several lines depicting various courses. Knowing exactly where he was, he quickly decided on his course of action and which route he would take. He ignored the order, turned the wheel to starboard, and pushed the throttle. He turned on the vessel's CP450C Sonar just in case. Ling knew from his research that the Cape-class vessel's maximum speed was less than the Midnight Express', but it wasn't his plan to outrun this one. More importantly, the draught of the pursuing vessel was three metres compared to his own vessel's one point five metres, which was why he was making for the shoals immediately to the north. He would disappear into the shallow channels and then hopefully make his getaway.

The pursuing vessel had altered course to track him, but with the Viking 48 having a top speed of thirty-five knots the Cape York was losing ground. Ling still needed to get to the shallow waters of the nearby shoals, where he could use the cruiser's narrow draught to his advantage. The Midnight Express was still illuminated by the powerful spotlight, but Ling could see its effect was diminishing by the minute. That could change quickly as he slowed to navigate through the jagged shoals. He also knew each Cape-class vessel was armed with two .50 calibre machine guns, but he didn't think they had ever been deployed in peacetime in Australian waters. He hoped that wasn't about to change.

The Midnight Express was now about one hundred metres from the gap in the shoals he had identified on the chart. He gently pulled the throttle back towards him, slowed the cruiser to five knots, and turned on his own spotlight. He had ordered Wang onto the bow to be his spotter.

'This is Captain Johnson of the Cape York. You will turn off your engines and drop anchor now! This is your final warning,' the voice boomed a third time.

Ling again disregarded the threat and carefully navigated the Midnight Express into what was at most only a thirty metre gap between the shallow reefs. Wang raised his arm to the right and Ling gently allowed the vessel to drift across to starboard as it entered the shallow channel. He knew the patrol boat couldn't follow him and if he could safely navigate the two nautical miles of the unnamed channel, then he would be back into open water again. The patrol boat would have to navigate around the large reef, which should take them nearly half an hour by his estimate, even if they could achieve maximum speed. He looked over his shoulder and saw through the glare that the patrol boat had come to a halt some two hundred metres astern. The captain made another threatening announcement, but Ling ignored him once more and kept his vessel creeping forward. His heart rate slowed as he put some distance between himself and the now stationary pursuit vessel. That didn't last long as he heard the loud rat-a-tat-tat of the Cape York's machine guns.

'La shi,' he repeated. That wasn't supposed to happen. Ling saw Wang drop flat to the deck, and he himself flinched as the projectiles whooshed above them. 'Wang, get up and keep looking,' he barked. He had a choice between being captured or risk holing his vessel on the jagged rocks and coral. The first wasn't an option, so he pushed the throttle forward and picked up the speed to ten knots. The Cape York could launch their RHIB's, but it would take some time to lower them into the water and be mobile. Anyway, they wouldn't be able to navigate these shoals any faster than he. The captain would undoubtedly be aware of this, so he had ordered another ear-splitting volley from the machine guns.

'Bǎochí lěngjìng,' Ling ordered Wang as he told himself to remain calm as well while the bullets whooshed overhead again. He was drawing further away from the Cape York, but there was no cover amongst the shoals, so he simply had to keep going.

'Dāngxīn,' Wang cried out as one of the eighteen-foot Shakespeare VHF antennas came crashing down onto the cockpit.

'Tā mā de,' Ling cursed. He looked up at the cockpit ceiling and fortunately for him, the antenna bounced across the roof and harmlessly into the water. Moments later, he was relieved to see the channel opening up into a wider expanse. He spotted another channel opening further across the water. Turning off his own spotlight and running lights, Ling pushed the throttle further forward. The effect of the pursuing vessels searchlight had diminished considerably and he felt slightly more comfortable now. Five minutes later, he reached the next channel, backed off on the throttle and cautiously steered the cruiser into the narrow neck. He was now in uncharted waters and the sonar told him this was slightly deeper than the previous channel, so he upped his speed to eight knots and held it steady.

Fifteen minutes later, he was out of the second channel and into the open water south of Ross Reef. He pushed the throttle all the way forward and accelerated up to the Midnight Express' top speed of thirty-five knots. The Cape York would lose even more time navigating around the second reef, so he and Wang should be safe now. They had fifty nautical miles of open water in front of him. It would take them an hour and a half to reach their destination at the shallow and sheltered bay. The patrol vessel would never catch them now. Wang rose from his knees and stepped from the bow into the cabin. 'That was too close, laoban.'

'Yes it was, Wang, too close. Gǎnxiè shàngdì,' he said to himself. This would be his last visit to this part of the world.

The Chinese Horizon was passing the leeward side of Hyde Reef and heading northwards into the open water of the Coral Sea when Captain Han heard a muted staccato sound coming from somewhere behind him. He hoped he was wrong in what he was thinking. He looked back from the bridge and could see a horizontal beam of white light about ten nautical miles to his stern. That sight and the sounds he had heard were not a good sign and it could only mean one thing. From his perspective, it was a good thing though; his ship wasn't the target, this time anyway. He wasn't waiting around to have his thoughts validated. He pushed the throttle power lever forward to its maximum position and took his ship up to twenty-four knots.

(**8**)

Oceanic Hotel Darling Harbour

After the frank discussion with his business partner and having had more than his fill of his Pipis, Li left the Golden Phoenix feeling quietly chuffed with himself. The fact that he was carrying a significantly heavier briefcase only further added to his hubris.

'Thank you, the Pipis were delicious as always; my compliments to the chef,' he said to Huang as he exited the restaurant and lowered himself into his waiting limousine. Upon his return to the hotel, he rode the executive elevator to his suite high above the city and immediately called the direct line for Client Services. 'I would like to speak to the Vice President.'

'Unfortunately, Mr Woodard is unavailable at this time, Mr Li, can someone else assist you?'

'No. I would like to speak only with Mr Tony Woodard, so could you kindly locate him and ask him to come to my suite.'

'I'll do my absolute best to locate him for you, Mr Li,' the woman said.

'I have no doubt you will.'

Li Qiang could be a high maintenance guest, but he was also a VIP, so it was no surprise to him that not more than five minutes later, there was a knock on his door. 'Why is it so difficult to reach you,

Mr Vice President?' Li wasn't one for pleasantries with the service staff, even if they carried an executive title.

'I was having a late dinner following the hectic evening rush if you must know,' Woodard responded indignantly.

'I thought you might have been having a siesta after the little present I gave you.' Li laughed at his own allusion.

'Some gift. I have bruising to my stomach thanks to that bitch,' Woodard complained as he leant forward.

'Don't call her that again if you know what's good for you.' He raked a critical eye over the younger man. 'You don't seem to have much luck with women, Tony.'

Woodard's nose and forehead scrunched up with confusion. 'What do you mean by that?'

'You know exactly what I'm referring to,' Li said smugly. 'Anyway, you're here now and we have an important matter to discuss.' He had a standing arrangement with the Vice President of Client Services and he wished to avail himself of his services again.

'What can I do for you on this occasion, Mr Li?'

'Open the briefcase on the dining table, Tony.'

'It is the hotel's policy that staff, no matter what their position, are never to interfere with guests' personal belongings.' Woodard said quietly, trying to maintain his composure.

'I give you my express permission, Tony, now open it. It's not like this is your first time.'

Woodard trudged across the suite to the dining area and paused momentarily, hovering above the designer briefcase. He had been put in this situation a number of times previously and since Li's last visit, had been seeking a way to remove himself from their arrangement. He should have said no the first time, but that would have resulted in Li taking his custom and substantial financial resources elsewhere. There were a number of resort casinos in Australia that also catered for clients of Li's stature who wouldn't be shy in obliging his every whim, including the request that accompanied the briefcase.

Li wasn't accustomed to service staff disobeying his instructions, even if they were nefarious in nature. This applied equally to the Vice President who was dilly dallying over the task at hand. 'Open it, Tony. I've already entered the padlock's combination, just flick the latch.' He demanded, savouring the man's tortured expression.

'No, I won't do it, Li.'

'Mr Li, to you, and yes you will if you know what's good for you.'

The Vice President of Client Services flicked the latches and hesitated before he lifted the flap. An inordinate amount of time seemed to pass. Finally, Woodard inhaled deeply, lifted the flap and took a step back from the table. He was looking down in the direction of the briefcase, but nothing was registering except for the blur of the layers of green polymer notes.

Unnamed Bay

With the harrowing near miss with the Cape York now firmly behind him, Ling had steered the Midnight Express into the shallow, unnamed bay. He had transferred to the tiny aluminium dinghy, and with Wang and their valuable cargo on board, was now drifting towards the shore. All they needed to do now was land the vessel, drag it across the mudflats, and stow it in their bush hideout. From there it was a manageable five hundred metre walk along the dirt road to their hidden vehicle and then twenty kilometres through the Dryander National Park to the highway.

'Wǒ kào,' Wang called out. 'La shi.' He was kneeling on the front cross bench of the small dinghy, LED torch in hand, as he guided Ling into the shallows of the bay. He suddenly jumped up and stumbled backwards over the bench seat. The beam of the torch had picked up two red eyes staring back at him from the shallow waters between them and their destination.

'What's wrong, Wang?'

'Kàn, kàn,' he yelled, pointing his quivering arm towards the shallows. Just then, the eyes disappeared under the water, much to Wang's horror.

'What are you pointing at?'

'Kräkə, dīl.'

'Where?' Ling stood up and balanced himself in the centre of the dinghy. 'I can't see anything.'

Wang turned to reply when he saw it again. 'Wǒ kào, kàn, kàn,' he yelled, pointing his torch at the large reptile. The beast was about three metres long and had surfaced parallel to their tiny vessel, only a metre away, its right eye sizing up its intended prey.

Ling had seen videos on YouTube of large crocs leaping out of the water in promotions for the Northern Territory. 'La shi.' He picked up the oars and handed one to Wang, who grasped it, but didn't move. The croc had risen slightly in the water and Ling could see the beasts powerful jaw, full of hungry teeth. He desperately tried not to overbalance as he repeatedly jabbed the crocodile's snout with his oar. 'Bùyào zhǐshì zhàn zài nà'er lái bāng wǒ, Wang.' Ling glanced to his left and could see that Wang was consumed with fear. He turned back to the prehistoric monster and resumed jabbing at it. The reptile lunged towards the dinghy and Ling caught it on the snout with a blow from the oar. He breathed a sigh of relief as the large croc twisted away, began swinging its tail from side to side in a wavelike motion and then disappeared out into the dark waters of the bay. *That was too close.*

'Nà tài jìnle, Wang.' Ling turned the key, pushed the choke and cranked the outboard motor. He wasn't about to venture further into the shallows with a large croc lurking in the waters, so he throttled up the outboard and began doing donuts in ever increasing circles to scare it and any others away. Hopefully, it didn't have any friends or family resting on the shore.

Ten minutes later, they were dragging the dinghy across the mudflats and up onto the narrow beach. Ling could see the look of dread in Wang's eyes as they darted back and forth, looking for more of the prehistoric creatures. 'Hopefully, it's like the old motherland and the parents only had one offspring, Wang,' he said, trying to calm his partner with humour. They safely stowed the dinghy in the tropical vegetation and covered it with loose branches and shrubs.

Then they retrieved the upright trolley with the tractor tires, stacked the coke aboard and, navigating by torchlight, began the ten-minute trek along the track to their waiting vehicle.

After their near miss with the patrol boat, Ling knew they would now have to avoid the Bruce Highway and take the longer inland route via the Leichardt Highway all the way to the border with New South Wales. This would keep them two hundred kilometres inland of the heavily patrolled major coastal route and hopefully out of harm's way. First, though, they had to navigate through the regional hub of Proserpine, then travel, hopefully undetected, the one hundred and twenty kilometres south to Hampden where they could quietly slip onto the inland highway. Ling wasn't an overly superstitious man, but he hoped that the age old saying of terrible things happening in threes was just that.

Forty minutes later, he steered off of Shute Harbour Road, about one kilometre north of Proserpine, and continued southwards on the Bruce Highway. There was no way of circumnavigating the town, as the surrounding area was dominated by national parks and state forests, with no public access roads allowing for any nocturnal detours. His worst thoughts were realised when he saw a conga line of red lights curving around the bend in front of him. This was an unusual sight for such a small town, and while it could simply be random licence checks, a vehicle accident, or even a booze bus, he didn't believe in coincidences.

He noticed the prominent blue sign with the white 'H' directing traffic into Taylor Street. He didn't need to be told twice. 'Wang, bring up Google Maps on your phone and find me a back way through this town, quickly. Use the hospital as your starting point,' he demanded as he made the right-hand turn.

'Hǎo de.' Wang brought up the Proserpine Hospital and shrunk the map with his fingers so he had an overview of the whole town. 'Okay, take first left past hospital; is Chapman Street and go to the end.'

'La shi,' Ling said as he passed a police car waiting to turn left out of the hospital driveway. He proceeded cautiously and watched as the car cut in behind his SUV. He slowed again and indicated before turning left into Chapman Street. He was trying to second guess the policeman's intention when Wang called out to him.

'It's okay, Ling, he going to the station,' he said, handing Ling his iPhone, which showed the police station's location on the next block across. Ling didn't realise he had been holding his breath and sighed heavily as he continued carefully down Chapman Street. He was jolted from his sense of relief by the yelp of a siren and the red and blue flashing lights of the police car accelerating up behind him. 'Bù hǎole,' he cried out as he pulled over to the kerb. He sat quietly in the driver's seat of the SUV. The police officer would be running his vehicle's registration through the database. Ling was full of trepidation while pondering the possible reasons for being pulled over. It had been over three hours since their near-miss with the patrol boat and he was desperately hoping this was insufficient time for the various law enforcement agencies to communicate with each other and coordinate any search for them. He would know soon enough.

In his rear vision mirror, he watched as the officer stepped out of his vehicle and walked towards their vehicle. Ling's heart was racing and his breathing became shallow as he thought about the one hundred kilos of coke hidden in the spare tyre wheel well. He had his Chinese made Type 67 semi-automatic pistol stashed under his seat, but using it would escalate the situation beyond his control. The officer would have undoubtedly already activated the ANPR technology in his patrol car that would identify his vehicle, and worryingly, Ling himself. He would also be easily identifiable from the footage from the officer's bodycam. Out of the corner of his eye, he noticed Wang reach down under the passenger's seat. 'Bùyào zuò, Biéguǎn tā, Wang,' Ling ordered. Wang gave him a nervous look, but returned his hand to his lap. 'Don't do anything to arouse suspicion, Wang. We don't need him searching the car.' Ling pressed the window button and waited for the window to descend before turning his head towards the approaching officer.

'Good evening, sir; can I see your licence and vehicle registration, please?'

'Good evening officer,' Ling replied evenly. He reached across and withdrew the registration paper from the glove compartment, handed it across to the officer and then lifted his wallet from the console, opened it and held it up.

'Thank you, sir. Do you know why you were pulled over?'

'No, I don't.'

'You were using a mobile phone while driving your vehicle.'

Ling breathed a sigh of relief that he tried to disguise.

'No, sir, that was my passenger.'

'Sir, I have you on video holding the phone while your vehicle was in motion. That is an offence under Section 300 of the Transport Operations Regulation. You can request a copy of the video when you receive your infringement notice. You will be fined one thousand dollars and have four demerit points recorded against your traffic history, Mr Ling.'

The officer printed out the infringement notice and handed it across. 'Have a good evening, sir and be careful. We've already had one accident in town this evening.' *Bugger.*

Ling slowly pulled away from the kerb and continued down Chapman Street. Less than five minutes later they were south of the town and driving through the sugarcane fields, depicted by the unbroken wall of leafy green storks illuminated in the SUV's headlights. They arrived at a T-Junction with the Bruce Highway, turned right and continued south on their journey. He was thinking about the police stop. Now the police would have a record of him being in North Queensland at a similar time to the earlier incident with the patrol boat, and that would provide another link to his illegal activities. That wasn't good and the boss wouldn't be happy.

$$(10)$$

Bondi Beach

It was still a balmy twenty-five degrees as Lucie Chan drove down bustling Hall Street in Bondi Beach, replete with its crowded sidewalks, blaring music and the smell of waffle cones. It was forecast to be thirty-eight degrees tomorrow, so she assumed many of these revellers had decided to party on tonight and pull a sickie tomorrow. That was good for business, which was why she was here. She had her window wound down so she could soak up the sights and sounds of this vibrant part of her delivery round. This might be one of the last times she would be able to enjoy this spectacle for some time if you listened to the persistent rumours about the impending lockdown brought on by the COVID-19 pandemic.

Much to her surprise, and delight, she found a parking bay in Chambers Avenue about fifty metres from Hall Street, adjacent to Vinnies and only two blocks from her destination. Star parking, she called it. Lucie grabbed the small gift-wrapped box from the passenger seat, placed it in her handbag and exited the vehicle. She strolled down the hill to the beachfront hotel which, given the idyllic weather conditions, would be packed to the rafters at this time of the evening. She took the stairs up to the first floor and made her way out onto the wraparound balcony. Given this was her last appointment for the evening she thought she might enjoy a glass or two of bubbles and see what was on offer. She had dressed in her favourite party dress; a silver sequined spaghetti strap bodycon number with a deep vee. She had matched the dress with silver pumps, which made her even taller and the dress even shorter. Even though it was a beach pub and most patrons were dressed accordingly, the swivelling heads confirmed she had made the right choice.

She recognised her client and walked across to his table. She knew him only as Jordan. He was wearing a light blue short-sleeved linen shirt, white dress shorts and navy blue loafers. He was handsome, tanned and physically appealing too and on previous occasions she had considered lingering and see what transpired. 'Hello, Jordan, how are you?'

He stood, and pulled her chair back. 'I'm well thanks, Lucie, and yourself?'

'You look very smart,' she said.

'Thank you. You look, well, just wow. Where are you going tonight?'

'Nowhere. You are my last client for the day, so I thought I might treat myself to a glass of bubbles.'

He smiled. 'Well, tonight's my treat then.'

She pushed the small package across the table and he reciprocated by sliding a present of his own, also gift-wrapped, but larger and flatter, in the opposite direction. 'I'm having a few clients over to my place later, so I needed something to ensure they remember who their favourite sports agent is.'

'I'm certain they will be pleased with your offering.'

He was staring, but this woman looked drop dead gorgeous tonight, particularly with her caramel skin glowing in the increasing night light. She sure was sexy as hell, especially with the sights on offer from her low cut dress. 'You're more than welcome to come too, Lucie,' he suggested as he poured her a glass of Moët.

'Thank you, but let's just enjoy the view and the bubbles first and see what transpires, shall we? Cheers.'

Well, at least that wasn't a no. 'Here's to the magnificent view and bubbles then. Cheers.'

She knew precisely which view he was enjoying, so she made it easier for him by leaning forward, softly asking, 'So, who are these clients that you need to ingratiate?'

'A few self-absorbed footballers from various codes.'

'Jordan, I'm up here,' she reminded him, watching his face colour with embarrassment.

'Sorry. Anyway, this is their last chance to have a little fun and let their hair down before their respective football seasons start, so I've arranged a little pool party for them.'

'And their fun comes gift wrapped too,' she responded with a coy smile. 'What about drug testing?' She asked as she sipped her on her champagne.

'These particular clients have a few days away from their clubs, so they'll be okay.'

'Do you have many clients, Jordan?'

'Quite a few, but I imagine not as many as you judging by the quality of your product,' he replied.

She laughed. 'It's just as well this balcony is so noisy that no one could possibly overhear our conversation.'

'Touché. Well, I really should get going as it won't be much of a party without the host, and especially my little treat,' he replied holding up the box.

'Thank you for the bubbles. I just love a glass of Moët.'

He handed her a business card with a Rose Bay address listed. 'I would love it if you could make it, Lucie.'

She tilted her head and smiled coyly. 'We'll see, Jordan.'

She was thinking about her handsome client as she walked back up Hall Street. He was a tad on the self-absorbed side, but physically he was very easy on the eye, so with nothing in her calendar, she had decided, *why not?*

Lucie crossed over Chambers Avenue and walked around to the driver's side of her CRV and opened the door. As she stepped up into the driver's seat she felt the coldness of a metal object pushed up against her temple, a hand tightly grip her nose and mouth and a strong body force her face down across the front seats. She was trapped and couldn't move or breathe.

'Do you know what this is about, Lucie?' She shuddered at the sound of her name from her attacker's lips. 'Yes, we know exactly who you are, you chink bitch.'

Stay calm, she told herself, even as her heart raced. Her dress had ridden up to her waist and she could feel him hardening against her bare skin. 'Naughty girl,' she heard him say. She flexed her glutes as tightly as possible in anticipation of what would come next. 'No, that's not going to happen, not this time, anyway.' She willed her body to relax. 'This is just a friendly warning, but next time we won't be so accommodating,' he said, pushing the weapon harder against her head. 'If we see you in or around our territory again, you know what to expect,' he said in his accented voice. 'Make sure your chink boss understands that too.' He pushed himself off and slapped her on the bottom. 'Great arse, Lucie.' With that, the man exited the vehicle and he and his accomplice calmly walked up leafy Chambers Avenue and into the dark of the night.

Yes, she really was Lucky Chan.

(11)

Coral Sea Queensland

Captain Stuart Johnson was on the bridge of the Cape York as it continued its search for the mystery vessel that had eluded them. They had lost valuable time having to navigate around the treacherous reefs and shoals and they were now heading in a westerly direction at a steady fifteen knots. He doubted they would see the fleeing vessel again tonight, but which direction did it go?

His digital map told him that after exiting the second channel his quarry could navigate below Ross Reef and that would give them a clear shot at the coastline to the west. The other option for them was to turn to port and make their way south. The latter meant they would have to navigate around the populated Whitsunday Islands. That would make the journey to the nearest coastline thirty nautical miles further than the alternative. He figured they would want to be off the water as soon as possible, so they would take the first option and head due west.

Johnson picked up the handset and connected through to the Maritime Border Command Operations Centre in Canberra. Moments later, Shane Williamson, the MBC Operations Manager called him back. 'What have you got for me, Stuart?' he asked.

Johnson walked him through the York's activities of the past hour.

'They could have headed south, but they would have to dodge and weave through the Whitsundays, which would have slowed them down considerably. My best guess is that they have headed due west, making for the nearest coastline. That would place their landing point somewhere north of Airlie Beach.'

'Did you identify the vessel?'

'No. Their transponder must have been deactivated. We only had a rear view and there were no identification markings on the hull.'

'Are you in a position to undertake a comprehensive search?'

'Not at this stage. But I'm going to search around the populated islands of the Whitsundays using our searchlight capacity, but with the number of bays, inlets and harbours to search, I'm not hopeful.'

'Okay. If you come up blank can you head for Bowen and commence a search of the coastline heading in a southerly direction towards Mackay?'

'Yes, we should be able to, but that won't be until early tomorrow at best guess.'

'I know, and that's fine. In the meantime, I will alert the local authorities and see if we can get some roadblocks in place at Proserpine and Mackay.'

'How will they know what they're looking for, Shane?'

'You said the skipper was Asian in appearance and they must have a vehicle stashed somewhere, so they need to KALOF for a vehicle with an Asian driver or passenger who may be acting suspiciously. That's all we have for now.'

'Before you go, Shane. There's a cargo ship, the Chinese Horizon, which was about twenty nautical miles east of Hydrographers Passage at its last position and was heading out into the Coral Sea. Its original location wasn't far from where we first sighted the suspect vessel, and given it's heading to Brisbane, it had no reason to be anywhere near there. There has to be a connection.'

'Okay, I'll follow that up too. Hang on a second, Stuart, did you really fire upon them?'

'Yes, I had no other option to slow them down. I'm sure I'll have some questions to answer from the desk jockeys and the brass in Canberra for doing that.'

'Okay, good luck, and keep in touch.'

'You too, please, Shane.'

AMSA Control Room Canberra

James Fairweather was sitting at his desk in the secure monitoring room of the national headquarters of AMSA. He was the only operator on duty to monitor the seven screens that showed the activity of over four hundred vessels traversing the eight million square kilometres of Australia's Exclusive Economic Zone. He had graduated with honours in information technology from Canberra's Australian National University and had held high hopes for a development role with a start-up tech firm or potentially even one of the social media giants that dominated the IT innovation landscape these days. Unfortunately for him, jobs in both these spheres were in short supply in the national capital. A friend had steered him to an online job advertisement seeking analysts to work for the Australian Maritime Safety Authority. James had always thought of himself as having an analytical mind, so, although the position wasn't within the IT sphere, he applied for one of the roles. To his surprise, he duly succeeded in gaining a position and had now been labouring in the role for an excruciatingly tedious six months.

Analyst, really, he reflected as he stared at the screens with their pretty little icons of varying colours dotted around the coastline. James' idea of an analyst's role was someone who interacted with a business's stakeholders, worked diligently to identify their needs and required outcomes. They then devised and implemented solutions, preferably IT based, of course, that would enable them to achieve their goals. Analysts used their brains, monitors used their eyes, but at least it was a job, particularly at a time when the Commonwealth Government was predictably downsizing the public service. So, having long ago dialled down his once lofty ambitions, here he was, settled in for another long, monotonous night.

Other than the giant ore carriers off the northwest coast, there wasn't much of significance to monitor along the extensive coastlines of the Indian and Southern Oceans, so invariably he would be more focused on the monitors depicting movements within the Coral Sea and Torres Strait to its north. Also, like environmentalists the world over, he had concerns for the welfare of the Great Barrier Reef and its world heritage listed marine park, so he tended to monitor this part of the country more diligently. In particular, James would focus on the precious reef's narrow passages that vessels, especially cargo ships and tankers, would have to navigate to access the numerous inner ports of Queensland's coastline.

At the commencement of his shift, he scanned the two monitors of most interest to him.

There was the predictably long line of cargo vessels depicted by green icons snaking their way from the Vitiaz Strait in Papua New Guinea down through the Coral Sea, with the majority heading for the eastern seaboard ports of Brisbane and Sydney. He studied the directional flow of vessels and but could see nothing out of the ordinary. In particular, the area around Hydrographers Passage was quiet with only one vessel in the near vicinity. Which, when he double clicked on the green icon, he saw was the cargo ship Chinese Horizon. The only other vessel in proximity was a tanker which looked to be about one hundred nautical miles to the north and also heading in a southerly direction.

Fairweather was wearing a track in the carpet as he paced up and down in front of the seven monitors to keep his blood circulating.

Three hours into his shift he noticed something slightly unusual. The green icon he had seen earlier just outside of Hydrographers Passage remained in a similar location, but the icon was now facing an easterly direction. In the time since he had first noticed the Chinese Horizon, she should have been at least seventy nautical miles to the south. Further confirming his observation, the tanker was now only thirty nautical miles from the cargo ship. *Where had the Chinese Horizon been during the preceding three hours?* He wondered as he started pacing again.

$$13$$

East of Hydrographers Passage

Captain Han was still on the bridge of the Chinese Horizon, and although his nerves had settled, he still wasn't comfortable with what had occurred far to his stern. He knew in his heart it must have had something to do with his earlier transaction. He blocked that thought out for now and completed entering the new coordinates into the electronic navigation system that would see his vessel make a quick turn to starboard and then another. Although the ship was now back on the seaward side of the reef and shoals, he was required to set a course for the Outer Marker to the south-east first. He still needed to round another group of shoals that jutted out into the Coral Sea. Then he would adjust his heading further to starboard and continue on south to Brisbane. Once safely away from the passage, and as required by SOLAS and LRIT, Han transmitted their identity, position and the date. It was a balmy, still night, so he collected his cigarettes and coffee and made his way out to the foredeck. He looked astern and couldn't see or hear anything. He finally relaxed, inhaled on his cigarette, sipped his coffee and soaked up the tranquility of the night and gazed across the calm dark waters.

The sound of his Inmarsat phone ringing loudly startled him and quickly released him from his all too brief bout of reverie. He hastily butted out his cigarette, grabbed his coffee and made his way back onto the bridge. *Why was the phone ringing now? And why so soon after they had left their secluded cove in Hydrographers Passage? Had they been spotted by the authorities? And which authorities; Border Force, Coast Guard, Maritime Border Command, Navy, AMSA—who?* He didn't believe in coincidences, so he prepared himself for the worst. Han sucked in a deep breath and having composed himself sufficiently, he depressed the green button on the satellite phone. 'This is the Chinese Horizon, Captain Hsin Han speaking.'

'Captain Han, good evening. My name is James Fairweather and I am from the Australian Maritime Safety Authority; you may know us as AMSA, Captain.' Han felt relieved knowing AMSA were mostly focused on marine safety, seafarer welfare and training, the marine environment and vessel seaworthiness amongst their many responsibilities. He did not think they were responsible for maritime security.

'Mr Fairweather, good evening. Yes, I am aware of AMSA. What can I do for you sir?'

'Captain Han, I have noticed something slightly irregular while monitoring shipping in the Great Barrier Reef Marine Park. In particular, your vessel's direction over the past few hours has varied from the traditional north-south course that would take you through the Coral Sea and directly to Brisbane. I can see you are now heading toward the south-east and the Outer Marker.'

'So, what is the nature of the irregularity you speak of, Mr Fairweather? We are on the correct heading for Brisbane, as you say.'

'Yes, you are now, Mr Han, but you weren't an hour ago. Then you were heading in an easterly direction away from the entrance to Hydrographers Passage. Furthermore, you seem to have lost time on your voyage. I was concerned that there may have been a mechanical malfunction with the Chinese Horizon and that you may be dangerously adrift close to the reef.'

The captain breathed a sigh of relief. 'Thank you for your concern,

Mr Fairweather. I am delighted that Australian authorities are so thorough in their monitoring of vessels that navigate the vast seas that surround your country. We had a minor electrical fault onboard that required attention. I could have waited until we docked in Brisbane. However, the seas are so calm tonight and there were no other vessels in the area, so I steered out of the shipping lane, dropped anchor and had the electrical fault repaired.'

'Where did you drop anchor, Mr Han?'

'Just outside of the Hydrologist Passage.' Han deliberately misspronounced the name to lighten the tone.

'You mean Hydrographers Passage?'

'I always get confused with that name, Mr Fairweather, hard for Chinese man to say.'

'The Chinese Horizon also seemed to disappear from my screen for some time.'

Fairweather paused and then cautiously asked. 'Did you turn off the ship's AIS transponder, Captain?' Fairweather was now calling him 'captain' so Han hoped that was a sign of the situation thawing. He wouldn't let his guard down and would stay respectful to this man, however.

'No, I would never do that, Mr Fairweather. That would be a very dangerous thing to do, especially in this busy shipping lane. Maybe it automatically shut down because of the electrical problem,' Han lied.

'Maybe it did just that, Captain.'

'I will definitely have it checked when we reach Brisbane.'

'Okay, Captain, as long as everything is fine with your vessel and you and your crew are safe, I will thank you for your time. Have a good night.'

'And the same to you, Mr Fairweather, and thank you for your concern.'

Macquarie Suite – Oceanic Hotel

Woodard finally regained his composure, inhaled deeply and turned to face Li. 'I respectfully ask that I be allowed to remove myself from this arrangement. You know these transactions contravene both the Commonwealth and New South Wales government's anti-money laundering laws and the Oceanic certainly won't take kindly to being investigated by Austrac. Any contravention of either government's money laundering laws would lead to fines in the millions being imposed on both the casino and its executive management. There is also the possibility of the casino losing its gaming licence and even prison terms to be considered.'

'Have you finished? Come, come now, Tony, stop with the dramatics. What do you Westerners say? This is not your first rodeo.'

'I should have never agreed to conduct these transactions for you in the first place, Mr Li and every single day I regret having done so. And now, judging by the brimming briefcase it appears this is another significant amount of money you want handled. I don't even know the source of the money. It could be from the sale of drugs or money used to support terrorism, which is another cause for my concern.'

'The source or use of the money is not your concern and you should keep it that way if you know what's good for you, Mr Vice President.' Li said sternly, raising the temperature of the conversation. 'And furthermore, I don't expect to have to explain myself to the service staff. I can assure you though that I don't sell drugs and I certainly don't finance terrorist operations; I love this country.'

'I'm the Vice President of Client Services, not just service staff, and I take exception to being spoken to in that threatening manner. If you don't like our service, you can…'

Realising what he was about to say would further escalate the conversation, Woodard allowed his voice to trail off.

'Yes, you're correct to stop right there. You don't want to finish that sentence, Tony if you know what's good for your wellbeing and your employer's operations,' Li said pointing his index finger in a threatening manner. 'Okay, if you don't like being threatened, how about some motivation?' Li suggested.

'What do you mean by that cryptic remark?'

'Have a look at this little video I came across.' Li held up his mobile phone and pressed play on the video button. He turned the mobile towards Woodard and held it in front of his face. 'Where the hell did you get that?' Woodard yelled.

'You know where.' Woodard was watching a video of himself naked, and a mostly naked Sophie Zhao massaging him on the rug in this very room.

'That's blackmail.'

'Not at all. It's just insurance in case you have finally developed a conscience, that's all it is. Shall I keep playing the video? It gets even more interesting,' Li said, chuckling. 'And, if you need more convincing, my dear Mr Vice President of Client Services, can you imagine the response from your federal and state authorities if they were to receive an anonymous phone call regarding you and your fine establishment facilitating illicit activities. Needless to say, that phone call would be an international one, a call that would place me at a considerable distance from your authorities. Now shall we go back in time fifteen minutes to the part where you were looking at the money and ascertaining how you were going to fulfil my simple request?'

'How much is in the briefcase?'

'Look, it's not much more than on previous occasions when you have handled your side of the transaction with such aplomb.'

'How much?'

'One million dollars.'

Good God, how am I expected to deal with that amount of money and go undetected?' 'You seem to be doing well in life, Tony, with your new townhouse overlooking that picturesque little bay, family holidays in Fiji and children in private school. Oh, and let's not forget how the children get to school. Your pretty wife appears enamoured with her new X5 it would seem. Somehow, I can't help but think our little arrangement may be linked to your family's improving lifestyle, so I am certain you will find a way.'

'You leave my family out of this. Anyway, how do you know so much about my life?'

'Naivety doesn't suit a man in your position, so let's drop the pretence, shall we? Do you really think I would trust a man to handle our delicate transactions without conducting my due diligence first? You were handpicked, Tony. I obviously needed a person with executive authority to achieve my ambitions. It was also important that it was someone who didn't seem to be reaping the rewards of their work and may be open to some incentivisation. And, judging by your wife's abundance of social media photos, she would not come cheap. I did my research and the rest, as you know, is history. Now take the briefcase and go transact some business on my behalf,' Li demanded. 'I should think one hour would be sufficient time for a man in your executive position.'

The firm knock on Macquarie Suite's oak door startled Woodard. He had momentarily forgotten that he had called security and requested an escort. 'You requested an escort, sir?'

'Yes,' Woodard replied to the suited security officer. 'I need you to accompany me to the Bennelong Room Treasury Office.'

(**15**)

Bennelong Room Treasury

'Thank you, I will be fine from here,' said Woodard, dismissing the guard as he knocked on the Treasury Room's reinforced door. The guard waited until Woodard was safely inside the room and once the door was secure again, returned to his appointed duties.

'Hello Michelle, how are you?'

'I'm fine, thank you. What can I do for you, Mr Woodard?' she said as she closed the door behind him and greeted him with a professional smile.

'Nothing, thanks, Michelle. I just need to exchange some cash for chips for one of our whales.'

The woman wearing a business suit of a graphite jacket and matching skirt frowned. 'You would think these highly successful businessmen would be able to handle their own transactions. How do they manage to get through life without someone servicing their every whim?' she said, bemused. Noticing the stylish briefcase in his hand, Michelle reminded him, 'Don't forget to record the transaction in the Austrac database.' She assumed the briefcase would surely be holding much more than the mandated reporting threshold. 'Would you like me to enter the details for you, Mr Woodard?'

He gave her a congenial smile. 'That's exceedingly kind of you, but I will take care of it, Michelle.'

Michelle Ironside was the Bennelong Room's Treasury Manager and, as well as her operational treasury responsibilities, she was also responsible for the governance of the department. That included all internal corporate reporting and external statutory reporting. Strict adherence to governance protocols was a crucial component of a casino's business culture and she was a stickler for timely and accurate reporting.

'Why don't you grab a coffee while I'm here, Michelle? I'm sure you could use one about now.' Woodard needed the woman to leave him alone for ten or fifteen minutes so he could complete his transaction in privacy.

'Thank you, I would like that.'

Later that night, Michelle was arranging the exchange of one hundred thousand dollars in cash for casino chips for a valued client. As was mandated by federal and state anti-money laundering legislation, she was required to record the details of any cash transaction in excess of ten thousand dollars in the Austrac database. The client handed over ten bundles of the green polymer one hundred-dollar notes. Michelle then pulled one note from each of the bundles and individually scanned them in the Safescan Counterfeit Money Detector. With no lights pulsing red on the detector, she then, one by one, fed each bundle into the note counter. Satisfied at the legitimacy and amount of the currency, she scanned the client's casino identification card. Then she entered the monetary details of the transaction into the database. Finally, Michelle handed over a sleeve containing twenty orange-coloured chips, and with the transaction complete, the client made his way back into the exclusive Bennelong Room.

Ever since earlier noticing the bulging briefcase Mr Woodard was carrying, Michelle had been curious as to the size of the transaction being handled for the anonymous whale. Treasury Managers, as part of their training, are taught to be alert, suspicious and enquiring, and Michelle regarded herself as having each of those skills in spades. Her curiosity finally won out and while she had the Austrac database open on her monitor she thought, *why not? Let's take a peek and see how big the transaction was.*

She clicked on the summary tab and scrolled down to the bottom of the transaction listing.

She couldn't see Mr Woodard's transaction, so she adjusted the filter to sort the listing into date order and then by the time of the day. This would show the most recent transactions first. Tonight had been relatively quiet. Michelle had only handled five transactions all evening that required reporting, so Mr Woodard's transaction should be near the top of the listing. Her eyes followed her finger down the column of figures, instantly recognising the amounts that she herself had transacted. There appeared to be no listing for Mr Woodard's whale.

Surprised, she returned to the top and placed her index finger on the screen below the first amount and slowly moved it down the listing. It didn't take long until she was looking at transactions that had occurred prior to her shift. Just to be sure, she scrolled back up the listing until she came to her client's one hundred thousand dollar transaction. There was definitely no entry for Mr Woodard's whale.

Michelle was certain there would be an innocent explanation, but she couldn't imagine what it would be. When collecting the one hundred thousand dollars in chips for her own client earlier, she'd thought that the stock of five thousand dollar chips, pumpkins they were called, held in the vault had diminished considerably. Maybe she was mistaken, but she knew of another way to ascertain out whether there had been a sizeable amount transacted. A quick count of the cash on hand would either confirm or eliminate her suspicions.

After completing another client's transaction, Michelle returned to the vault and began her count. Treasury only handled notes of two denominations, one hundred-dollar notes and fifties. Both denominations were in bundles of one hundred notes and then ten bundles were grouped, in what they termed a 'brick.' Each brick contained either one hundred thousand, or fifty thousand dollars, dependent on denomination. It only took her five minutes to inventory the notes and then conduct a double check.

With her notebook in hand, she locked the vault and returned to her computer monitor. All she had to do now was subtract the value of the recorded transactions on the database from the cash on hand figure she signed for at the commencement of her shift. Michelle recalled the two unreported five thousand dollar transactions during the evening. She added the ten thousand dollars to her database total and subtracted the sum total from her open cash holding.

She suddenly felt quite unwell, both nauseous and light-headed. She wasn't prone to anxiety attacks, but she was now suddenly feeling extremely anxious. She had never been in this position in her career as the Treasury Manager. Trying to regain her composure, she sat upright in her chair and breathed deeply. Treasury's cash on hand figure was exactly one million dollars higher than her reconciliation figure. And she surmised, quite rightly, that the value of the stock of 'pumpkins' on hand would be one million dollars less. She couldn't reconcile the pumpkin transactions, as they didn't record the denomination of chips handed out to clients. *Oh, what the heck do I do now?* She thought. Michelle loved working at the casino and had managed her career prudently since commencing as a croupier many years ago. It was her life. She had always been highly regarded because of her punctuality, honesty and integrity, and was considered to be beyond reproach, qualities which had eventually been rewarded with the Treasury Manager's position. Now she felt horribly compromised by Mr Woodard's activities.

What options do I have available to me? She contemplated a number of possible options open to her and wrote them down in her diary.

1. Ignore it completely and hope the discrepancy in cash versus gaming chips wasn't discovered in the next day or two, after which it would be too late to attribute blame to a specific person.

2. Enter a transaction for one million dollars into the Austrac database, listing an anonymous client.

3. Raise her concerns with the Bennelong Room General Manager, as her immediate superior.

4. Contact Mr Woodard and confront him with her concerns.

The first was a possibility, but it still came with inherent risks to her and her career if the discrepancy was discovered during a random audit and the second really wasn't an option at all unless she wanted to go to prison. It was only fair that she allow Mr Woodard the opportunity to explain his actions before acting on her third option. *At least I have eliminated two options, well maybe,* she mused.

She would have to sleep on it and evaluate the best way to deal with the conundrum with which she was now faced. Michelle quickly inventoried the gaming chips and then added the value to the cash on hand figure she had counted earlier. The total was exactly twenty million dollars, as it should be. The complication was that, if there was a forensic audit conducted prior to her next shift tomorrow evening, it would show a variation of one million dollars in both cash on hand and gaming chips. Having completed the handover to the incoming Treasury Supervisor, she ventured out into the cool, dark night, stepped up into the rear seat of her Uber and headed home to her apartment.

$$\textbf{16}$$

AMSA Control Room Canberra

James Fairweather disconnected the satellite call, leant back in his chair, and reflected on the exchange with Captain Han. As part of his induction and training as an analyst, he was provided with an overview of some of the basic mechanical, electrical and hydraulic failures that can befall a large ocean-going vessel. He was also advised on the potential impact of such failures and a vessel's ability to continue its voyage. Even though the technical training was quite limited, he had a couple of thoughts rattling around in his analyst's brain. There were responses from the captain that were inconsistent with his understanding of the circumstances as described. First, he understood that most ships had some kind of back-up generator, not to power the ship itself, but to maintain emergency signs, corridor lighting, key instrumentation on the bridge and most importantly, the mandated navigation lights. Similarly, even without knowing the model of transponder, he was certain that all AIS transponders would have an in-built back-up power supply. *So why did it cease transmitting?* he pondered.

And the other thing bothering him was the location where Han said he had temporarily anchored while the ship's electrics were supposedly being repaired. The captain, by his own admission, had said that it was a calm night on the water, so why would he steer the vessel west towards the passage and drop anchor there? On such a calm night he could have dropped anchor anywhere in the waters adjacent to the shipping lane.

For obvious reasons, mostly in case of potentially damaging litigation, all calls made by the AMSA Control Room were recorded, so he listened intently to the recording, seeking to confirm his thoughts. The left side of a person's brain performs tasks that involve logic and James's was in overdrive as he listened to the recording for a second time.

Even though AMSA was not a government security agency, James felt there were enough inconsistencies in the captain's story that he should at least write a summary of his conclusions and forward it, along with the recording, to the Maritime Border Command. His boss, Jonathan Caldwell, was your typically cautious public servant, and if he sent the report to him, it may never see the light of day. He drafted the email, attached the recording and momentarily hovered the cursor above the send icon. Public servants didn't have a reputation for being proactive, but James wasn't an ordinary civil servant. Many were cautious about escalating scenarios without cause or proof of an incident, but James was convinced that he was right to raise his concerns about the Chinese Horizon. He waivered, wondering whether this was too far removed from his job description and could lead to repercussions. *No*, he thought, his gut feeling told him he was *right to have concerns*. He bent forward and clicked on the send icon. He leaned back in his chair again and reflected on the least boring night he had experienced in his role since joining AMSA. *Maybe I am an analyst after all*, he chuckled to himself.

At seven o'clock in the morning, Shane Williamson was sitting at his desk sipping an extra hot latte as he scrolled down his inbox and read his emails. He was a career public servant and committed to whatever role the Commonwealth Government needed him to fulfil. Currently, he was the National Operations Manager at the Maritime

Border Command. He always checked his emails first thing in the morning, in case there were any overnight incidents that required his attention. This was particularly the case following the incident with the Cape York last evening.

The most recent email had been forwarded by the Operations Centre at two o'clock that morning. The original email was from a James Fairweather, a young analyst who worked the night shift in the AMSA Control Room. It made for interesting reading. Apparently, a Chinese-based cargo vessel had disappeared off the monitor for three hours in proximity of Hydrographers Passage on the Great Barrier Reef. When the vessel reappeared on the monitor, it was positioned contradictory to its intended voyage to Brisbane. Fairweather had, probably correctly, Williamson thought, contacted the vessel to enquire as to its welfare. He had interrogated the captain, and apparently not satisfied with the responses which had raised his suspicions, he filed his report. Given Captain Johnson's concerning observations about the location of the same vessel, a picture was beginning to develop in Williamson's mind. He read the remainder of the report and listened to the voice recording from the email attachment. Then he called his assistant on the desk phone's intercom. 'Sally, good morning. Can you contact Jonathan Caldwell from AMSA for me and ask him and his analyst, James Fairweather, to meet with me in my office this afternoon, please?'

'Certainly, Mr Williamson.'

The Chinese Horizon wouldn't be arriving in Brisbane until tomorrow morning, which gave Williamson time to decide on a course of action. He was in no doubt as to what that course of action needed to be.

Balmain Inner West Sydney
Monday 2nd March

'What time is it?' Jack asked as he leant across Julie-Anne's naked body, looking for the alarm clock.

'It's time we continued from where we left off last night,' she murmured as she teasingly trickled her hand down between his legs. Given that it was still early, and he was rapidly hardening, Jack rolled Julie-Anne over, kissed her passionately and entered her.

'That was fast,' she said, mildly surprised while wrapping her legs around his hips and drawing him further in.

'I'm just doing what you said, picking up where we left off last night.'

'You're a funny man, Jack Wagner.'

They went back and forth, arching and lowering rhythmically until they were both close to peaking. She liked him to pick up the pace when she was close, and his timing was perfect.

'I love morning glories,' she panted.

He kissed her on the forehead and untangled himself from the one thousand thread count Egyptian cotton sheets. With hands cupped protecting his modesty, Jack circumnavigated his king-size bed and headed to the bathroom.

Julie-Anne had propped herself up on the pillows. 'Oh, puh-lease, why are you holding your hands like that for god's sake? You look ridiculous.'

'I'm quite shy if you haven't noticed,' Jack replied, offering a cheeky grin.

'Really, you didn't seem very bashful last night when you were jumping my body, and again this morning, for that matter.'

'That was different. It was dark.'

'Well, Mister Modesty, you had better leave the bathroom light off then 'cos I'm coming to join you.'

Afterwards, over coffee, they discussed what they both had in their schedules for the ensuing day. 'Do you have any mysterious investigations that you care to share with your lover and some-time girlfriend?' she asked mischievously, eyeing him over her coffee cup.

'Nothing exciting, really. A criminal informant of mine wants to meet for coffee, so I'll catch-up with him and see what he has to offer. Apparently there's been an increase in the volume of a higher purity cocaine being distributed around the eastern suburbs. It seems that the bad guy's business model is evolving. I'll see what my informant has to say about that and then take it from there, assuming he has anything of substance to offer. What about you, JA?'

Julie-Anne was an investigative journalist for the Sydney Daily News. Until recently, it was a broadsheet newspaper, but had now been trimmed down to tabloid size to reduce costs. Even though some journalist positions had been made redundant for the same reason, she was proud of the fact that the Daily News was still committed to investigative journalism. That could change in a heartbeat given the ever-evolving media landscape and the digital giants reposting freely obtained content from traditional media publishers. She would need to stay at the top of her game.

'Not that different to yours, really. Your STG is looking into the impact of Triads in Sydney and in particular how the profits of their criminal enterprises are generated and where the funds are directed.

I think there's a link with China's increasing interference activities, and if there is, I am going to find it.'

'Good for you. What does STG stand for?' Jack asked.

'You're the detective. Work it out, genius.' Julie-Anne rose from her stool, kissed him farewell and with a swish of her hair and a cheeky wink, made for the front door.

$$\textbf{(18)}$$

Sydney Daily News Surry Hills

Julie-Anne loved her electric blue BMW 3 Series. It was a stunning blue-sky morning and a balmy twenty-six degrees for the first working day of autumn. With only the whiff of a breeze, she flipped back the soft top, cranked up Beyoncé and headed across the Anzac Bridge, down through Darling Harbour and into Surry Hills. The weather forecast was for a maximum temperature of thirty-eight degrees, and as much as she loved the sun, she wouldn't be venturing out of the office today into that oppressive heat. She was in a buoyant mood after her sleepover at Jack's and their tumble this morning. Julie-Anne was suitably stimulated for the day ahead as she pulled up to the entry to the newspaper's underground carpark. She waited patiently while the carpark's sensor confirmed her vehicle's number plate. All being as it should, the roller shutter clanged upwards, and she drove through the concrete maze to her dedicated parking spot.

In the new world of digital and social media, and television's obsession with the twenty-four hour news cycle, newspaper reporters, and their profession, were no longer held in the high esteem of their twentieth-century predecessors. *And no wonder,* she thought. Read any of the country's tabloids and be treated to a headline that championed "the Ten Best Pizza Restaurants in Parramatta" or pointed the finger at the "Sydney Suburbs Most Prone to Burglaries". Or heaven forbid, "Love Rat Outed on The Bachelor." It's not even journalism, she thought, it's just cut-and-paste fodder for the vicariously living, poor, unfortunate masses.

Julie-Anne's career in journalism began in her hometown of Lismore, in the Northern Rivers region of New South Wales. She cut her teeth in the newspaper industry as the local health reporter, which was a challenging role given the proliferation of anti-vaxxers in the region. It seemed like everyone in the area had an opinion on vaccinating children. When in the role, Julie-Anne made sure she kept her opinions on the highly controversial subject strictly to herself and avoided like the plague discussing the topic.

Then she scored the role as agriculture reporter, another challenge, especially for a woman who knew next to nothing about farming. While reporting on everything agricultural, she also had a brief stint as the evening weather presenter at the local television affiliate. It was in this role that she was noticed by a newspaper executive from Sydney whilst he was holidaying with his family in Byron Bay. In an industry increasingly requiring multi-taskers, the editor was looking to employ an all-round reporter. Julie-Anne was successfully recruited and had covered similar industries until she was eventually promoted to her current role as investigative journalist.

She investigated issues of national and state public interest and, after years in the role, she had become damn good at it. As such, she was highly respected at the Daily News and kept a couple of benefits of the old profession. Julie-Anne was free to conduct her own investigations and manage her own timeline just as long as she kept her editor in the loop. And she had been allocated her very own dedicated car parking space, which, given the prices of parking in Sydney, was a blessing. She also got to attend the morning editorial meeting, which was where she was heading now.

The meeting still resembled somewhat of a boy's club, but Julie-Anne was one of three women invited to the meeting. She gathered it was three more than would have been in the same room anytime in the last century. Chris Russell, the Editor-in-Chief, called the gathering to order and one by one, the departmental editors provided an update on the stories they were developing for the following day's edition. They discussed both federal and state political events unfolding, finance with banks behaving badly, increasing crime in the western suburbs, the ice scourge, climate change and, of course, the elephant in the room, the unfolding COVID-19 pandemic.

'JA, how is your investigation progressing? Can we have a quick update?'

Julie-Anne was usually one of the last to update the gathering and had her time quarantined to sixty seconds. Not for any negative reason, just that she wasn't on a deadline like the others in the room, so she didn't have to submit copy by four o'clock.

She leaned forward in her chair. 'With all the hysteria about China putting its political finger in other country's domestic pies, I'm trying to ascertain how that process is operating in Australia. There is anecdotal evidence that there are links between the Triads operating here in Sydney, Chinese Australian residents doubling as spies and Chinese government agencies hiding behind the now defunct Confucius Institute program. With the Institute being removed by the state government, China will be looking for other avenues or vehicles to continue their program of interference.'

'What have you got so far?' enquired Russell.

'It's early days, but I am making progress. I just need to nail down the key players, find out how they're linked and what their end game is. And of course, if I can find the source of the funding, then I may be able to follow the money and see where it leads.'

'Okay, keep at it and keep me in the loop. This investigation, if it develops as you obviously think it will, could cause significant angst for many prominent people in this country at a time when our relationship with China is fragile. I don't want to be blindsided. And watch your back.' With that, Russell closed the meeting and Julie-Anne returned to her desk, determined to make progress.

$$\textcircled{19}$$

Milk and Honey Café

Jack drove his ten-year-old silver Holden Commodore along New South Head Road in Rose Bay, making his way to the agreed meeting point. He also owned a mustard MGB-Roadster which he had lovingly restored with the help of his father. It was a soft- top convertible, and he fancied a drive around the various bays that jutted into New South Head Road, but it was a little too conspicuous for a meeting with a criminal informant.

On the drive to the café, he passed through the leafy suburbs of Darling Point, Double Bay, Bellevue Hill and Point Piper. These were some of the more exclusive suburbs of Sydney whose wealthy residents, Jack assumed, were no doubt availing themselves of the higher purity cocaine he and JA were discussing over coffee earlier this morning. For this reason, he irreverently referred to the café as Coke and Money. He slowly, but not too obviously, drove past the café twice, looking for people that weren't doing what they should be doing, someone pretending to read a newspaper, a man not talking into his phone even though it was held to his ear, or even the obvious, an overdressed person sitting on a park bench in thirty degree heat. Instead, he saw young mums in their active wear trotting along behind their prams, lycra-clad twenty somethings with buds in their ears jogging around the park, schoolboys training on the football pitch and pretty little things in pink gently hitting the ball back and forth at the Lyne Park Tennis Centre. Only when he was comfortable that he had cleared the area did he park his car in a side street one block from the café.

He walked back along the sidewalk to the Milk and Honey Café, made his way through the courtyard at the front and into the café proper. Jack quickly spotted his CI sitting at a table with his back to the wall. He made his way through the sea of babbling well-to-do milfs, their tables chock full of kale and egg white omelettes and soy lattes. Stevie was as unassuming in appearance as any CI Jack had ever known. He always seemed to be wearing a lumberjack shirt that hung loosely over his baggy jeans. His well-maintained George Michael beard was contradicted by his gap-toothed smile and perpetually bloodshot eyes. His hairstyle was a throwback to the nineties Beastie Boys with a mullet that Jack thought more closely resembled a mudflap.

'You look like the poster boy for criminal informants.'

'What does that mean, Mr Wagner?'

'Never mind. Swap seats,' Jack ordered. In his years as a detective, Jack had never sat with his back to an entrance and he wasn't about to start now. *Old habits.*

'How come?'

'Use your head. I want to keep an eye out for any unexpected visitors, and you don't need to be recognised having coffee with one of the force's finest. Now, what have you got for me, Stevie?'

'Straight down to business, hey, Mr Wagner.'

'You are my CI and outside of that we don't have much in common, so forgive me if I skip the small talk. You contacted me, so what have you got?' Snitches were notoriously unreliable, so he needed to keep Stevie focused.

'Can I at least have a coffee while I'm here?' The waitress was approaching the table, so Jack ordered two lattes.

'How much is it worth to you?'

'For God's sake, how would I know until you tell me what you've got? You're wasting my time and I've got better things to do,' Jack said as he started to rise from his seat.

'Okay, calm down.'

The coffees arrived and Stevie tentatively took a sip. 'I've heard on the street that there's a new batch of cocaine doing the rounds of the eastern suburbs.'

'I live on the other side of town and even I've heard that for myself.'

'Yeah, but this has levels of purity not seen in Australia before. I have heard it's as high as forty-five percent, which is well above the street level average. And that's what's got the stockbrokers and financiers of the eastern suburbs so excited. They're happily paying upwards of five hundred dollars a gram for the new gear.'

'I could have found that out in about five minutes in a cocktail bar in Bondi and all for the cost of a Jack and Coke. You got anything else for me? I have to go.'

'There doesn't seem to be a big supply, which is interesting. I've heard that it is being distributed by a gang out of Chinatown. The Chinks don't normally stray far from Haymarket, so this is new turf for them. That's gotta be worth something to you.'

Jack was becoming frustrated again. 'As usual, I could have found that out at the corner pub within five minutes of ordering a beer.'

'Okay, okay.' Stevie's eyes darted around the room. 'Supposedly, there's a hot chick with a model's looks and body doing the rounds of the eastern suburbs and dropping off baggies to her toffee nosed clients.'

'Do you know who she is?'

'Nah, all I know is she is a part Chink chick from Chinatown and she is new to the area.'

'You mean Eurasian, Stevie.'

'What?'

Jack sighed. 'Never mind.'

'I only found this out earlier this morning. Apparently, the camel jockeys whose territory it is weren't too impressed and they ambushed her in Bondi last night.'

'What happened?'

'What I heard on the street is that they threatened her at gunpoint, gave her a serious warning and then let her go.'

'Do you have a name for me?'

'No. But if she's from Chinatown, then I'm sure you can work out which crew she's with.'

Jack handed over a one hundred dollar note as he rose from his chair.

'Is that all? A lousy hundred dollars. Surely it's gotta be worth more than that.'

Get me something I can actually use rather than street gossip and maybe, just maybe, there'll be more in it for you next time. And don't forget your change when you pay for the coffees.'

'Mr Wagner, that's hardly—' but Jack was already heading for the door.

Whilst taking the short drive to AFP headquarters in the heart of Sydney, Jack mulled over the conversation again. He didn't learn anything new from his CI, but it added fuel to his suspicions of a subtle change occurring in the retail cocaine trade. The AFP and Border Force had made numerous large seizures of cocaine in the past year that had resulted in a shortage in the market. Cocaine must still be arriving, and the AFP had suspected for a while that smaller shipments of higher purity coke were now entering the country. This change in business model was intelligent as the smaller shipments reduced the chances of detection, the higher purity commanded significantly higher prices, and as a result, the distributors still made their required margins.

As he pulled his Commodore into the Australian Federal Police headquarters in Goulburn Street, he recalled something that Julie-Anne had said over coffee that morning. Something about her investigating the Triads and where their profits were being directed. He wondered if there might be a link between their investigations, especially given Stevie's revelations about the Chinks. Jack and JA respected each other's professional boundaries, so they both kept their work conversations general and avoided getting into specifics. He wondered if that was all about to change.

Macquarie Suite

Woodard had made a timely return to the Macquarie Suite the previous evening and Li now had one million dollars in gaming chips in his possession. To finish the laundering process, he would need to spend time in the Bennelong Room, pretending to be the 'whale' the casino thought he was. The Chinese traditionally favoured baccarat, but Li found it boring and really just a game of chance. He much preferred blackjack, it was more about skill and strategy than just plain luck.

He would wait a day or two before availing himself of the plush surroundings of the Bennelong Room. He hoped the time delay would minimise anyone connecting him with Woodard's activities. When he did play, he would only play a few hands of blackjack, then feign illness and request an electronic funds transfer for his remaining chip holding. Of course, feigning illness would only be a necessity if he happened to lose. If he did lose a few hands, he wasn't bothered because he would ensure his losses were limited to less than ten percent. This was an acceptable price to pay for laundering his chips into legitimate currency. And of course, if he won, then the overhead security cameras would clearly show just that and any suspicion would be minimised. In the meantime, the chips were securely locked away in his room safe, under both key and combination lock. Now, down to business and one of the key reasons behind this visit to Sydney. He took out his mobile phone and dialled a number he had memorised.

'Melissa Wu speaking.'

'Hello, Miss Wu, my name is Li Qiang. I believe we have a mutual associate.'

'Hello, Mr Li, yes, although I have never met you, apparently, we do. How is the Consul General?'

'He is well and enjoying his new role. Miss Wu, I would like to meet with you to discuss a proposition I have for you. Are you available this morning?'

'Can you give me an idea as to the nature of your proposal? I wouldn't want to waste your time.'

Li allowed himself a smile. 'I think you will find my proposition most amenable to you.'

Melissa had no idea as to what the proposition might be, but she was inquisitive by nature. 'Okay, I have an hour free from eleven o'clock.'

'That would be acceptable to me. Where can we meet?'

'There is a café called Jimmy Chan's on Burwood Road in Burwood. I will see you there. How will I know you, Mr Li?'

'It's okay, I will recognise you, Miss Wu. I'll see you at eleven.'

Li called Client Services and ordered a car and driver for ten thirty. He had an hour to fine tune his strategy for hooking Melissa Wu. His planning session was interrupted by the ringing of his burner phone. It could only be one of the three people to whom had given the number.

'Wie, my friend, how are you?'

'It seems your warning came too late.'

'What are you talking about?'

'Ling Jun, Wang Wei and our cruiser were intercepted and fired upon by an Australian naval vessel last night.'

Li was biting his tongue and again desperately resisting the temptation to give Wie the "I told you so speech." 'What happened? Were they captured?'

'Luckily no, but they were tracked through the reef and fired upon twice. It was only through Ling's excellent seamanship and good fortune that they managed to escape. The pursuing vessel was the Cape York which was apparently too large to enter the many shallow channels within the reef, so Ling was able to evade them, eventually.'

'Are they both okay?'

'Yes, fortunately, but then there was another concerning incident. They were pulled over by a policeman as they were detouring through a small country town. Ling was caught using his mobile while driving, but luckily for him the vehicle wasn't searched.'

'Nà zhēnshi yúchǔn.

'Yes, it was just that; stupid. Ling's getting careless and I will need to speak with him. And earlier, they apparently had a near miss with a crocodile.'

'Huò bù dān xíng, Wie.'

'No, it seems their misfortune does not come singly. I concede you were correct with your suggestions yesterday. We need to change our method of delivery and product transfer. We could have easily lost a hundred kilos of coke, had Ling and Wei arrested and exposed ourselves to the authorities. This can't be allowed to happen again.'

Li was smiling to himself. 'No, it cannot. Have you spoken to our contact in the mother country, Wie?'

'Yes, and he agrees.'

(**21**)

Oceanic Hotel Corporate Offices

'Mr Woodard, there's a call from you on line three. It's Michelle Ironside.'

Michelle had never called him and their only interactions had always been limited to providing corporate and treasury services to Bennelong Room members when their roles overlapped. Woodard didn't believe in coincidences and knew in his mind this had to be in relation to his transaction the previous night. It couldn't be anything else. He needed time to think and develop a plausible response to the inevitable question she would pose to him. He started to sweat profusely, and his breathing accelerated. *This isn't good at all,* he mumbled to himself.

'Sage, can you get her contact number please? I will call her back shortly.'

He needed time to compose himself, so he waited an hour before calling Michelle's number. He also thought it an appropriate amount of time to wait to avoid displaying any sense of urgency.

'Hi, Michelle, it's Tony Woodard here. You left a message for me.'

'Yes, hello, Mr Woodard, thank you for calling back.'

'My apologies for the delayed response, but Client Services have been inundated this morning. What can I do for you, Michelle?'

Michelle had always been impeccably honest and wasn't accustomed to being deceitful, but neither could she discuss her concerns over the telephone. She thought generalisation was the best tactic for now. 'Mr Woodard, I noticed a slight irregularity within the Treasury operations last night and I need advice from someone outside the department,' she stated cautiously.

'What sort of irregularity, Michelle?'

Not wanting to neither alarm nor forewarn him, she said. 'Nothing major, but I would value your opinion and advice, Mr Woodard.'

He was fairly certain he knew exactly the irregularity she was referring to, but wasn't convinced of the precise reason behind the call. 'Okay, what can I help you with?'

Trying to remain calm and not sound flustered, she said, 'I usually have a coffee on my way to work at the Bayside Café on Pyrmont Bay near the HMS Endeavour replica. Perhaps we could have a quick chat there before I start work at three o'clock,' she suggested.

That sent the alarm bells ringing inside Woodard's head. *Why would she want to meet with him away from their workplace?* he asked himself. Well, he had a few hours to think about it and formulate a plausible response, if indeed he was to be asked the obvious question. If Michelle was certain of her facts, she would have doubtless lodged a report. That she wanted to meet for a coffee suggested to him she wasn't yet at the point of formalising her concerns. Maybe he had some wriggle room to manouevre, or even negotiate if she put forward any allegations. *I guess I'll know in a few hours,'* he surmised.

'I'll see you at two o'clock then, Michelle, if that suits.'

'That's perfect, thank you, Mr Woodard.'

Having had his worst fears confirmed, Woodard now needed to develop various scenarios to respond to whatever specific allegations the Treasury Manager was going to put to him. His actions had breached state and federal anti-money laundering laws, but one thing was for certain; he wasn't going to prison. Whatever happened this afternoon that would be his default position and he would do anything and everything to ensure it stayed that way.

(22)

Desk of Julie-Anne

There had been two episodes of the national broadcaster's nightly current affairs program dedicated to rising Chinese influence in Australian politics and one particular thought-provoking article published in the national broadsheet on the same topic. Whilst all raised considerable issues, none reached a definitive conclusion, nor did they provide any actionable intelligence.

Julie-Anne intended to change all that with her investigation. She needed to read her notes again and clearly understand the quality of the information she had to this point. So far all she had was rumour, innuendo and unsubstantiated intelligence. *I need to whiteboard this and start building a flow chart to plot the links between the various players,* she thought, looking up at the ceiling in frustration.

Her thoughts were interrupted by her mobile phone ringing. She was excited to see that the Caller ID said Jack. Julie-Anne had met him six months earlier at a crime scene near her apartment in inner city Newtown. She didn't need a man in her life, nor the validation that comes from having a boyfriend. Apparently, that's what some women felt, but most definitely not her. Although, if someone appealing to the eye stumbled into her line of sight, then who was she to ignore the sonar going off in her head? At the crime scene, Julie-Anne had noticed this ruggedly handsome, tall man, with an athletic build, black hair and deep brown eyes. And he was around her age, too. *I'll have to find out who this guy is.* Then, much to her disappointment, she noticed the lanyard dangling down across the front of his suit jacket. *'Nup, well there goes that idea. I don't date policemen,'* she had grumbled at the time.

'Hi, Jack, is that you?'

'Yeah, it's me, STG, don't you have Caller ID?' he jokingly enquired.

'Of course I do, but two conversations in one day. I thought maybe someone had *hi jacked* your phone. I Just knew I could find a way to get that into our conversation,' she said, chuckling.'

'Get what into our conversation? I'm confused.'

'You'll get it one day. So, did you work out the STG acronym yet?' 'I'm still working on it.'

'Well, now, you have two things to work on detective. What's up?'

'I've scored a couple of tickets to see Diesel at The Bridge Hotel in Rozelle tonight and thought we might go along. We could have tapas at Alegrias and then stroll up to pub for the show. What do you think?'

'What do I think? I think that would be three catchups and two sleepovers in twenty-four hours. Are you feeling okay?'

'Who said anything about a sleepover?' he responded tongue in cheek.

'I did, detective. I'll see you at Alegrias around seven.'

Julie-Anne and Jack had been dating for six months. Even after all that time, Julie-Anne still didn't know what they had, nor where it was heading. She didn't have to attach a label to it, but some clarity would be nice. Jack ran hot and cold. He appeared to be happy spending time with her at the moment, probably because things were quiet at his work, she guessed. They were enjoying each other's company, so she would make the most of it while it lasted, knowing there would be the inevitable downtime not too far into the future. As soon as Jack became busy with an investigation the dinner cancellations would come. Whereas, even if she were busy with an investigation of her own, she would still always make time for him. Probably, she thought, because she was always playing catch-up. She didn't know how long she could accept the spasmodic nature of their relationship, or whatever it was called, but for the time being, it was fun, so she would roll with the flow. *And the sex was awesome*, she mused, recalling their romps of the past twenty-four hours. She cleared her mind of the mental images, went back to her whiteboard and began charting what little information she had so far.

$$\left(\textbf{23}\right)$$

Jimmy Chan's Café Burwood

Melissa Wu was seated next to the large floor to ceiling window of Jimmy Chan's Café, lost in her thoughts, when she noticed a portly man of Chinese appearance alight from a limousine and cross the road towards the café. *This must surely be my appointment*, she thought. Although men of Chinese appearance were common in the area, limousines were not.

He entered the café, immediately turned to his right, and made his way to her table. 'Mr Li, I assume,' she said as she stood and offered her outstretched hand.

Li thought she was an extremely attractive woman, unusually tall and dressed in a bold red two-piece business suit that was unfortunately hiding what he suspected was a trim and taut physique.

'Yes, hello, Miss Wu. Please take a seat.' Li first needed to put her at ease, so he made small talk, which did not come naturally to him. 'This is a cosmopolitan part of Sydney; I almost feel as if I am back in Shanghai.'

'Yes, it is, diversity abounds here in Burwood and is no more evident than with the number of residents of Chinese ancestry in the area. It is a vibrant part of Sydney.'

'You must be very comfortable here.'

Melissa frowned; she was slightly taken aback by his inference. 'I am Australian. I was born in Burwood and have lived here for my entire life, so yes, I am extremely at ease here,' she stated, too sharply.

That was what he wanted to hear.

'Would you like tea, Mr Li? They serve only Golden Leaf here, so you will definitely feel at home here, too.'

'Yes please, just a simple green tea will be fine, Miss. Wu.'

'I have another appointment at twelve, so can you please tell me why we are here?'

'It is a long, complicated story and we don't have time to delve deeply into it on this occasion, but I will provide you with an overview. Put simply, Miss Wu, the people I represent are concerned with the anti-Chinese rhetoric that is pervading this country at this time. China is a responsible global citizen that contributes significantly to the world economy. We manufacture and export products that make life more innovative, efficient and liveable for more than half the world's population. And we have taken giant steps with our Belt and Road Initiative that in particular assists the poorer nations of the world.'

'I am sure that China feels enormously proud of its global commitments, but what does any of that have to do with me?'

'China is Australia's largest trading partner with over a quarter of its exports going to China, which in turn, contributes over seventy-five billion dollars to the Australian economy. Yet all we seem to hear in the Australian media are stories about China's human rights record, their poor environmental record, annexing the islands and shoals of the South China Sea and political interference, amongst an extensive list of negatives, Miss Wu.'

Melissa wondered where this conversation was heading. 'As I said, I'm certain China is very proud of its achievements.'

'Allow me to continue, please. The New South Wales government has removed the Confucius Institute program from the thirteen schools in which the program operated. The program was even paid for by the Chinese government. And now, China is unfairly being held responsible for the virus outbreak that is sweeping the world. So, you can understand that the people I represent want to change the public discourse, if you will, in this country.'

'Who do you represent, Mr Li?'

'The people I represent have the best interests of China and the Chinese people at heart and to ensure the continued advancement and success of our country. Who they are is not important.'

'*Your* country, Mr Li,' Melissa said. She again wondered where this conversation was leading. 'And you've come to tell me this why?'

'You are a well-known and highly regarded long-term resident of this area, are a successful businesswoman in your own right, are an accomplished lawyer, have served on the local council and as such, understand the robustness of political life.'

Melissa cupped her hands under her chin. 'And of course, it doesn't hurt that I am of Chinese ancestry.'

'Nearly twenty percent of the population of this area have Chinese ancestry and in Burwood itself the figure is as high as thirty-two percent. I don't see your ancestry as a negative, Miss Wu.'

'I'm sure you don't,' she responded. 'So, what is it that you actually want of me?'

'We would like you to represent the interests of China and the Chinese people in the New South Wales state parliament.'

Melissa straightened herself and sat upright. 'Let me remind you, I am Australian by birth, so when I was a local government councillor my focus was on representing the entire electorate, not just one ethnic group, even if they do share my ancestry, Mr Li.'

He held his hands out like a preacher. 'Okay, maybe I could have said that better. We just want someone with a voice inside the state parliament that can promote the benefits of working cooperatively with China and provide an alternative viewpoint to the pervasive negative sentiment. Of course, as you rightly pointed out, your primary role will be to represent the people of this electorate.'

'Let me guess. I imagine one of the first priorities of your chosen candidate would be to lobby to have the Confucius Institute reinstated into New South Wales schools. How close am I?'

'It's good to see that you still have an interest in New South Wales politics. Certainly having a member sitting on the cross benches in state parliament could enable us to achieve significant positive change in the public discussion surrounding China.'

After taking a sabbatical from local political life, Melissa had recently been deliberating whether it was time to again to serve the people of inner western Sydney and how she would go about achieving that ambition. She had been considering re-entering politics at either the state or federal level, but didn't really want to get involved in the sometimes dirty machinations of pre-selection for the major parties. Maybe this was her opportunity.

Melissa rested her chin on her clasped hands. 'If I were to consider your proposal, you and the anonymous people you represent need to understand that I won't be a puppet for anyone,' she said.

'Given your integrity and stellar reputation within the community we would expect nothing less.'

'I have to go to my next appointment, so thank you for your time. It was an interesting chat.' Melissa Wu said as she rose from the table and offered her hand.

'Yes, I have a luncheon appointment as well. Farewell for now, I hope. I will be in touch, Ms Wu.'

Chinatown Sydney

'Welcome, Mr Li. It is good to see you again so soon. How are you?'

'Thank you, Huang, I am still very well. Has my guest arrived yet?'

'I'm not sure, who is your guest today, Mr Li?'

'I'm sure you would know if he was here, Huang.' Li looked around the restaurant, and not seeing his guest, made his way to the bar where he ordered his usual, a fifteen-year-old Glenlivet.

Five minutes later, Huang, now gushing with pride, was ushering Li's guest towards him.

'Mr Consul General, it's good to see you, how are you?'

'I'm well thank you, Li, how are you?'

'I am always excellent when I have my favourite drink, and I am in my favourite restaurant in my favourite city. Life is good.' Li escorted the Consul General past the wall of aquariums to his table in the rear corner.

'Huang told me this was your favourite restaurant, twice in two days, he said.' Li would need to have a quiet word with Huang and remind him of the meaning of discretion, he thought, while the Consul General ordered a green tea.

Li had first met Zhang Xiao at one of those cocktail parties that Consuls General are obliged to host. Consular staff, bureaucrats, social columnists, B grade celebrities and even minor politicians of no influence seemed to delight in such gatherings. Not Li. He found the attendees mind numbingly boring with their trivialities and pasted-on insincerity. He had to reluctantly attend because it was courteous and declining the invitation would have caused offence to the Consul General.

'Consul General, would you like me to order for you?'

'I know all too well what you are going to order, Li, the Pipis in XO Sauce. Am I correct?'

Li smiled politely. 'You know me too well, sir.'

'Go ahead, I haven't had them since I was here last. Did you read the article in The Australian this morning, Li?'

'Which one, sir?'

'Can we dispense with the formalities? Please, call me Xiao. The story siding with the so-called democracy protesters in Hong Kong.'

'Yes, I did and once again I noticed an anti-Chinese sentiment running through the story.'

'Li, we need to change the direction of the dialogue in this country. Have you considered what we discussed on your last visit?'

'Yes, I have, and I have also discussed it with our mutual friend in China. I might have found the ideal candidate.'

The Consul General looked up from his Pipis. 'Tell me more, please?'

Li told Xiao about his meeting with Melissa Wu, her ancestry, business acumen, legal background, political experience, and suitability for the demographic of the electorate she would be representing.

'I think I met her once at a local government reception. That all sounds very promising, but does she share our concerns and is she sympathetic to our cause, Li?'

'Well, she made it abundantly clear that she is proud of her Australian citizenship and her first priorities are always to her constituents. She seems to be fiercely independent, and of her own mind, so we would have to massage the messages we want her to deliver. Wu is articulate, attractive with a trim figure, dresses smartly and has engaging smile, not that she shared it with me. She would present very well on camera and in person.'

'This Wu sounds like a suitable candidate, so what more do we need to do to convince her?'

'It will take some time, but she has the best profile for the candidate we are looking for; we will just need to influence her ideologies along the way. Anyway, the next state election is six months away, so time isn't of the essence just yet.'

'I understand the timeline, Li, but it would be preferable to lock her in as soon as possible. You know what they're like in Beijing. Patient like the ox one minute then scurrying around like rabbits the next. What is your next step?'

'Do you have any of your boring consular receptions coming up?'

The Consul General folded his napkin, turned to Li and sighed. 'Li, Li, you really need to learn something about diplomacy. As luck would have it, I am actually hosting the State Government's Trade Minister, his staff and a couple of DFAT representatives two nights from now to celebrate our most recent trade agreement. I assume you would you like me to invite Miss Wu along.'

'Yes, and me too, Consul General. I will send you her details. Now, have you discussed this scenario and our plans with the Ambassador in Canberra, Xiao?'

'Yes, and he agrees with our approach, but for obvious reasons, does not want to be linked. Li, I have to leave for another engagement. That is good progress and hopefully will lead to a successful outcome. And as always, those little creatures were delicious. Thank you.'

Li held back briefly while the Consul General departed and signalled for Huang to join him. 'Huang, you and I have a good relationship and if you would like it to remain that way, then I would appreciate it if you could be discreet about my activities.'

'Oh, I always am very private about our clients. What have I done?'

'You told the Consul General I was here yesterday. Yes, he is surely an acquaintance of mine, but I still like to maintain my privacy and I don't need everyone knowing my movements. Is that clear, Huang?'

'It will never happen again, Mr Li.'

'Thank you, now can you call up my car, please?'

While Li was waiting at the bar, Wie walked in the door. He looked agitated and was bouncing on his toes.

'What's wrong?'

'One of my dealers was threatened at gunpoint in the eastern suburbs last night. And don't give me any of that 'I told you so' bullshit either.'

'Well, I—'

Wie bounced on his toes again. 'Don't go there; I am not in the mood.'

Li could see the rage still evident. 'Which dealer and what happened?'

'Lucie. She had made her last delivery in Bondi and was heading home when she was ambushed as she reached her car.'

Li was very fond of Lucie and had made numerous overtures towards her, but unfortunately for him, she had never reciprocated the sentiment. 'Is she okay?'

'Yeah, she's a tough cookie, that one, but I know she has to be concerned, especially with her minder still away. She wants to carry a gun now, but I fear she will use it if she sees those guys again.'

'Do you know who they were?'

'She said the main guy had a Middle Eastern accent. I'm guessing it was those lowlife Lebo's who think they own the eastern suburbs.'

'What are you going to do?'

'As soon as Ling and Wang are back from Queensland we'll go find those sand monkeys and give them a message of our own. In the meantime, I worry that Lucie might take matters into her own hands.'

'Would you like me to speak to her?'

'I know you would like that, but no, I will deal with it.'

'Okay, good luck, Wie.'

Bayside Café Pyrmont

Once again, Woodard didn't want to show any outward sense of urgency, so he took his time on the walk from the Oceanic through Darling Harbour to the Bayside Café. He enjoyed the stroll under the endless blue sky and was pleased to see Michelle had secured a table overlooking the shimmering waters of the bustling harbour. *Less chance of being overheard too, mmmm clever, but that worked both ways,* he thought.

'Hi, Michelle, how are you? Sorry for the delay. I took the opportunity to stroll down and enjoy this beautiful weather. And well done on the table too, a wonderful outlook.'

'Hello, Mr Woodard, no problem at all. I was just admiring the view.'

There was an awkward, pregnant pause, with neither person knowing what to say or do next. 'Would you like a coffee, Mr Woodard?' Which came out more rushed than she intended.

'I'll order them. What would you like?'

'Okay, just a skinny latte please.'

Woodard returned from the café, took his seat and once more they endured a prolonged silence. While this was her meeting, someone had to break the impasse, so he thought it may as well be him.

'Michelle, you mentioned on the telephone that you needed some advice on a matter of a possible irregularity within the Treasury Department. As you know, in my role as Vice President – Client Services, I'm not responsible for overseeing Treasury functions, so I'm not sure how I can help.'

Michelle was still having reservations about raising her concerns directly with him, so she was pleased once the coffees arrived. The timely interruption bought her a few more precious seconds to gather her thoughts. She took a hopefully, not too noticeable deep breath and began.

'Last night when I conducted my cash on hand reconciliation prior to handover, I picked up the irregularity I mentioned earlier on the phone.'

'What was the irregularity, Michelle?'

'Treasury's cash holding was one million dollars higher than it should have been.'

Woodard struggled to maintain his outwardly calm demeanour. 'Maybe one of the whales had a big loss last night,' he offered, knowing it was a ridiculous thing to suggest.

'Treasury doesn't work that way, Mr Woodard and I suspect you know that. We don't collect losses or pay out winnings, we just exchange cash for gaming chips and vice versa. And anyway, the total value of cash and gaming chips on hand balanced to Treasury's allotted holdings, as it always does.'

'So, if your reconciliation balanced, I fail to see the problem then, Michelle.'

'The stock holding of the five thousand dollar gaming chips was considerably lower than is usually the case. I'm sure you know these chips are orange in colour and as such, they stand out. Last night there were noticeably less on hand at the time of reconciliation. I'm pretty certain they were one million dollars light on.'

'That would seem to be perfectly understandable then; cash has increased by one million dollars and the gaming chips decreased by the same amount. I fail to see the irregularity nor what this little scenario has to do with me.' He was oversimplifying, but he also knew where the conversation was heading.

'The irregularity, Mr Woodard, is that someone conducted a one million dollar transaction on my watch, and it wasn't entered into the Austrac database.'

'What is the Austrac database, Michelle?' he asked, feigning ignorance again.

'You know damned well what it is. Any cash transaction of ten thousand dollars or more must be entered into the Austrac database complete with the client's details and identification.'

'Okay.'

'What was the value of the transaction you conducted in my absence, Mr Woodard?' This was the moment of truth, the elephant in the room, the sixty-four-thousand-dollar question, and how he responded would determine the future actions of both of them, their careers, and probably their destiny.

'One million dollars, Michelle.'

(26)

Maritime Border Command Canberra

'Hi, I'm Sally Rowethorn, Mr Williamson's personal assistant.' Rowethorn arranged for Caldwell and Fairweather to sign in at the security station and then escorted them through the security doors and into a large meeting room. The windowless room contained a highly polished burgundy coloured boardroom-sized table. All that sat on the table was an opened laptop, a UFO shaped contraption used for conference calling, numerous computer cables, a glass jug of water and half a dozen glasses. At the opposite end of the room, a large white screen was suspended from the ceiling.

'Mr Williamson is still in a meeting but he will be with you shortly. Make yourself comfortable please, gentlemen,' said Rowethorn, ushering them to the table.

'Judging by these facilities the government has Maritime Border Command higher up the food chain than AMSA, Mr Caldwell.'

'How do you arrive at that assumption, James?'

'Well, Mr Williamson has his own personal assistant, and we're sitting in a rather large boardroom. You have neither at AMSA.'

'Conservative governments will always have border security ranked higher than maritime safety, James, so that's where the money goes. Thanks for the reminder though,' he replied sarcastically.

The door burst open and a tall, formidable looking man with a military bearing entered the room. He had a slightly ruddy, cottage cheese complexion with a short back and sides that was greying at the temples. Dressed in a navy blue business suit and carrying a manila folder, he strode confidently up to his two visitors.

'Sorry to keep you waiting, gentlemen, but as you know, these are busy times for border security. Thank you for coming over so promptly and I won't keep you long. Now let's see what we have here, shall we?' he said, taking a seat at the end of the table and opening the folder. 'Firstly, I want to say thank you for bringing this matter to my attention. It's always preferable to be overly cautious rather than dismissive when it comes to potential national security issues.' Fairweather felt more comfortable now that his decision appeared to have been vindicated already.

Williamson continued. 'I have read the report and listened to the audio file. Before deciding on the next course of action, I have a couple of questions that I need to have clarified. How certain are you that the vessel had detoured from its designated course?'

'I'll let James respond if that's okay. He is more familiar with the specifics of vessel monitoring.'

'That's who I was addressing, Jonathan.'

'Well, Mr Williamson, it's fairly straightforward,' Fairweather began. 'The Chinese Horizon was originally positioned in the shipping lane about ten nautical miles to the north-east of the Great Barrier Reef in a straight line off the coast from Mackay. It was tracking in a southerly direction, which is correct if it was heading to Brisbane from the north. Then, three hours after I first noticed the Chinese Horizon in the shipping lane, the icon representing the vessel was now positioned adjacent to Hydrographers Passage and facing in an easterly direction.'

'So, you're saying that the ship had obviously altered course for some reason?' Williamson enquired.

'Exactly, with the vessel being so close to the passage and now facing east, it had to have been exiting the passage. The only vessels that need to navigate the passage are those bound for Mackay or the various coal terminals dotted along the coastline. And the Chinese Horizon was doing neither.' Fairweather glanced at Caldwell, concerned that he might have overstepped his authority. Receiving no acknowledgement either way, he continued. 'Furthermore, most ships travelling from Chinese ports to Brisbane, Sydney or Melbourne would navigate through the Vitiaz Strait near Papua New Guinea and then continue south in a straight line to their destination. As they pass through the latitude for Mackay, they should be at least two hundred nautical miles off the coast. Here, I took a screenshot.' Fairweather handed both Williamson and Caldwell a copy. This was the first time Caldwell had seen or heard of the screenshot and he glanced sideways and raised his eyebrows at Fairweather.

'So, what was it doing there?' Williamson asked, more to himself than the others.'

'Well, I guess that's for you to find out, sir.' James replied.

'Yes, thank you for reminding me of my obligations, Mr Fairweather.' Williamson retorted. 'And, I'm guessing you don't accept the captain's explanation about needing to drop anchor near the passage to fix the electrical fault either?'

'No, not at all. It was a minor fault; he could have fixed it anywhere at any time. He certainly didn't need to go parking in the passage to resolve the problem.'

'Okay, gentlemen, I can now enlighten you on an incident that took place late last evening, that, given the information you have presented to me this afternoon, I would suggest is linked to your findings.' He looked across at Fairweather and noticed him beaming a satisfied smile. 'Yes, James, it seems you were correct in bringing this to the attention of MBC.'

'Thank you, sir.'

'One of our vessels, the Cape York, challenged a cruiser last evening near where you noticed the Chinese Horizon take its little detour. They even fired warning shots over the vessel and lit it up like daylight. The crew on board the cruiser didn't take kindly to being confronted and manage to hightail it into the nearby shoals and escaped through a network of shallow channels. By the time the Cape York had skirted around the shoals, the target vessel had disappeared. I have ordered the captain to undertake a grid search of the wider area, so let's see what he turns up. The captain of the York also thinks there is a link between the vessel he challenged and your Chinese Horizon, so we'll follow that up as a matter of priority. As a professional courtesy, I will keep you informed of any developments. Thank you for bringing this to our attention.' He rose and escorted the men back to reception.

With Williamson taking on the Chinese Horizon case, AMSA was now absolved of any responsibility over the issue. 'I thought it went well, don't you think, James?'

Fairweather was feeling quite chuffed with himself as they walked to the car. 'Well, it seems like the events of last night may have corroborated my own findings, Mr Caldwell.'

'I think we might make an analyst out of you yet, James.'

Following the AMSA officer's departure Williamson opened his binder again. He re-read Fairweather's emailed report and the Cape York's draft report and compared the key points and timings indicated by both. The AMSA kid seemed to be on the ball. Finally, he double clicked on the audio file and listened to the recording for the second time. Fairweather was correct in escalating the report to Maritime Border Command and whilst the kid appeared slightly impertinent and cocky, he seemed to know his stuff.

Maritime Border Command is responsible for countering civil maritime security threats such as illegal arrivals, people trafficking, prohibited imports, piracy, and even attacks on environmental and commercial infrastructure. In being off the grid for three hours, Williamson knew that the Chinese Horizon could have been involved in any of these illicit activities. His gut feeling and common sense told him that whatever it was had to be linked to the vessel pursued and fired upon by the Cape York. He thought of the York's captain and the explaining he would have to do to the bureaucrats in Canberra regarding his use of live munitions in Australian waters. He leant back in his chair, put his feet on the table, clasped his fingers together and stared at the ceiling. This was his thinking position. The Chinese Horizon would dock in Brisbane tomorrow morning, so if he were going to widen the investigation, it would need to be this afternoon. After running various scenarios through his mind, he pressed Sally's extension number on the conference phone. 'Yes, Mr Williamson.'

'Sal, can you get me Damian de Vries on the phone, please?' De Vries was the Brisbane based Operations Manager for Queensland.

'Certainly, sir, just a moment.'

'De Vries speaking.'

'Damian, it's Shane Williamson from Canberra HQ. How are you?'

'I'm well thank you, yourself?'

'Glad to hear it, Damian. I assume you have heard about the incident involving the Cape York last night?'

'Yes, I received a copy of the draft report from the captain earlier today.'

'Good. We have another situation that I'm pretty certain is linked to the York incident. I could do with your assistance. At this stage it's nothing definitive, but I have received a report from AMSA, and I would like to follow it up and see if there is any merit in it.'

'What do you need from me?'

'I am about to email you AMSA's report. There is an audio file attached which you should listen to. I would like you to ascertain whether your office has any corroborating intelligence of its own particularly any unusual occurrences that may be linked to either incident. So, do your research, collect your thoughts on the matter and then call me back.'

'Okay, will do Shane. Give me an hour and I'll get back to you.'

Almost exactly an hour later, Sally called through on the desk phone intercom. 'Mr Williamson, Mr de Vries is on line two for you.'

'Damian, how did you go?'

'I agree there is nothing conclusive in either the report or the audio file that would precipitate our taking action. My guys here in Brisbane haven't been made aware of any suspicious activity in that region in the past twenty-four hours other than the incident with the York.' Williamson sat at his desk patiently waiting, knowing there was more to come. 'I think any potential suspicious activity within the marine park, no matter how trivial it may seem, is worth a follow up. The incident reported by AMSA and the York incident occurred within ten nautical miles of each other. That can't have happened by chance. What would you like us to do?'

'I think you and your staff should wait at the Port of Brisbane tomorrow morning when the Chinese Horizon docks. No uniforms, I don't want to alert the captain before you confront him, but you are required to carry your official identification, though. I know you have an office at the dock, but I would like you to transport him to the Border Force offices at Brisbane Airport. Being taken away from the dock and out of familiar surroundings will give him further reason to be concerned. Let's sweat him so to speak. Once at the airport, you can then interrogate him, find out what he's been up to and if his vessel is linked to the incident with the York last night.'

'We're assuming he's been involved in illegal activity, Shane?'

'Yes, and given his proximity to the Cape York incident, you should too, so let's find out, shall we?'

(**27**)

Bayside Café Pyrmont

'One million dollars. What in blazes were you thinking, Mr Woodard?'
'I guess I wasn't, Michelle,' he replied soberly.

'Really, do you think?!' she exclaimed. 'I can't believe you would put me in this position. I have spent the past decade building a career with Oceanic and now you do this to me. I started as a croupier, for God's sake! I have worked diligently in every position on the way up, while pushing through the glass ceiling, and I was finally rewarded with the Treasury Manager's position. Now what happens to my career and, more to the point, my reputation? They're both in tatters thanks to you,' she hissed.

'I don't know what to say, Michelle.'

'Well, you had better think of something, and soon, *Mr Vice President*,' she retorted with a heavy emphasis on his title. 'And what about the deception, I trusted you? *"Michelle, why don't you go and grab yourself a coffee? You could probably use one about now. Blah, blah, blah."* And you used me, Mr Woodard.' She was determined not to cry but she could feel her eyes moistening, the anger building and her face flushing. Michelle was normally quite reserved, but she was now more worked up than she could ever remember. 'What do you have to say for yourself?' she demanded.

Woodard was leaning forward, arms on his knees, head bowed and eyes staring at the ground below him. He couldn't look Michelle in the eye, thereby inviting another period of silence between them. He looked up. 'It's no excuse, but I got myself in financial trouble at home with the new mortgage, school fees and the wife insisting on a new car. And of course, we just had to have a family holiday in Fiji, didn't we? I earn a good salary but not sufficient to match my wife's expectations.'

'Blame the wife? Do you know how pitiful that sounds?' Michelle blurted in disgust; her eyes boring into him.

'I know nothing mitigates the blame, but one of the whales somehow found out that I was struggling financially and approached me to conduct a transaction for him.' Woodard wasn't about to tell the Treasury Manager that this had been going on for some considerable time. 'He is a valued, repeat client of the Oceanic, so I knew him through previous visits. I know I should have said no, but the incentive offered provided timely financial relief for me, and my family.'

After composing herself, Michelle proffered; 'A manager from my past used to say to me, "don't bring me a problem, bring me a solution", so what's your solution, Mr Woodard?'

'I'm not sure what the solution is at this point, Michelle.'

'Well, I have an idea for you, Mr Vice President. Why don't you contact your whale and ask him for the gaming chips back and we'll return his cash? We could do the exchange tonight and hope there wasn't an audit conducted today.'

'That's not an option. You don't know this man, Michelle; he, nor his associates, are people to be messed with,' Woodard said as he stared at her.

'Mr Woodard, this scenario is not of my making, so the onus is on you to provide a suitable solution, and one that completely absolves me of any responsibility. If not, then I will have no option but to submit a report to my General Manager tonight; a report which will undoubtedly implicate you. Then it will be up to Oceanic as to what action is taken. If they forward the report to Austrac, which they surely will, there will then be the appropriate forensic and criminal investigations. You will no doubt be charged, convicted and probably imprisoned for a considerable amount of time. I don't see how you can avoid that, Mr Woodard.'

The word imprisoned set alarm bells ringing for him and he bolted upright. 'I'm not sure I can let you do that,' he said with a steely resolve. 'Michelle, I can imagine a scenario that goes something like this: *"Mr Woodard, how were you able to be in a position to launder money through the Treasury Department? Well, Mr Auditor, I had an arrangement with the Treasury Manager. When I visited Treasury with the briefcase in-hand, she was to take a coffee break for a previously agreed twenty minutes. The Treasury Manager would inadvertently leave the vault unlocked, conveniently allowing me access. I would simply swap the money for gaming chips, lock the vault and be gone before she returned. She was well-rewarded for her complicity, probably the most expensive cup of coffee in history."* Woodard leant back in his chair and folded his arms across his chest. How does that sound, Michelle?'

'That would be dishonest, and frankly vile behaviour. That's hardly a dignified approach befitting a man in your position.' She glared at him. 'You're a coward, Mr Woodard.'

His nostrils flared in anger. 'Fuck the dignified approach. I can't do this to my family and I'm certainly not going to prison.'

Michelle lived a quiet existence in her cosy apartment in Drummoyne near Birkenhead Point and would spend her downtime reading novels by her favourite authors, a cup of Earl Grey by her side and her cat nestled on her lap. If she was feeling energetic, she might venture to the gym, but didn't go often, as she usually felt out of place amongst the ubiquitous, lycra-clad twenty somethings that pervaded the place. She was a career woman, had never married nor had children, and her job was her whole life. It brought her a profound sense of satisfaction and she couldn't imagine being without it.

Now her simple lifestyle and fulfilling employment were being threatened through no fault of her own, just this man's greed.

'How often are Treasury audits conducted, Michelle?'

She sighed. 'We're never forewarned. They're always random checks conducted by the Finance Department; they can occur at any time. Why, what are you scheming up now?'

'Well, give me an idea of the frequency. Are they usually weekly, monthly, how often?

How long since your last audit?'

'Probably every week or so, and the last one was two days ago.' Michelle thought she knew where this was leading, and as it turns out, she was right.

'Chances are that there won't be another audit for a few days then. By that time, I imagine there will have been dozens, potentially even hundreds, of sizeable transactions. The auditors could still conduct a forensic reconciliation of the cash and gaming chips and will undoubtedly discover the discrepancy. But with the time lag, they won't be in a position to attribute blame to any one individual.' Woodard explained, self-assuredly.

Michelle clasped her hands together to stop them shaking. 'In my twenty-five years of working life, and most certainly over the past decade at Oceanic, I have never even had a dishonest thought, never mind being involved with criminal activity. And now you want me to throw my career away by participating in a cover-up, all so you can take the high-maintenance wife and snotty-nosed private school kids to Fiji. I just won't do it.'

Woodard leaned in close. 'Yes, you will, Michelle, or your career and life as you know it is over.'

Desk of Julie-Anne

Later that afternoon, while immersed in her whiteboard process, Julie-Anne's desk phone rang.

The desk phone never rang, she didn't even know the number, but someone obviously did. 'Hello,' she said absentmindedly, still focused on the whiteboard.

'Julie-Anne Granger, the journalist?' enquired the slightly accented female voice on the other end of the handset.

'Yes, this is Julie-Anne. What can I do for you?'

'I need your assistance. I know of someone acting suspiciously and I wanted to bring him to your attention.'

'First, can you give me your name, please?'

'I would prefer to remain anonymous.'

'Then you should contact your local police station or Crime Stoppers where you can provide information anonymously,' Julie-Anne replied indifferently.

'I don't have enough information to do that, so I fear they will dismiss my claims. You are an investigative journalist and I thought you would like to hear my story.'

Julie-Anne wanted to get back to her whiteboard, but she detected a faint hint of sadness in the woman's voice. 'Okay, whatever your name is, tell me in sixty seconds or less what you think you know.'

'It's not what I think I know, it's what I do know. You don't believe me?' she quizzed.

Julie-Anne was scribbling on her whiteboard as she spoke. 'You haven't told me anything yet and you're now down to forty-five seconds.'

'Okay, wait. There is a man I know who is doing illegal things in this country.'

Trying to hide her growing exasperation, Julie-Anne asked again. 'What sort of illegal things?'

'I don't know exactly, but he comes here often, has meetings in Chinatown with gangsters and gambles substantial amounts of money at the casino.' *That narrows it down to half the men in Sydney,* Julie-Anne guesstimated. 'I think they call him a shark at the casino.'

Julie-Anne knew what the woman meant and she chuckled to herself. 'How do you know this man?'

'I would rather not say for now, but I promise I will tell you if you investigate.'

Slightly intrigued after the mention of Chinatown, gangsters and substantial amounts of money, Julie-Anne softened her tone slightly. 'What else can you tell me? You said he comes here often. Where from?'

'He is Chinese and lives in Shanghai, but he must have a visa as he visits Australia a lot. He always stays at the Oceanic Hotel and Casino in Darling Harbour.'

Trying one more time, Julie-Anne asked. 'If I decide to have a look at this, then at least tell me your name and how I can follow up with you. You haven't given me much usable information so far, therefore I wouldn't even know where to start, even if I was interested.'

'I won't give you my name just yet, but I will tell you his name. It is Li Qiang.' The tone of the woman's voice suggested she was glad to get that off her chest.

'Okay, that helps somewhat. If I start an investigation, I will need to talk to you again. Write down my mobile number and call me in a few days.'

'So you can track me by my phone?'

'I'm not ASIO. I can't track people's phones for heaven's sake. Do you want to write down my number or not?'

'Okay, give me the number.'

$$\textbf{(29)}$$

Alegrias Spanish Tapas Restaurant

Jack Wagner was raised on a cattle farm in Pine Hills just outside of Bathurst on the Central Tablelands of New South Wales. His father toiled away every day for years working the family farm and Jack learnt the value of a hard day's work early in life. His mother taught English during the day at McKillop College, an all girls' school, and ran the family homestead at night.

Jack had two sisters and his mother would often have students over after school for extra tutoring. Throughout his childhood and teenage years, he was always surrounded by girls and young women. He learned early on in life how to behave in the company of the opposite sex and treated women and girls with the utmost respect. He was proud that this principle had remained deep-rooted into his adult life.

As a result, he had never liked the idea of women sitting alone in bars or restaurants. It left them potentially vulnerable in any manner of ways, depending on the circumstances. Invariably, men with over inflated egos and bulging wallets, and thinking with the wrong part of their anatomy, would see that as an open invitation to intrude into the woman's space, uninvited. In a world where women were stronger and more independent than ever, the brief exchange invariably ended with the ego being given a sharp reality check and the wallet never having the left their pocket.

Jack arrived at Alegrias fifteen minutes early and secured two stools at the bar. He sat facing the entrance. You never kept a lady waiting and he wanted Julie-Anne to be able to spot him easily. *Call me old fashioned.* Being a warm day, Jack felt like something refreshing, so he ordered a Sapphire and Tonic with lots of ice and extra squeezed lime. As he turned back to face the door, he spied Julie-Anne crossing the road in front of the restaurant.

'Wow,' he said too loudly, attracting the attention of the bartender. Julie-Anne was tall with a toned athletic figure, lustrous black locks, piercing blue eyes and nicely tanned skin. In the time that he had known her, he had never seen her look *this* gorgeous though.

He was breathless as he watched her strutting confidently across the street, dressed in what Jack guessed was a silver sequined sleeveless top with matching shorts. Her hair was gently bouncing as she walked, and he couldn't help but notice her cleavage moving in time with her hair. A black clutch and patent killer heels completed the stylish look. Jack was wearing a buttoned down, white linen shirt over black dress jeans and chestnut coloured brogues. He initially felt quite smart, but seeing Julie-Anne's spectacular outfit, he now felt decidedly underdressed. *Just as well I got here early otherwise she'd have surely been swamped by men with egos and bulging wallets batting well out of their league,* he laughed to himself.

'Hi, Jack,' she said with a mischievous chuckle as she breezed up to the bar.

Jack began to stand, but she leaned in and kissed him on the lips, stopping him in his tracks. She held the kiss just long enough to stir his emotions and even his other brain. As she pulled back from the kiss, she saw him staring at her all wide eyed.

'What was that all about?' he asked, having been knocked for six twice in the last minute.

'I've had a productive day at work, have been looking forward to our date-night all afternoon and I'm feeling quite special tonight, so I shared my sunny disposition with my favourite detective. Is that okay?'

'I could get used to your sunny disposition. I'm having a Sapphire and Tonic. What would you like, Julie-Anne?'

'Wow, you just called me by my name; you never do that. I'll have something bubbly to suit my mood; a Bellini would be great, thanks.'

'You look so stunning that JA just wouldn't cut it tonight.'

'Thank you.' She looked around the room and admired the wooden ceiling beams, curved archways, highly polished hardwood floors, classic chandeliers and the candlelit tables. 'I love this place Jack, it's very romantic.' Judging by the uncomfortable expression on his face she sensed that her comment had made him feel uneasy. *Aaahh, men.*

'Yes, it is.'

The maître d' sauntered over to the bar and invited them to accompany him to their table. Once seated, he laid their linen napkins across their laps and poured them still water.

'If I could offer a couple of suggestions, senor y senorita? I would recommend the Champinones Rebozados and the Fritto di Calamari to start with. The drink waiter will be with you shortly. Disfruta tu comida.'

'I think I heard calamari in there somewhere and maybe something about fruit too, but I have no idea about the rest.'

'Aaahh, poor, Jack.' Julie-Anne reached across and patted his hand. 'The first dish was crumbed mushrooms and yes, you heard correctly, the second was calamari fritters. And he wasn't recommending we order fruit, disfruta means enjoy in Spanish.'

'I'm glad I brought you along,' he responded with an exaggerated wink.

After the appetisers, and while struggling to navigate their way through a large dish of traditional Paella, Jack, with saffron juice dripping onto his chin, asked her. 'What made your day so productive, any journalistic gossip you care to share?'

Surprised, she eventually responded. 'You've never asked me about my work before. I always assumed it was like quid pro quo in reverse. You don't ask me about mine, then you don't have to discuss your work.'

'No, it's not like that at all, JA. There's not much light in my role, I spend my days on the darker side of society and discussing it would just dampen the mood during the dawning of our evening.'

Oops, we're back to JA again, time to back off Julie-Anne, she thought. 'That's very considerate, but I'm a journalist who investigates all manner of crimes and bad behaviour and there's not always a rainbow hovering over my desk either. I'm a strong, clear-thinking woman, and I can compartmentalise and switch-off quite easily.'

'Okay, what was so productive about your day? What are you investigating?'

'I think I touched on it this morning over coffee. There is anecdotal evidence that there are links between the Triads and their involvement in the cocaine trade, potential political interference, who's funding what and probably an arm's length link to some Chinese government agencies.'

Jack was leaning forward and being unusually attentive. Julie-Anne dabbed at his chin with her napkin then continued.

'Then there's all the media hype around the local Confucius Institutes and their political connection to the Chinese Communist Party. It's all linked; I just need time to make the connection. I set up a whiteboard today and started an organisational chart to try to plot the key players and their links to each other. I am a long way from putting the puzzle's pieces together, Jack.'

Jack had picked up on the words Chinese and cocaine and he thought back to his meeting with his CI this morning. Stevie had implied that the Chinatown based Chinese were now dealing a higher purity product across the eastern suburbs. If the coke was coming out of Chinatown, then the Triads would certainly be involved. Surely Julie-Anne's investigation wasn't heading in the same direction as his. Alarm bells were ringing in his head for any number of reasons, not the least being concern for her safety. The Triads didn't play nice.

'That's a formidable challenge, yet exciting and potentially rewarding work. Well done.'

'Thank you, what about your day, handsome?'

Not wanting to create reverse suspicion and reveal exactly what he was working on, Jack reverted to cop speak. 'A nothing day really. The meeting with my CI went nowhere, then I had an hour in Federal Court as a witness in a drug trial. Then I had the joy of writing reports and shuffling paperwork at the head office for the rest of the day, which worked out well really as we might not have been here otherwise. Wanting to change the subject he said, 'I'll grab the cheque and then we can go and see if Diesel in his fifties sounds as good as he did in his twenties.'

Bondi Junction

Wie Ping Lie parked his Audi A6 across the road from BJ's in Spring Street and settled in for the impending wait he would have to tolerate. The glitzy bar was obviously named after the suburb of its location, but he could imagine the connotation applied to it by its snotty nosed guests following an evening of intoxication. Some of those same guests would be his clientele, but the less well-to-do; well they were clients of the street dealers. He didn't see his operation as being in opposition to that run by the lowlife Lebos; his product was far superior to theirs. Unfortunately for them, they obviously held a different view and that was why he was here now. It was important to avoid a turf war, but Wie couldn't, and wouldn't, abide an attack on one of his key people. And the response would be swift and merciless.

'There he is,' Lucie blurted out as a black Subaru Impreza pulled into a parking bay across from where they were parked. 'That didn't take too long at all.' Her breathing accelerated as her heart rate increased. Wie could see Lucie's anger levels rising as she became increasingly agitated at the sight of the man. She reached to open the car door, but Wie firmly grabbed her arm.

'We wait,' he ordered. She glared at him, but knew he was right.

Wie couldn't believe their good fortune. Amir Abboud was alone. 'This will be easier than we thought.'

They watched as Abboud, dressed in a black tracksuit and ballcap, walked to the entry, palmed something to the black clad doorman and entered the bar. Lucie reached for the door handle again. 'Not yet. We stick to the plan, woman,' Wie demanded as he exited the car. What is it about these Lebos and their fascination with Impreza's, he wondered as he evenly walked across to the car. While the doorman was occupied Wie walked along the driver's side of the car. He glanced towards the doorman to ensure he hadn't been noticed and then leaned down very slightly so as not to attract unwanted attention. He flipped the CSAR-T knife over, slashed at the front tyre and then repeated the process on the passenger's side. He heard the gentle hissing sounds as he calmly returned to his vehicle. After twenty minutes, the line at the entrance to the bar had diminished, leaving only the huge doorman at the entry. Then they watched as Abboud exited the bar, his business obviously completed. He spoke briefly to the doorman, shook hands and then walked towards his vehicle. 'Okay, time for you to play your part, Lucie. And please stay calm,' Wie pleaded.

Abboud walked up to the driver's door and Wie saw him look down at the near front tyre before throwing his hands in the air in anger. Lucie took a deep breath, exited the Beemer and walked across the road towards the Impreza. As she neared the vehicle she slowed as Abboud opened the trunk, bent over and rummaged around.

'Hello, Amir,' she said with composure. In accordance with their plan, she was wearing the same party dress with the deep vee she had worn last night when she was attacked by the same man.

He stood upright and turned towards her. 'What the fuck,' he blurted out. 'I thought we had an understanding,' he said, staring at her cleavage.

'That's well out of the reach of a lowlife like you,' she smarted. 'You're ambitious, but not stupid.'

'I should have fucked you last night, you Chink bitch.'

Contrary to how she was feeling internally, she remained calm. 'Yes, you should have. Now you're about to be fucked yourself, you camel jockey.'

She could see the rage building, his face colouring and distorting, but she had his attention, which was all she needed. 'Now, hear this, you come near me again and I will kill you. Do you understand me, you miserable goat fucker?' He clenched his fist and drew his arm back, but before he could launch at her, a vicious knifehand strike caught him on the side of his neck. As his knees buckled, Wie grabbed him under his shoulders. 'Take that, you fucking towel head,' Lucie screeched as she launched a vicious kick into Abboud's groin with the pointy end of her stiletto.

Wie swivelled his head towards the bar and noticed that the doorman was trying to break up a fight that had broken out in the opposite direction to the Impreza. *Nice timing, no witnesses.* Lucie bent down, grabbed Abboud's legs and with Wie holding his torso, they threw his unconscious body into the trunk. She rifled through his pockets and retrieved the car keys and his mobile phone, neither of which he would be needing anytime soon. Wie was now on the phone, confirming the prearranged tow truck. She slammed the trunk lid down.

'It was thirty-eight degrees earlier today and I reckon it's still in the low thirties, so that miserable, lowlife, desert dweller should feel right at home in the trunk.'

Wie chuckled. 'Remind me never to upset you, Lucie.'

'I'm not finished with them just yet. There's still the other one who needs to be given a message,' she said as they entered their Beemer.

'Lucie, let it go. You've had your retribution and we don't need this to escalate into an all-out turf war. They've got the message that we're not to be messed with. Now you need to back off. Anyway, it's made me realise that I have to fine tune our method of operation.' He turned onto Oxford Street for the short drive back to the CBD. 'I've been thinking that I should set up a dial-a-dealer style operation especially for our high worth eastern suburbs clients using an encrypted messaging app.'

'Like WhatsApp?'

'Exactly.'

31

Tip of My Tongue

Jack and Julie-Anne made the short walk along Victoria Road to the Bridge Hotel and arrived just in time to catch the start of Diesel's show. The darkened entertainment lounge was packed to the rafters, although it didn't stop the lads from swivelling their heads as Julie-Anne walked past. *Dream on boys*, Jack thought while walking a little taller and smiling inwardly.

Diesel had a distinctive blended musical sound which was influenced by his father's record collection and blues and soul music from the likes of Sam Cooke and James Brown. He was also a guitar player of note and his quality playing underpinned his music. As usually is the case, recording artists preferred to showcase their new releases. Julie-Anne was standing in front of Jack and bopping away, so she at least quite liked his latest stuff.

It was no surprise when he was raucously called back to the stage for an encore. 'Diesel..., Diesel..., Diesel...' chanted the excited crowd. 'Here we go, here comes the good stuff.' Julie-Anne wanted Jack to dance with her. It was too crowded, and he couldn't dance to save himself. He compromised, wrapped his arms around her bare midriff, snuggled in, and swayed from side-to-side to the beat of the music.

Diesel launched into two of his biggest hits, Soul Revival and then Cry in Shame. Julie-Anne was pushing back into Jack and brain number two was firming up nicely as they swayed together. He nuzzled in, kissed her neck and trickled his hand down her bare midriff. He was tempted to keep going, but thought better of it. *Too many people; go easy tiger.* He turned back to the music. Diesel finished the show with the classic, Tip of My Tongue, with the crowd joining in the chorus. Once the show was finished and the room had quietened down, Julie-Anne turned to Jack. 'Let's get out of here and go make some music of our own.'

Jack's apartment wasn't far from The Bridge, and with the evening still quite balmy, they decided to ditch the Uber idea and enjoy a stroll. They paused a couple of times for a passionate, deep kiss. Such was the passion, Jack fleetingly thought maybe they should prop on a park bench and take the next step. Julie-Anne was in a great headspace, but he wasn't sure he should push it that far. He was singing and humming Tip of my Tongue most of the way home.

'You've got that song stuck in your head.'

'Yeah, I know, it inspires my best work.'

'What do you mean by that?'

'If you're lucky, you might just find out,' he responded, offering a sly grin.

Arriving at his apartment, he asked, 'Would you like a nightcap?'

'Do you have any champagne? We could have a toast and celebrate our wonderful evening.'

'Sounds good, I'll meet you out on the balcony.' The rear balcony overlooked native bushland which afforded him complete privacy, especially for nights like this. In the mornings, Jack would invariably have his coffee out there and soak up the sounds of the myriads of lorikeets and wattlebirds that inhabited the eucalyptus trees. He brought the bubbling glasses out onto the balcony and handed one to Julie-Anne.

Looking her in the eyes, Jack said, 'And here's a toast to the most interesting, intelligent, amazing woman I know. Cheers to you, Julie-Anne.' Jack placed his glass on the patio table, stood gazing into her eyes then leaned forward and kissed her passionately. He drew back momentarily, admired her beauty again and then placed his hand on the nape of her neck, pulled her in and kissed her again, more deeply this time.

'Wow, Jack,' she exclaimed. 'Who's this new man in my life?'

'I didn't have a very productive day at work, but I have also been looking forward to our date night all afternoon and I'm feeling quite special tonight, too. So, I shared my warm, fuzzy feelings with my favourite investigative journalist.'

'I'm sure I've heard that line somewhere before.' Julie-Anne said with a chuckle. 'Who writes your stuff? She must be exceptionally good.'

Jack leaned in again, kissed her slowly on the neck. His hands move to her bare shoulders and inched down to her breasts. Upon feeling her erect nipples, he was reminded that she wasn't wearing a bra. He slid his hands back to her shoulders, dropping the straps down her arms and coaxed the top down to her waist. Her full, teardrop shaped breasts enamoured Jack, they looked breathtaking in the night light. He arched forward and kissed one, then the other, and slowly moved left to right and back again across her chest, pausing to lick her erect nipples.

Julie-Anne whispered an agreeable sigh. 'Oh, Jack, that's wonderful.'

He knelt down in front of her and placed his hands at the waist of her shorts. She let out a soft moan of anticipation. He slowly folded the waist over, gently encouraging the sequined shorts down over her thighs, then her knees, from where they fell onto her heels. That revealed the sexiest lace underwear he had ever seen. He lightly coaxed the sheer navy see-through panties off and allowed them to drop. Julie-Anne slowly stepped out of her clothes and with a flourish, kicked them to one side. She was now only wearing her heels and leaning against the balcony railing. Her nicely tanned body was arched back and she was breathing deeply. *Just breathtaking*, Jack thought.

He eased her legs apart, then caressed his fingers along her inner thighs, following with his tongue. Teasing her with a soft motion, getting higher and higher along her thighs, he listened to her breath deepen in anticipation. Then he heard her gasp as his tongue massaged higher. Her soft groans grew louder as her hips shifted and her back arched once more. With his hands now on her hips, holding her in place, he gently ran his tongue up and down her. She was wet, warm and welcoming, and Jack liked the taste. He wanted to please her. Julie-Anne released a loud gasp as Jack pushed into her with his tongue.

She opened her eyes and gazed up into the pitch black, star filled sky. *Is this what heaven is like?*

Then he began slowly flicking his tongue in an upward motion. She gasped again, louder this time, responsive to his touch, and Jack felt himself growing harder. Julie-Anne released a loud, elongated groan. He kissed her firmly, yet meticulously and had her moist and trembling. She placed her hands on Jack's head to steady herself and to hold him in place. Then, to her amazement, right at that precise moment she heard humming. He can't be surely, not now!

Right on the tip of my tongue.

On the tip of my tongue.

Still breathing heavily, she panted. 'Oh, my God, Jack, are you really humming that song?'

'I warned you on the way home honey, it inspires me.'

'You are so funny you should do stand-up.'

'Nah, I do my best work on my knees.'

She stood upright. 'Yes, you do. Now take me to bed and let's see what you're like on your back, funny man.'

'Cos she only comes when she's on top,' Jack was singing merrily as Julie-Anne led him inside.

Port of Brisbane

Tuesday 3rd March

It was a partially overcast but warm and humid morning as Damian de Vries arrived at the Brisbane Container Port on Fisherman Island. Queensland didn't have the common-sense to implement daylight saving, so the day dawned around five o'clock, even at this time of the year. To maximise the daylight hours, the container companies started their day shifts at six o'clock in the morning, so it was no surprise to de Vries that the docks were already a hive of activity. A typical sub-tropical day was forecast where the uncertain weather could serve up anything and everything. He wondered if the investigation he was about to embark on would do the same.

He parked his Jeep Cherokee next to the Maritime Border Command office and walked up the steps and into the building. Having checked the arrivals schedule the previous evening, he knew that the Chinese Horizon would dock at seven o'clock, so De Vries had arranged for his two MBC investigators to meet him at six.

Agents Scott Harvey and Sam Benson were already reading the report that Shane Williamson had forwarded the previous afternoon, making notes in their respective diaries as they went. As ordered, they were in civilian dress, both wearing jeans, loose-fitting shirts and lightweight hiking boots. They didn't think they would need to be armed for a seemingly minor matter, so neither had bothered signing-out their weapons.

De Vries walked into the meeting room with his coffee mug in hand. 'Good morning, gents, how are we this fine morning?'

They were both hard edged, experienced investigators who had cut their teeth in the late noughties dealing with the huge volume of illegal boat arrivals under the previous Labor Government. Given their extensive experience, and particularly the tragedies they had witnessed off the north-west coast, they would no doubt be wondering why they should be involved in a nondescript activity such as the one they were about to embark on.

'We would be a lot better if we weren't wasting our time on a low-level bureaucrat's hunch boss,' came Benson's gruff reply.

'I hear you, Sam. But, be that as it may, this kid Fairweather seems pretty smart to me. He obviously has a unique knowledge of marine traffic and might just be onto something. Now, you both know I don't believe in coincidences, so we should assume there is a direct link between the Cape York incident and the kid's report about the Chinese Horizon, so let's go find out what it is. Have you prepared your questions for the good captain?'

'Yeah, we're good to go, boss,' confirmed Harvey.

'Okay, then. As you know, under the Maritime Border Command charter, we have arrest and detain powers, so let's go do just that and see what the good captain has to say for himself.'

As they made their way towards the container terminal they could see the Chinese Horizon's mooring lines being tied off to the wharf and the gangway about to be lowered. Once it was secured, the three agents produced their identification lanyards and hung them around their neck. Then they proceeded up the gangway and followed the starboard side railing towards the stairs leading to the bridge of the vessel.

Now the vessel was secured, Captain Han had shut down the engines, grabbed his coffee and walked out onto the narrow walkway surrounding the bridge. He lit a cigarette and surveyed the wharf and surroundings. As he turned back towards the stern of the ship, he noticed three casually dressed men walking up the gangway. He was about to call Angel on the radio and ask him to intercept them when to his dismay, he saw the laminated cards dangling from their necks.

This is not good at all, he thought to himself. *Who are they and what do they want?* He started panicking and taking frequent pulls of his cigarette in an endeavour to calm himself. His nerves were jangling and he felt the onset of nausea. He butted his cigarette, then took deep breaths to calm himself, sucking in as much of the salty air as he could. *Maybe they are from AMSA.* As the three men made their way up the stairs to the bridge, their physical appearance and focused demeanour became apparent to the captain. They obviously weren't safety inspectors. He cast his mind back to the events of two nights ago. 'La Shi.' He would have to regain control of himself, and quickly.

Han held his coffee in one hand, put on his captain's hat, and pretended to flick through the navigational maps on the desk, all the while trying to look important.

'Captain Han.' He turned quickly, pretending to be startled.

'Sorry, I was checking the charts for the next stage of my voyage. Anyway, we don't allow unauthorised boarders on the ship,' he trumpeted, pretending not to notice the lanyards. 'You will need to disembark immediately.'

'No, I don't think so, Captain. We are from Maritime Border Command and we have every right to board your ship,' de Vries replied with conviction.

'Can I see your identification, please?' asked the captain. The three agents lifted up their ID lanyards and held them in front of Han's face.

'Okay, what can I do for you gentlemen?'

'Captain Han, I am Damian de Vries, the Operations Manager for the MBC and this is Agents Harvey and Benson. We have a few questions for you.' *They knew his name,* Han noticed, now becoming even more concerned.

'Certainly, sir. What questions do you have?'

'We would like you to accompany us to the MBC office where we can talk privately.'

Han was trying to think his way around this problem. 'You can speak openly here, gentlemen. Let me get you a coffee, I have a fresh pot on the bench.'

'No, thank you, captain, will you come with us now please?' de Vries demanded.

'I will have to speak to the crew first and give them instructions for unloading.'

'You can call your crew on the radio if you need to.' Han reluctantly called Angel and said he had to go to a meeting onshore.

Angel thought that was most unusual, so he went to the starboard side of the ship and looked out over the dock. The captain was being escorted to a waiting Jeep parked beside the Maritime Border Command offices. Although the three men with the captain were dressed casually, Angel could tell by the way they carried themselves that they were definitely law enforcement. *No me gusta nada,* he mumbled to himself. *No, I don't like this at all.* Angel had been with Captain Han for many years, had been treated well by him and he in turn had rewarded the captain with his loyalty. He would need to act quickly if he was to help his captain now.

(33)

Macquarie Suite

Li Qiang was dressed in his bathrobe and relaxing on the chaise lounge reading the Sydney Morning Herald. He had arranged for room service breakfast and subsequently decided to have the morning to himself. His burner phone rang. He had only given the number to three people since his arrival in Sydney; the Consul General, Wie Ping Lie, and his contact in China. He couldn't imagine why the Consul General would be calling so soon after they had lunch, so it must be one of the remaining two. Neither had any reason to call him at this stage of his visit, so this wasn't going to be good news.

He reluctantly picked up his mobile. 'Yes,' he answered gruffly.

'Li, we have a problem,' said his master from the party in China.

'I know that, otherwise you wouldn't be calling me. What sort of problem?'

'There were agents waiting for the Chinese Horizon when it docked in Brisbane this morning.'

'What do you mean, waiting?'

'There were three agents on the wharf. They boarded the ship, made their way to the bridge, spoke briefly to the captain and then escorted him away.'

Li sat upright and swivelled on the lounge. 'What agents, what department, why?'

'Apparently they were from Maritime Border Command.'

Li ran his fingers through his thinning hair. 'How do you know this?'

'One of the ship's English speaking crew noticed the identity tags they were wearing.'

'Where have they taken him?'

'I do not know, Li.'

'How did you find out this information?'

'Angel, the ship's mate, called the shipping company's office in Shanghai by satellite phone about an hour ago. They then contacted me.'

'Okay, there is nothing you can do from there, so leave it to me. I will make a call and see if I can uncover more information.'

'Now, before you hang up, the party is keen to know your progress in recruiting our political candidate. Where are you up to?'

'I have found a suitable candidate who is perfect to fulfill our requirements. She is Sino-Australian, well known in what will be her local constituency, articulate, intelligent and attractive.'

'Knowing you, I knew she would be attractive, Li. Let us hope that the electorate finds her an attractive candidate too. May I remind you how crucial this appointment is. I am fed up with the continuing onslaught by the Australian media, criticising our supposed poor human rights and environmental records, the South China Sea, political interference, Hong Kong protests and disparaging the Belt and Road Initiative amongst a long list of negatives. And they will no doubt be blaming China for the spreading of this virus next.'

Li had long had to endure the rantings of his master in China. Fortunately, it was a small price to pay for the privilege of undertaking his responsibilities on his regular visits to this wonderful city. The pleasures that the Emerald City offered weren't lost on him either as he lit a cigar and settled in for another speech.

'My comrades within the party are becoming increasingly agitated at what they see as Australia's growing anti-China sentiment. And now the New South Wales government has cancelled the Confucius Institute Program, which was supposedly full of student spies. We urgently need an elected official in the state parliament who can use their position to turn the tide of this negative discourse, and in particular, lobby to reverse the Confucius Institute decision. If we are successful, then we can turn our attention to the federal parliament. What stage of her recruitment are we up to?'

'Melissa Wu is attending one of Xiao's consular cocktail parties tomorrow night where I hope to finalise the arrangements.'

'That is good. Let me know when you have secured her candidacy and we can begin her induction into our program of requirements. In the meantime, I will arrange for the Global Times to publish a series of articles about Australia's shortcomings as a so-called responsible global citizen. With their own lamentable human rights record around the treatment of their Indigenous population, placing corporate spies here in China, destruction of the Great Barrier Reef and their standoffish approach to climate change we should be able to gain some traction. That might give the Australian governments and their complicit media pause to consider their own inadequacies and cease their incessant China bashing. We need to push back, Li. Now, I will leave you to rectify Captain Han's situation.' Li's contact then disconnected the call without further comment.

Li thought back to his conversation with Wie Ping Lie two nights ago. *Are we becoming complacent as a result of our success?...If it seems too good to be true, then it probably is,* He remembered himself saying.

As far as any risk to his own involvement in the captain's predicament was concerned, he wasn't unduly worried, as he thought he was sufficiently removed from the importation process. There were other ramifications, however, and certain people in prominent positions of power in China wouldn't be so untroubled by this untimely occurrence. For everyone's sake, he hoped the arrested captain was discreet. There was also Wie to consider. Whilst they had a cordial dinner and held amiable discussions, he was a Triad leader and they were known to resort to violence when circumstances weren't to their liking. Li would have to avoid that occurring at all costs.

Either way, he would ensure that this would be Captain Han's last voyage. Li drew on his cigar, sipped his whiskey and looked out across the gleaming waters of Darling Harbour. God he loved this city.

He knew he had no option but to place a call he really didn't want to make. 'Consul General's office, can I help you?'

'This is Mr Li; can I speak to Mr Zhang, please?'

'Mr Zhang is unavailable at the moment; can I have him return your call, Mr Li?'

Li paced up and down impatiently on the suite's plush carpet. 'How long will he be unavailable?' he asked brusquely.

'I don't know, Mr Li, but I will have him call you as soon as he is available.'

'I expect you will, miss.'

Li hated not being in control of all situations at all times. He was what westerners called a control freak, but he didn't care. This particular incident though was clearly out of his control. Even though this component of the operation wasn't within his sphere of responsibility, he felt certain that each step in the process had been well planned and implemented, so how had this been allowed to occur? Maybe Wie had become complacent after all. Even though it wasn't even midday, he poured himself a Glenlivet fifteen-year-old and took a gulp. His burner phone rang a few minutes later.

'What is so urgent that you were rude to my assistant?' Xiao said firmly, offering no introduction.

'We have a problem.'

'Li, we don't have problems, we Chinese always have challenges. What is this latest challenge that is confronting us?'

'A Captain Han from a Chinese cargo ship has been detained in

Brisbane by Australian border authorities.'

'That is never good, but what does this have to do with me, and with you for that matter Li?'

'Xiao, it is a long story and not one I'm prepared to share with you now. Suffice to say, I need you to ascertain what the situation is surrounding Captain Han, and I need it done quickly.'

'I can't be seen to be meddling in the affairs outside of my jurisdiction; that will immediately raise suspicions. I will need to contact the Consul General in Brisbane and seek his assistance. Where is the captain being held?'

'I have no further details. I am sure the Consul General in Brisbane will have the appropriate contacts and I would like you to contact him immediately, Xiao.'

'Don't push me; what is the name of the cargo ship?'

'Chinese Horizon. Can you ensure the Consul General in Brisbane is not aware of my involvement? Just tell him that you received a call from the shipping company's office in China.'

'Okay, but I don't want any blowback from this.'

'There won't be, now make the call,' he demanded. Li was conscious of how unusually tense he was. He knew exactly the remedy he needed to release the tension. He leaned back on the chaise, took a sip of his Glenlivet and called Kaili Wang's number.

Sophie Zhao arrived in the Oceanic's foyer a little more than an hour later. She was wearing a red crepe Carla Zampatti jacket and matching knee length pencil skirt. She confidently strode through the lobby in her favourite Jimmy Choos and headed for the elevators. As she did so, she saw Tony from two days ago, waiting in the foyer. He was wearing a corporate badge that, much to her disgust, said he was the Vice President - Client Services. He gave her a dark, angry stare. She returned the stare and called out, 'nice to see you with your clothes on, Mr Vice President.' His face reddened and Sophie noticed two smartly dressed, middle aged women now looking at him keenly. She held up her hand and gestured with her thumb and index finger two inches apart, the inference being obvious. 'He's all yours, ladies,' she said as she turned back to the bank of elevators, immediately regretting having said anything at all. It was beneath her but damn him, that was the least that he deserved.

She pressed the Macquarie Suite's doorbell, also knocked politely on the mahogany door and then let herself in with her swipe card. Li was in his favourite bathrobe again, slouched on the sofa with a whiskey glass in one hand and a Monte Christo in the other. *Some things never change,* she thought. He invited her to take a seat with him on the sofa. Sophie was glad for its expansiveness and sat at the opposite end to him. She was very surprised when he told her she looked stunning, as always. Then, unusually, he opened up a conversation with her. 'How are you, my child? How is your day?'

What's going on here? This is most unusual, she asked herself. 'My day is going well thank you, I've had a wonderful morning at the beach.' Sophie was correct in thinking that something troublesome must be happening in one of his business transactions for him to be even remotely cordial.

'Well, since you didn't ask, my day has turned sour with one of my business deals hitting a minor snag,' Li offered anyway. Sophie didn't like the miserable little man, but thought she should reciprocate the politeness.

'I'm sorry to hear that, Mr Li. Is there anything I can do to help?'

'Why do you think I called you? I need a massage to release me of all this tension so you could start by getting undressed.' *So much for politeness.*

Li stood up, dropped his bathrobe where he stood, naked from head to toe, and then made his way to the bedroom. *What middle-aged paunchy little man would parade around naked?* Sophie pondered, incredulous at his lack of pride. She wasn't going to put on a floor show for him today, so she removed her outfit in the living room, collected the massage oils from the bathroom and hesitantly ventured into the bedroom.

The bedroom contained a king-size bed and Li was lying face down and spread-eagled in the centre of it. She hated his positioning as she wouldn't be able to massage him from the side of the vast bed; rather, she would have to climb onto the bed. *How predictable.*

Sophie knelt to the side and massaged his left leg from the ankles to his upper thighs, being careful with her long sweeping strokes. Then she swapped sides and repeated the process on his right leg. *Now comes the hard part,* she despaired. *Focus Sophie. You know you have no choice but one day, hopefully soon, this will all be over.* She straddled him, being careful to remain up on her knees, and began massaging his back from his shoulder blades down to his lower back. He released one of his miserable little sighs. Then she clenched her fists and forcefully guided her knuckles in long flowing movements up and down the indents on either side of his spine. 'You are so strong and have a magnificent touch, Kaili Wang,' he complimented, deliberately referring to his preferred Chinese name for her.

It was time to massage his neck and shoulder region, so she had no option but to move forward. Wearing only her French knickers, she wasn't going to sit on his back, so she carefully knelt above him again. She slowly kneaded and manipulated the tissue and muscles around his neck and shoulders, and she could feel him starting to relax. He released another sigh. Moving aside, she held his arms out one by one and massaged both sides, finishing with the ubiquitous finger clicks. Whilst none of this was a pleasant experience for Sophie, the worst was still to come. She paused momentarily, trying to fill her mind with visions of inanimate objects.

'You need to roll over.'

Li rolled over and Sophie, ignoring his ugly protrusion, massaged the front of his legs, his chest and then his shoulders again, all the while trying to subtly avoid leaning in too close. Finally, hoping she was nearly finished, she stood, walked to the foot of the bed, massaged his feet and one by one clicked his toes. Thinking she should be polite, and also to intimate that the massage had ended, she stood back and enquired, 'How do you feel now, Mr Li?'

He tilted his head up and admired her near-naked magnificence. 'I feel very relaxed, thank you. That was an excellent massage, but I don't think you're quite finished yet, Kaili Wang.'

'I really have to go,' she said in a soft, pleading voice.

He noticed the glistening of tears in her eyes but could care less. 'I assume your family in China are still safe and well, Kaili Wang.' Sophie immediately recognised yet another veiled threat against her family.

She picked up the massage oil and slowly stepped back towards the bed.

ABF Offices Brisbane Airport
Tuesday 3rd March

The Border Force offices at Brisbane Airport were only five kilometres from the container terminal as the crow flies. Unfortunately, the mouth of the Brisbane River separated the two facilities, so it was a twenty kilometre drive from the port to their destination via the M4 and M1 Motorways. Wanting to keep the captain guessing as to their intentions, the agents rode in silence as the Jeep Cherokee made its way across the Gateway Bridge on the M1.

The quietness was unnerving Han, but he tried to remain calm and to clear his head for the inevitable questions he knew were coming. He looked through the bridge railings and saw a large cruise ship moored at Portside Wharf. Han decided there and then that when he returned to China he would take his wife on a cruise up the wondrous Yangtze River. *If he returned to China.*

Forty minutes later they arrived at the Border Force's airport offices. The three agents signed in and then escorted Han through the security doors and placed him in an interview room. 'We'll be with you soon, Captain,' de Vries said as he left the room. Han heard the unnerving click of the steel bolt against the door lock.

After the team had finished morning tea in the Operations Manager's office, de Vries stated, 'okay gents, I think Captain Han has sweated long enough. Are you both clear on the events of two nights ago?'

'Yep, we're ready to go,' replied an eager Benson.

'Okay, I'll leave you two to do the initial round of interrogation and see what you can learn from him. Now go find out what the good captain's been up to.'

'Captain Han, my name is Agent Harvey, this is Agent Benson and we are duly authorised offers with Maritime Border Command. MBC is an Australian government agency responsible for this country's maritime security and protecting our maritime borders. It is our role to investigate any incidents or suspicious behaviour that occurs within those borders. Do you understand so far, Captain?'

'Yes, I think so. Though I do not know why I am here.'

'We'll get to that in a minute. First, you should know that this conversation is being recorded. Can you confirm your name, position and the name of your vessel, please?'

'Yes, I am Captain Hsin Han of the Chinese Horizon.'

'How many times have you visited Australia, Captain?'

'I have only been here for work and only as captain of the Chinese Horizon. I think this is number twelve.'

'And how many times has the Chinese Horizon been to Australia?'

'Same number, I have been captain since beginning.'

'And where is your port of departure? Is it always the same port?'

'Yes, we leave from Dailan in northern China and travel to Brisbane, Sydney and Melbourne and then we go back. Sometimes we leave from Qingdao, but route always same, Mr Harvey.'

'Explain the route to me please.'

'We leave Dailan through Yellow Sea, then we go through East China Sea. After that we go into Philippine Sea and all the way to Bismarck Sea near New Guinea. Then we go through Vitiaz Strait, pass by Solomon Islands, enter Coral Sea and go to straight to Brisbane.'

'Thank you for that explanation, Captain,' said Harvey, maintaining a firm but cordial approach. He wanted Han to get comfortable with the questioning, become relaxed and hopefully Benson would catch him off guard with his more intensive interrogation shortly.

'Would you say that you know the route of your voyage very well then?'

'Yes, I think so, Agent Harvey.'

'And would you say that is the most expedient way to get from Dailan to Brisbane?'

Han tilted his head. 'What you mean expedient?'

'The fastest way to Brisbane, Captain.'

'Yes, for sure.'

'Okay then, explain this to me, please: If you navigated through the Vitiaz Strait and were heading in a straight line to Brisbane, you should have been two hundred nautical miles off the coast of Queensland when you passed the point level with Mackay. Why weren't you?'

Benson had been chomping at the bit to get involved and that was his cue. 'So, captain, given everything that you have just told Agent Harvey about your route, I have a simple question for you. Why was the Chinese Horizon near Hydrographers Passage two nights ago?'

'Where is Hydrologist Passage?' Han remembered what he said to the AMSA man and he tried to be cute again.

'It's called Hydrographers Passage, you know that, and it's where you navigate through the Great Barrier Reef to enter the Port of Mackay, captain.'

'Oh, okay, I know where you mean now.'

'So, captain, you need to answer the question. Why was the Chinese Horizon near Hydrographers Passage two nights ago?'

'As I told man from AMSA who call me, we had electric fault on board that need fixing. I could have wait until we dock in Brisbane. However, seas were so calm two nights ago, that I navigated out of shipping lane, drop anchor and have fault repaired.' Han had reverted to clipped sentences in order to feign innocence.

'What was the specific nature and cause of the electrical fault, captain?'

'One of power boards get too hot and then safety breaker drop out. It affect the corridor and bedroom lighting. We could have kept going using emergency lighting, but I decide to repair then.'

Benson continued. 'That's when you navigated into Hydrographers Passage and dropped anchor?'

'No, I no go into passage, Mr Benson.'

'Again, that's bullshit, captain.' Benson slammed his fist down on the table for effect.

Han lurched back in his chair. 'Why you yell and swear at me?'

'Because you aren't telling the truth. The Chinese Horizon was flagged on the Marine Traffic monitors moving in a direction away from the passage. There is nowhere to anchor near the passage entrance, so where did you anchor then, Captain?'

'I drop anchor far out near shipping lane.' Looking on, Harvey also noticed that Han was now responding in faltering English.

Benson continued. 'I'm calling bullshit again Captain; you've lied twice now.'

Han knew that he had no option but to keep avoiding the truth if he valued the safety of his family back in China. 'No, I no lie to you.'

'Yes, you did, twice. Firstly, you said you navigated a straight course from the Solomon Islands to Brisbane and you have just confirmed yourself that wasn't true. Secondly, you are lying about accessing Hydrographers Passage.' Benson took the printed screenshot out of his folder and slid it across the table.

'What is picture?'

Benson pointed at a spot on the screenshot. 'That picture, as you call it, Captain, clearly shows your vessel moving away from the passage,' he said tapping on the screenshot. 'You are lying again.'

Harvey stood up, gave Han a steely stare and said. 'Captain Han, under the Maritime Border Command charter, we have arrest and detain powers. As such, we are going to keep you in custody while we continue our investigations. We would like you to think carefully about your answers to our questions. If there is something else you would like to tell us then press that green button on the wall and we might come back and hear what you have to say, but no more lies?'

'What happen to my ship now?' Han called out.

The agents were already heading out the door and then Han heard the heavy bolt click against the door lock once more. 'La shi.'

De Vries, Harvey and Benson had finished their lunch after discussing the Chinese Horizon situation at length. They were no further advanced with their investigation. They were fully aware that they didn't have proof of any maritime security related offences that they could charge the captain with. There was no doubt in their mind that the captain had entered Hydrographers Passage, but they had no idea as to the pretence for him doing so or any evidence of any illegal activity, other than potentially breaching a Commonwealth maritime law. Having nothing to charge the captain with, they discussed placing him under more pressure and see whether ramping up the intensity would produce a result. 'I think I should conduct the interview alone,' Benson suggested.

De Vries, for reasons of appropriate governance, always had two agents in attendance when interviewing suspects, so he was wary of allowing a solo interview. On this occasion though, he thought Benson's more aggressive approach just might intimidate the mild-mannered captain. 'Okay, Sam, but be sure not to overdo the aggression.'

It was more than three hours since the agents had first interviewed him. Captain Han was becoming more nervous by the hour. He was thinking about his ship, the crew and the unloading of their cargo back at the dock when he heard the door bolt slide back. But he was mostly concerned for his family back in China, wondering if he would ever see them again. What would become of them if he were detained permanently? Then the door opened with a rush and banged loudly against the side wall. Han flinched at the sudden, loud noise. It was the angry agent coming back, and he was alone.

'Captain Han, I am going to resume the interview now, so let's get to the nitty gritty, shall we?'

'What is this "nitty gritty", Agent Benson?'

'It means serious, captain.'

Han nodded furiously. 'Oh, okay.'

'Explain this to me, please? You didn't answer Agent Harvey last time. If you navigated around the Solomon Islands and were making for Brisbane, why weren't you two hundred nautical miles off the coast when you passed Mackay? Why weren't you?'

'I tell you sometimes we go different way.'

'That's not what you said earlier. You said, "then we pass Solomon Islands and enter Coral Sea and go to straight to Brisbane." I can play the tape for you if you like. So, Captain Han, if you always go straight to Brisbane, why was the Chinese Horizon near Hydrographers Passage two nights ago?'

'I tell you before, we had electric fault on board that require attention.'

Benson thought he might see if he could get the captain to slip up. 'That's when you navigated into Hydrographers Passage and dropped anchor?'

'No, I no go into passage, Agent Benson.'

'Yes, you did. You and I both know that's bullshit. What were you doing in the passage? Dropping off illegal immigrants, drugs, arms, what, captain?' Benson slammed his fist down on the table again.

Han shuddered in his seat. 'You yell and swear at me again,' he pleaded.

'Because you're still not telling the truth.' Benson continued. 'The Chinese Horizon was flagged on the Marine Traffic monitors moving in a direction away from the passage. So you must have been in the passage prior to that.'

'I no go into passage. Maybe AMSA have wrong ship. I tell you before, I drop anchor far out near shipping lane.'

'Rubbish, you're lying again.'

'No, I no lie to you.'

There was a knock on the door, which then opened slightly. De Vries poked his head through the gap and asked Benson to step outside into the corridor. Benson harrumphed loudly, showing his displeasure. 'Can't it wait until I'm finished here, boss?'

'No, I need to see you outside now,' came de Vries' gruff reply. Benson stood up, slammed his chair against the table and left the room. 'I was just starting to get somewhere and you've bloody cost me the momentum, boss.'

'Yeah, yeah, okay cool it, Sam. Shane has received a call from the Minister's Office. They have been contacted by the Chinese Consul General in Brisbane who has been enquiring as to Captain Han's detention.'

'So, what does that have to do with my interview?'

'Obviously, the Consul General wants to know the nature and reason for his detention. He is insisting that unless we have evidence of criminal activity that the captain be released immediately. Whilst Home Affairs are supporting us at the moment and are prepared to allow us some leeway, they won't do so forever. So, finish your interview and then we'll make a decision on the next step.'

'Bloody bureaucrats,' grumbled Benson as he walked back to the interview room. He slammed the door, both out of frustration at the interference and to regain the captain's undivided attention. 'Now, captain, tell me about the cruiser you rendezvoused with on Sunday night and the two men aboard.'

Han was alarmed that they knew more than he had originally thought. This was getting serious now. 'I no meet with anyone, Agent Benson,' he replied, clasping his trembling hands.

The agent slammed his fist down on the table again. 'Yes, you did, Captain. A Viking Cruiser was seen leaving your location at the same time you were exiting the passage. That didn't happen by accident.'

'I no see any other boat,' he pleaded.

'Yes, you did and I'm sure you heard the gunfire too. We can place the cruiser and your ship in the same area at the same time.'

'No, no, no, Agent Benson. I no hear any gunfire or see any cruiser.'

'Of course you did. You couldn't have missed hearing the gunfire from your position. We both know sound travels further across water.'

'No, I no hear anything.'

'You're lying again,' Benson shouted. He took a deep breath to calm himself. *One last try.* He suggested to the captain that his family might be in danger back in China and that he should consider that when answering his questions. 'Are you certain you don't want to provide the answers we both know that you have, even for the sake of your family?' Captain Han was either very smart or very stupid, but he offered nothing more.

'Captain Han, you are free to go. Maybe we will see you again in Sydney or Melbourne.'

'How will I get back to ship?'

'I'm sure you will find a way,' smarted Benson.

Benson was sitting across from his boss, frustrated at what he knew were the undeniable facts. 'He and I both know he's hiding something, boss; he had no valid reason for being anywhere near the coastline or Hydrographers Passage,' an exasperated Benson said to de Vries. 'His explanation regarding the electrical repairs is complete bullshit and he had to have at least heard the gunfire if not witnessed it. And he's certainly involved in whatever went down out on the water.'

'I completely agree with you, Sam, so I'm going to ask Shane to put him on the Movement Alert List.'

'He's a ship captain, so what are you hoping to achieve by doing that?'

'Assuming he is involved in illegal activities, then his employers will be extremely nervous about his detention. I'm thinking that they'll want to eliminate any potential risks and therefore might try to remove him from the country expeditiously. And if they do, we'll be waiting for them, Sam. He will undoubtedly be worried about the consequences of his detention from his employer back in China. And he also has the ramifications for his family to consider, so he might just be a little more forthcoming next time.'

Sydney Daily News

'I had a fabulous time last night, Jack. Thank God your balcony overlooks a nature reserve. It was just a wonderful evening and I especially loved the encore.'

'Me too. I thought Diesel was great,' he joked.

Julie-Anne rose to her knees, grabbed her pillow and playfully pummelled Jack with it.

'Diesel was great'… *wham*, 'Diesel was great'… *wham*, 'Diesel was great'…*wham*, she repeated with every swing of the pillow. I'll give you Diesel was great, buddy. You know very well what I meant.'

Jack was curled up in the foetal position, pretending to be hurt. 'Mercy, please, no more, I surrender. You're killing me honey.'

'You'll get no mercy from me after that comment, buddy.'

'Hey, Julie-Anne,' he called out from under the pillow.

'What?!' came the barked reply.

'You, on your knees, naked, hair and breasts swaying with every swing of the pillow, reminds me of someone.'

'Who, funny man?' Julie-Anne halted the pillow onslaught, expecting a compliment.

'Xena Warrior Woman.'

'Aaahh, I'm really gonna kill you now, Jack. Xena…' *wham*, 'Xena…' *wham*, 'Xena…' *wham*.

Later, they had showered and dressed and were having coffee on the balcony, Jack asked Julie-Anne. 'So, what's on the agenda for today, JA?'

'Oops, business as usual. We're back to JA,' she replied.

'It's not like that at all, just that as a serious investigative journalist, JA suits you better.'

She let it slide. 'Well, I finally got some information onto the whiteboard yesterday and today I'm going to follow up a lead I received and see if it has any merit.'

Jack's interest piqued now. 'What sort of lead?' he pretended to ask casually.

'A woman telephoned me unexpectedly yesterday afternoon and claimed to have some knowledge about illegal activities involving a whale, casinos, large amounts of money, etc. That narrows it down to half the men in Sydney, I told her. She wouldn't give me her name, so I told her to ring Crime Stoppers.'

'What did she say to that?'

'I was about to hang up when she told me his name and where he was from. That garnered my attention, but I didn't let my enthusiasm show.'

Jack was facing away from Julie-Anne, pouring another coffee. Trying not to sound overly enthusiastic, he half turned his head and quietly asked. 'So, who is this mystery man about town?'

'Apparently, he's Chinese and lives in Shanghai, but spends a lot of time in Australia. I'm guessing he has an extended stay or residency visa or something.' Jack tilted his head slightly and stared at the coffee beaker.

'Really? Did she tell you who he was?' he asked nonchalantly.

'Yes, Ms Anonymous eventually told me his name. She said it's Li Qiang. So, I'm going to do what I do. I'm going to research Li Qiang today and see what I can find out about the man.'

Jack was thinking he would do the exact same thing. 'JA, you really need to be careful, especially if you're trying to connect the dots with the Triads. They won't take kindly to your investigation and they don't play nice.' As shaky as the connection might be, Jack was again left wondering if there was a link between JA's investigation and what Stevie had told him the previous morning.

Julie-Anne finished her coffee and walked across to Jack. 'Thank you for last night. I had a fabulous time, and again this morning, Mr Modesty.' She placed her hand behind his head and pulled him into a kiss. 'Now, I have to get going.' As she started to walk away, she stopped and looked back over her shoulder. 'And just for the record, you weren't bad on your back either,' she said, winking at him. 'Have a good day, Jack, I intend to. Bye.'

An hour later, Julie-Anne was sitting at her desk thinking about what Ms Anonymous had revealed to her yesterday. There were some tenuous links to her investigation and she would have to try to firm them up, if that were at all possible. She could spend days online researching casinos, money laundering, whales, triads, newspaper articles, etc, and get nowhere. The only new piece of information that she could act upon was the name Li Qiang. So common sense suggested that's where she needed to begin her search. Julie-Anne opened her browser, typed in the letter 'g' and of course the Google website appeared instantly. *Okay, let's start with the simple search first,* she thought. She typed Li Qiang into the search box and hit enter. The result was pages and pages of hits for numerous versions of the name. There was Li Qiang itself then Qiang Li, Dr Qiang Li, Li-Qiang Qin, Prof. Li Qiang Zhu and even ya li Qiang.

One by one, she double clicked on all the links to the obvious candidates, Li Qiang and Qiang Li. It took almost an hour to glance over all the articles related to the two names. There was nothing that closely resembled the topics that her caller had alluded to. Then, one at a time, Julie-Anne searched for anything noteworthy for the less obvious names. *Nada again.*

Then she started adding suffixes to the name Li Qiang, starting with the word gambler.

Google found over 600,000 results in a split second. She scrolled down the first half-dozen pages and nothing caught her trained investigative eye. *Okay, let's try whale*, thinking that gambling exploits in the millions of dollars might just have made headlines somewhere. *Nothing.*

Becoming mildly exasperated, she had another thought. *Okay, let's try Li Qiang Sydney.* Google found 824,000 results in less than half a second this time. 'Bloody hell,' she murmured too loudly, attracting a look from a colleague at the next desk. There was a Li Qiang who had authored an acclaimed scholarly article, a Le Qiang who may or may not have been a Chinese spy according to whichever article you read and a Qiang Li with a master's degree from Sydney University. None of these were her Li Qiang.

Not one to give up lightly, she ploughed on, scrolling, clicking and reading. She came across an article where the Google subject line contained nothing but a list of names, one of which was a Li Qiang. What attracted her attention though, was not the name Li Qiang, but two other names that appeared in the subject line. One was a New South Wales member of parliament and the other, a well-known lobbyist. *Here we go.*

Julie-Anne double-clicked on the link. There was no story contained within the link, just the same list of names she had read in the link's subject line. But the names were attributed to individuals who had posed for a photo together. The photo was taken at a cocktail party held at the Chinese Consulate located in a leafy inner-city suburb. It had taken her four hours of eye- straining research, but she thought she may have found her man. Yeah, *may have* being the operative words, she thought with some uncertainty, not really knowing whether she had the correct Li Qiang or not.

There was one interesting aspect of the photo that gave Julie-Anne mild encouragement.

If the names attributed to the photo were in the same sequence as the subjects, then Li Qiang was the man third from the left. In the photo he appeared to be trying to minimise his presence. *Interesting.* She emailed the link to the computer geniuses in the IT department requesting a large copy of the photo and a separate blown up photo extract of just Li Qiang. As an experienced investigative journalist Julie-Anne knew she didn't really have anything definitive, but she did have a hunch and that was enough for her. 'Now where to from here?' she mumbled to herself.

(36)

AFP Headquarters

Jack was in a buoyant mood as he drove over the Anzac Bridge and headed into AFP headquarters. It was another blue sky morning in the Harbour City, with the waters of Jones Bay to his left shimmering silver in the morning sun. He had the driver's window down in his beloved Commodore to soak up the warm breeze drifting across the harbour. With the seat reclined, he was driving one-handed, right elbow resting on the window frame and humming Tip of My Tongue. He had a little chuckle to himself as he revisited the activities of the previous evening.

On a professional level, he was even more buoyed by the tip that Julie-Anne had inadvertently given him over coffee this morning. She wouldn't be too pleased that he was using her intel to progress his own investigation, but he was a federal police officer and was obligated to use all information and resources at his disposal. It wasn't a lot to work with anyway, but it was a start. After his unproductive day yesterday, he was determined to make some progress by the end of today.

He arrived at his desk and immediately went to work looking for this mysterious Li Qiang.

While Julie-Anne would be restricted to conducting her research through her sources and publicly available online databases, Jack had access to contacts at other federal government agencies. That is where he would start. His first call was to his contact at the DHA in Canberra. 'Lucas, it's Jack Wagner.' Lucas Bourne had been his go to man in Home Affairs since Jack was promoted to detective five years ago. The two of them had never met in person but had an effective working relationship, albeit by telephone.

'I've been given the name of a Chinese national who may be linked to an investigation I'm working on. Apparently, he somehow spends quite a considerable amount of time in the country, in Sydney in particular. I'd like to check on his recent movements. All I have is a name and possibly his city of residence. His name is Li Qiang and he's from Shanghai, supposedly.'

'I've got a couple of pressing issues to deal with for the Minister, but I should be able to get back to you by the close of business.'

'Thanks, Lucas, I appreciate, it as always.' Jack disconnected the call and pondered his next move. Then he suddenly remembered the line 'follow the money' from All the President's Men, the movie about the Watergate scandal. If Li Qiang really was a "whale" then he had to be acquiring large sums of money from somewhere with which to gamble. And it would probably be in cash, so there would be records kept of his transactions. Jack was fully aware of the statutory reporting requirements for large cash transactions.

Once again, needing the resources of another federal government agency, he called Chris Coleman at Austrac. The agency was responsible for preventing, detecting and responding to criminal abuse of the financial system, particularly by organised crime figures, so if anyone would be able to assist him it would be Coleman. Jack wasn't a close associate of his, but they were known to each other. He detailed the information he required and why. Initially, Coleman wasn't all that enthusiastic, so Jack upped the ante.

'Chris we're both public officials, work for the same government and we both investigate money laundering.' Jack deliberately placed emphasis on "we both", in the hope the reminder of their status as contemporaries would yield a more willing collaboration. *Let's see if it worked,* he pondered. 'Look, if I find any evidence of money laundering, the resulting charges will potentially be laid by your office anyway. Call it a joint investigation if you want; I couldn't care less. I just want to catch this guy, especially if he's laundering money to fund criminal activities. And by the way, I'm more interested in the criminal activities themselves than the money laundering, so you can have all the credit for that, for all I care.'

'All right, calm down, spell the name for me.'

'Li Qiang.' Jack spelt the name.

'Okay, call me back in a couple of hours.'

Call me back in a couple of hours. Really, you don't know how to use a phone? You twat. Bloody Canberra bureaucrats. He agreed and hung up the phone.

'Calm down Jack,' he said to himself. He started his online search for Li Qiang while he waited for Lucas to call him back and to fill in the two hours before he could call Austrac back. There were dozens of variants of the name listed and hundreds of thousands of results. He would need to narrow the search parameters, so he did just that, starting with the most obvious; Li Qiang Sydney.

He was all too aware that all he needed was just one piece of information, one lead to kick start his investigation. That one piece would be the base or rock on which to build it. Then that would lead to another piece, then another and so on as the investigation developed. And, like any good detective, he would also have to corroborate each snippet as he proceeded.

Bugger, there are still hundreds of thousands of results; *is this the John Smith of Chinese names?* he said to himself, exasperated. Among the closest results he found centred in Sydney were a scholar, a Master's graduate and a potential spy, but none were his Li Qiang. He imagined that JA would have discovered the same useless information.

In the middle of his frustration, his mobile rang.

'Jack, it's Lucas here. You just might be in luck. If it turns out that I have the correct Li Qiang then he's in the country as we speak.'

'That would be too much to hope for. What have you found?'

'Let me walk you through this. As you would know, everyone entering the country has to complete an Incoming Passenger Card and the information they supply is recorded and uploaded into the Home Affairs database. They are allocated a reference number and then their passport number is used as a cross reference. There are quite a few versions of Li Qiang with your spelling listed in the immigration records. So, I eliminated Australians returning from overseas, and any Li Qiang's that arrived from the myriad of Chinese cities, other than Beijing, being the capital, and Shanghai.

'Lucas. You wouldn't be telling me all this if you didn't have something.'

'Just let me walk you through this from start to finish, that way you'll be comfortable with the due diligence I applied to the search and the efficacy of the information.'

'Sorry. Carry on, please,' Jack apologised.

'Okay. Then I searched their frequency of travel and one particular Li Qiang had significantly more arrivals than those not already eliminated. This Li Qiang has visited Australia over a dozen times in the past three years, so I focused on him.'

'You didn't mention why you were looking for a Li Qiang, Jack, but I can speculate through what I'm about to tell you next. During every one of his visits he stayed at the same hotel. He listed the Oceanic Hotel and Casino at Darling Harbour on his Incoming Passenger Card.'

'Voila,' Jack exclaimed. 'Thanks Lucas, you're incredible. Can you email his file across?'

'No can do. Our country's privacy laws don't allow that. There's information contained within the file that is not for general consumption.'

'Alright, I get that. Can you send me a summary listing all of his inbound and outbound travel dates then?'

'That I can do. I'll extract his arrival and departure dates, put them into a one-pager and send that across.'

'Just one more question, Lucas. How is he able to travel to Australia so frequently?'

'He uses the Business Owner Visa which allows him to visit Australia for business purposes.'

'What restrictions are attached to the visa?'

'Not a lot, really. He has to own a business here and spend at least one year in Australia over a two-year period. There are some other minor clauses related to turnover and assets, but I'm sure your man would qualify.'

'I really appreciate your help and I'll buy you a beer next time I'm in Canberra.'

'Yeah sure, you hate the place, so you'll never come down here.'

'Bye, Lucas.'

(37)

AFP Headquarters

By the time he had finished with Lucas's call, the *couple of hours* had elapsed that Chris Coleman had requested. Jack dialled the Austrac number again.

'Hi, Chris, it's Jack Wagner calling again as requested. Did you have any luck?'

'Yeah, I think so,' Coleman said.

'You sound unsure.'

'Well, there were quite a few transactions for various Li Qiangs, so I had to go through a process of elimination. Most were for small amounts that I thought you wouldn't be interested in. Once I had completed that, there was only one Li Qiang remaining.' Coleman paused.

Jack had his metaphorical fingers crossed. 'Continue, please, Chris.'

'Well, on three occasions there were two transactions conducted in a twenty-four-hour period in 2017 and 2018 for a Li Qiang for amounts between eight hundred thousand and nine hundred and eighty thousand dollars.'

Jack thought, *here we go*. Unable to hide his enthusiasm, he said to Coleman. 'And let me guess where the transactions were carried out: the Oceanic Hotel and Casino in Sydney.'

'How did you know?'

Jack wasn't about to reveal his source for fear of Coleman starting up his own investigation and compromising Jack's. 'Call it an educated guess.'

'Okay, then.' Coleman replied, seemingly quite startled by Jack's revelation.

'Chris, can you tell me if there was any follow-up investigation conducted by Austrac?'

'We got his contact details and conducted a telephone interview. Li stated that he won original his stake money at the races. Apparently, the timing of the transactions lined up with the Sydney spring and autumn racing carnivals, so I guess no one thought anymore of it.'

'So, that would be between September 2017 and April 2018 if my knowledge of Sydney racing is any good,' Jack suggested.

'You're on the money, pun intended.' *Geez, maybe they do have a sense of humour in Canberra.* Jack kept that thought to himself.

'And there were no other transactions, none more recent, Chris?'

'Well, actually yes there are and this is where it gets interesting.'

'I'm all ears.'

'On seven other occasions there are single transactions where the casino has obviously cashed in his chips and transacted an Electronic Funds Transfer on his behalf. All transactions were for either six or seven-figure sums. I know what you're going to ask next, Jack.'

'Hang on a second. Is there no record of him exchanging cash for casino chips on or around any of those dates?'

'Nope, none at all Jack.'

'So, where did he get his original stake from on those occasions?' Jack asked, as much to himself as Coleman. 'Can you give me the exact dates for all his transactions, please?'

'Yeah sure, got a pen? Better still, give me your email address and I'll send you a summary .'

'If you don't mind me saying so, Chris, I'm surprised that Austrac didn't investigate further, given the sizeable amount of the transactions and the focus on money laundering these days.'

'Me too, but there may have been more pressing investigations underway at the time and potentially, we didn't have the resources to initiate another one. And by the way, they're not that large in the scheme of things.'

'You're kidding, right?'

'You would be surprised at the size of some of the transactions we investigate, Jack.'

'Okay, thanks, Chris you've been a big help. If anything comes of this that falls within Austrac's purview I'll be in touch again and give you the heads-up,' he replied, although he had no intention of doing any such thing.

'I would appreciate it.'

Jack hung up the telephone and thought about his next move. He maximised his inbox and saw that Lucas had already sent through the list of dates showing when Li Qiang had entered and left the country. He opened his notebook and compared the three dates Coleman had given him. All three transactions were conducted within the first three days of his arrival in Sydney. Jack then checked the dates against the Australian Turf Club racing fixtures and each transaction had been conducted on the night of a major race day. *So, where did the cash originate for the other seven completed transactions?* Jack asked himself. He knew what his next move needed to be.

Oceanic Hotel Darling Harbour

'Security Office, Jim Brennan speaking.'

'Hi Jim, it's Jack here. How are you?'

'Yeah, all good here, long time no speak, buddy.'

Jack had worked with Jim Brennan at the Australian Federal Police for a number of years and Brennan had been a mentor to him in his early days with the force. The increased adoption of technology by the AFP had led to introducing voluntary redundancies for the first time in the agency's storied history. As a long-term employee, Brennan was entitled to fifty-two weeks redundancy pay, which, after some earnest consideration, he understandably accepted. State and federal police officers, especially those with seniority, were highly sought out for private security roles and Brennan was no different. He had been headhunted by a recruitment agency and was now the Director of Security for the Oceanic Hotel and Casino.

'My apologies, Jim, but you better than anyone know what life is like at the AFP, buddy, especially in these changing times.'

'Isn't that the truth. What can I do for you, Jack?'

'I am in the early stages of an investigation and my research has led me to one of your regular guests.'

'What's it about and who is the guest?'

'Well, there isn't a lot that I can tell you, but the guest is a Mr Li Qiang. All I know is that he is a regular at the hotel, gambles large amounts of money, is a person of interest to me and he is staying at the hotel as we speak.'

'I know of the man you refer to and have even met him a couple of times when escorting him to the Bennelong Room. That's the high rollers room where they have access to anything and everything laid on by the hotel and casino. And I mean anything and everything, Jack. How do you know he is a high roller gambling large amounts of money?'

'You know I work for the federal government and have access to significant volumes of information from other agencies.'

'Okay, what do you want from me, Jack?'

'I would like to know if he has been involved in any suspicious or unusual activity, or if the casino has had any reason to investigate him. And I would appreciate a photo of Li Qiang if possible; I assume you have one on file.'

'Let me see what I can find out. Give me your email address and contact number and I'll get back to you?'

'Thanks, Jim, I appreciate it. Chat soon.' Jack disconnected the call, leaned back in his chair and pondered his next move. From previous AFP investigations Jack knew of the Bennelong Room, where the high rollers preferred to gamble, drink and entertain without being observed by the great unwashed. Given Austrac's record of Li's transactions at the Oceanic, and the fact he was staying at the hotel, it was reasonable to assume he could be found there most nights during his stay.

Jack read through the information he received from Austrac and Home Affairs again for a refresher. He rang Jim back.

'Jim, it's me again.'

'I haven't even got around to researching your target, Jack.'

'That's okay, no hurry.'

'Then, what can I do for you buddy? It's quite hectic here at the moment.'

'I'll be quick. Can you get me access to the Bennelong Room tonight?'

'That's pushing the friendship. The high rollers expect absolute privacy and discretion from the casino when they're in the Bennelong Room. How would it look if one of them found out there was an AFP officer prowling around in their private domain?'

'Come on, Jim, you know I can be discreet,' he pleaded.

'Those guys can smell a cop miles away.'

'I'll wear something stylish and I guarantee I won't stand out. Come on buddy, help me out here? I wouldn't ask if it wasn't important.'

'Okay, okay. I will leave your name with Bennelong Room reception. If anyone pushes the point, just say you are a consultant working with the Director of Security on the potential redesign of the security systems in the room. That will baffle them for a while and they won't be able to verify it anyway, as I'll be home asleep.'

'One more thing, can you text me Li Qiang's photo, so I have it on my phone?' Jack didn't wait for an answer. 'Thanks, Jim, I owe you one.'

Jack was expected to have dinner with Julie-Anne tonight, but she would understand this would have to take priority. As an investigative journalist, she more than anyone understood the importance of acting upon information as expeditiously as possible. Anyway, they had been together for the past two nights and Jack could use a night off. He was fond of Julie-Anne, but he wasn't going to rush into a new relationship after knowing her for only six months. She was probably too busy to be interrupted, he said to himself, justifying the text message he was about to send.

Sydney Daily News

Julie-Anne was still sitting at her desk, now with her third latte of the day. She was wondering with the little information she had, how would she progress the investigation. Then it came to her in a flash. If Li Qiang was photographed at the Chinese Consulate General with a lobbyist and a member of state parliament then she had to assume that he had a connection to one of the three entities, if not all. Otherwise, why would he be there.

She dialled the desk number for the paper's entertainment reporter. Deborah Atkinson, the best known entertainment reporter in Sydney, was equally well connected and if anyone could get Julie-Anne into the Consulate, then Deb surely could. 'I need some information on a story I'm researching.' Julie-Anne asked the reporter, who'd picked up on the second ring. 'I can't go into all the details just yet, but it may have a connection to the Chinese Consul General.'

'Really? That sounds juicy already. Anything in it for your favourite entertainment reporter?'

'No, not at all, well not yet anyway, Deb. Do you have any connections with the Consulate by any chance?'

Deb knew JA was onto something. 'Aaahh, you'll love this. There's a cocktail party being held to celebrate an insignificant something or other at the Consulate tomorrow evening and I'm going along. Wanna come? I could use a plus one who's not going to get on my nerves all night.'

'That would be fabulous. I'll try and tell you more tomorrow evening,' said Julie-Anne excitedly.'

'I'll meet you at the QV Wine Bar for a cocktail at six and we can go from there.'

'See you there, Deb.'

Okay, I'd better get busy then, Julie-Anne thought. Just in case she found herself in conversation with the Consul General, she knew she had to conduct research on the Consul General's activities in Sydney and wider New South Wales. She Googled *Chinese Consulate Sydney* and began her research.

The leading story on the website was the Consul General's consternation at the decision by the NSW Department of Education to end its Confucius Institute program. She searched *Confucius Institute political interference* and was surprised at the volume of articles. An article posted on abc.net.au seemed to sum up the New South Wales government's concerns.

The New South Wales Department of Education has expelled a Chinese Government language program from the state's public schools due to fears of potential foreign influence. The Confucius Institute program is overseen by Chinese Government agency Hanban and teaches Mandarin in thirteen public schools across Sydney and on the mid-north coast. Intrigued, she kept reading.

Following concerns of potential propaganda in Australian schools, the NSW Department of Education ordered a review last May. Handing down its report, the department said the review found no evidence of "actual political influence". That's the typical politically correct response, she thought.

But it said there was a perception that "the Institute is or could be facilitating inappropriate foreign influence, and that NSW is the only government department in the world hosting a Confucius Institute".

The review said the arrangement placed Chinese Government appointees inside a NSW Government department.

This was of particular interest to Julie-Anne, given her own suspicions surrounding the Confucius Institute's activities. China would have to find other ways to influence public policy and potentially even insert Chinese appointees inside the New South Wales government, she surmised. She was drawn to the Consul General's response to this, scrolled down and kept reading. The CG was demanding clarification from the state government. The article continued.

On the so-called political influence through Confucius Institute programs, China has been always committed to developing relations with other countries based on principles of mutual respect and non-interference in each other's internal affairs. It is noted that the relevant review by the NSW Department of Education found no evidence of actual political influence through its Confucius Institute program. We hope relevant parties will discard their ideological prejudice and view China's development and foreign policy in an objective and rational manner. 'Yeah sure, tell that to the people of Taiwan, Tibet or Hong Kong,' she mumbled to herself.

"*Principles of mutual respect and non-interference in each other's internal affairs.*" Really, you expect us to believe that? she thought. She kept reading. Next came an article on the South China Sea.

China reaffirming its territorial sovereignty and maritime rights and interests in the South China Sea, enhancing cooperation in the South China Sea with other countries, and upholding peace and stability in the South China Sea. Yeah sure, after you've stolen, colonised and militarised Vietnam and Philippines claimed islands, Julie-Anne lamented.

And of course, no Chinese Government website would be complete without referencing the Belt and Road Initiative.

Leaders of forty countries and international organisations attended the leaders' roundtable, focused on the theme of "Belt and Road Cooperation: Shaping a Brighter Shared Future". They exchanged views on topics such as advancing connectivity, strengthening policy synergy and promoting green and sustainable development. Of course, the article was accompanied by a large photo of Xi Jinping himself.

It seemed to Julie-Anne that the Consulate's website was more interested in promoting China's activities worldwide than in fostering relations between China and New South Wales. She clicked on the 'NSW in Brief' link and the page was blank. She then went to each of the Tibet, Taiwan and Human Rights links and they too were all blank pages. Too controversial to publish in Australia, she assumed. The website was probably authored in Beijing anyway, or at the very least, authorised there.

Well, if she was going to attend a cocktail party at the Consulate, then she had better focus on the positives, although she was struggling to find information on the website that was anything but propaganda. She had been to Hong Kong, but thought the timing might be wrong to mention that, given the street protests that were prevalent in the former British colony at the moment. *Maybe I'll just tell them of my love for Peking Duck,* she mused while chuckling to herself. *Okay, be serious Julie-Anne.*

Just then, her mobile phone buzzed with an incoming text message. She read the message and a frown came across her face. Jack had cancelled dinner. 'Stood up by text message. *Far out, it was only a few hours ago I was naked in his bed for the second time in two days.* How's the guy's form, a bloody text message?' she mumbled and grumbled. *Don't push it, let it go.*

She composed herself and went back to Google where she searched Chinese economic impact on Australia and memorised some key facts. Next, she researched Chinese economic growth. And finally, in an effort to be topical, she searched China—New South Wales where she found interesting articles about early Chinese settlers in Parramatta, eleven thousand Chinese seeking their fortune on the New South Wales goldfields in the 1800s and the history of Sydney's Chinatown. 'That's more positive,' she said to herself as she memorised the statistics.

And finally, she undertook research on Zhang Xiao, the Consul General himself. There wasn't much information available other than his diplomatic history, which was extensive, and his Chinese Communist Party membership. There was, however, a small article referencing suspected corruption, but he was apparently exonerated by President Xi's corruption officers. Maybe that's how Xiao ended up in the New South Wales CG's posting rather than a full-blown ambassadorial role, she pondered.

That should be enough for tonight that I can sound reasonably intelligent regarding all things China. Still smarting from Jack's rejection text message, she thought, *'maybe I'll even meet someone at the cocktail party who knows how to dial a phone number.'*

Bennelong Room

Li's thoughts were interrupted by a knock on the door. He slowly rose from the chaise and walked across the vast living area to the entry foyer. Following a cursory glance through the peephole to be sure it was Woodard, he opened the door. 'Give me a minute while I freshen up. I've been busy, Mr Vice President.' After he had cleaned up, they exited the suite, made their way to the private elevator and rode it down twenty floors to the Bennelong Room.

'How do you propose to exchange your chips without drawing unwanted attention to yourself, Mr Li?'

'I can't very well just walk up to the cashier and hand them over, can I? As usual, I will play a few hands of blackjack, betting reasonably large amounts and the overhead cameras will no doubt capture my activity as usual. Whether I win or lose is irrelevant as long as the size and frequency of my bets are captured, which will mitigate any suspicion and validate my exchange when I eventually make my way to the cashier. And I will request an electronic funds transfer and the money will then be clean.

'Good luck.'

Li projected a dark stare. 'Luck has nothing to do with it, Mr Vice President.'

Li took a seat at his favourite blackjack table, placed a soft leather, navy toilet bag on the adjacent chair, unzipped it and pulled out a sleeve of pumpkins which he duly stacked on the table. The croupier was in the middle of shuffling the eight decks of cards which suited him as he preferred to play with a full chute of cards. His strategy was to gamble nominal amounts initially and then slowly up his bets to one hundred thousand dollars. His plan was to lose no more than that. That equated to ten percent of his funds, which was an acceptable cost to pay for laundering illicitly gained money.

Li placed four chips in the yellow rimmed rectangular box in front of him. The croupier dealt the first hand and Li had a ten and a seven, seventeen against the dealer's eight. As always seems to happen, the dealer drew a ten and Li's first twenty thousand disappeared into the croupier's chip holder. He played a few more hands, still betting the same amount each time, with mixed results. Forty minutes later he raised his next bet to fifty thousand dollars. As luck would have it, he was handed an ace and a jack. 'Blackjack,' called the croupier as he pushed seventy-five thousand dollars in chips across to Li.

The next few hands were once again a mixed bag for Li. He had now been playing for nearly an hour and his blackjack collect was the difference between his winning and losing. Okay, time to up the stakes, he thought. He placed two stacks of ten chips in the yellow-rimmed box.

The croupier dealt Li a seven and a four. 'Eleven double, Mr Li?' enquired the dealer. The dealer had an eight, so assuming the dealer's next card was a ten, then Li would only need an eight of his own to win the hand. Unless the dealer drew an ace of course. The odds were still in his favour. He took out another sleeve of chips from his bag and added twenty chips to his original stake, doubling the bet. He now had two hundred thousand dollars riding on one card. The dealer slowly slid a card from the chute and turned over the ten of hearts. Li now had the maximum of twenty-one and couldn't lose the hand. The dealer did, in fact, turn over and ace for himself, but to no avail. He then measured up a stack of chips against Li's and pushed them across the table. Li pushed the eight stacks back into his betting box.

A few guests had discreetly gathered around the blackjack table to watch the previous hand. When Li left the four hundred thousand dollars in chips in place for the next hand, word spread quickly around the Bennelong Room and the crowd grew even further. This was good news for Li as he knew the pit supervisors, and more importantly, the overhead cameras would definitely be focused on his table now. He needed that. The dealer dealt him a ten and a nine and himself an ace. There was an anguished, collective groan from the assembled crowd, reflecting their concern for Li's predicament. They knew he would have to 'sit' on nineteen and the dealer only required a nine or ten to better his hand, cards which comprised thirty-eight percent of the card deck. Li himself wasn't concerned, as even if he lost the hand, his total losses wouldn't be much more than one hundred thousand dollars. It was slightly more than he was usually prepared to lose but it was still a reasonable price to pay to launder nearly a million dollars.

There was a pause from the dealer as he waited for the crowd to quieten. With the crowd now hushed, the dealer looked at Li and then began sliding a card face down from the card chute. His hand seemed to be moving in slow motion as the crowd waited for him to turn over the card. As the card turned, Li could already see that it wasn't a picture card. Now he needed the card to be an eight or less. 'Dealer has eighteen,' was all Li heard as the seven of clubs landed next to the ace. The gathering erupted in congratulatory applause and polite cheering.

As he gathered his chips, and to further draw attention to himself, he pushed two chips across to the dealer and waved his hand backwards, indicating that it was a tip for his services. He knew it was against house rules for gaming staff to accept gratuities and the dealer duly pushed them straight back to Li. 'I'll escort you to the cashier, Mr Li,' offered Woodard as he walked up to the table.

'Excuse me while I use the men's room.' Li walked into a cubicle and closed the door. He pulled out the unused sleeves of pumpkins, stripped off the plastic covers and poured the loose chips into his bag. He wanted it to appear to the cashier, and more importantly, the ever-present closed-circuit cameras, that he had been gambling his entire chip holding and any unopened sleeves would raise unwanted suspicions.

As they walked into the Treasury Offices, Woodard was alarmed to see that Michelle Ironside was in attendance as the Duty Manager. He knew immediately what she would make of the association between him and Li, referring to the mystery whale he had mentioned during their tense meeting at the Bayside Café.

'Hello, Mr Woodard,' said Michelle tersely as she turned to greet his companion.

'Hello, Michelle.'

'Ms Ironside, if you don't mind.'

Li picked up on the brusque exchange and reminded himself to query it with Woodard later.

'Mr Li would like to cash in his winnings,' advised Woodard, emphasising the word *winnings*. He accepted the navy blue bag from Li and handed it across to Michelle. 'How much is here?'

'Mr Li has just had a significant win at the blackjack table, but he's not sure as to exactly how much. Probably in excess of a million dollars.' Michelle's tried to hide her disgust at the mention of a *million dollars*. She was pretty certain she knew exactly where the majority of the chips had been sourced. *Her vault.*

'In what form would you like your funds, Mr Li?' He handed over a business card with his banking details handwritten on the reverse side. 'It will take some time for me to count and verify the value of your chips; probably twenty minutes or so.'

'I am in no hurry, Ms Ironside,' said Li reading from the name badge attached to her graphite coloured business suit. Nearly twenty

minutes later Michelle had completed counting the chips and advised
Li of the final amount.

'If you agree with the amount, I will now deposit 1.715 million
dollars into your nominated account, Mr Li.'

'That will be fine.' Five minutes later, Michelle returned and handed
Li a printed receipt confirming the deposit.

'In the interest of transparency, and in accordance with federal
law, this transaction will be recorded in the Threshold Transaction
Report, which is remitted to Austrac, Mr Li.'

Without acknowledging Michelle, Li stood and looked at Woodard.
'I'm going to my suite; can you arrange for a bottle of my favourite
whiskey to be delivered? You might like to join me; we have something
to discuss.'

'I bet you do,' smarted Michelle under her breath as they walked
away.

Woodard had escorted Li back to the Macquarie Suite. 'So, Mr Vice
President, do you want to tell me what is going on between you and
that cashier?' Li was now leaning back on his sofa holding a Glenlivet
in his left hand and a Monte Christo in the right.

'There is nothing going on between us. She's too old for me.'

'Don't be coy, Tony, we both know that's not what I meant. Now
explain that little interaction.'

'On the night I exchanged your million dollars in cash for gaming
chips, Ms Ironside checked the Austrac database and couldn't find
any record of your transaction. She then conducted a reconciliation
of her cash and chip holding and noticed a discrepancy of one million
dollars in both.'

'So, what action have you taken, Mr Vice President?' Li was
accentuating his casino title expecting Woodard to utilise his
position to mitigate the problem.

'I have made it abundantly clear to Ms Ironside that if she can't
maintain her discretion then her career and life as she knows it are
over.'

'I hope for your sake that she does maintain discretion. Otherwise the same will apply to you.'

'Are you threatening me, Li?'

'*Mr* Li to you and your understanding of English appears to be particularly good, Mr Vice President.'

'I only have two more transactions that I need handling and then our business relationship will cease. And, of course, I look forward to your ongoing accommodation with both transactions. I won't allow anything to complicate matters. Do you understand?'

'Of course.'

'Now leave, Mr Vice President.'

(**41**)

Bennelong Room

Jack rode the hotel's elevator up to the eighteenth floor and alighted into a subtly lit, but grand looking foyer of decorative marble, heavy burgundy velvet drapes and plush gunmetal grey carpet. He had dressed smart casual with charcoal coloured, tapered trousers, a slim fit white linen shirt hanging over his belt and a lightweight black leather jacket. He didn't think he looked like an undercover cop, but hey, who knew? If he were recognised, he could always just disappear into the carpet, such was its thickness, he chuckled to himself.

Given the obvious harbour views that would be available from the eighteenth floor, Jack was surprised that there were no windows to highlight the location. He guessed the casino didn't want its high-flying guests to know what time of day or night it was, for obvious reasons.

He walked across to the reception area and introduced himself. He provided the requested identification and was ushered through the large mahogany doors and into the Bennelong Room itself. The stylishly dressed, attractive hostess gave him a tour of the facilities and explained the house rules, room etiquette and gaming. 'If there's anything else I can do for you, Mr Wagner, please let me know. I'll be at reception. In the meantime, enjoy your evening,' she gushed like a broken pipe while offering a practiced, beaming smile.

Jack made his way across to the bar and ordered a Jack Daniels and Coke from another stylishly dressed, tallish, attractive young woman. He guessed she was in her late twenties. The bar attendant also wore a long sleeve silver blouse tucked into a tight-fitting black pencil skirt. Her blonde hair was wrapped around itself and looped up into what Jack guessed was called a bun. Just like the reception hostess, the bar attendant had her blouse open at the top two buttons. *Are they all clones in here?*

'I'm sorry sir, we don't stock Jack Daniels. We have Woodford Reserve, Makers Mark, Blanton's Gold Edition or Wild Turkey Rare Breed. Which one would sir prefer?'

'I'm a fairly rare breed, so I'll try the Wild Turkey please, Miss.'

'That was very amusing, sir. You can call me Danielle.' She had worked long enough in the casino to recognise a detective and she made him straight away. *I wonder what he's up to*, she pondered, while pouring his bourbon.

The Bennelong Room wasn't large by any means, and it was dimly lit compared to the main casino floor eighteen levels below. The carpet was a dense plush pile similar to that in the foyer, the burgundy velvet drapes were here as well, and the dim lighting was provided by crystal chandeliers. Downlights were strategically placed above each of the gaming tables. From his viewpoint at the bar, Jack counted eleven gaming tables in the room. Four blackjack, a similar number for baccarat, two pai gow and a large poker table which he assumed was restricted to pre-arranged games between the high rollers. Looking at the mix of tables, it was obvious to Jack that the target market was certainly wealthy Chinese and the gamblers were mostly just that. He had refreshed his memory of Li Qiang's face through the photo on his mobile as he made his way up in the elevator. Surveying the room, Jack couldn't see Li in attendance, so he would bide his time at the bar.

After about twenty minutes, the reception clone pushed open the entry door and Li walked in accompanied by another suited man, who to Jack, looked like he was probably from corporate relations or maybe even security. *Why the escort?*, wondered Jack. He would find out who the suited man was before he left. The suit escorted Li to a blackjack table in the far corner of the room, but close enough to the bar that Jack could survey the action. Li sat by himself in the centre chair, which looked like a leather Chesterfield to Jack's untrained eye. He was obviously going to play one on one against the casino. Why wouldn't you? Jack thought. Why let other players ruin your strategy when you can stay in control of your destiny by playing alone? He noticed for the first time that Li was carrying a navy blue toilet bag which he had placed on the adjacent chair. Jack watched him open the bag and extract a sleeve of orange gaming chips. He guessed the sleeve contained about fifty casino chips.

Jack turned to Danielle and ordered another of his new namesake bourbons. As subtly as he could, he asked who the man dressed in the navy blue suit was.

'Oh, that's Mr Woodard, he's the Vice President of Client Services.'

'Oh, okay, I thought it was someone I know, but obviously not.'

Yep, definitely a detective.

Li played a few hands over the next half hour with mixed results, judging by the lack of movement in his chip stacks. The very next hand the dealer pushed a stack of about fifteen orange chips across to him.

'Danielle, what is the value of the orange gaming chips?'

'Five thousand dollars, Mr Rare Breed.'

Okay he's just won around seventy-five thousand, let's see what happens now. Jack watched as Li appeared to count out about twenty chips and placed them in two stacks behind the card box. One hundred thousand dollars by Jack's calculation. A small group of spectators were now gathering around Li's table, obviously eager to watch the ensuing hand. This was a good opportunity for Jack to blend in and get a closer look, so with bourbon in hand, he casually walked over to the table and stood at the rear of the enthusiastic crowd.

He watched as the dealer gave Li a seven and a four. 'Eleven double, Mr Li?' queried the dealer who had dealt himself an eight. Given the odds were seriously in his favour Li naturally doubled the bet. Jack knew enough about blackjack to know that if Li's next card was a ten, he couldn't lose the hand. Li now had two hundred thousand dollars riding on one card. The dealer slowly slid a card from the chute and turned over the ten of hearts. The assembled crowd gave a muted cheer, consistent with the etiquette of the room.

Jack was stunned when Li left the entire four hundred thousand dollars in chips in-place for the next hand. *Wow!* More guests were drifting across to the table as word spread around the room. The dealer waited for the crowd to quieten, then dealt Li a ten and a nine and himself an ace. The crowd groaned at the sight of the dealer's ace. Li was stuck on nineteen and the dealer only required a nine or ten to win the hand. With the crowd hushed, the dealer looked at Li and then slid a card out of the chute. 'Dealer has eighteen,' Jack heard as the seven of clubs was turned over. The crowd erupted in applause, and Jack found himself joining in. Li had just won another four hundred thousand dollars, bringing his winnings to over half a million dollars.

Li gathered his chips and then picked up the bag. Jack could see the outline of more sleeves pressing against its side. That told him he had significantly more than the two hundred thousand dollars he had placed on the blackjack table. And now he was about to add more than half a million dollars to his kitty. Li then surprised Jack by going to the bathroom by himself, toilet bag in hand. He thought the suit should have accompanied him to provide a level of security.

Upon his return, Li and the suit made their way to an unmarked room, which Jack guessed was the cashier or treasury where Li would exchange his chips for an electronic transfer as he had obviously done on previous visits. He was about to transact at least one million dollars by Jack's reckoning. After nearly half an hour Li and the suit exited the room. Jack then spied a well-groomed, mid-forties woman conservatively dressed in a grey business suit, exit the same room. She didn't know it yet, but she would be having a conversation with Jack in the near future.

'Mr Rare Breed?'

Jack had been waiting at the bar for Li and the suit to exit the Treasury Office. 'What's up, Danielle?'

'I finish work in a few minutes, and I know a bar nearby that serves your brand of bourbon.'

That came out of left field, but Jack wondered if this was an opportunity to learn more about Li and Woodard's activities. She was thinking the same thing about him.

'I have an early start in the morning, but I guess I could squeeze in a couple more.'

42

Macquarie Suite
Wednesday 4th March

Li's burner phone rang, and he hoped it would be the Consul General advising of the outcome of his intervention. He pressed the green button. 'What took you so long?'

'Good morning to you too, Li,' came the sarcastic response. 'Matters of diplomacy are never rushed. It takes time for the wheels of government to turn.'

'Not where I come from, Xiao, now what information have you got for me?'

'Well, apparently Captain Han was detained by Maritime Border Command and taken to their Brisbane Airport office, rather than to their Brisbane Port office for some reason. I'm guessing that the officers were hoping the drive to an unfamiliar location may unsettle the captain.'

'That doesn't surprise me. What else?'

'Well, the good news is that the Consul General in Brisbane was able to speak to Home Affairs officials. The CG was quite forceful, apparently accusing the government of being xenophobic towards China, which, given all the unfavourable media coverage lately, made the officials quite nervous. Anyway, it seems the captain was released yesterday afternoon, but we have nothing further as we can't contact him.'

'That is a good outcome, I will take it from here.'

'Why is this captain so important to you?'

'You don't need to know the details, but trust me when I say this. He is important to you and your causes, also.' Li pressed the red button on his phone. With the burner still in his hand Li pressed the number one and speed dialled his contact in China.

'What news do you have for me, Li?'

'Captain Han has been released, but we are unable to contact him,' he replied.

'It is just as well that one of us knows what is happening with our business, Li. I have spoken to the captain myself. Angel arranged for him to call me on their satellite phone immediately upon his release and return to the ship. He was asked many questions about his route of navigation and why he was in certain places at particular times. Apparently, the border agents didn't believe his answers, but they couldn't prove any criminal activity, so they eventually released him.'

'I arranged for the Consul General in Brisbane to intercede on our behalf, that's why he was released.' Li retorted, trying to regain the initiative.

'Li, I am concerned about the captain and his ability to keep quiet. He will still be in Australian waters for another two weeks at least. If the authorities collect further evidence they could easily detain and question him again in Sydney or Melbourne and we might not be so fortunate next time. I want him out of the country.'

'We can't just leave a twenty thousand tonne cargo ship in a foreign port without its captain. The ship will be seized by the port authorities,' snapped Li.

'Li, may I remind you of a favourite Chinese saying? "The lone sheep is in danger of the wolf." I want Captain Han out of Australia and on a plane to Shanghai today, even if you have to fly to Brisbane and arrange it yourself. I have a replacement ship's captain booked on a flight to Brisbane. He will be there tomorrow afternoon.'

'Okay, I will arrange it.' Li responded submissively.

(**43**)

AFP Headquarters

Danielle had taken Jack to a Melbourne laneway style bar in the side streets of Ultimo, not far from the casino. He had waited on the main casino floor while she changed out of her uniform in the basement staff room. She had swapped her clone outfit for a white sleeveless and backless short mini dress with a deep vee neck that highlighted her tanned skin and showed more of her ample cleavage than Jack thought possible. She had sashayed across the room towards him, her blonde hair bouncing off her bare shoulders. *Is this the same Danielle?*

'Let's go have some fun, Jack,' she had teased as she looped her arm into his.

'What can I get you?' he asked her.

'I would really love a Rare Breed,' she whispered into Jack's ear before giving him an impish smile.

'How did I know you were going to say that.'

'God, I hate being predictable. I've had a long boring day in that dingy room and I need something to stimulate me.'

He looked at her uncertainly, wondering what she was intimating.

'I'm serious,' she said, gazing into his eyes. 'Oh God, I love this song. Come on, Mr Rare Breed.' She grabbed his hand and pulled him onto the dance floor. This free-spirited young woman obviously loved to dance and put on a floorshow of her own with her arms, legs and body bopping, gyrating and twirling in every direction. Jack loved the twirling the most, as it caused her mini dress to flutter high up above her thighs. *Yep, definitely an all-over tan.* He liked the song, Uptown Funk, and was doing his best to keep up with Danielle, in spite of his two left feet.

'That's better,' she said breathless, as the song ended. Danielle moved into Jack, looped her arms around his neck and kissed him with a hungry mouth.

What have I started, he thought? It seemed to Jack that his connection to JA was more liaison than relationship, given their dedication to their respective careers. Or was he justifying his current circumstances to himself. He wanted Danielle, but it had only been two days since he was intimate with JA and letting things escalate with Danielle didn't seem appropriate, even to Jack. 'I'm going to head home, Danielle; I've got an early start in the morning,' shouted Jack, trying to be heard as the next song began playing. He had to extricate himself from this situation before he changed his mind.

'Have another dance and then we can go home and have more fun,' she laughed, leaning into him again.'

'Seriously, I can't. Will you be okay by yourself or do you want me to get you an Uber?'

'I'll be fine. Will I see you again, Jack?' she asked, the sentence fading as she made her way back to the centre of the dancefloor.

Jack was eager to make an early start and get to the bottom of Li's activities after his observations the previous night. He slept through both his mobile phone and clock radio alarms, so that put an end to that. *Bugger.* It was now ten o'clock and Jack was finally at his desk at AFP Headquarters. His focus for the day would be to ascertain where and how Li got his starting stake for his previous evening's gambling. Given his original stake on the table, and adding that to the other sleeves that Jack noticed in his bag, it had to be a minimum of five hundred thousand dollars, if not more. Before getting down to business for the day, he texted JA asking her if she would like to have dinner tonight. He felt a prickle of guilt about cancelling their catch-up last night and then going drinking and dancing with Danielle. Now it was time to hit the phone.

'Chris Coleman speaking.'

'Hi, Chris, it's Jack Wagner again. We spoke about a high roller named Li Qiang yesterday.'

'Yes, I remember.'

'I've been following his activities as part of my investigation. Last night he gambled sizeable amounts of money in the Bennelong Room at the Oceanic here in Sydney.'

'Do you know how much?'

'Not exactly, but it was in the hundreds of thousands.'

'How do you know?'

'I was there, undercover.'

'Wow! So, what can I do for you?'

'Can you let me know once you receive the Oceanic's Threshold Transaction Report for yesterday's date please? And, in particular, I would like to know the details and size of Li Qiang's transactions. He should have two transactions listed. I realise they don't have to provide yesterday's TTR report for another week, but if you receive it early can you give me a call please?'

'Consider it done.'

Jack's phone buzzed with an incoming text message. It was from Julie-Anne saying she was unavailable tonight due to a work function.

What about tomorrow night? He returned the text. She said yes. *Come over at seven and I'll make a Caesar,* he replied.

Next, he called Jim Brennan. 'Hi Jim, it's Jack again, how are you?'

'Good thanks, still busy. Now, what can I do for you?'

'I want to interview the woman who is the cashier in the Bennelong Room.'

'There's more than one.' Jack then described the woman who had managed Li's transaction the previous night.

'That's Michelle Ironside. She's the Treasury Manager and is responsible for all Treasury functions in the Bennelong Room. Jack, she is well respected, very competent at her job and has been here for many years. I can't imagine she would be involved in anything untoward.'

'I'm not suggesting that she is. I don't want to conduct the interview at the casino.

Can you give me her contact number, I'll call her and arrange to meet her off-site?'

'No can-do, buddy. Company policy prevents me from giving out employee information, even to you.'

'Okay, can you contact her, give her my number and ask her to contact me as soon as possible?'

'That I can do. I'll call her now.'

An hour later Jack's mobile rang with an unknown incoming mobile number.

'Jack Wagner speaking.'

'Mr Wagner, this is Michelle Ironside. I have been asked to contact you.'

'Hello, Michelle, thanks for calling so promptly. I'm don't know what Mr Brennan told you, but I am a detective with the Australian Federal Police. I am currently undertaking an investigation and I would like to speak to you about certain matters.'

'Okay, go ahead, Mr Wagner,' she responded unsurely.

'Thank you, but I would like to speak to you in person and to ensure discretion, I am prepared to meet with you away from the casino.'

'I'm unavailable today, but I can meet with you tomorrow before I start my shift. Does two o'clock suit?'

'Yes, that's fine.'

'Do you know the Bayside Café by the water in Pyrmont? It is only a short walk from the casino.'

'That's fine, I'll find it.'

'Can I at least ask what this is all about, Mr Wagner?'

'Not at this stage, and please keep this conversation to yourself. See you tomorrow at two, Michelle.'

Maritime Border Command Brisbane

Things had been relatively quiet since their interviews yesterday with Captain Han, and unless there was any new intelligence in the offing, de Vries knew the investigation was dead in the water. He chuckled at his own quip. Agents Harvey and Benson had been in contact with Maritime Border Command posts up and down the Queensland coastline and none had any suspicious activity to report. Just as he was contemplating which investigation would be their next priority, his mobile phone rang.

'Damian, it's Shane, how are you?'

'Well, to be honest, I'm a little flat after our unproductive interviews yesterday, but we move onwards and upwards.'

'Not so fast. Where are Harvey and Benson?'

'At their desks reviewing outstanding cases to ascertain our next highest priority. Why?'

'Well, your suggestion to put Captain Han on the Movement Alert List has paid dividends already. It seems his employers must have been nervous when they heard of his detention. He's booked on a flight to Shanghai this afternoon.'

De Vries bounced out of his chair. 'Okay, we'll go grab him and start over.'

'There's no urgency. He got red-flagged on the MAL going through immigration and is currently being held in a Border Force interview room at Brisbane International waiting for you and your guys.'

'Thanks, that's great news. He'll be aware by now that he's not getting on his scheduled flight, so let's see if the captain is more forthcoming this time around.'

'Harvey, Benson, my office,' came the page over the intercom. The agents logged off from their desktop computers and proceeded down the corridor to de Vries' office.

'Gents, it appears that our hunch has paid dividends. The good captain was flagged as he attempted to pass through immigration a few minutes ago. He was detained, of course, and is being held in an ABF interview room. Plan your strategy, develop your line of questioning, and then get over there and give it your best shot. Good luck.'

It only took Harvey and Benson half an hour to develop a plan, make the short drive across to the international terminal, park their SUV, pass through security and be badged into the ABF offices. The colour noticeably drained from Captain Han's face as the two agents entered the interview room.

'Aaahh, Captain Han, we meet again,' said Benson, grinning. Prior to entering the interview room Harvey had turned on the video camera to record the interview. 'Captain, for the record again, I am Agent Harvey. This is Agent Benson, and we have some more questions for you.'

'Why I here, Agent Harvey?'

'We all know why you're here captain. Tell us what you know, and we can make some progress. Who knows, maybe you'll even be on your way to Shanghai in the next few days.' Harvey's last remark captured Han's attention. He wasn't going anywhere soon.

'Let me be clear here. We are not going to go over old ground again.'

'What you mean, old ground?'

Harvey sighed.

'Don't play dumb. We know you are a reasonably well-educated man, otherwise you wouldn't have a ship captain's licence and you certainly wouldn't be in charge of a twenty thousand tonne cargo ship. To answer your question anyway, we are not going to ask you the same questions as we did yesterday. We know you were in Hydrographers Passage three days ago, so let's not dispute that anymore, shall we?'

'I no go into passage,' Han pleaded once more.

'Shut up, captain, yes you did,' bellowed Benson. 'Let's not go there again, shall we?'

Harvey noticed the colour draining from Han's face again and he waved Benson away. *Good cop, bad cop.* 'Captain, who arranged for your ticket out of the country and how were you going to collect it?'

'I get call on satellite phone at lunchtime, no name, no number, they tell me come here for ticket.'

'Come where, captain?'

'China East Airline at airport.'

'Who were "they"?' asked Harvey, making the quotation sign with his fingers. 'What did they say to you?'

'They no tell me name; just say you have to go home to China.'

'Did you recognise the voice on the phone?'

'No, I not hear before.'

'Why didn't you just ignore them and what about your ship?'

'I have family in China and not want them to have trouble, so I go home.' The captain's facial expression soften as he mentioned his family.

'Why do you think your family will be in trouble, as you say?' Harvey asked.

Han wasn't about to tell them about the threats made against his family. 'I just think much better to go home,' he replied quietly.

'What about your ship, captain?'

'Man on phone say, ship not my problem, just go home.'

'And, Captain Han, why do you think they want you out of the country?'

'They did not tell me; just say I must go home.'

'Come on captain, that's bullshit, and you know it,' interjected Benson, a little less forcefully this time.

'You swearing at me again...'

Han's voice trailed off as Benson interrupted him. 'You are being sent home because we detained you yesterday. Someone you know is anxious that you are going to reveal their illegal activities to the Australian authorities. And captain, whatever the illegal activities are, and you know what they are, your employer simply can't let that happen.'

The interview room door opened, and de Vries walked in with a photocopy of Han's airline ticket in his hand. He was delayed in getting to the interview, but arrived at the observation room just in time to hear the captain mention China Eastern Airlines. He had arranged for an ABF clerk to hastily obtain a copy of the ticket from the airline.

'Mr Han, I have a copy of your airline ticket here. We know where the ticket was purchased, and it will take us no time at all to figure out who purchased the ticket on your behalf. You may as well save us the trouble and tell us yourself.'

'I not know who buy ticket.'

Benson placed both his palms on the table and leant forward, came face to face with Han. 'Do you know what will happen, captain? When we eventually find out who is behind all this, and we will, I will personally tell them that you, Captain Han, informed us of their identity. It doesn't matter if it is true or not, he or she will think it is and you know what happens then? The safety of your family back in China will be put at risk, and it will all be your fault. We'll give you a few minutes to think about that.'

The three agents left the interview and adjourned to another meeting room. Harvey asked de Vries. 'Where was the ticket purchased, Damian?'

'I have no idea yet, but he doesn't know that. We'll find out eventually, but I thought it was worth a try to speed things up. He might just give you something after he reflects on today's events.'

'Yeah, boss, and he will be petrified about his family's safety,' offered Benson.

'I'm not sure I agree with threatening a man with his family's safety, but I'll ignore it for now,' de Vries uttered as a mild rebuke to Benson. 'Go back in there and let's see if he's still pleading ignorance.'

Captain Han was deep in thought when the door opened again. The troubled look on his face confirmed to the agents that he was indeed extremely worried about his family's safety. Harvey and Benson sat down at the interview table again and waited for de Vries to turn the camera back on from the control room. Upon seeing the green light flicker Harvey continued the questioning.

'Captain, have you had time to consider your family's safety? Do you have anything you want to tell Agent Benson and I?'

'I don't know what to do,' muttered the captain who had visibly paled again and Harvey detected a slight quivering of his hands. *Here we go, time for good cop.*

'Captain Han, give us something to work with and we can assist you to ensure your family's safety. I am also a family man with young children. I can see you are worried about your family and I would be too if I were in your situation. Let me help you to help your family remain safe.' Benson, sensing that Harvey's empathetic approach was working, excused himself and left the room.

'How will you do that, Agent Harvey?'

'When we solve this case, and we will, Captain, I will personally inform the culprits that you weren't helpful at all and you refused to cooperate with our investigation.'

'If I'm not on the plane this afternoon they will know something is wrong.'

'Give us something worthwhile that aids our investigation and we might be able to get you on tomorrow's flight. That's the best I can do.'

The two men sat in silence for some time, the captain staring disconsolately down at the table and Harvey looking at him for a response. The captain, to financially help his growing family, had got himself involved in a criminal enterprise. Now he himself was in a world of pain.

'I know the name of the boat,' Han mumbled.

'What did you say, Captain?'

'I know the name of the boat that collects the packages from my ship.'

'What packages?'

'I don't know what they are, but there're always twenty of them and they're maybe five kilograms each.' Harvey noticed Han had dropped the clipped accent now.

'How does the process work?'

'I don't really know, Agent Harvey. The packages are already on board when we leave Dailan or Qingdao and we're met by a fast boat in the passage you keep talking about.

'What type of boat is it, captain?'

'I think it's maybe fifteen metres long with diesel engines and a cabin.'

'How does the courier boat know when you are in the passage?'

'They must see my ship on the Marine Traffic website. I navigate my ship into a cove near to Wackett Reef and they always know we are there.'

'Captain, how many times have you undertaken these drops in the passage?' 'I think maybe ten or eleven.'

'Who collects the packages?'

'It is always the same two men; Chinese men, but I don't know who they are. They look like bad men.'

'And what is the name of the courier boat?'

'Funny name for a boat, Midnight Express.' Harvey understood the significance of the name.

'Okay, that's good. Now we know you're telling the truth. Did you notice the registration number of the boat?'

'Maybe, but I don't remember.'

'Did you see or hear anything three nights ago?'

Han guessed that the agent already knew the answer to his own question. 'Yes, as we were exiting the passage, I heard gunfire and saw a bright light maybe ten nautical miles astern of my ship.'

'What did you think was the cause of that?'

'Someone was chasing the Midnight Express.'

'Is there anything else you would like to tell us, Captain?'

Han felt relieved to have unburdened himself and hoped things will be okay now. 'No, that's everything I know.'

'Okay.' The agent leant back in his chair, closing the file in front of him. 'We're going to transport you back to the ABF offices where you will be held in custody while we continue investigating. You've been here for some time now, so I will arrange food and drink for you while I follow-up on your information. You may be with us for some time.'

'Will I be on a plane tomorrow?' Han asked, his hands twisting together.

'We'll see, Captain.'

Outside the room, the agents discussed the unfolding events. 'Good work, now let's get back to the office and find out what Midnight Express is all about. Where is it registered, who owns it, what's its home port, is there a registered skipper, etcetera?' directed de Vries. 'I will talk to Williamson and get him to contact each of the Maritime Border Command outposts within range of the drop zone and see if they know anything. Then I'm going to see if I can track down who paid for the captain's airline ticket. Given it is now after office hours all of this could take some time.'

Consulate General Cocktail Reception

Julie-Anne went to her wardrobe and flicked through the clothes hangers until she found one of her little black cocktail dresses. 'This should do the trick,' she mumbled to herself. Her favourite LBD had the cleavage cut out and replaced with a sexy polka dot lace overlay with a low back and its hem resting halfway up her thighs. She wouldn't wear a bra, hoping the bodycon fabric would hold her together. It was perhaps a little too sexy for a Consul General's cocktail party, but it was stylish and would be a useful tool for this evening. If Julie-Anne wanted to find out more about Li Qiang she needed to ensure she stood out and hopefully garner his attention. She would complement the LBD with her Manolo Blahnik black silk satin pumps with a Swarovski crystal buckle. If she didn't stand out in the LBD, the heels would definitely do the trick.

She alighted from her Uber and walked into the QV Wine Bar at a quarter to six. Deb was doing her an enormous favour, so Julie-Anne didn't want to keep her waiting. The QV was a hip bar with a hint of chic. Along one wall ran a deep chocolate banquette and subtle lighting gave the place a cozy atmosphere. Even so, Julie-Anne still felt slightly uncomfortable walking into the bar in her revealing LBD and killer heels. Dressed as she was, she certainly wasn't going to take a seat alone at the bar, so she took a corner seat on the banquette and waited for her friend.

Deborah Atkinson walked in moments later wearing her own little black dress, although not as revealing or as short as Julie-Anne's. 'You look fabulous, Deb,' she said as she stood, and the women air kissed left and right.

'Wow, you look stunning! If you're hoping to get noticed at the cocktail party you've certainly nailed the look.'

'Thanks, Deb, I do want to be highly visible, and for good reason, but I do feel a little self-conscious. Is it too much?' she asked glancing at her neckline.

'No, not at all, you look gorgeous,' Deb replied, looking up to her impossibly tall friend.

The women sat on the banquette and both ordered a Sapphire and Tonic from the attendant waiter.

'So, what's with the highly visible, JA?' Julie-Anne told Deb about her investigation and explained the reasons for her wanting to attend the Consul General's cocktail party, including wanting to make Li Qiang's acquaintance. 'Sounds like something out of a spy thriller, JA, how exciting,' Deb said.

'Well, not yet, but it could have the makings of something extraordinary if my hunch is correct. But it's early days in my investigation.'

'It's a whole lot more interesting than writing nothing articles about B-List celebrities, social media influencers and reality TV stars, JA,' Deb lamented. 'Okay, let's go do some spy stuff,' she said finishing her drink and checking her lipstick, which remained flawless. JA would have to ask her friend for that trick sometime. Julie-Anne signalled to the waiter to bring the bill while Deb ordered an Uber.

The Chinese Consulate was a grey, austere building with a central flagpole surrounded by a floodlit ornamental fountain in the forecourt. Naturally, the bright red Chinese flag with its five golden stars fluttered proudly atop the flagpole. Julie-Anne and

Deb jostled their way through the group of forty or more chanting protestors demonstrating against China's increasingly vice-like grip on Hong Kong. They walked into the foyer and were surprised to be greeted by the Consul General. Zhang Xiao, dressed in a black suit, white shirt and red tie, introduced himself, and Deb and Julie-Anne reciprocated.

'You stylish ladies will certainly add some sophistication to my cocktail party,' he remarked, completely ignoring the loud protest just metres away. 'I believe you are both journalists for the Sydney Daily News. That must be fascinating in a dynamic city such as Sydney.'

'Yes, Consul General, we are, and it is very interesting. I am the entertainment reporter and Julie-Anne is an investigative journalist.'

The Consul General seemed impressed. 'What do you investigate, Ms Granger?'

'Criminal enterprises including people and drug trafficking, corporate fraud, illegal activities by corporations and sometimes even government collusion and interference. The role is truly diverse, Mr Consul General.'

'Well, that must be a very challenging undertaking for a woman working in a man's world.'

'It is a challenging role for anyone, male or female,' replied Julie-Anne, offering a mild rebuke.

'Well, I sincerely hope that you can just relax and enjoy yourself tonight, Ms Granger.'

'Thank you, Consul General, I will.' The man strode away at JA scowled at his back. 'I'll give him woman working in a man's world, what century is he living in, Deb?' Julie-Anne snapped as they walked into the cocktail party and made their way towards the bar. It was impossible not to notice the heads turning in their direction as they passed through the crowd. To Julie-Anne's delight, she spied a man she thought to be Li Qiang being distracted from his conversation.

'Well, if you wanted to be conspicuous, JA, you've certainly achieved that. Was that short man in the pewter-coloured suit and red tie, who couldn't help himself but stare, your target?'

'I've only seen an enlarged, downloaded photo of him, but I'm pretty sure that's him. Let's have a drink and see what evolves.' The two women stood at the bar with their glasses of champagne in their hand, people watching.

'We need to mingle. Who do you know here, Deb?'

'I noticed a couple of mid-level DFAT bureaucrats and a few B-List celebrities on the walk through. The conversation won't be very interesting or enlightening, but it's a start. Let's take a walk.'

'Deb, the Consul General is now talking to my target. How about we walk into that conversation instead? I can guarantee you it will be more interesting,' Julie-Anne suggested.

'Sounds good to me.' Deb linked arms with Julie-Anne and the women ambled across the room.

'Ms Atkinson, Ms Granger, how are you enjoying my cocktail party?'

'We are just starting to mingle Consul General and we thought we would start at the top,' Deb said, offering a cheeky grin.

'Aaahh, you flatter me, Ms Atkinson. Can I introduce you to my colleague, Li Qiang, ladies?' Julie-Anne turned first to face Li Qiang and offered her hand to the short, pudgy man.

'Hello, Mr Li, nice to meet you,' JA said as she looked into his eyes and held his gaze. 'Ms Granger, I assure you the pleasure is all mine. You look exquisite if I may be so forward.'

'That is exceedingly kind of you, Mr Li. You look quite smart yourself,' she lied.

'Mr Li, I am Deb Atkinson, pleased to meet you,' she said, offering her hand.

The quartet continued to converse, and the women were astute enough to avoid discussing any of the contentious topics that surrounded China these days. Both the Consul General and Li were surprised at Julie-Anne's knowledge of the history of the Chinese people in New South Wales. While Julie-Anne was holding court,

Deb more than once observed Li's eyes lingering on Julie-Anne's cleavage when he obviously thought no-one would observe him. The initial phase of Julie-Anne's plan was working perfectly, and Deb was equally impressed with her level of knowledge.

'Ms Atkinson, can I please introduce you to some of my other guests?' The consul general offered, extending his elbow to Deb, which she accepted with a mischievous gleam in her eye.

'That would be wonderful, lead the way.'

As the Consul General and Deb walked away Li turned to Julie-Anne. 'Ms Granger, I am going to get another drink, would you like one too?'

'What are you drinking, Mr Li?'

'My usual, fifteen-year-old Glenlivet. It is a Scotch Whisky with a lovely vanilla and spice character.'

'Yes, I know that, Mr Li, and I will have one too, with ice please.'

'Ganbei, Ms Granger.'

'Cheers to you too, Mr Li.'

'Aaahh, you know the meaning of ganbei.'

'Mr Li, I always do my research when I'm entering into an environment to which I'm unaccustomed. And it's also respectful to my host.'

'You are a very wise and intelligent woman. What is your role at the Daily News?'

'How did you know I work at the Daily News?'

Julie-Anne thought this exchange was getting interesting already.

Li had Xiao send him the guest list so he could see if his prospective candidate was bringing a significant other. He had also made a mental note of the names of the two journalists on the list. He had a deep mistrust of journalists.

'I also do my research, Ms Granger.'

Julie-Anne remained silent, but offered him a coy smile in response. Eventually she said, 'I am an investigative journalist.'

'What do you investigate, Ms Granger?'

'Mainly illicit activities such as people smuggling and drug trafficking, corporate fraud, illegal undertakings by corporations including collusion and price fixing and sometimes, foreign affairs.'

'That must be very exciting,' Li said with an uneasy smile.

At that moment, a photographer walked up to them and introduced himself. He was from the Sydney Daily News and was at the function to snap shots for the weekly entertainment supplement. 'I don't want a photo,' grumbled Li.

'Oh, come on. It's fun and we might become famous.' Julie-Anne said as she laughed, put her arm around Li's waist, and pulled him in close. Unbeknownst to him, Julie-Anne had arranged with Deb for the photographer to snap photos of him for her investigation.

'Okay, just for you, Ms Granger.' She tousled and flicked her hair, adjusted her cleavage for effect and leant into Li.

$$\textbf{46}$$

Consulate General Cocktail Reception

'Mr Li, there you are. I've been looking for you.' An attractive, toned, and unusually tall woman of Eurasian appearance strode up to Li and Julie-Anne. She had intelligent eyes and was wearing a body-hugging, fire engine red, knee length midi dress with killer red heels. Maybe she wants to be highly visible as well, thought Julie-Anne. *Well, if so, she certainly nailed it.*

'Miss Wu, nice to see you.' Li tried to greet her with a kiss on the cheek but the woman pulled back ever so slightly, Julie-Anne noticed.

'This is Ms Granger.'

'Julie-Anne is fine, nice to meet you, Miss Wu.'

'Melissa, please.'

'Can I get you a drink, Miss Wu?'

'I'll have what Julie-Anne is having please.' While Li was ordering her drink, Melissa turned to Julie-Anne.

'What is your involvement with the Consulate?'

'Nothing really, I'm just a handbag for a friend, but it's lovely to be here and Mr Li is an interesting man,' Julie-Anne said searching for a response.

'I'm sure he is.' Melissa said too sharply as Li returned with her drink.

'A toast to beautiful and intelligent women, ganbei.' Both women offered a polite 'cheers.'

'Ms Granger, I have some business to discuss with Miss Wu, so will you excuse us please?'

'Of course, Mr Li.'

'Miss Wu, let us go somewhere quiet where we can talk.' He led Melissa into an adjoining function room where they sat opposite each other in leather lounge chairs.

'Thank you for coming tonight. I appreciate it. Have you had time to consider my initial proposal, Miss Wu?'

'I would be lying if I said I wasn't interested in your proposal as I have been considering re-entering political life for some time. Engaging in state politics would seem the next logical step for me. As I mentioned before, I am Australian by birth, so I would only entertain your proposal if I was to appropriately represent the entire electorate, not just one ethnic group or whoever 'we' is.'

'I would expect nothing less, Miss Wu. You will be free to conduct your candidacy and hopefully, your subsequent representation as you see fit. All we want is someone with a voice inside the state parliament that can promote the benefits of working cooperatively with China. We also need someone who can provide an alternative viewpoint to all the negative discourse surrounding China that is prevalent in this country.'

'I'm pretty certain I know exactly what you want, Mr Li, but I will not be a puppet for anyone. I am more than willing to promote better cooperation between New South Wales and China, and I am well aware of the benefits of a better accord between the two states. I will not, however, be a puppet for Beijing, for you or your backers. Tibet, Taiwan, Hong Kong, the South China Sea and the Belt and Road initiative are all issues for the federal government, not me or the New South Wales parliament, should I be fortunate to be elected. Is that clear?'

'We would expect nothing less, Miss Wu and we are committed to your success,' he replied through a fake smile.

Melissa leaned forward in her chair, clasped her hands and rested her elbows on her thighs. 'Now, who is the 'we' you keep referring to? And please don't insult me by telling me I don't need to know, otherwise you can find another *potential* candidate.' Melissa emphasised the word to be sure he knew she wasn't hooked yet.

Li also leaned forward in his chair and spoke quietly. 'Okay, I will tell you in complete confidence what I can. There are three principal supporters. There is a successful shipping magnate from China, the Consul General himself and me. The finance for your candidacy will come through me and will have no link to China.'

'If I may ask, how much financing is available for the campaign?'

Li smiled for the first time. 'A multi seven-figure sum to start with is not out of the question, Miss Wu, if that gives you the confidence to know you will be able to run an effective and robust campaign. I have a legitimate business here in Sydney from which the campaign funds will be disbursed,' he lied. 'The Consul General will provide whatever support you require, if you so choose to avail yourself of his services.'

'And what of the shipping magnate?

'He undertakes significant trade with Australia and shares our desire for better communications and relations between the respective governments. He will be a silent partner but will gladly contribute if needed.'

'Political donations are a hot button issue. As such, all donations need to be in accordance with the state's political disclosure and donation laws. This is also non-negotiable, Mr Li.'

'We would not want to do anything that would undermine your integrity and reputation in the community, nor compromise your candidacy.'

Melissa rose from her chair and projected her best professional smile. 'Thank you. Now I have received more definitive information from you I should soon be in a position to give your proposal the appropriate consideration. I just need to conduct some due diligence.'

'I was hoping for a commitment from you tonight, Miss Wu.'

'I'm sure you were. Now shall we go find Ms Granger? She seems like a fun girl and I would like to know her better.' That made him decidedly nervous. He didn't need his prospective candidate being best friends with an investigative journalist.

'Yes, I could do with another Glenlivet, too,' he responded.

Melissa spied the woman in question standing at the bar. 'What are you doing at the bar by yourself, Julie-Anne?'

'My host is talking to a couple of boring DFAT guys, so I excused myself, and here I am.' Melissa looked confused. 'What's DFAT?'

'It's the federal government's Department of Foreign Affairs and Trade. I think the guys are more trade than foreign affairs, judging by the nature of the conversation.'

'That's funny, I like it. I much prefer foreign affairs myself.' Melissa had a twinkle in her eye as she regarded Julie-Anne. *Is she flirting with me?* mused Julie-Anne.

She wondered what was happening between Li and Melissa, so she thought the best way to find out would be to gain her confidence. 'I love that dress, Melissa. It's a bold colour and provides a whole new meaning to power dressing. And the shoes are to die for.'

'That's really lovely, thanks. I knew that Mr Li would want to meet with me tonight, so it was important that I felt confident and projected an image of self-assuredness.'

Julie-Anne was chomping at the bit to know about the meeting with Li, but now certainly wasn't the time to ask. 'Well, you've certainly achieved that.'

Melissa stifled a laugh. 'In my circle of friends and co-workers I am known for my red attire. I think I embarrass them on occasions.'

'Well they shouldn't and that dress is an absolute eye burner.'

'I haven't heard that expression before.'

'Me neither until I read it in a fashion article in an online magazine. I've been just dying to use it forever, so thank you for coming to my rescue.'

'Now, tell me about that gorgeous little number you're wearing,' Melissa said, trying to avoid staring.

'Unfortunately there's no fabulous story behind this,' Julie-Anne said as she self-consciously fiddled with the lace overlay. 'I saw it in the window of Cream on King, an upcycling shop in Newtown, and I simply had to have it. When I tried it on again at home I wasn't quite as enamoured with it. I took it to a dressmaker friend and she came up with the idea of cutting out the chest and replacing it with the polka dot lace overlay. Now I absolutely love it.'

Melissa risked a glance down at the revealing overlay. 'I thought you said there wasn't a story behind it. I think that's a wonderful tale and you look fabulous.'

They were interrupted by the Daily News photographer. 'How about a photo of the two most beautiful women in the room. Grab a glass of champagne and I'll get a celebratory shot for the paper.'

Just then, a tall handsome looking man called out. 'Hang on, can I be the thorn among the blooming roses? Hi, I'm Jackson from DFAT.'

'Sure, why not?' The women ruffled and flicked their hair, placed their arms around Jackson's waist and posed for the camera. The photographer snapped away. 'You look great ladies, nice shots.'

'We seem to have lost Mr Li, Melissa.'

'Between you and me, Julie-Anne, he's been ogling both of us and my body could do without his beady eyes boring into it.'

Julie-Anne raised her glass. 'Ganbei to that, Melissa.' The women tittered as they clinked glasses. 'That didn't last long. Here he comes now.'

'Aaahh ladies, here you are. Ms Granger, will you excuse us? I would like to reintroduce Miss Wu to the Consul General. After all, it is his party.'

'That's perfectly fine, I should probably find my friend Deb anyway.'

As they walked away Melissa whispered to her. 'I'll see you before I leave.' Julie-Anne wanted to see Melissa again too, but probably for different reasons. Given their instant attraction to each other this was going to be a tightrope walk for Julie-Anne, and unusually for her, she wasn't comfortable with the idea of interrogating Melissa. She banished the thought and walked across the room to Deb's conversation group.

'Deb, there you are. I thought you'd gone on a trade mission to some far-flung country,' she said, doing her best to sound humorous.

'The DFAT guys were just telling me about Australia's trade with China and how important it is to our economy; it's fascinating stuff Julie-Anne,' Deb replied with a grin. She promptly introduced Julie-Anne to the bureaucrats and then made their excuses to exit the conversation. 'Thank heavens you came along when you did; those guys were boring me to tears, JA. Where have you been hiding?'

'Well, I was having a drink with Li when a Melissa Wu walked into the conversation. She's the tall, attractive woman in the red midi over there talking to the Consul General.'

'Wow, she's hot, JA,' exclaimed Deb, admiring the woman.

'Anyway, Deb, her and Li went off to a private room for a discussion. I have no idea what the conversation was about, but I just know something's happening here that's related to my investigation and I intend to find out exactly what that is. Melissa made it clear afterwards that she is no fan of Li, so what was the private chat about?'

'How do you propose to find out then, JA?'

'I'm going to befriend Melissa as best as I can and see where it leads.'

'Are you sure that's all your interest is? She's an attractive woman.' Deb asked, eyeing her friend over the rim of her drink. 'Speaking of which, she is walking our way now.'

'Hey, Melissa. Can I introduce you to my friend Deb? Deb, please meet Melissa.' The women exchanged pleasantries and Julie-Anne continued. 'How was your chat to the Consul General?'

'Far less stimulating than our conversation.'

Deb picked up on the nuanced response and thought, yep, someone's definitely flirting here. Melissa continued. 'Julie-Anne, why don't we vacate this stuffy place and grab a drink somewhere livelier?'

Before Deb could say anything, Julie-Anne jumped in. 'You don't mind do you, Deb?' This was Julie-Anne's opportunity to get closer to this intriguing woman.

Deb quickly realised what JA was up to. 'Of course not, I'm going to have a quick chat to the Consul General myself and then call it a night. Enjoy ladies, I'm sure you'll have fun,' she said mischievously. As Deb turned around, she noticed that the Consul General and Li appeared to be having a serious conversation, given their earnest facial expressions. She went back to the DFAT guys while she waited for an opening with the Consul General.

'Li, have you read the article I wrote earlier this week, the one about the state government abandoning the Confucius Institute?'

'Yes, I saw it, which is why we need Miss Wu in the state parliament more than ever.'

'I know, we have to address the imbalance in the conversation in this country.'

'Xiao, did you notice by any chance, who our star candidate just left the cocktail party with?'

'No, why is that important?'

'Miss Wu just left with the Granger woman and that concerns me.'

'But why should that concern you, Li?'

'She is an investigative reporter for a major newspaper. You don't find it unusual that she would be attending a joint China, New South Wales trade celebration, one to which she has no connection?'

'Ms Granger was my guest's partner for the evening.'

'How convenient. Wake up, Xiao. Now, she has departed with her new best friend, our potential political candidate. And you're going to tell me it is all a coincidence. We can't allow that relationship to develop; it is not in our mutual interest. Do you have one of your cultural attaches available now? And I mean *now*.'

(47)

The QV Wine Bar

'Where shall we go, Julie-Anne?'

'Well, Deb and I had a pre-cocktail party drink at this cosy, New York style bar a few blocks from here in Surry Hills. It's called the QV Wine Bar. Want to check it out?' Ten minutes later, the two women alighted from their Uber and entered the bar. The same banquette was surprisingly, for this time of night, still vacant, so Julie-Anne ushered Melissa across to it.

'I like this. It's nice and private,' offered Melissa. Once again Julie-Anne agreed. She liked the privacy too, but for differing reasons she felt sure. Melissa could potentially provide her with a lead into the life of Li Qiang, so she would endeavour to steer the conversation in that direction at some point. Although she had just met Melissa, Julie-Anne had taken a shine to her already; she felt they were kindred spirits of sorts, so she would be careful with her emotions.

'Did you enjoy the cocktail party, Julie-Anne?'

'I have been working quite hard on an investigation lately, so when Deb invited me to be her handbag, I thought, why not? I could do with some fun,' she fibbed. 'I feel bad for Deb though, getting stuck in conversation with those bureaucrats.'

'Yeah, I can imagine, foreign affairs would have been a whole lot more interesting though.' Melissa laughed; the connotation now being obvious.

'What about you?'

'Other than meeting you, no, not really. It was more of a business meeting for me. I needed to meet with Mr Li.'

'Did your meeting go well?' Julie-Anne asked evenly, not wanting to sound too obvious.

Melissa wanted to avoid that particular conversation, for now anyway. 'Let's not ruin the night by talking about that lecherous, corpulent, little man, shall we?'

'Nice description, but you left out the plastered down comb-over. Huh, that reminds me of a joke, Melissa.'

'Okay, let me have it.'

'What do you call a group of rabbits hopping backwards?' Melissa put her thumb and index finger on her chin, tilted her head upwards and struck the thinking pose.

'I give in, what do you call a group of rabbits hopping backwards, Julie-Anne?'

'A receding hairline.'

Melissa burst out laughing, and as she did so, she leaned forward amid the frivolity and subtly put her hand on Julie-Anne's arm. *Maybe that was a little tester,* thought Julie-Anne, enjoying Melissa's soft touch. As the laughter subsided, she found Melissa gazing into her eyes. Julie-Anne held her gaze and felt Melissa's hand drift up and down her arm. Julie-Anne briefly thought of Jack, but it was banished by the sensitivity of Melissa's touch.

'That was just too funny,' Melissa said, as she pulled back and leant against the banquette. There was a lull in the conversation, and Julie Anne bumped her shoulder gently against the other woman.

'You look miles away. What are you thinking, Melissa?'

'I'm trying to remember a joke. Okay, I've got it.' As she said that, she leaned forward, placed both her hands on Julie-Anne knees and looked into her eyes. 'Here we go.'

'*A panda bear walks into a restaurant, sits down, and asks the waiter to bring him a plate of bamboo. After the panda eats all of it, he takes out a gun and kills the waiter right then and there. The restaurant owner was horrified. He says to the panda bear: "Why did you do this?", to which the panda replies: "Look it up in the encyclopedia."*'

Melissa started rocking backward and forward with laughter as she neared the punch line. 'Sorry, where was I?' she asked calming herself.

'Look it up in the encyclopedia,' Julie-Anne prompted.

'Right. *The restaurant owner takes out his encyclopedia, and under the entry of panda bear, he finds: "Panda. Giant mammal indigenous to China, eats bamboo and shoots".*'

The women burst into sustained, raucous laughter, which attracted the attention of nearby guests, including two well-dressed guys, who were doubtless wondering what was so funny. As the laughter subsided, Julie-Anne found herself leaning forward, this time with her hands on Melissa's. Their laughter was fading, replaced by a look of longing as they gazed into each other's eyes. Without saying a word, Melissa leaned further inward, placed her hand on the nape of Julie-Anne's neck. Giving Julie-Anne time to withdraw if she'd wanted to, Melissa slowly pulled her forward and kissed her softly. Julie-Anne's eyes were still open, stunned as she was. She momentarily thought of Jack again, but that quickly dissipated, such was the tenderness of Melissa's kiss. Her eyes briefly glanced around, and satisfied that they were safely cocooned in the privacy of their banquette, she allowed her mouth to open. She closed her eyes, leaned into the kiss and placed a hand on Melissa's cheek.

Melissa's tongue slid gently into her mouth, exploring, while her free hand was softly caressing the inside of Julie-Anne's thigh. 'Aaaahh.' Julie-Anne felt a soft sigh caress her lips, but wasn't sure whether it was hers, or Melissa's. She could feel her nipples hardening and something was stirring inside her. Sensing a shadow passing by the banquette, she gently removed Melissa's hand from her neck and withdrew from the kiss. Julie-Anne had never been kissed by a woman, unless you counted the usual pecks on the cheek between friends and relatives—and with the flush of passion still racing over her skin, she knew this was something different entirely. She was also questioning her own actions and why did her body respond like that? 'Wow, where did that come from?' she asked, as she leant back, exhaled and attempted to regain her composure. She knew the answer of course, thinking back to Melissa's flirting at the cocktail party.

'Let's get out of here,' said Melissa, without answering the question.

'Well hello, ladies,' came a cocky voice from behind them. The two women were waiting for their Uber on the vacant footpath outside the wine bar on Crown Street.

The two suited men obviously had the women in their sights and were walking towards them. 'That was quite a show you girls put on inside. Care to share the love with a couple of tall, dark, handsome, upwardly mobile young men?' The women disregarded the comment whilst keeping the men in their peripheral vision.

'Apparently, it wasn't such a private area after all,' whispered Melissa.

'You weren't so shy inside girls. What, you don't like the opposite sex?'

The women continued to ignore them. 'Come on, Mr Uber' muttered Julie-Anne, shuffling closer to Melissa.

'Do you have anything useful inside that clutch of yours?' Melissa asked her.

'I do. I always carry something for protection at night-time,' she replied nervously.

'Okay, you might want to keep it handy.'

Julie-Anne discreetly took the slim canister from her clutch and concealed it in her palm.

The two men were now growing bolder with their comments

and were approaching the women. Julie-Anne heard the taller one talking, more slurring, about her cleavage and what he would like to do with her breasts.

'Come on girls, you've had your little entrée, now how about trying the main course? What do you say?' the women heard the taller one say, in a self-assured voice.

'Okay, here we go, Julie-Anne, game time,' Melissa warned. The men had reached the women, with the shorter one leaning into Melissa's neck as if to sniff her fragrance. She stiffened, but maintained her composure. At the same time, the second guy reached out to touch Julie-Anne's breasts.

'Now!' Julie-Anne heard, as she saw Melissa take half a step back. Julie-Anne brought the spray can up towards the taller man and glimpsed a red blur out of the corner of her eye. Melissa had risen on the ball of her left foot and was pivoting one hundred and eighty degrees at blinding speed towards the second guy. Her right arm was crooked at a ninety-degree angle at the elbow as the joint smashed into the man's throat. Julie-Anne heard the unmistakeably sickening sound of bone or cartilage being crunched. Simultaneously, she aimed the spray can at the second guy and depressed the nozzle.

Both men were doubled over, clutching their throat and face respectively while moaning and groaning. They were trying to scream obscenities at the women, but neither man was capable of speaking. All that was emanating from them were strange animal like utterings. Julie-Anne thought she heard Melissa's hapless victim crying. Whilst she was astonished at Melissa's moves, she felt surprisingly emboldened herself. 'Now, what were you saying about my breasts, tough guy? You won't be seeing *anything* for a while,' Julie-Anne glanced at Melissa, who was standing over her own victim.

'How's your main course looking now, you neanderthal? Enjoy your smoothies,' Melissa yelled. Just then, the Uber pulled up to the curb. 'Take two. Let's get out of here, Julie-Anne.'

The two women were quiet in the back seat of their Uber as it made its way to Julie-Anne's apartment in Newtown. Melissa's hand was resting on Julie-Anne's, more for reassurance than anything else. Julie-Anne broke the silence. 'Nice move. Where did you learn that?'

'Given my surname, I'm guessing you worked out my father is of Chinese heritage. There is a martial art called Wing Chun that is a close-range combat system invented by a Chinese woman. My father thought I should learn a self-defence skill and the basic moves of Wing Chun were the easiest to master.'

'I bet you didn't train in a red midi and Jimmy Choos though.'

'No, that was quite a risky move in heels, but fortunately it worked out okay. You weren't bad yourself.'

'Thanks, I've been practicing on the insects at home.'

The women were still laughing as the Uber pulled up outside Julie-Anne's apartment building.

'It was a pleasure to meet you, I mostly had a lovely time tonight, Melissa.' Julie-Anne leaned forward and gave her a farewell kiss on the cheek.

Melissa put her hand under Julie-Anne's chin and turned her head towards her. 'Are you going to invite me in? I would love that.' She was about to kiss Julie-Anne on the mouth when she felt a finger come between their lips.

'Raincheck?' Julie-Anne was attracted to Melissa, but she really needed to seriously consider everything that had occurred this evening in the cool light of the day. And she needed to come to terms with her surprising physical reaction to Melissa's tender kiss; *where had that come from?* The next step was a serious escalation in their newfound friendship. First, she needed to find a way to separate Melissa the person from Melissa the link to Li before allowing things to move to the next level. She wasn't sure they were separable. And she had whatever her relationship with Jack was, to consider.

'I need time to clear my head. Text me when you're safely home, please.' Melissa blew her a kiss as the Uber moved away.

(**48**)

Unnamed Bay
Thursday 5th March

It was five o'clock in the morning and the day was dawning already as Benson and the CSI walked down the stairs of the pier and stepped onto the Gemini Rigid-Hulled Inflatable Boat.

Stuart Johnson, the captain of the Cape York, had located the Midnight Express the previous morning, just in time for Benson and his CSI to catch yesterday's evening flight to Proserpine. The Cape York was too long to safely enter the marina at the tourist town of Airlie Beach, so the captain had dropped anchor just outside the rock wall in the turquoise waters of Pioneer Bay. As the RHIB made its way to its mother vessel the sun began to poke up over the horizon, casting an array of red, pink and orange hues across the nearby Whitsunday Islands. Captain Johnson introduced himself, welcomed them aboard, and showed them to a vacant cabin where they could store their equipment. James Andrews was Benson's CSI on this case and he knew him well. He had been with Maritime Border Command since the agency's inception and was well regarded for his meticulousness. If there were traces of human activity on the Midnight Express, James would find them and that hopefully would lead to the identity of the culprits.

'It will take us some time to reach your destination, so in the meanwhile come and join me on the bridge, grab a coffee and enjoy the magnificent, panoramic views. I've been traversing the Coral Sea for more years than I care to remember, but I never cease to be amazed at the beautiful scenery and all-encompassing views up here.' He pointed to the coastline on the port side of the vessel. 'Just check that out.'

Benson turned to his left and was astounded at the blaze of rich oranges and yellows that were caused by the rising sun's rays reflecting off of the mangrove leaves. 'Wow, that is a spectacular sight, Captain.'

'Yes, it is. Now, just so you are up to speed gentlemen, yesterday morning we finally spotted a vessel which we feel could be your target. It looks like the vessel we fired upon a few nights ago, but someone has tried to remove the name from the hull. I'm fairly certain it's your target vessel though. Unfortunately, the little bay where it was anchored was too shallow for this baby to enter, so I launched a team on a RHIB to investigate. They confirmed that there was no- one aboard your vessel. The bay is unnamed and juts into the Dryander National Park. The map shows an isolated dirt track leading through the national park almost to the bay. At this stage it's unknown just how navigable the track is, hence, why you're accessing from the water. I had two of my guys camp near the shoreline of the national park overnight and they watched over your vessel.'

An hour later the Cape York cruised into the unnamed bay and dropped anchor about two hundred metres from the Midnight Express. 'The bay gets too shallow further in, so this is as far as this baby goes. The RHIB will take you two the rest of the way,' the captain advised.

With its shallow draught, high buoyancy and maneuverability, Benson knew the RHIB was ideal for this type of work. It was manned by two ABF seaman who were both armed with what Benson identified as Glock 22 pistols. As they approached the vessel, he noticed the ugly scarring on the hull of the sports fishing vessel where someone had unsuccessfully endeavoured to remove its name, Midnight Express. Unfortunately, there was no registration number painted on the hull of the vessel, as required by Queensland law.

'I think that could be our vessel alright. Let's go check it out.'

'Shouldn't we get it checked for booby traps first?'

'The Cape York's seamen checked it out yesterday, so we should be fine. Besides, it's worth too much money to blow up.' The RHIB tied up to the Midnight Express. Benson and Andrews donned latex gloves and forensic booties, collected their equipment, climbed over the railing and boarded the vessel. Benson knew from experience that it was a Viking 48 with twin one thousand horsepower diesel engines. *More than enough to get them to Hydrographers Passage and back in quick time.* The Midnight Express was probably about fifteen years old, but it would still be worth around half a million dollars in today's market.

'This is a lot of money to be left moored in the middle of nowhere.'

'Not if you're running a multi-million dollar drug enterprise.'

'I suppose not.'

'I am going to hide a tracking device on board so we can monitor and tail these guys when they come back. Therefore, it's crucial that we don't leave any evidence of our presence on board. So, let's be very careful how we go about our search. James, if it's alright with you, I'm going to have a look around for non-forensic evidence. I won't contaminate your crime scene, if that's what this is. Okay?'

'Sure, just don't touch anything that would be capable of retaining a fingerprint. You know, like the helm, any levers, instrumentation, handles of any sort, rails and nothing in the galley, especially cups and glasses. Use your knife if you need to open drawers, cupboards and the like. No hands, even if you're wearing gloves. I don't want you smudging any potential prints. Got it, Benson?'

'Yeah, I got it. This is not my first time.'

Benson made his way down the stairs to the staterooms and began searching. In the first of the two rooms he eased open the benchtop cupboards with his knife, then the wardrobe and finally the bedside chest. He lifted the double mattress from all sides and that revealed nothing. He carefully replaced the mattress, tucked in the covers and then knelt down and searched under the bed. Then he went into the tiny bathroom, opened and checked the under-vanity cupboards and finally inspected the small air conditioning duct, all to no avail. He repeated the systematic process in the second stateroom and came up empty handed again.

He next went down into the galley and couldn't believe his good fortune. There on the floor under the galley table was a barely noticeable, minute quantity of white powder. It would only be visible when entering the galley and he guessed that once the culprits had validated the product, they packed up the cocaine and left the boat in a rush. If any of them had returned to the galley or looked behind them, they would have surely noticed, just as Benson had, the white powder highlighted against the dark navy carpet. Whoever these guys were, they were sloppy. They had evidently cut open one of the twenty packages mentioned by Captain Han, firstly to ensure it was the real deal, and secondly, to test for level of purity. In their haste they had spilt a tiny quantity on the floor.

Benson wet the tip of his index finger and rested it on the tiny powder particles. He then brushed his finger against his tongue. Sure enough it quickly numbed his tongue. He wasn't tasting for flavour but rather the purity. The higher the purity, the higher the strength, the increase in numbness. His tongue was now very numb. He scraped up a minute sample and put it in the small plastic evidence bag and then repeated the process, so he had a back-up sample. He would have it tested for purity and with any luck identify the country of origin. The sample could also be invaluable in matching to any future cocaine seizures and linking the Midnight Express to the culprits.

If these guys were in a hurry and had been sloppy with their testing of the cocaine, then he guessed Andrews would probably find a few patent fingerprints on the vessel too. That was especially likely knowing the crew must have panicked when fired upon by the Cape York. Given they didn't want the culprits to know they had been on board the Midnight Express, Andrews had been unable to dust with fingerprint powder. He would have to rely on his naked eye and maybe even his trusty magnifying glass. If he did find patent fingerprints, he would lift them from the surface with clear tape and then transfer them to another contrasting surface before taking them to the ABF's laboratory for analysing.

'Sam.' Benson heard Andrews call out, so he made his way back up to the deck.

'What have you got?'

'These guys were careless. I have had no trouble lifting a few fingerprints just from the bridge alone.' Andrews held up a few little plastic evidence bags and waved them in Benson's direction as he broke into a wide grin.

'For guys who are handling cocaine with a street value of upwards of thirty million dollars ,they are extremely sloppy. For heaven's sake, just look at the slapdash attempt to remove the name from the hull.'

'Maybe they've been getting away with importing their illegal contraband for so long they've become complacent. And if so, we'll make them pay for the error of their ways.'

'Let's hope so. I'm almost finished here.'

'Okay, if we're all done here, I'm going to place an Asset Recovery Device on the vessel. Then I will get the technicians back in Canberra to set up a geofence.'

'What's a geofence?'

'It's a virtual boundary set up around a geographical location. It's pretty simple really. I'll just get the technicians at head office to set up the geofence around the vessel with a circumference covering the exit to this bay. As soon as the Midnight Express breaches the geofence, the software will trigger a response and send a signal to the techs. As a back-up, it is also fitted with a shock/tilt alarm, so if the vessel tilts or rocks, the ARD will wake up and begin transmitting its position via a nominated satellite network. The head office techs will then be able to monitor its every movement. The tracking device I planted earlier will act as a back-up. More importantly, the Cape York will also be able to track the vessel, hopefully to their handover location. If they get lucky, they'll catch the culprits in the act.'

Andrews was fascinated. 'Where are you going to position this device so it won't be found?'

'I'm guessing the guys aren't interested in fishing, so I'm going to install it behind one of the empty tackle drawers. When I get back to Brisbane I'll file a report on our findings and send you the link to the file number in the database. Can you please advise me once you have uploaded the fingerprint results into the file? I will then distribute the file to Williamson and de Vries for further investigation.'

'Consider it done, Sam.'

'Okay, let's get back onboard the RHIB and get out of here. It's only midday, so the York should get us to Airlie Beach by one thirty, which will give us ample time to get to Proserpine and catch the 3:55 flight back to Brisbane.'

Seafarer's Mission Brisbane Port
Thursday 5th

Captain Hsin Han was enjoying the surroundings of the colourful, manicured garden inside the Seafarer's Mission. As a mariner he worked, lived and slept in a largely colourless environment aboard the Chinese Horizon, with his entire life dominated by rusted blacks, browns, whites and greys. The Mission, with all its greenery and flowering shrubs was an oasis nestled amongst the steel and concrete jungle of the port and he felt at peace after his recent ordeals.

Han was sitting on a timber bench under a blooming Bougainvillea, reading a Chinese language novel from the Mission's library. He delighted in the fact that his concentration was constantly interrupted by the squawk of the pretty parrots playing in the upper foliage of the tree, which strangely, had a calming influence on him. The captain thought about his wife and two children. The children in particular, would be in awe of the cheeky birds with their vibrant blue, green and orange plumage. He had always wanted to bring his family to this wonderful country, but given his current predicament, that seemed to him like a long-lost dream now.

The Mission didn't traditionally provide overnight accommodation, but once he had explained his extraordinary circumstances to the pastor, the captain was allowed to access the Day Sleeping Room for the duration of his stay. Hopefully, Agent Harvey would finish his enquiry soon and he could go home to his family. He returned to his book and continued reading.

His state of reverie was interrupted by the sound of the common room door opening. He looked up to see two men walking through the doorway and out into the garden area. Alarm bells began ringing as he watched the two men he recognised from the Midnight Express walk towards him. *What were they doing here? Was this a coincidence?* Maybe it was nothing to worry about and they were just seafarers utilising the Mission, just like him.

'Yǒuhǎo de nǐ hǎo.' He stood, smiled, and offered a friendly, if cautious, greeting. As the two men approached him, he noticed a sudden flash of light as the morning sun gleamed against the steel blade held by the taller man. His approachable smile was now replaced by a look of sheer terror as he realised what was about to befall him. He thought again of his family and how they would get through life without him. They wouldn't. He couldn't leave them, not now.

Han turned to run, but the smaller man was quicker and extended his leg, tripping him. He crashed onto the brick paving, hitting his head with a thud that momentarily dazed him. You must keep going, he thought, you have to. The taller man was almost upon him now and he didn't have time to stand. He scrambled on all fours as he tried to reach the doorway that led to the Mission building. 'Jiùmìng, juiming. Help, help,' he cried out, hoping the Mission's pastor or other seafarers would hear him. His hopes faded as he saw that the smaller man had outflanked him and was now standing between him and the doorway.

The taller man grabbed the belt of Han's jeans and pulled him to a halt. He was caught between the two men. He lashed out, kicking wildly with his legs while trying to free himself, but the taller man agilely side-stepped him. In desperation, he swung his torso around and tried to wriggle free, but the smaller man grabbed the collar of his shirt and trapped him. He yelled out as loud and long as he could in a final act of desperation. No-one was coming to his aid and he finally surrendered to the hopelessness of his situation as he felt the steel blade slice into his side, again and again.

Han lay prostrate in the garden bed where they had dumped him, thinking about his family. He could feel the warmth of his blood as it continued to ooze out of the wounds in his side. With every breath, he could feel himself becoming weaker and he knew he was fading. He prayed to the God Shang-ti for his life and for his family's safety. 'Qǐng bǎohù wǒ de jiārén ānquán,' he implored faintly.

(50)

Golden Phoenix Restaurant

Julie-Anne was at the desk in her cubicle when her mobile phone buzzed. *Nice photo JA* was all the message from Jack read. No good morning, no hello, JA, no how are you? *What is he talking about?* she pondered. She was trying to recall any recent photos she had taken when it suddenly hit her. *The cocktail party, of course.* She assumed Jack was reading the Daily News at work, so she began flicking through one of her copies, looking for the entertainment section. There appeared an article in the lifestyle section covering the Consul General's cocktail party and the celebration of a joint trade agreement between China and New South Wales. There was a photo of the DFAT bureaucrats shaking hands with the Consul General and another with the bureaucrats on their own, posing with a celebratory champagne.

Maybe there's something to be said for foreign affairs after all. She laughed to herself as she recalled Melissa's flirting joke from last night. Below those photos were two more. One was of her with Li Qiang. *Bang!! Got you in print buddy,* she rejoiced. The last photo was of her and Melissa with Jackson, the DFAT guy. The photographer had taken numerous shots of the three of them, but the entertainment editor had chosen this particular one to publish. It was a good shot of the two women, but Jackson appeared to be gazing more towards

Julie-Anne rather than looking directly into the camera. *Nothing to see there*, thought Julie-Anne.

She wondered which photo had pissed Jack off and led to his sarcastic text. The one with a gazing Jackson, or was it the one that showed she had obviously made the acquaintance of Li Qiang? Probably both, she guessed. Maybe it was neither. Julie-Anne hadn't seen Jack to tell him about Deb's timely invitation to the cocktail party, so maybe he was simply surprised. Anyway, he was the one who stood her up two nights ago, and by text message no less. He should be pleased that she was progressing her investigation, but maybe he was worried about her safety, given the subject matter. He would also notice that Melissa was partly of Chinese descent and therefore he could reasonably assume that she might also have a connection to her investigation. *So, what's the problem?* Julie-Anne had spent considerable time with Jack earlier in the week; maybe it had been overkill and Jack was getting jittery. Maybe she would back-off. As for being stood up by text message, well what's with that? *Aaahh men!!*

She was interrupted by the ringtone on her mobile phone. There was no caller ID and she didn't recognise the number. 'Julie-Anne Granger speaking.'

'Ms Granger, this is Li Qiang.'

'Nice to hear from you.'

'Did you enjoy yourself last night at the Consul General's celebration?'

Julie-Anne thought she would tease him. 'Yes, and I met some interesting people, too.'

Li let that comment slide. 'Ms Granger, I was wondering if you would like to have lunch with me today? I know it is short notice, but I was going to be eating alone at my favourite restaurant, and then I thought of you and our interesting conversation last night.'

'I don't know, Mr Li; I have a heavy workload at the moment.' Julie-Anne was dying to go, but she didn't want to appear overly eager, particularly given he was the subject of her investigation. And she had to be very careful not to arouse his suspicion.

'Ms Granger, the restaurant is only ten minutes from your office and their signature dish is superb.' Julie-Anne paused for effect before responding. 'Okay, where and when, Mr Li?'

It was another lovely blue-sky day, so Julie-Anne decided to walk the kilometre and a half from her office to the restaurant. Along the way, her mobile rang and she answered to find a cheerful Melissa following up on their connection from the night before.

'You sound like you're out walking; I can hear traffic in the background.' Melissa commented after the pleasantries were exchanged.

'I'm off to lunch in the city and it's a beautiful day, so I decided to walk in.' She wasn't about to tell Melissa who her lunch companion was just yet.

'Yes, it is a beautiful day, so I thought we might have dinner on my deck tonight; what do you think?' she asked.

Julie-Anne stopped at the crossing and waited for the little green man to make an appearance. 'I would love to, but I have something else on tonight, sorry.' She hadn't mentioned Jack to her yet, so she was being deliberately vague. 'I can do tomorrow night though, if that works for you.'

'Yep, lock it in.'

'What time and what would you like me to bring?' she replied while crossing George Street.

'Make it seven and just bring a bottle of your favourite wine. I have a bottle of Veuve chilling in the fridge. I'll text you the address.'

'Thanks, Melissa. I'll see you tomorrow at seven.'

'Welcome madam, my name is Huang. Can I help you?' *Madam, really, how old does he think I am?*

'I am having lunch with a Mr Li Qiang.' Just at that moment Julie-Anne spied Li sitting at the bar. 'It's okay, Huang, I can see him.' Julie-Anne noticed Li give her the once over as she walked across the restaurant. No cleavage for you today buddy.

'Aaahh, Ms Granger, nice to see you.'

'You too, Mr Li. Thank you for the invitation.'

'I'm having my usual, what would you like to drink?'

'The same then please, with ice.' After some polite conversation and small talk, they were escorted to their table by Huang, who attended to Julie-Anne's chair and napkinned her. 'There's no need for the menus, Huang as I know what I am going to order, if Ms Granger will allow me.'

'I'm in your hands, Mr Li.'

'Huang, let's surprise Ms Granger shall we, I'll have two serves of my usual. And, we'll also have a bottle of Tyrrell's Vat 47 Chardonnay 2015.'

Julie-Anne was looking round and admiring the bustling, yet comfortable restaurant with its wall of aquariums, red Chinese Lanterns hanging above the tables, lighting tracks winding through the restaurant, countless timber wine racks built into the wall and white linen table cloths.

Huang served the meals. Julie-Anne thought it unusual for the maître d' to be serving the food and the wine. Li would have to be more than just a regular guest for that to occur in a packed restaurant.

'Mmmm these little creatures are just divine and the sauce is just delicious,' Julie-Anne said while juggling one on her spoon.

'I'm very pleased that you think so,' replied Li, smiling.

'And the wine is excellent and nicely matched. Cheers.'

'Ganbei, Ms Granger.' Li had a message he wanted to deliver to the Granger woman and she had just unknowingly offered him a segue to deliver it. 'I think you'll agree, both are considerably better than what was served at the cocktail party last night.'

'This is heaven compared to that, but I am never critical of my hosts' offerings.'

'That is very wise.'

Julie-Anne caught a man looking at her and he appeared to be making his way directly towards their table. He was a tallish, handsome man of Asian appearance with high cheekbones and black hair. He was fashionably dressed in a gainsboro grey designer suit that highlighted his strong physique and he was wearing patent leather shoes. As he drew near she could just make out a tattoo of what she thought could be a dragon on his neck.

'Aaahh, Li, how are you? 'Wie said, greeting her host with a warm handshake.

Just when Li was about to enter the door that Granger had opened for him Wie had shown up. Li would come back to the issue at hand later. 'I am well thank you.'

'Good to hear. And who is your beautiful lunch companion?' he asked as he turned to Julie-Anne.

'This is Ms Julie-Anne Granger. Ms Granger meet Wie Ping Lie.'

'I am delighted to meet you, Ms Granger. How do you like the Pipis?'

'They are delicious thank you.'

The two men then spoke briefly in Chinese. Wie bade them farewell and as he started to walk away, he paused.

'Don't forget to call me, Li.'

Julie-Anne noticed that his charm had now been replaced by a brooding, almost menacing expression. She needed to know more about that man. 'Your friend was a very snappily dressed guy. 'Is he a business acquaintance, Mr Li?'

'You could say that.'

Julie-Anne was aware of Li still staring where Wie had been standing moments earlier and judging by the glare on his face he wasn't happy. 'What line of business are you in?'

'Import, export,' he replied without looking at her.

She could imagine what he was importing. 'What sort of products?'

'I import figurines and send boutique wines the other way.'

She needed to get the conversation back on track otherwise she wasn't going to glean anything from this man today. 'Is that why you were at the Consul General's celebration last night?'

'Yes.' Judging by the short answers she was now getting, Julie-Anne reasoned that Li was preoccupied and less than overjoyed with the outcome of the conversation with Wie.

'You and Miss Wu seemed to be getting along well last night.' Li suggested, changing the subject back to the reason behind the luncheon invite.

'Yes, we did. She is an intelligent, articulate and interesting person; we had fun and I enjoyed her company. She intrigued me.'

'She is also extremely attractive to the eye; wouldn't you agree, Ms Granger?' Julie-Anne looked up from her Pipis in time to see the smug look growing on Li's face. She paused while she worked out where this conversation was now heading.

'Yes, she is, but beauty is only skin deep. I prefer her other, less superficial, qualities.'

'I'm sure you do,' he replied arching a brow.

Julie-Anne was concerned about Li's sudden interest in her friendship with Melissa. She cleared her throat and fiddled with her napkin, taking a breath to compose herself.

'Mr Li, how did you get my mobile number and how did you know where I worked, specifically?'

'Like you said last night, "I do my research," Ms Granger.'

'It seems you do,' she replied. Julie-Anne furrowed her eyebrows, conjuring up a look of indignation. 'And pray tell, why would you find it necessary to research me?'

His look had darkened again. 'Miss Wu and I are working on an important project and I wouldn't like to have that undermined. You seemed to have become close to her very quickly. And you are an investigative journalist, after all, so my suspicious nature wondered whether there was a connection.'

Julie-Anne took a sip of her wine to buy a few precious seconds then placed the glass on the table. 'Let's just say hypothetically, that even if I were investigating something, if there were no illegal activities occurring, then the investigation would surely amount to nothing and your concerns would be unfounded. Wouldn't you agree?' The man's cheeks flushed and she smiled sweetly at him, 'Hypothetically speaking, of course, Mr Li.' He made no reply. She felt a smug warmth in her chest. Gotcha. With that she stood up, thanked him for the lunch, and made her way to the exit.

'Thank you, Huang, that was lovely,' she called out in farewell to the maître d' as she pushed the door open and strode out into the warmth of the afternoon sun.

(51)

Bayside Café Pyrmont

Jack strolled along the Jones Bay Wharf admiring the sights and sounds of a lively Darling Harbour. He looked across the sparkling water to the almost completed new casino building that dominated the skyline and seemed to disappear into the clouds. The tourist and charter cruise boats with their blaring music didn't appear to be in any hurry as they calmly chugged along while the city's ferries were taking evasive action as they dashed in and out of Barangaroo Wharf. In the distance he could just make out the shapes of people undertaking the Sydney Harbour Bridge climb in their blue coveralls. While sightseeing he was also subtly looking for anyone out of place. He hadn't told anyone about the location of his meeting with Michelle Ironside, but he couldn't be sure about the depth of her involvement in his investigation, so he wasn't about to take unnecessary chances. He cleared the area and then made his way to the Bayside Café, where he sat inside away from any prying eyes. He also wanted to provide comfort to Ironside that he was being discreet and maintaining her privacy, at least until he ascertained the depth of her involvement. As always, he sat with his back to the rear wall, facing the entry.

He watched as Ms Ironside enter the café and glanced around the room. She wouldn't recognise him, so he signalled to her with a subtle wave. She walked across to his table and he introduced himself.

'Take a seat, Ms Ironside. Thank you for agreeing to meet with me.'

'Did I have a choice?' she asked. Jack then pulled his AFP identification out of his wallet and showed her. They ordered coffees and made small talk about the scenic location and harbourside views. Once the coffees arrived, Jack got down to business.

'Ms Ironside. The only person who is aware that we are meeting is the Director of Security at Oceanic. I would imagine, given that you work for the casino, you don't want to advertise the fact that you are meeting with an Australian Federal Policeman, so I have been discreet.' Jack needed her to feel comfortable and wanted to build some trust early in the conversation. 'Depending on the outcome of our meeting today, I will endeavour to keep it that way.'

'Thank you, but I have no idea why I am here,' she stated.

'I doubt that's true. I didn't draw your name out of a hat.' Michelle was aghast at that remark and suddenly knew that the detective must know more than she had originally hoped was the case.

'I'm investigating suspected laundering of illicitly gained money through the Bennelong Room. In particular, I am looking at the activities of a Mr Li Qiang.' If Michelle was aghast at the detective's previous remark, she was now horrified at his latest pronouncement. She tried to maintain a calm demeanour, but her stomach was churning and she felt the colour draining from her face.

'I believe you are the Treasury Manager for the Bennelong Room, is that correct?'

'Yes, Detective Wagner, I am,' she replied proudly.

'That being the case, you would therefore be responsible for all cash management, financial transactions and reporting for the room, would you not?'

'Yes, I am.'

'Okay, that's good. I'm speaking to the right person then.' That was Jack's way of letting her know that she wouldn't be able to defer to anyone else now; this would all be on her. He would now carefully walk her into a scenario from which she wouldn't be able to extricate herself.

'Okay, let's go back to Mr Li Qiang. Do you know who Li Qiang is, Ms Ironside?'

'Yes, I do. I met him officially for the first time two nights ago.'

'Officially?' Jack queried.

'Yes, I knew of him previously and I had seen him in the Bennelong Room before, but I had never met him. He's a high roller.'

'And these high rollers, they all bet with gaming chips provided by the casino?'

'Yes, they do.'

'So how do they obtain these gaming chips in the first place?'

Michelle sat forward in her chair. 'There are three primary ways they buy their chips. With cash over the Treasury counter, by electronic transfer or through an account established with the casino.'

'And given they're all high rollers, I assume the amounts involved in these transactions are significant.'

'Yes, they are, sometimes in the millions of dollars.'

'And through various federal and state laws, there are numerous reporting requirements that the Oceanic is legislated to undertake?'

'Yes, once again.'

'And these would be TTR's, SMR's or an IFTI'S? I assume, as Treasury Manager, you are responsible for the compilation and submission of these reports.'

'Yes, I am.'

'Okay, I have a couple more questions for you then.

Only a couple to go thank God, thought Michelle as she relaxed in her chair.

'Firstly, let me preface these questions by saying that I know Mr Li has stayed at the Oceanic Hotel and Casino on eleven occasions in the past eighteen months. That being the case, how is it that you have never met Mr Li until his eleventh visit?'

'Well, maybe he didn't visit the Bennelong Room on every visit detective.'

Jack gave her a look of disbelief. 'Ms Ironside, really! If I went back through the CCTV footage for the Bennelong Room at the times Mr Li has stayed at the Oceanic, I'm sure I will find him sitting at his favourite blackjack table. You do know that CCTV footage is retained for a legislated period of time, don't you?'

'I have no idea detective; I don't work for security.' Jack stared at her, but let the rebuff pass.

'Moving along to my second question. On Mr Li's first three stays at the Oceanic his financial transactions conducted within the Bennelong Room were recorded in the Threshold Transaction Report on each occasion, as required by federal law. On his subsequent seven visits there is only a TTR record of him cashing in his chips and the casino transacting an Electronic Funds Transfer on his behalf. There is no TTR record of Mr Li purchasing the chips in the first place. Don't you find that somewhat strange, Ms Ironside?'

'I have no idea, detective. Maybe he got his stake downstairs on the main floor of the casino.'

Jack leant back in his chair and folded his arms. 'Ms Ironside, do you really expect me to believe that the cashiers on the main floor of the casino carry seven figure chip holdings just in case a high roller turns up wanting to exchange a million dollars?' Michelle mirrored his pose, folding her own arms across her chest, and remained silent.

'Or just maybe, someone stopped recording all of Li's transactions after the first three and only recorded his cashing out,' Jack said.

This got Michelle thinking. She was meticulous with her record keeping, so how *had* he obtained his gaming chips on those seven occasions? A scenario of her own was beginning to form in her mind and she broke her stare with the detective. She took a sip from her coffee and the cup rattled against the saucer as she set it down again, betraying her nerves.

He did notice.

'Ms Ironside, you said you had never met Mr Li before two nights ago, but you "knew of him."'

'Yes.'

'How is it that you *knew* of him?'

'Maybe it was from his earlier visits that you mentioned.'

'What, you can remember someone from eighteen months ago?'

'That must be the case, detective.'

'I'd like to remind you of the availability of CCTV footage and my ability to access it Ms Ironside.' Jack didn't really know whether the casino had retained the entire eighteen months of CCTV footage or not, but it was worth the bluff.

'Moving along, Ms Ironside. You said that you first met Mr Li two nights ago.'

'Yes, I did.'

'How did you meet him?'

'He came to the Treasury Office to cash in his gaming chips.'

'Did you give him cash?'

'No, he requested an electronic transfer.'

'Okay, that's fine, there will be a record of that. And did you only meet with Mr Li once that night?'

'Yes, why do you ask?'

'Isn't it obvious?'

There was a pause while Michelle wondered where the detective was heading with this line of questioning.

Jack continued. 'You would have had to have met Mr Li twice that night, otherwise, how did he get his gaming chips in the first place? And please don't tell me again that it was on the main floor of the casino.'

Michelle knew very well where Li had got his gaming chips, and she was also aware that she was between a rock and a hard place now. She shifted uncomfortably in her chair. 'I have no idea, detective.'

'Are you certain, Ms Ironside? You are the Treasury Manager and you strike me as someone who would be professional, diligent and honest in your duties.'

Jack leaned forward, his elbows braced against the small table. 'You do know it is an offence to lie to an Australian Federal Police Officer, don't you?' He paused and she felt her palms sweating in her lap. The officer lent back, pursing his lips. 'Well, I'm sure I will get the answers that I'm seeking when I view all of Oceanic's Threshold Transaction, Suspicious Matter and Electronic Funds Transfer Reports for that day. In fact, I am going to request them for the entire eleven visits. Let's move onto something else.'

'Who was the suit with Mr Li that night? He looked like security, maybe a bodyguard or perhaps client liaison or one of those fancy titles that get people excited about.'

'Which suit, detective?'

'Now you're just being clever and I'm now wondering why that would suddenly be the case? You know very well which suit I'm referring to. The one that shadowed Mr Li the entire evening and who accompanied him to your office.'

Realising the detective must have been in the Bennelong Room two nights ago and that she now had no loyalty to Mr Woodard, she needed to be honest. 'He's the Vice President—Client Services.'

'Does he have a name?'

'Tony Woodard.'

'Do you have any idea why Mr Woodard has such a vested interest in Mr Li?'

'What do you mean, "vested interest", detective?'

'He arrived with Mr Li, didn't leave his side all night long, stood watch outside the bathroom door while Li did his business, accompanied him to your office and then departed with him. Does the Vice President—Client Services only have one client? Corporate business must be slow if that's the case, wouldn't you think?'

'I have no idea.'

'Ms Ironside.' Jack paused. 'I don't think you're a criminal or even a bad person, but you are involved in something that is beyond your control.'

'Why would you say that, detective?' Michelle felt her face flush which belied her response.

'That you even asked that in itself validates my question, otherwise you would have denied it outright. You likely would have become very angry, or at least, agitated. You did neither. I have checked you out, Michelle.' Jack used her first name to create an impression of empathy. 'You are highly regarded within your workplace, are known for your professionalism and diligence and you are a stickler for detail and accuracy of reporting. For you not to provide definitive responses to most of my questions beggars belief.' Jack paused, but there was no reaction from her. 'That will do for now.' He offered her his business card. 'If you think of anything else you would like to tell me, please call.'

'Okay, Detective Wagner.'

Michelle thought she handled the interview quite well, considering. She knew the detective would keep digging and the CCTV tapes would contradict most of her responses. She was in trouble, big time, but she had bought herself some time to think through her situation. And what was the detective's last remark about? Did he already know about her dilemma with Woodard?

The CCTV cameras would show Woodard entering the vault two days ago and exchanging the cash, but it would also show her conducting her own reconciliation, and she never reported the cash versus chip discrepancy. And who would have conducted the cash transactions on the other occasions? It certainly didn't happen on her watch. While walking through the afternoon sunshine to the casino, she thought about her options. Whatever they were, she had better make a decision, and soon.

Macquarie Suite

Li arrived back at his suite after the interesting lunch with the reporter woman and made himself comfortable on his sofa. As usual, he had a Glenlivet in his left hand and a Monte Christo in his right. He was thinking about the exchange between himself and Wie earlier this afternoon. What was so concerning to Wie that he wanted Li to call him so urgently? His issues with Woodard and the Ironside woman were no concern of his. Maybe he had found out about the captain being taken off his ship. Li knew he should have told him sooner.

'Yes.'

'It's me; you requested I call you.'

'It wasn't a request. We need to talk.'

'What about?'

'Not on the phone. I'll meet you back at the restaurant in half an hour.' With that, Wie terminated the call.

Li entered the Golden Phoenix, pausing to savour the exotic mix of sweet, savoury and sour aromas that penetrated his senses and transported him back to his native Shanghai.

'Mr Li, welcome back. So soon.'

'Where is he, Huang?'

'I'm right here.' Wie had entered unnoticed behind Li. The two of them made their way to their usual table in the back corner of the Golden Phoenix and sat facing the entrance.

'When were you going to tell me about the captain, Li?'

'There's nothing to tell. He was taken by the authorities for interviewing and as I understand it, told them nothing. He doesn't know anything anyway other than where he does the handover. I arranged for his expeditious release. Our mutual friend in China became nervous and wanted the captain out of the country, which I duly arranged.'

'So, he's gone. Is that what you're saying?'

'Yes, he left yesterday.'

Wie smiled and took a sip from his drink, enjoying the warmth of the alcohol across his palette.

'Why the smug look, Wie?'

'No reason. Anyway, it seems our friendly travel agent received a visit from some border control guy yesterday. He wanted to know who purchased the captain's airline ticket. She is very loyal to me, so of course she told him she didn't know and couldn't remember the face of the purchaser. That, combined with the captain's detention and Ling's near miss with the patrol boat, tells me that there must be some sort of wider investigation going on into our business venture. Maybe it's all just a coincidence, but I don't think so.'

'If you remember correctly, Wie, it was I who suggested, right here in this restaurant four days ago, that we should review our activities. And do you remember your response? "If it isn't broken, then don't fix it." How do you feel about that now?' Li smarted.

'Well, we have another shipment due in a couple of weeks, so it is too late to stop that. We can stop the final shipment leaving Dailan though. Can you arrange that, Li?'

'Finally, some common sense, yes I will.'

Li noticed a concerned look wash over Wie's face. 'Good, because I now I have another issue to deal with thanks to Lucie.'

'Let me guess. She couldn't wait for Ling Jun to return and she took matters into her own hands.'

'You should be a clairvoyant, Li. Yes, she did some investigating of her own and an informant of hers in the eastern suburbs gave up the name of the other assailant from Sunday's not so subtle warning. Abboud's accomplice is Jasar Khoury. Of course he's a lowlife Lebo like I told you.'

'So, what happened, Wie?'

'She conducted her own research through her connections and quickly found out where he lived; some shithole down in Columbia Avenue in Punchbowl.'

'That young woman is very resourceful.'

'Yes, she is, but I don't need to be involved in a turf war and I had clearly told her I didn't want the situation to escalate. She was told to leave matters alone.'

'With respect, she was the one who had a gun held to her head, not you, Wie. I'm guessing she wanted to send her own message that she herself wasn't someone to be messed with. What did she do?'

'She firebombed their house.' Li laughed loudly. 'Really?'

'Didn't you see the news this morning?'

'Aaahh, Shàngdì ài nàgè niánqīng nǚrén. I love that young woman,' Li said with pride. 'How did she do that?'

'Evidently, she made two Molotov Cocktails, drove to his house and waited until the time was right. Once the occupants had settled in for the night she walked across the road to their front yard, lit one and hurled it through their dining room window. Then she calmy walked across the lawn to the living room window and repeated the process.'

'What happened to the occupants?'

'Unfortunately, or fortunately, they only suffered minor injuries, but that's not the point; she disobeyed an order. Let's just hope the Lebos didn't see who it was and aren't smart enough to put two and two together. And the cops too, for that matter.'

'Oh, come on, Wie, you would have done the same thing.'

'Probably. Anyway, tell me, who was the woman at lunch?' Wie asked pointedly.

'What concern is that of yours?' Li responded.

'I have seen her face somewhere before.'

'There are five million people in this city, so it could have been anywhere.'

'She was very attractive and you of all people know I never forget an attractive woman.' Li sighed.

'She is a reporter for the Sydney Daily News.'

'What's her name, what does she report on and why was she having lunch with you?'

'Her name is Granger and she is an investigative journalist.'

Wie was becoming nervous the further the conversation proceeded. 'What does she investigate?'

'Criminal activities, corporate fraud, illegal activities by corporations, political interference, those types of criminal activities.'

'And you invited her to lunch? Ben Dan.' Li had been called many things, but never a stupid egg.

Li hated having to explain himself, but when dealing with the volatile Wie it was occasionally prudent to do so. 'She seems to have befriended a woman, a potential candidate, who is crucial to a political project of mine, so I thought I would give her a subtle message and warn her off.'

'I hope for your sake that's all it is. What do you propose to do about her?'

'I intend to maintain a watch over my candidate and as long as this Granger woman stays away from her, I won't have to do anything.'

'Fú wú chóng zhì, huò bú dān xíng, Li.'

'I know what that means, Wie. Blessings come along alone; troubles often come together.'

'And if she doesn't stay away?'

'Then the next message will be less than subtle.'

'If she starts investigating our joint business activity, I will be less than pleased. That's a little message of my own, Li.'

'Our activities are not connected to my political project.'

'Your share of the profits from our business dealings are funding your political project, are they not?'

'You know they are.'

'Then there is a direct connection between the two. And, if she is any good at her investigating job, she will make the connection one day. You need to deal with her. Stay in touch and don't hold back on me again,' Wie demanded as he rose from the table. 'You know the consequences.'

(**53**)

Balmain Inner West Sydney

Julie-Anne pressed the call button next to the front door and waited. Arriving at Jack's apartment, she wasn't sure what to expect or what the atmosphere would be like given the missed catchups, including Jack standing her up by text, which still irritated her. And let's not forget his sarcastic message this morning about the newspaper photo. She would normally wear something sexy to get his juices flowing, but not tonight.

'Sorry, I was in the middle of sautéing the bacon. How are you, Julie-Anne?' he asked, ushering her inside. *Oops, no JA*, she picked-up on. *What's he up to?*

'Yeah, I'm well, thank you. Yourself?' Jack made to kiss her, but she turned her head and his kiss landed on her cheek. He followed her into the living area in silence. She knew him well enough to know what he was up to.

'You're checking my arse out, am I right?' she said with a stifled laugh. 'Anyway, I hope so, I love these jeans.' Julie-Anne wore a rose coloured long sleeved linen shirt, her new favourite white, lace-up skinny jeans, comfortable sandals and had left her silky black hair to drift across her shoulders.

'Caught again,' he said.

'It's not hard, you're so predictable.'

'I know, but I can't help myself. You have a magnificent figure.'

'You don't look too bad yourself.' Jack was dressed smart casual with firm fitting navy chino shorts, a light blue linen shirt with the sleeves rolled up the forearms and tan loafers. 'And speaking of predictable, you haven't cleaned up since I was here last; it's starting to look like a bachelor's pad,' she taunted.

Jack wondered whether that was meant as a tester, but if it was, he wasn't going to take the bait. 'Would you like your favourite sav blanc? It will go nicely with the chicken caesar.' Julie-Anne loved the Shaw and Smith Sauvignon Blanc from the Adelaide Hills and Jack usually had a bottle chilling for her.

'Sounds good to me.' Jack one: Julie-Anne: zero, she thought. Despite her best efforts, she could feel her irritation melting away in the face of his thoughtfulness.

''So, how have you been, Jack?'

'Quite busy with the investigation really, hence why I had to cancel the other day.'

'You could have rung me you know,' she replied, striking the teacup pose.

'We had only left each other a few hours earlier, so I thought a text message would be okay.' She let it slide. He passed her a glass of her favourite. 'Cheers, JA.'

'Ganbei.'

'What does that mean?'

'Cheers in Chinese.' She couldn't resist teasing him, hoping that he would make the connection with the Li Qiang photo, but alas, he didn't.

'Dinner is almost ready so why don't you go out on the balcony, get comfortable and dinner will be served in a minute.' Julie-Anne cackled in response.

'What's so funny?'

'Oh, nothing.' Julie-Anne was thinking about the last time she had gotten *comfortable* on his balcony. She walked outside and breathed deeply inhaling the minty aroma of the eucalypts while her mind wandered.

'Okay, here we are, Chicken Caesar a la Jacques.'

'It looks great, funny man.' *Another point for Jack.*

'I put the anchovies on the side just in case you don't like them.'

'I love all seafood, even the hairy little fish.' She heard a repeated soft hollow hooting sound. 'Did you hear that? Ozzie Owl is still here.'

'I haven't heard him for a while, so I'm guessing his return must be because he's attracted to you too.'

'Great answer, Jack.'

He raised his glass. 'Cheers again, here's to successful investigations, JA.' *What no toast to happiness, romance, me, us, beautiful warm evenings, anything but work?*

'Seeing as how we're toasting investigations, where are you up to with yours?' she asked.

Here we go. 'Well, I've been focusing on a Chinese national who I'm fairly sure is laundering money through the Oceanic Casino.'

That quickly got Julie-Anne invested. 'Really? tell me more,' she asked as she mustered a neutral expression.

'He's a high roller or whale as they sometimes call them and has spent considerable time in the Bennelong Room over the past couple of years.'

'Really, that's sounds fruitful. How did you come across this particular high roller?'

Jack guessed where the conversation was heading and thought carefully about his response. 'I have contacts at DHA and Austrac and they were both very accommodating in helping me identify him.'

'Yeah, but how did you know which high roller to look for in the first place?' Julie-Anne asked casually while picking at her caesar salad. 'One of them must have had a line on him already,' he replied, trying to sound dismissive, but he knew she would see through it. He'd always been careful with what information he shared with JA, but he'd never lied to her.

Julie-Anne prodded at an anchovy. 'So, who is this mystery man?' she asked, knowing very well what Jack was about to say.

'His name is Li Qiang.'

She fumed and slammed down her fork. 'Rubbish, Jack, I told you his name two days ago over coffee.'

'No, you didn't, I would remember. When, JA?'

'Don't *JA* me now, Jack. You were pouring coffee, and as I now realise, were obviously trying to not sound overly interested. You asked, "So, who is this mystery man about town?" Then I told you. Are you going to deny it now after I've just recited it back to you verbatim?'

'Okay, if you say so.'

'Yes, I most certainly do.' *I guess his points have run out tonight.* 'Christ, Jack. I've been Googling my heart out, pounding the streets, literally, and getting threatened and intimidated, all while you used the name I gave you and ran it through all your fancy government databases.' She pushed her plate back and stood, wrapping her arms around her middle as she paced the length of the balcony. Her heart was pounding, as she reevaluated their previous encounters. Had it meant anything to him? 'I thought I could trust you,' she said. 'But I guess everything that happened the night before and earlier that morning meant nothing to you once you heard the name you needed. Oh, and let's not forget "on your knees, naked, hair and breasts swaying with every swing of the pillow" blah, blah, blah.' Julie-Anne was on a roll now. 'I feel used, Jack. Do you know what that feels like? Do you?' She took a deep breath and returned to her seat.

'I don't know what to say, JA.'

'And stop the JA crap too, my name's Julie-Anne.'

'Look I'm sorry. I guess I just had my detective head on and wasn't thinking.'

She rolled her eyes. 'You think so? There's a revelation, genius.'

'Okay, what do we do now?' Jack asked, running a hand through his hair, his cheeks flushed.

She took a sip of her wine and stared up into the dusky evening sky, considering what to say next. 'Right, I know what we have to do. I want in on your investigation, Jack. You need to give me everything you've got so I can get my own investigation back on track. You should have done that in the first place instead of keeping information from me.'

'You know I can't do that, Julie-Anne.'

'Ha, you remembered my name, and yes you can, Jack. I don't want to know about your government secret agents' boys' club stuff. Just tell me what you know about Li Qiang's illicit activities and anyone else involved,' she demanded. 'Oh, by the way, I had lunch with him yesterday too,' she said while savouring a mouthful of the caesar.

'You did what?' he blurted.

She relished the astonished look that had washed across his face. 'You heard me. I just maybe have some interesting titbits that might fascinate you too.'

There was an awkward silence between them, but eventually Jack relented. He told her as much as he could without breaching any government acts or privacy laws. He spoke about Li Qiang's activities in the Bennelong Room, the amounts he suspected were involved, Woodard's proximity to Li and the Oceanic's TTR requirements. 'There you are, open and transparent.' He hadn't mentioned Danielle.

'What's your next move, Jack?'

'I'm waiting for more information from a government agency.' He wasn't ready to reveal the results from his coffee with the Treasury Manager just yet. Now his investigation was gathering momentum, he first needed to strategize his next move.

She sighed. 'Thank you, that wasn't so hard now was it?'

'What about you? Where's the quid pro quo?' Julie-Anne told Jack the little information she had learned at the cocktail party. She briefly mentioned meeting Melissa Wu and her private meeting with Li. Then she recalled the conversation with Li over lunch and the veiled threats he made about her friendship with Melissa.

'Melissa, was she the attractive woman in the red dress in the photo who looked a bit like Lucy Liu?'

'Yeah, a younger, improved version. Why?' *Did I really just say that?*

'Oh, really, no reason,' he said dismissively.

'Anyway, back to my story, Jack. During lunch a fashionably dressed, quite tall, athletic looking Asian guy came to the table. He and Li spoke in Chinese for a brief period and then the visitor started to leave. As he walked away he stopped, turned back to Li and made a pointed remark. He appeared to be threatening Li, "don't forget to call" he said.'

'What did he look like?'

'I just told you. Hang on, I just remembered something; he had a dragon tattoo on his neck.'

'Christ, that's simply great, JA. That is probably Wie Ping Lie and he is the head of the Triad that controls all illegal activities in Chinatown. You need to be very careful around him.'

'Yeah, that's him. We should assume they have a relationship of sorts, but we just need to establish what the nature of that relationship is. So, where does our investigation go from here, Jack?'

'There's no "our" investigation,' he said, making quotation marks with his fingers.

'You know I hate clichés, but two heads are better than one, and I'm sure I'll have more information in the next couple of days. And in the spirit of quid pro quo, I'll share it with you, Jack,' Julie-Anne said, projecting her best saccharine smile.

'Alright, give me a couple of days to think about the ramifications of that and I'll call you. You know that I work for a federal law enforcement agency, so there is only so much information I can legally share with you.'

'Well, I am an investigative journalist for a respected newspaper. I never divulge my sources, so there is only so much I can share with you, too,' she replied smugly.

Jack didn't respond and with head bowed he continued enjoying his Caesar. 'So, tell me about the cute blond bimbo?'

'What cute blonde bimbo?' Once again knowing full well who Julie-Anne was asking about.

'The one at that laneway bar in Ultimo the other night.'

'Oh. Her,' he replied trying to sound dismissive. 'She works in the Bennelong Room and invited me for a drink after she finished work. I thought Danielle might be able to tell me more about Li, so I went.'

'Aaahh, Danielle is it?'

'Nothing happened, Julie-Anne,' he said firmly.

'I know. But you weren't going to mention it though, were you?'

'How did you find out about that anyway?' he replied, ignoring her assessment. Even if she was correct, he had no intention of confirming it.

'Sydney is a big city, but sometimes it's just a small town, Jack. The paper's entertainment photographer happened to be at the bar and snapped the two of you together, probably enamoured by her plunging neckline as I'm sure you were. My friend Deb is the entertainment reporter. She saw the photo and showed me. Don't worry, the snapper told her you left by yourself.'

'Thank heavens for the photographer then,' sighed a relieved Jack.

'Well, thank you for the lovely Caesar and for my favourite wine. It's been an interesting evening. I'll see myself out.'

'What, you're not going to stay? You always stay, JA,' he said with a pout.

'Not this time. You used me, Jack, made me feel like nothing more than an informant and you hurt my feelings. The last time I stayed, you got what you wanted out of me: sex and a name. This time I willingly gave you a name, but sex is out of the question. See you.'

She left Jack sitting alone on the balcony, nursing his wineglass and a bruised ego.

ABF Offices Brisbane Airport
Friday 6th March

Benson arrived at work early the following day following his sojourn to Airlie Beach and the unnamed bay to the north. His first task was to provide de Vries and Harvey with an overview of his findings aboard the Midnight Express. After completing the briefing, he asked. 'How's our captain doing?'

'Well, I didn't think there was anything else of use he could tell us, so I released him and told him not to try to leave the country again until our investigation was complete. Harvey drove him around to the Seafarer's Mission at the port. He's still listed on the watch list for international departures, so he won't be going anywhere in a hurry,' de Vries confirmed.

'Okay, I have to write up the report on my findings and contact Andrews and see where he's up to with the fingerprint identification.'

'Keep me in the loop, Sam,' instructed de Vries.

Benson logged onto his desktop and opened his MBC email account. To his surprise, there was already an email from Andrews, time dated earlier this morning. He read the contents. "Sam, I need the file set up ASAP so I can upload the fingerprint results." *That was pretty damn fast*, thought Benson. He rang Andrews straight away.

'I thought you would want the results quickly, so I went straight to the office after we landed. I had already rung the techs in Canberra from the airport and asked them if they could stay back for a few hours. When I arrived at the office, I scanned the fingerprint impressions and emailed them immediately. I received their response first thing this morning. Normally it would take at least twenty-four hours for a result, but the quality of the prints was surprisingly excellent, so they worked through the night and expedited the process,' Andrews said proudly.

'That's great news, James. I will set the file up now and then you can upload the results. Give me fifteen minutes and it'll be available for you.'

There was already an investigation file in place, but Benson needed to add the details of their search of the Midnight Express before Andrews could upload his results. He did so immediately and then waited on Andrews. His impatience caused him to click on the refresh button a few times, but nothing had been uploaded. To ease his frustration, he went to the kitchen and made himself a coffee.

'Voila, here it is.' Upon his return, Benson had clicked on the refresh button and was thrilled when he saw Andrew's email with the link to the file included. 'Okay, here we go,' he said to himself.

The fingerprints lifted belonged to two Chinese nationals, Ling Jun and Wang Wei. They are residents of Australia and currently live in Sydney. The two men were in the Australian Border Force database as part of the information sharing relationship the ABF had with state-based police forces, in this case New South Wales. Both had been arrested for minor drug charges in Sydney, and being Chinese nationals, they were included in the ABF database. And, not surprising to Benson, they both had Haymarket addresses listed as their places of residence. Haymarket being the inner-city suburb that encompasses Chinatown. A picture was emerging in Benson's mind.

He walked down the corridor to de Vries' office. 'Come in Sam. What have you got for me?' Benson talked de Vries through the information he had garnered through the fingerprint identification.

'Damian, where have I heard the name Wie Ping Lie?' De Vries reiterated an earlier conversation he'd had with Charlie Romano from their Sydney office and in particular, referenced the potential links to the Chinatown triad group.

'This gets more interesting by the day. I think we need to involve the Feds. We are a civil maritime security and safety authority, but it seems to me that this investigation is becoming land based, and also crosses state borders. In which case we need to involve other agencies, if not hand the entire investigation over to the AFP. I'll call Williamson, discuss it with him and get back to you and Harvey.'

'Harvey, Benson, my office please.' The guys heard the page from de Vries and, as they had done many times previously, made their way along the well-worn carpet to his office.

'Take a seat gents.' They obeyed the instruction and settled in before their boss continued, 'I have spoken to Shane and given him an overview of where our investigation stands at the moment. He agrees that this is obviously a cross border operation, so we now need to involve the Australian Federal Police. And gents, don't get all bitter and twisted if they take over the investigation. Remember, we are a maritime agency.'

'There's an AFP detective who is working on an investigation into an increase in the supply of a higher purity cocaine across the eastern suburbs of Sydney. This may, I emphasise may, be the end market for the product delivered by the Midnight Express. The test results will provide us with a better indication when we receive them, I hope. Harvey, the detective's name is Jack Wagner. Here are his contact details. Maybe give him a call and introduce yourself first and then we can set-up a video conference call with Wagner, Williamson, ourselves and whoever else Wagner involves. Harvey and Benson went back to their workstations and Harvey immediately called the contact number for Jack Wagner. The call went through to voicemail, so he left a detailed message.

'Harvey, Benson, my office please,' came de Vries voice over the in-house intercom ten minutes later.

'What now?' moaned Benson.

The guys headed back down the corridor they had traversed only fifteen minutes earlier. 'I've got some bad news I'm afraid.' De Vries gloomy expression went from Harvey across to Benson and back again. 'Captain Han's body was found yesterday at the Seafarer's Mission.'

'Oh, no,' drawled Harvey. De Vries thought he noticed a slight watering of his eyes. 'What happened, how did he die, boss?' he asked, after a long pause.

'He was stabbed to death as a result of an argument apparently.'

'An *argument*, really? That's bullshit. He was a mild-mannered family man who was just trying to do the best for his wife and children,' Harvey lamented.

'Well, unfortunately he got mixed up in something illegal that probably got him killed.'

'That doesn't sound kosher at all; you interviewed him; he was harmless. Someone was obviously concerned enough about his detention to ensure he didn't get interviewed again. They, whoever they are, murdered him. We should have protected him, boss.'

'Scott, if I had thought he was in danger I would have placed him in protective custody. We didn't know how far this investigation would go, now unfortunately, we do. Anyway, the state police will investigate his death and will keep MBC in the loop. And make sure the AFP are aware of our suspicions surrounding his death as well,' de Vries instructed.

Harvey grumbled all the way back down the corridor. He had liked the captain. And after all, he had confirmed the Midnight Express to them. *And probably died for it,* he thought to himself.

'I liked him too, Scott. I played the bad guy 'cos I had to, but he was an okay guy,' said Benson. 'He didn't deserve to die.'

$$\left(55\right)$$

Milk and Honey Cafe

At a quarter to ten Jack was, for the second time this week, driving his Commodore along New South Head Road in Rose Bay, heading for the Coke and Money Café. His CI had rung him the previous afternoon, supposedly with new information, and given the investigation seemed to have stalled, hopefully temporarily, he had thought, *why not.*

So, here he was once again, slowly, but not too obviously, driving past the café, peering through the windscreen wipers for anything or anyone out of place. Criminal informants weren't an entirely reliable species and they're certainly not competent in the art of detection, so Jack needed to ensure, for both his and Stevie's welfare, that the area was clear. It was pouring with rain and certainly not the weather for the pretty young things to be out jogging or gently lobbing tennis balls across the net.

CIs are extremely common in every-day police work, including homicide and narcotics investigations. Enlisting and managing informants is one of the crucial ways in which law enforcement, and its officers, collect information. It can be a high-risk activity and some cases, if it is not done prudently, people can suffer. Stevie was a low level CI, but Jack still took the appropriate precautions.

Satisfied that the immediate vicinity of the café was clear, he parked his car on the main road, grabbed his umbrella from the passenger side footwell and walked back along the sidewalk to the café. He was early and there was no sign of his snitch, so Jack again made his way through the slippery courtyard, into the café proper and to the rear table. The babbling Milfs were conspicuous by their absence this morning, so he could clearly see the comings and goings of the café.

He noticed his CI crossing the road wearing a tatty bright yellow PVC raincoat. So much for going undetected. Jack ordered two lattes from the attendant waitress. Stevie was smiling as he walked through the café to Jack's table. 'No yummy mummies here today, Mr Wagner.'

'No, they all ran out the back door when they saw you crossing the road.'

'That's very funny, Mr Wagner.'

'Okay, let's cut to the chase; what have you got for me?'

'Well, the latest batch of blow that has hit the leafy streets around here is pretty good gear.'

'How good, Stevie?'

'My sources tell me it's well over forty percent.'

'You told me that last time. Any idea where it comes from and who's distributing it?'

'That hot Chink chick I told you about last time. She's distributing it for the Triads from Chinatown.'

'I already know that, too. This is fast becoming a waste of my time,' Jack said as he rose and made to leave.

'Okay, okay, hold your horses, Mr Wagner.' Jack's CI glanced around the room, before continuing. 'Apparently, after she was threatened by the Lebos, they changed their modus operandi.'

Jack laughed. 'Modus operandi, really. Are you trying to sound like a spy? Come on, get on with it.'

'Alright, alright. The chinks have started up what they're calling a dial-a-dealer operation in the eastern suburbs and the model chick is heading it up.'

'And?'

'She drives a shiny black Honda CRV.'

Jack rolled his eyes. 'Well, that sure as hell narrows it down for me.'

'What's that worth to you?'

'Give me the CRV's registration and I won't shoot you. How's that?'

Stevie looked uncertainly at Jack. 'You're joking, right?' Jack stared blankly back at his CI, but remained silent.

'It's FGL 81H.'

'There you go. That wasn't so hard, was it? Now I don't have to shoot you.'

Stevie laughed nervously in response. 'You're still joking, right?'

Jack leaned forward in his chair. 'Listen to me carefully. It is reasonable to assume that, if this woman is based out of Chinatown, she is working with Wie Ping Lie's crew. You don't want to end up being a snitch in a ditch, so you be careful, okay, Stevie?'

Jack took his wallet out of his pocket and laid two hundred-dollar bills on the table.

'Oh, Mr Wagner, that's hardly fair, a lousy two hundred dollars.'

'It's two hundred dollars and you're still alive to spend it.' Jack winked as he rose from the table and walked towards the exit. He could still hear Stevie grumbling. This time, he paid for the coffees himself as he made his way out.

$$\textcircled{56}$$

AFP Headquarters

Arriving back at his office after meeting with Michelle Ironside the day before, Jack had drafted a letter to the Oceanic Hotel and Casino's Chief Executive Officer on an official AFP letterhead. He had then sent it upstairs to the Deputy Commissioner's office, had it authorised and signed before having it couriered to the Oceanic. The letter requested access to Closed Circuit Television footage from the Bennelong Room and listed the dates coinciding with Li Qiang's previous seven visits and his current period of occupation. He requested a delivery receipt to confirm that the CEO had received the letter and now all he could do was wait.

Subsequent to the meeting with his CI, Jack was now sitting at his desk at AFP Headquarters in Goulburn Street, pondering his next move in the investigation. Chris Coleman hadn't called back and Jack didn't really expect him to for a few days, given the Oceanic weren't required to submit their latest Threshold Transaction Report for another week. He had only discussed the investigation with JA the previous evening, so it was unlikely she would have sourced any new information in the intervening period. And Jack knew he wouldn't receive a response from the Oceanic's CEO until he had spoken to his legal department. He hated this stage of any investigation.

He had forgotten to check his voicemail and sure enough there was the little red icon overlaid on the call button. *Not very professional, Jack.* He listened to the message and was intrigued. It was left earlier that morning by a Scott Harvey from the Maritime Border Command in Brisbane. Jack returned his call.

'Hello, Jack. I imagine you're busy, so I'll be quick.' Harvey provided Jack with a brief overview of their investigation and why they needed to involve the AFP. Jack remained silent throughout while listening intently. 'Essentially, we want to set up a video conference call with all the relevant authorities and network our investigation as a first step. Can you do four o'clock this afternoon?'

'Yeah, that will work fine.'

'Alright, I'll set up the call for four. Feel free to include anyone from your organisation you deem appropriate. I'll send you through the link to the video conferencing app and log in details shortly.'

'Thanks for the heads-up, Scott, it's appreciated.'

There was always a point in every case where a detective would have exhausted all avenues of investigation and was sitting on his hands awaiting new information and responses. Everything was up in the air and all Jack needed was something of consequence to land. *Shit, he hated this.* While he was grumbling to himself, his mobile phone rang. He saw the number on the display but didn't recognise it. 'Jack Wagner,' he answered tersely.

'Detective Wagner, this is Michelle Ironside.' He should have saved her number when she first called two days ago.

'Hello Michelle, how are you?'

'I've been thinking about our conversation yesterday.'

'That's very wise of you, Michelle.'

She picked up on the detective's choice of words. She was right to call. He does know more than he's letting on, or at the very least, what he suspects. 'Can we meet again, detective?'

'Sure, when and where?'

'Today, same place, same time?'

'I'll be there.'

For the second time in two days, Jack was walking along the Jones Bay Wharf looking for signs of anyone who didn't belong. While scanning the area for threats, he marvelled at the millions of dollars in luxury launches that were tied up in their pens. How many of these boats were purchased with dirty money? Michelle Ironside would probably know some of the owners, given the casino wasn't too far from here. He hoped she realised the gravity of her situation and would reveal details of her involvement in the money laundering. This would escalate his investigation, which in turn, could also potentially expose her to danger. He would have to be increasingly vigilant and alert, which was exactly what he was being now. He was early again and as usual sat with his back to the rear wall and facing the entry.

For the second time in as many days, Michelle entered the café hesitantly and look around the room. She would recognise him this time, so her obvious reconnaissance told Jack that she was extremely nervous. She spotted him and walked across to his table.

'Hello, Michelle.'

'Hello, Detective Wagner.' She took her seat and remained quiet for a few moments. Jack guessed she was still gathering her thoughts, so he remained silent and gave her some headspace.

'I'm really not sure where to start, detective,' she sighed.

'Take your time.'

She sighed again. 'A few days ago, I noticed something that concerned me. A senior executive within the hotel and casino acted in a suspicious manner within the Treasury Office...' Michelle then explained to Jack what had occurred throughout the evening, including her cash and chip reconciliation and discovery of the discrepancies.

'I didn't want the particular person to be investigated, and potentially have his career destroyed without definitive proof. I also wanted to provide him with an opportunity to remedy the situation if I was correct in my assumptions.'

'It's a male executive then?'

She continued without confirming his deduction. 'I contacted the person and arranged a meeting to explain my concerns and afford him the opportunity to provide his own explanation. The meeting was here, just outside on the pier, actually.'

'And how did that go?' asked Jack, guessing what the response would be.

'Not very well I'm afraid.'

'Do you want to tell me his name?'

'In good time.' Michelle paused again, tapping her finger against her coffee in a staccato beat. 'He threatened me,' she said at last, her face pale.

'What did he say exactly?'

'He said, "my and career and life as I know it would be over".'

'Okay, it's time, Michelle. Who threatened you? And how would he be able to achieve that? How do you know it wasn't a bluff?'

'Why should I give you his name, detective? How does that help me with my predicament?'

'Maybe it doesn't and that's a risk you need to consider. But, Michelle, I promise I will do everything within my power to bring the person in question to justice. If I achieve that, then hopefully it will mitigate your involvement in the eyes of your employer.'

She looked around the café and Jack assumed she was using the time to reach a decision. Eventually, she turned back to Jack and sighed. 'Mr Woodard. The Vice President of Client Services you enquired about yesterday.' Michelle gave Jack the abbreviated version of what Woodard had said. 'In short, he said he would just say that I was conveniently absent at a prearranged time and that I was well-rewarded for my timely absence.'

'He would blackmail you?'

'Yes, I guess you could call it that,' she surmised. 'In my twenty-five years of working life, and most certainly over the past decade at Oceanic, I have never, ever been dishonest, never mind being involved with criminal activity, Detective Wagner. This situation is not of my making, but I could lose my career at Oceanic over it.'

'How so, Michelle?'

'I was a fool thinking Mr Woodard would do the right thing. I should have reported what I discovered immediately, and now it's too late.' Jack had completely changed his opinion of Michelle in the space of twenty-four hours. He believed her when she said she was trying to do the right thing by Woodard.

'Who do you think he laundered the money for?'

'I don't really know.'

Sensing she was avoiding giving him a name he raised an eyebrow. 'Take a well-educated guess.'

She sighed again. 'Mr Li Qiang. He's a high roller that frequents the Bennelong Room.'

'I know who he is Michelle; we discussed him yesterday if you remember. Would it surprise you if I told you that Mr Li has stayed at the Oceanic eleven times and yet his monetary transactions seem to be inconsistent with his activities? He initially appeared on the casino's Austrac TTR Report six times, as would be appropriate covering two transactions on each of his three initial visits. On his subsequent seven visits the only transactions that appear are his EFT transfer at the end of each gambling session. There is no record showing how he obtained the gaming chips in the first place. Do you have a theory regarding how that would be possible? And please don't tell me again how he could have conducted the exchange downstairs on the main casino floor.'

She sat quietly, looking down at the table while considering her response. 'Yes, I just realised what you're insinuating. It's obvious really, given what we just discussed.'

'Yes, my guess is that Mr Woodard has been conducting transactions for Mr Li behind your back and probably during periods of your absence from the Treasury Office. And, I'm deducing he has done that at least seven times in the past twelve to eighteen months. I will certainly find out,' Jack said doggedly.

Michelle was fiddling with her necklace. 'I'm so embarrassed. I don't know how I could have missed noticing that. I need to get to work if you don't have anything else for me.'

'No, that's all for now, Michelle. Thank you for contacting me. I'll be in touch.'

'Do I need protection, Detective?'

'If you notice anything suspicious, call me straight away and have someone walk you to your cab every night.'

(57)

MBC / AFP Conference Call

At four o'clock that afternoon the invited participants logged in to the scheduled video conference call. There was Williamson calling in from Canberra, de Vries, Harvey and Benson from Brisbane, all representing Maritime Border Command. Jack and John Robertson, the Deputy Commissioner from the AFP, were seated in the AFP's Sydney Head Office conference room along with Charlie Romano from MBC Sydney. A representative from Australian Border Force and Detectives Michael Sanderson and Nathan Billingsley from Day Street Police Station in Chinatown were also connected to the call.

The MBC's report had been distributed to all participants prior to the call, but Jack hadn't had time to read it after his meeting with Michelle Ironside. Williamson assumed the chair and provided an overview of the case to date. 'Before we continue, you should all be aware that the Captain Han mentioned in the report was found deceased yesterday. He died of stab wounds inflicted at the Seafarer's Mission at the Port of Brisbane. You should also know that Harvey and Benson don't think this was an accident and the Queensland state police are now investigating.'

Harvey jumped in. 'Whoever is involved with this drug smuggling operation couldn't afford to let the captain be questioned by us again.

Ironically, the sad thing is, he had already provided us with the very little information he had, so he died for nothing. And the Cape York found the Midnight Express anyway. I want to get these bastards, gents.'

Jack finished reading the report provided by Williamson and addressed the group for the first time and provided a summary of his own investigation. 'I actually have two separate investigations running concurrently and with the information provided by MBC, I think they might be linked. To explain, the two guys you identified from the Midnight Express have links to Wie Ping Lie, a Triad leader here in Sydney. A supply of higher purity cocaine has hit the streets in the eastern suburbs. A CI of mine thinks it is linked to the Chinatown based Triad headed up by Wie. My CI also gave me details of a vehicle that is registered to one of your Midnight Express guys. Apparently, according to him, an attractive woman of Asian appearance has been using it for her deliveries.'

'Hi, this is Michael Sanderson in Sydney. We oversee the Haymarket and Chinatown precincts. 'The woman you mentioned is probably the elusive Lucie Chan; she is known to us, but we've never had sufficient evidence of her activities to arrest her.' Jack knew Sanderson was the typical hard-nosed cop that would be assigned to Chinatown. Conversely, from their shared experience out on the high seas it was clear that Sanderson still had the enthusiasm for the job.

Damian de Vries spoke for the first time. 'Back to the coke. We have received the laboratory results back on Benson's sample from the Midnight Express. I can confirm that it is forty-three percent pure which, as you would know, is a higher grade than usually found on the street. Unfortunately, we have been unable to identify the source of the product.'

'Thanks, Damian.' Jack continued. 'My second investigation centres around money laundering where Wie is a known associate of my key suspect. I believe the profits from the sale of this particular cocaine are being laundered at the Oceanic by a Li Qiang, my primary target in the investigation. As a priority, I think we should place Li Qiang, Wie Ping Lie and the two Chinese nationals on the Movement Alert List. If this investigation develops quickly, they may want to make a run for the sanctuary of their home country, and we should be prepared for that. The ABF officer asked for the details of all four men to be sent to him this afternoon and he would have them duly listed on the MAL.

It was pretty clear to Harvey and Benson that Wagner and Sanderson were going to assume control of this investigation from hereon in. They didn't like it, but were resigned to the fact. Williamson summarised the meeting and echoed their thoughts. 'This investigation appears to be Sydney centric, so I'm not sure if MBC can contribute much more to the case at the moment. I would, however, like Charlie Romano involved in interviewing the two Chinese nationals. We still need to know the intricacies of the drug smuggling operation and we may want to initiate charges of our own. If we receive any further information relative to the death of the good captain, of course we'll pass it on immediately.

'It appears that way, Shane, and I think Michael and I should take it from here. 'Michael, can Charlie and I catch-up with you later this evening and hatch a strategy for going forward? I'm only around the corner in Goulburn Street, so I'll come to you if that works.'

'About five-thirty would work for me, Jack, if that suits you?'

'A moment if you will please gents, interrupted DC John Robertson. There is something else you all need to consider while working this investigation. The cases of COVID-19 are on the increase across the country, which will inevitably lead to lockdowns being imposed at some point in the near future. That being the case, business as usual will be severely curtailed, so we need to expedite this case as a priority. We're on the clock, gents.'

Jack, Michael Sanderson and Charlie Romano walked into an empty interview room at the Day Street Police Station on the western edge of Chinatown. 'Very salubrious, Michael.' The ten by eight room with muted grey walls and no window contained a cheap metal table, three chairs a working air conditioner and not much else. 'No carpet?' Jack asked looking down at the tiled floor.

'Not with the late night drunks we have in here, Jack.'

'Good move.'

Sanderson continued. 'Before you start, Jack. I called a colleague of mine at Queensland Police and had him conduct a search in the QPRIME database for our two Chinese nationals. It seems that Ling Jun was pulled over in Proserpine on Sunday night for a minor traffic infringement.'

'Jesus, really. I thought Williamson said they had arranged for roadblocks to be set up in Proserpine and Mackay.'

'Well, somehow they evaded them.'

'That could have been just the stroke of luck we needed, too, Michael.'

'They should be back in Sydney by now.'

Jack raised his hand. 'Maybe not if they were involved in the demise of Captain Han yesterday. Ling and Wang had plenty of time to stop off in Brisbane on their way home.'

'If that's true, then they should be back in Sydney tonight or tomorrow, so I think Billingsley and I should round them up and bring them in for questioning. If nothing else, that will stir up Chinatown and we might learn something from the fallout,' Sanderson suggested.

'While you're rounding them up, you should keep an eye out for Lucie Chan. Given we know that she's been a target for the incumbent dealers, she might be looking for a way out and that could work in our favour.'

'I wouldn't count on it. I hear she's a tough, street-smart cookie, that one.'

'Can one of you also check with the ABF guy and ensure our four suspects have been added to the MAL?' Jack asked. 'We should add our girl Lucie to the list, as well.'

'I know the guy through various joint investigations we have conducted, so I'll do that,' offered Romano.

'What do we do about Wie Ping Lie for the moment; if anything guys?'

Sanderson jumped back in. 'Jack, I don't think we can move on him until we get these two guys talking. Wie will find out about their arrest soon enough, so I'll have one of my undercover guys keep an eye on him and see how he reacts. That sound okay?'

'Yep, and remember, we're on the clock now gents.'

(**58**)

Melissa's Townhouse

It was another balmy evening, so Julie-Anne opted to wear a casual lightweight dress. She selected one of her favourites, a white daybreak dress with silver sequined overlay, frilled hem and scooped neckline. The look was complemented by a pair of white strappy sandals. She felt like summer itself, even though it was now officially autumn.

She pressed the button on the wall and heard chimes sounding inside the townhouse.

While she waited she thought back to the cocktail party of two nights ago and her seismic reaction to Melissa's kiss. She still didn't understand her feelings from the night. Yet here she was at Melissa's.

After a moment, the door opened to reveal Melissa welcoming her wearing a skimpy bright red string bikini.

'Hi, welcome to my humble home,' Melissa said enthusiastically.

'Hey. Why do I suddenly feel overdressed?' Julie-Anne glanced down at her dress. Melissa had looked stunning in the body- hugging red midi two nights ago, but she looked hot enough to melt the Antarctic tonight.

'Oh, don't mind me, I was just getting the last of the evening sun on the deck, which luckily for me, faces west. Come in and I'll put that in the fridge and get us a glass of bubbles.'

Melissa's townhouse was stylish and modern, with combinations of dark charcoal greys, bluish hues, trendy blacks and the vitality of peach, wood, and beige accents. 'I love your design, it's so chic. And the transparent screens that separate the different areas, Melissa. There is so much natural light. I love it,' she gushed, and Melissa's cheeks flushed.

'I think we have about fifteen minutes until the sun dips behind the Blue Mountains, so let's go out onto the deck and make the most of it shall we?' The women walked through the living room and out into fading the sunshine.

'My God, you've got a pool too.'

'Well, it's more like a large spa, but it suits me. It's only seven metres long, but if I do enough laps it adds up to a reasonable workout.' The women sat down on the poolside lounges.

'Cheers, Julie-Anne, good to see you,' toasted Melissa, raising her glass.

'You too, Melissa, I love this place.'

'The area has developed quite a lot since I moved in, but once I arrive home I'm in my own private little sanctuary.'

'Sanctuary alright. I almost feel like I am immersed in a jungle out here. Look at those palms guarding the corners.'

'They're Kentias. They were about four feet high when I bought them and now they've grown well above the fence line. Why don't we jump in and have a quick swim before dinner?'

'I'll pass for now. I'm happy to just sit here, feel the warmth of the sun and enjoy the bubbles.'

'Okay, enjoy. I'll be back in a minute.' And with that, Melissa stood up, placed her drink on the side table, shallow dived into the pool and proceeded to swim a few laps. Afterwards, she propped her elbows against the side of the pool and the women chatted easily until dusk arrived.

'How is your elbow?' Julie-Anne asked with a wry smile.

'Good as gold. Those jerks got what they deserved,' Melissa replied, her eyes sparkling.

'I know. What's the world coming to if a couple of women can't even have a night out without being hassled by egotistic men who confuse their ambitions with their capabilities.'

'Maybe we should consider ourselves lucky; in some parts of the world where they have these archaic laws and misogynistic practices, we wouldn't be able to have a night out together at all. And we'd be stoned for any public displays of affection, that's for certain,' said Melissa. 'That was just wonderful. I needed that,' she said as she exited the pool. To Julie-Anne's amazement, Melissa then unclipped her top, untied the bottom of her bikini and dropped them both to the deck. Julie-Anne felt her face flushing, but not from discomfort. She wasn't even slightly embarrassed, quite the opposite, she felt something stirring inside her again as she was confronted with Melissa's naked body. She looked sexy as, with her wet hair dripping over her shoulders and across her firm, rounded breasts and her smooth caramel skin glowing from the light reflecting off the pool.

'Can you reach that towel behind you, please?'

'Sure, here you go.'

'I'll just get dressed quickly, check on dinner and then I'll be back. I think you'll love what I have in store for you,' she said playfully. *She's flirting again,* thought Julie-Anne.

While Melissa was away, Julie-Anne took the time to think about her friendship with Melissa and what lay ahead for both of them. Why had something stirred inside her when she had undressed in front of her? This was a completely new sensation for her. She chuckled to herself when she thought about *foreign affairs* again. Contrasting that, she knew she had to have the Li conversation tonight and find out what the nature of the relationship was between the two of them. Julie-Anne was certain it had something to do with her investigation. And she thought the impending exchange just might spoil the night and ruin their newfound friendship.

'Okay, dinner's up,' Melissa called out. She had changed into a white floral patterned summer dress of her own and wore strappy turquoise sandals. When Julie-Anne walked back inside, she was placing a large platter on the dining table.

'Wow, what have we got here? This looks like a challenge, Melissa.'

'Well, I hope you're okay at assembling your own Peking Duck Pancakes. It's nice and casual and I thought it might be fun. I cheated and bought the pancakes from the local Asian grocery but they're still light and fluffy. I did cook the duck and make the sauce from scratch though. Oh, and I also bought the spring onions and cucumber myself.'

'Haha, too funny,' chuckled Julie-Anne. 'I was going to bring my favourite sauvignon blanc but at the last minute I changed my mind and grabbed a pinot. The sav blanc simply wouldn't have worked with the duck.'

'Cheers, Julie-Anne.'

'What, no ganbei?'

'No, and damn that horrible, repugnant little man, too.'

Julie-Anne picked up on the vehemence of that remark and thought, *okay that's my lead.*

'Cheers, Melissa and thank you for inviting me.' The women clinked glasses. 'You seem angry at the reference to Li. I'm guessing there's some history between you guys,' she asked while trying to roll up her pancake.

'God no, and certainly no history like that.'

'I wasn't inferring anything, but you criticised him at the cocktail party and now the implied mention of him has made you angry, that's all I'm saying.'

Melissa sipped her wine. 'There's no history other than recent, really. He contacted me earlier in the week and asked to meet. I didn't know him before that. We met at a café down the road in Burwood and he put an interesting proposition to me.' Julie-Anne was listening intently now. 'I was an elected member of the local council in Burwood for many years and had harboured an ambition to maybe one day enter state or federal politics. And Li's proposition presented me with an opportunity to potentially achieve exactly that.'

'That sounds very exciting. You must be pleased.'

'Yeah, I should be, but I have concerns over the integrity of Li and his backers.'

'In what way?' Julie-Anne was trying not to appear overly curious, but this was becoming interesting.

'Well, I would be running as an independent candidate and therefore wouldn't have access to the significant resources of the major political parties. Li has guaranteed the financial support from himself and a mysterious Chinese businessman and the Consul General's staff would provide administrative support.'

Julie-Anne was slightly puzzled. 'So what are your concerns?'

'As you would know, political donations are a hot topic these days. All donations need to be in accordance with the state's new political disclosure and donation laws. As such, all financial contributions need to stand-up to scrutiny by the New South Wales Electoral Commission, and I have concerns about that. The other issue is the involvement of the Consul General. With all the negative publicity surrounding China's poor human rights and environmental record, their annexation of nearly everything in the South China Sea, buying favours through their Belt and Road initiative and their ongoing interference in Australian life, I fear they will pressure me to do their lobbying for them. And I just won't be a puppet for anyone, let alone a foreign power. I would want to represent all my constituents equally and fairly. I'm quite excited by the opportunity, but those concerns temper my enthusiasm somewhat. So that's my dilemma, Julie-Anne.'

'Wow, you've certainly got something to think about.'

'I know. How are you coping compiling your duck pancakes?'

'Yeah, good actually, they're very tasty and I love the freshness added by the spring onion and cucumber.'

'Enough about me. What are you working on?' Melissa enquired as she topped up their wineglasses.

Okay, here we go, thought Julie-Anne anxiously. 'Well, I'm not sure where to start. I've been working on an investigation for a few days now and things are moving slower than I would like.'

'What's the nature of the investigation?'

'It's a hotchpotch of issues really. Money laundering, drug trafficking, gambling and political interference. I haven't been able to link them yet, but I think it's all centred around Chinatown.'

'Well, that's topical.'

'More than you know.' Julie-Anne replied as she returned Melissa's gaze.

'What do you mean by that?' Melissa asked, her lips pursing. She'd picked up on the intimation. Julie-Anne sipped her wine. 'Julie-Anne, what do you mean?' Melissa asked again, her tone sharper this time.

Julie-Anne took a deep breath. 'I think Li Qiang is involved.'

'What?' Melissa cried.

'I'm really sorry,' Julie-Anne could see her eyes misting and she leaned across and placed her hand on Melissa's.

After composing herself, Melissa spoke. 'How do you know? Are you certain?'

'No, not yet.'

'Well, what *do* you know then?' Melissa demanded.

'As I alluded to earlier, nothing definitive yet. I had heard rumours on the street regarding the illegal activities I told you about earlier, so I started investigating. I wasn't making much headway, then I received an anonymous phone call from a woman who told me about Li Qiang. I did my research and I identified your Li Qiang as a tentative suspect in my investigation.'

'And let me guess; that's how you ended up at the cocktail party,' Melissa said.

'Yes. I thought I had made the connection between Li and the Consul General through a photo I found online, so I went to the cocktail party to see what I could find out. I didn't learn anything new, but then you and Li went off for your private meeting. Later, when we were at the wine bar you made it clear you were no fan of

Li's. I think you called him a lecherous, corpulent little man if I'm not mistaken.'

'Yes, I did, and he is just that.'

Julie-Anne continued. 'So, I was thinking, if this woman doesn't like the guy, why were they meeting in the first place? And now I know. I should also add that I had lunch with Li yesterday.'

'Oh fuck, the hits keep on coming,' blurted Melissa, throwing her arms in the air.

'Listen to me,' Julie-Anne said, reaching her hand out to place it on Melissa's arm. 'Somehow he found out exactly where I work and he also got my mobile number. That's scary enough, but I thought I could potentially glean some new information from him, so I thought, why not, I can do lunch.'

'So, what exactly did you glean?' Melissa asked, keeping up the sarcasm.

'A couple of things. He said that you and he are working on an important project and he wouldn't like to have that undermined. And secondly, he is not too enamoured about you having an investigative journalist for a friend and is suspicious of the reasons behind our friendship.'

'He's not the only one.'

Julie-Anne remained calm. 'Oh, come on, Melissa, you drove our friendship right from the very beginning. It was your idea to go for a drink after the obvious flirting at the cocktail party. *You* kissed me at the wine bar, and *you* suggested I invite you into my apartment. And it was *you* who opened up to me about your thoughts on Li. I never once probed you for information.'

Melissa scowled. 'So, Julie-Anne, does having dinner with me tonight constitute part of your investigation, too?'

'Melissa, please, of course it doesn't. Anyway, you invited me remember? I was pleased when you asked me to dinner as I was sincerely hoping it would provide me with the opportunity to do exactly what we are doing now: talking about it.'

'Do you have any more surprises for me?'

Julie-Anne thought about her conversation with Jack last night and his separate investigation. If she told Melissa now, it might be a bridge too far, but if she didn't open up, then she would be deceitful. 'No. I think that's enough drama for now,' she responded, artfully dodging answering the question.

'I feel like I'm in a haze after that revelation and I really need to clear my head. I'm going to swim a few more laps. I always feel relaxed afterwards, which I most definitely need right now.'

'Okay, I'll head-off then,' Julie-Anne offered.

'No, don't go. I'd rather not be alone right now.'

(**59**)

Melissa's Townhouse

Julie-Anne sipped her pinot as Melissa walked out onto the deck. She had quickly grown fond of Melissa and felt sad that her disclosures had brought on her current bout of despondency. She would make it right. Melissa reached down to the hem of her summer dress, pulled it up over her shoulders and placed it on the lounge. She was naked again except for the sandals. For the third time tonight, Julie-Anne found herself admiring Melissa's figure, her body glowing as the reflected pool lights washed over her again.

Julie-Anne took her glass of wine out onto the deck, sat on one of the lounges, and gazed admiringly at Melissa's form as it glided up and down the pool. She was chilling out to the smooth jazz mix wafting out from the deck's speakers and became lost in her thoughts while Melissa swam. She was right to have the Li conversation, and open up about her investigation and she was pleased to now have it out in the open. Melissa was intelligent, fun, articulate, obviously successful, and an attractive woman. She thought they were kindred spirits of sorts and she very much enjoyed her company. For that reason alone, she felt sad at being the cause of the gloom that had overcome her. She hoped the swim was the panacea she needed.

Still lost in her thoughts, she hadn't noticed that Melissa had finished her laps and was now leaning on her elbows, propped against the side of the pool again. 'Come for a swim Julie-Anne, it's invigorating in here,' she asked, appearing to have perked up now.

Julie-Anne was comfortable in her own skin and quite liked her own body. 'Sure, why not.' She put her wineglass on the patio table and rose from the lounge. Kicking off her sandals, she grasped the hem of her dress, lifted it high up over her head and placed it on the pool lounge. She eased out of her French knickers and walked down the steps into the sparkling waters of the pool.

'Now, that's what I call a golden tan,' Melissa commented. Julie-Anne had laid out on Jack's balcony numerous times to get her share of the sunshine vitamin and had finished up with a nice, even colour. 'We almost look like sisters, except for the obvious.'

Julie-Anne glided and frolicked herself for a while then joined Melissa who was still propped against the side of the pool.

'I always feel sooo much better after a swim. It relaxes the muscles, soothes the body and for some reason, clears my head, Julie-Anne. My frame of mind has improved immeasurably.'

'I'm glad. I felt sad at being responsible for your unhappiness.'

'It's not entirely your fault. I should have conducted my own research and due diligence on Li earlier, but everything seemed to be happening so quickly. I haven't found the time, but I should have made the time. I'm usually better than that.'

'Don't be so hard on yourself; it's only been a few days at most.' Then Julie-Anne took Melissa by the arms, turned her towards herself, wrapped her arms around Melissa's waist and gently pulled her into an embrace. Melissa rested her head against Julie-Anne's shoulder, released a contented sigh and remained there silent. After a while, she lifted her head and looked at Julie-Anne.

'It's been like a roller coaster of emotions these last few days. You know, the excitement of potentially going back into politics, having to deal with those guys outside the bar, my concern about Li and his friends, your revelations tonight and of course, meeting you.'

'That's a lot to deal with and think about in a short space of time.'

'And I'm glad you didn't leave.' Melissa put one hand on the nape of Julie-Anne's neck, the other on the small of her back, leaned in with her leg and pulled her into a tight embrace, their bodies now melded as one. The kiss was long, deep and passionate. Julie-Anne pulled back, turned Melissa's body around, leaned into her arched back, softly cupped her breasts and nuzzled her neck.

'What's the music?' Julie-Anne whispered.

'It's a smooth jazz chillout compilation that I found online; I love it.' The women swayed back and forth in silence.

Julie-Anne whispered. 'This could be complicated.'

Melissa burst out laughing at the reference to the classic movie line. 'This is all new for me,' she replied.

'And for me too.'

'No raincheck?' Melissa asked, cheekily.

Julie-Anne smiled. 'Not tonight. Take me to bed or lose me forever.'

The women were lying in bed, their bodies entwined, merrily chatting away and enjoying the warmth of the morning sun peeping through the curtains. 'You know I couldn't take my eyes off you earlier.'

'Really? When, Melissa?'

'When you were getting undressed by the pool and you lifted your arms over your head. I just went, *wow*. You looked magnificent, like a bronzed goddess. And I love your navel ring with that cute little dolphin,' she said, admiring the gleam of the stud in the soft light of the bedroom.

'Thank you, that's lovely, but you're embarrassing me. I might be guilty of the same.'

'When?'

'After your pre-dinner swim when you undressed and dropped your bikini to the ground right in front of me. Your wet body was gleaming and glistening in the light and I felt something stirring inside me. I knew at that precise moment I wanted to stay.' Melissa rolled over on top of Julie-Anne, kissed her enthusiastically and then slowly slithered down beneath the sheet.

The women were having coffee on the deck, enjoying the morning sunshine and discussing their day ahead. 'Was it really that obvious?' Asked Melissa, darting a shy glance at Julie-Anne from beneath her lashes.

'Was what so obvious?' Julie-Anne asked, puzzled.

'My flirting.'

'Well, maybe just a little.' They laughed, and she kissed Melissa's cheek. 'Okay, time to go,' Julie-Anne said as the laughter subsided.

'Can you please drop me in Burwood on your way?'

'Of course.'

Melissa set her house alarm, closed the front door and the women walked across the road to Julie-Anne's BMW. As she was driving down Burwood Road, Julie-Anne asked. 'Did you notice that black Subaru Impreza with the tinted windows that was parked down the street from your townhouse?'

'What's an Impreza?'

'Don't take this the wrong way, but it's a very fast car seemingly favoured by young Asian gangsters.'

'No, I didn't. Why?' Melissa was wondering where this conversation was heading.

'The Impreza is now two cars behind us; we're being tailed.' Julie-Anne didn't bother trying to lose their pursuer. Whoever it was surely wouldn't try any sort of intervention in such a populated area. She also knew she could never outrun the Impreza, even in her Beemer, so what was the point trying?

'How do you know about this stuff?'

'I'll tell you one day, Melissa.'

The Impreza made the rookie mistake of getting too close and Julie-Anne could read the number plate clearly in the rear vision mirror. She dropped Melissa off at her office in Burwood and then headed back northwards to the M4 Motorway and on into the city.

She should probably call Jack, especially after he expressed his concerns about Wie Ping Lie. Julie-Anne didn't know why someone was following her or even if she was the target. The tail was now gone, so maybe it was Melissa they were following in which case it might have no connection to her or Jack's investigation at all. She had a contact in the New South Wales Police Force, so she would instead call him first and then decide what to do next.

Julie-Anne's Desk
Saturday 7th March

Due to the traffic jam on the M4 Julie-Anne arrived at her office later than usual. *A traffic jam on a Saturday, really.* Of course, the lie-in with Melissa hadn't helped matters either. *What a lovely way to start the day,* she mused. Her first task for the day was to find out who had staked out Melissa's place and had tailed them earlier that morning. She dialled Harry Gorman's number. Harry was head of the state's Financial Crimes Squad and Julie-Anne had met him when they were both investigating corporate fraud and their cases had coincided. He was a hard- working, honest cop and she respected him enormously. Harry was also exceptionally good at his job; you didn't get to be the head of FCS without earning your stripes.

'Harry Gorman.'

'Hi Harry, it's Julie-Anne. How the heck are you?'

'Better for hearing from you darlin', how are you?' Harry was ten years her senior and had been immensely helpful in the past so she let him get away with calling her darlin'. They had a quick catch-up on what each other had been doing since they last spoke.

'Okay, now what can I do for you, darlin'?'

'Harry, I need a favour please. I was followed leaving a friend's place this morning.'

'Where were you?'

'I was driving a friend to work from Canada Bay to Burwood.'

'How do you know you were followed?'

'A black Subaru Impreza with tinted windows was parked outside my friend's house when we went out to my car. Then I noticed it following close behind me a couple of kilometres later.'

'Did you get the registration number?'

'Yes, he followed too closely at one stage and I was lucky enough to get a glance at his plate.'

'Okay, recite it to me and I'll see what I can find out.' She did so, and Harry confirmed the details back to her.

'I know you're not supposed to conduct unofficial investigations, so I am incredibly grateful for this Harry,' she said.

'We need to have a catch-up. Are you okay for dinner one night darlin'?'

She knew Harry liked the idea of more than just friendship with her and had asked her on a date once under the pretence of catching up. She had politely declined. *Surely not again. My private life's complicated enough already.*

'I've been working late most nights, so you might have to settle for coffee or lunch if I can find the time. I'll call you next time I'm heading out to Parramatta.'

'Darlin', what are you involved in this time that would cause you to be followed?'

'Nothing serious. I'll tell you over coffee, Harry.'

'Okay, I'll get back to you.'

Right, what's next on my list? After her lunch with Li yesterday, she had become curious to find out more about his associate Wie Ping Lie. She opened up her web browser, went to Google and typed in his name.

Julie-Anne heard the ringtone of her mobile phone and saw Harry

Gorman's name listed as the incoming caller. 'Hi, Harry, that was darn quick.'

'Yeah, I know, darlin', but I am even more concerned about your welfare now.'

'Why, what have you found?'

'The person who followed you is a man named Fan Chen and I'll save you the trouble of researching him. He is a cultural attaché at the Chinese Consulate here in Sydney.'

'You're kidding!' Julie-Anne said more as an exclamation than a question.

'What have you got yourself involved in this time, Julie-Anne?' He only called her by her given name when he was serious.

'I'm really not sure yet.'

'Well you'd better work it out soon. You know what a Cultural Attaché typically is don't you?'

'Yes, I do. It can be a pseudonym for something far more sinister. Thanks, I appreciate it.'

'You know you can call me anytime, so don't hold back if you have any further concerns.'

'I won't, I promise. Thanks heaps as always, Harry.'

Julie-Anne disconnected the call and went to her whiteboard to review what little hard information she had. She was a long way from completing her investigative puzzle and she required more pieces to insert before she had a clearer picture of what was occurring. Even with Li's implied threats, the car parked outside Melissa's, and then being tailed, the whole scenario could possibly be related to Melissa and not her at all. Julie-Anne surmised that no political party of any persuasion would relish the thought of their candidate having an investigative journalist as a friend. If she was being watched and tailed by a Consular Attaché, then it was reasonable to assume that the Consul General must be involved as well. If he and Li were involved in illicit activities as she suspected, then they certainly wouldn't want her anywhere near their candidate. And if she required any proof of that, it wasn't long in arriving.

Julie-Anne's desk phone rang. *The desk phone never rang.* 'Julie-Anne.'

'I have an envelope here at reception for you. Would you like me to bring it up?'

'Yes, please, I'm in the middle of something.'

Two minutes later, one of the receptionists arrived and handed her the envelope. 'It arrived by motorbike courier a few minutes ago.'

'Okay, thanks.' She sat down at her desk and unpicked the A5 sized envelope. She put her hand inside the envelope, slid out the white sheet of thick paper and flipped it over.

'Oh fuck!' she exclaimed. A colleague called out asking if she was okay. *'No, I'm not,'* she roared, more to herself than him. It was a photo of her and Melissa at the QV Wine Bar and not just any photo. Those in the paparazzi industry would call it the money shot; the journalist and politician entangled in a passionate embrace. Julie-Anne felt her cheeks burn as she studied it. Researching Wie Ping Lie would have to go on the back burner for now. She needed to compose herself, and quickly. She took a few long, deep breaths, loudly exhaling each time. She called reception.

'This is Julie-Anne. Did you see the courier who just delivered my envelope by any chance?'

'Yes, why?'

'Is he one of our regular couriers? Do you know him?'

'No, I've never seen him before.'

'Describe him.'

'He was just a courier, Julie-Anne. Black leathers, helmet under his arm, smartly groomed for a courier.'

'Any logos visible?'

'Not that I saw.'

Julie-Anne paced up and down in front of her whiteboard. 'Did you see his vehicle?'

'No, but that's not unusual.'

'I'll decide what's unusual,' Julie-Anne retorted. 'Appearance?'

'I don't know nationalities very well and he was wearing dark sunglasses, but I think he was of Asian appearance.'

'Did you sign for the delivery?'

'Now I think of it, no. Oddly, he never had any paperwork.'

'Thanks.'

Julie-Anne's morning had begun so beautifully at Melissa's, but had gone to shit ever since; and it wasn't even lunchtime. She had been tailed by a probable Chinese agent, assumed that it must have been sanctioned by the Consul General, who is obviously complicit with Li. Now the inherent threat implied by the compromising photo was clear. *What a morning; my world's just been turned upside down.*

She gathered her composure, went back to her whiteboard and added what she had learned this morning. She then linked the characters by lines, like an organizational chart.

Now, who did she talk to first? Her editor, Chris Russell, had told her to keep him in the loop. He wouldn't be happy about her *going off the reservation* as he liked to phrase it. Oh well, it's easier to beg for forgiveness than seek permission. Did she call Harry back and have that coffee sooner rather than later? Maybe she should call Jack; after all, he had warned her to be careful around these guys and the new information could assist his own investigation. And what about Melissa? She would be horrified, and if the photo made it into the public domain, then her potential career in state politics was over, if it wasn't already. She didn't deserve that.

Julie-Anne was so deep in thought she didn't even hear her phone ringing.

Absentmindedly, she picked up her mobile and eventually noticed the name of the caller. 'Oh no,' she groaned. She paused for what seemed like an eternity then swiped right.

'Hi, Melissa.'

'Do you know what's just happened to me, Julie-Anne?' she asked in a soft, faltering voice.

'I can guess, but tell me anyway.' Melissa started to speak, but Julie-

Anne could tell she was struggling, so she interrupted her. 'I received one as well.'

Melissa then seemed to compose herself somewhat. 'Oh, no, not you too.'

'Yep.' Both women were now sniffling and spent moments consoling one another. 'Melissa, we shouldn't talk about this on the phone. Come over to my place tonight and we can discuss it properly. I might have more information by then. I'll text you my address. Try and remain calm; we will work this out.' Julie-Anne then blew her a comforting kiss. 'Mwah.'

The aim of the photo was obviously to intimidate Melissa and get her to end her friendship with Julie-Anne. Or vice versa. Either way, Julie-Anne wasn't going to let that happen without putting up one hell of a fight. She had been an investigative journalist for nearly a decade and knew her way around the streets, but the subtle intimidation by Li, the Cultural Attaché and not so subtly, through the photo, did give her reason for pause. She called Jack.

'Jack, we need to talk,' she said relegating the pleasantries to the bench.

'Yeah, we do. You surprised me when you left the other night.'

'No, about our investigation,' she said, shutting down his personal thoughts.

'Oh, okay.'

Julie-Anne started pacing again. 'A few things have happened that you need to know about.'

'Well, come over tonight and we can workshop what we know.'

'I can't, I have a prior commitment.'

'You've been quite busy lately, JA,' he complained.

'Comes with the territory, I guess,' she said, avoiding his insinuation.

'Tomorrow night then?'

'No, it can't wait, Jack. Where are you now?' she demanded.

He picked up on the urgency in her voice. 'Not far from the city.'

'Alright, can I meet you at that café in Crown Street around the corner from my office? The Rogue Café I think.'

'Yeah, alright, give me half an hour,' he said, in an exasperated tone.

This was going to be a difficult conversation to have with Jack. Their liaison was fun, but it wasn't going anywhere, she had finally decided and neither of them was twenty-five anymore. They had been dating for six months, but how long does one date before it should become a relationship? *Not six months, that's for sure.* In the absence of any commitment, they were both focused on their respective careers, or vice versa. Maybe that was just an excuse. Julie-Anne thought she could commit to Jack, but he wasn't showing any signs of feeling the same way. As a result their catchups were spasmodic and usually spontaneous. And now Melissa had come along; talk about spontaneous. This *could* be complicated. But, for now her focus needed to remain on the investigation.

(**61**)

Rogue Café Surry Hills

Julie-Anne walked into the Rogue Café exactly half an hour later. Jack was already there seated at a rear table in the courtyard with his back to the wall. Yep, once a copper…

'Good choice of table, Jack, nice and quiet and we won't be overheard.'

'Hello to you too, JA.'

She offered a weak smile. 'Sorry, hi. My mind is overloaded at the moment.'

'I guessed that by the sound of your voice on the phone and the short notice. What's up?'

'It's a long and complicated story, but I'll give you the short version. Either way, I think it will add some fuel to your investigation.'

'Okay, go on.'

'Alright.' She breathed deeply and exhaled. 'I mentioned the other night over dinner that Li had made veiled threats and tried to intimidate me about my friendship with Melissa Wu. Well, I think I now know why Li is so concerned. Apparently, he and some mysterious backers want Melissa to be their political candidate and champion their causes in the New South Wales parliament.' Jack was listening intently now. 'The Chinese Consul General is involved too.

If he and Li are involved in illicit activities as I suspect, then they certainly wouldn't want an investigative journalist anywhere near Melissa. And I also suspect that the money Li is laundering through Oceanic is the source of funding to support Melissa's political campaign. There's the potential link to your investigation, Jack.'

'This gets more interesting every day.'

'I haven't finished.'

'Okay, go on.'

'Melissa and I have become quite close in the past few days.' She looked directly at Jack, so he knew where this was going and waited for his reaction.

He looked apprehensive. 'How close, JA?'

'I drove her to work this morning.'

'Well, that's certainly taken the wind out of my sails.'

'It shouldn't, but that's beside the point, Jack,' she said, stopping the conversation from getting personal. 'Anyway, as we went out into the street to my car, I noticed a black Impreza with tinted windows parked further down the street.'

After her revelation, Jack was trying his darndest to keep his detective head on. 'Where was this?'

'Melissa's townhouse in Canada Bay. Then, as I was driving down Burwood Road I detected the Impreza in the rear vision mirror.'

'Burwood Road's terribly busy and there aren't that many roads leading out of Canada Bay. It could have had a legitimate reason for being there.'

'There's more, Jack. I made a mental note of the Impreza's registration and had a friend check it for me. Are you ready for the kicker?' Jack had quickly cast aside his concerns about their personal relationship as JA's story unfolded.

'The Impreza is registered to a Fan Chen. He is a Cultural Attaché with the Chinese Consulate here in Sydney.'

'Oh, shit,' he blurted out too loudly. 'Are you certain?'

'Yep, and you better than anyone understand the nefarious activities that Cultural Attachés can become involved in.'

'Yes, I do, and it seems your Mr Li wasn't bluffing with his veiled threats and it also suggests the Consul General has to be aware of his activities, if not complicit himself. You need to be very careful, JA; this could escalate very quickly and turn nasty. *If only you knew how right you are,* she thought.

'So, where do we go from here?' she asked.

'What are you referring to?'

'Our investigation. Stay on track, Jack.'

'Oh, okay. Well, I need to accelerate my investigation into Li's Bennelong Room activities.' Jack then brought her up to date with the new information provided by Michelle Ironside yesterday.

'You're kidding. The Vice President—Client Services is laundering money on behalf of Li. There's another link.'

'Keep your voice down, JA. You never know who might have followed you here as well.

And, while it sounds extremely plausible, the information provided by Michelle is a long way from being evidential. I need to get my hands on their CCTV footage ASAP and then I might take a run at the Vice President, if the footage is as definitive as I think it will be. And we both know that the Oceanic will stall releasing those tapes for as long as possible. They will want to avoid, at all costs, being implicated in a money laundering scandal. Not only will it scar their reputation, but there will be a mass exodus of high rollers to other casinos around the country, which will savage their profits. They won't let that happen.'

'What about their statutory reporting requirements, Jack? They would be a matter of public record, although we might have to lodge an FOI application to access them,' she queried.

'I am waiting on the TTR Report for Li's last transactions. Depending on what is included or excluded in that report, I might be able to go harder at the Oceanic's CEO. As for Michelle Ironside, she is a decent person that faces potential criminal charges and loss of her career, so I want to find a way to extricate her from this mess, unscathed if possible. And, just to keep you in the loop, I have a name for one of the dealers peddling the cocaine around the eastern suburbs.'

'That's good news.'

'It will be if I can find her and bring her in for questioning. And, just so you know, she is a known associate of Wie Ping Lie. Do you remember I mentioned him yesterday and advised you to be careful around him?'

'Yeah, thanks, I will, Jack. So, do we think the money Li is laundering is his share of the profits from the coke sales linked to Wie Ping Lie?'

'Obviously we have no proof, but you did link them together from your lunch with Li, so my guess would be yes. If Li's money wasn't illegally earned there would be no requirement to launder it.'

'Okay, let's assume that for now and proceed on that basis.'

Jack was silent and appeared deep in thought. 'Do you want to talk about you and Melissa, you and me?' he asked awkwardly.

She heaved a sigh. 'No, not really. There will be plenty of time for reflection after we close this investigation out.' Julie-Anne was good at compartmentalising competing issues and would have no trouble keeping their investigation separate from whatever was or wasn't transpiring between them personally. She hoped she could be just as clear and strong with Melissa. 'Thanks for coming, Jack. I hope that piece of intelligence helps your own investigation. I'll see you later.' She rose and walked out through the courtyard.

'Don't forget to be careful,' he called out as she walked away.

After her meeting with Jack, Julie-Anne went back to her office and continued her research. She typed G into her browser and of course it again took her straight to Google. Then she typed in Fan Chen, Fan Chen Sydney, Fan Chen Chinese Consulate, even Fan Chen Subaru Impreza, all to no avail. Next, she typed in Chinese Consulate Sydney and opened up their webpage.

The Chinese Consul General in Sydney is concerned about the decision of the NSW Department of Education to end its Confucius Institute program blah, blah, blah. Okay, I've read that already; nothing new here, although it would explain why Li, and Xiao for that matter, are so keen to get Melissa into state politics and have a voice inside the parliament. And of course, isolating Julie-Anne would be a necessary part of the process.

Next she researched Michelle Ironside. She thought that with such a distinctive surname, any information on her would stand out, and it did. One whole link to her LinkedIn account which highlighted her Oceanic career and a couple of administrative roles prior to that. *Oh well, at least I know what she looks like.* She then Googled Tony Woodard and didn't find much information on him either other than his own LinkedIn account. She scrolled down through his posts and saw a photo of him and his wife, Bree, attending a function. *Let's check you out, honey.* Julie-Anne opened up Facebook and logged in. She typed Bree Woodard into the search box and up she popped, top of a short list. No private account for this woman. She clicked on photos of which there was an overabundance and had a quick scan. Trophy shots, Julie-Anne called them, not seeing anything posted of human interest at all. 'Let's have a closer look shall we.' She mumbled.

A few recent photos showed her being handed the keys to her new BMW X5. She must have attended a couple of fancy functions as there were two shots of her wearing full length Jadore gowns. *They're not cheap,* sneered Julie-Anne. Photos dated the previous year showed two boys wearing Trinity Grammar uniforms standing next to their beaming mother. She quickly searched "expensive private schools Sydney" and sure enough, there was Trinity Grammar, fifth on the list with fees topping over thirty thousand dollars a year per student.

She kept scrolling down. The next batch seemed to be focused on a new townhouse overlooking the Parramatta River at Chiswick. These photos highlighted the river views, pool deck and spacious living areas and Bree Woodard was pictured in every one of them. Mingled amongst the remaining photos were shots of her on numerous holidays abroad, including two at the exclusive Turtle

Island in Fiji. In all of them she was overtly posing in various skimpy, revealing bikinis that showed-off her trim figure. In one of them she was beaming as the photographer, which Julie-Anne assumed wasn't her husband, had captured her posing between two tall, tanned lifeguards. An image of this woman was starting to form in Julie-Anne's mind—self- absorbed and high-maintenance.

Okay, I get the trophy wife, and in return, she gets to live the life of comfort without having to worry about something as trivial as a job. Sure enough, there was no mention of a job in her profile and very few of the photos showed or even mentioned the husband. Julie-Anne logged into Instagram and searched Bree Woodard on that platform. More of the same self-aggrandisement from this narcissistic woman, and again Tony Woodard was conspicuous by his absence. The high-maintenance wife seemed to like to show off the trimmings provided by her husband on social media without affording him any recognition at all. *That would make for interesting conversation over the dinner table.* And where did she think the money was coming from to pay for her extravagant, hedonistic lifestyle? Julie-Anne knew the answer and wondered whether the wife ever asked herself the same question.

Other than some background and confirmation that the Woodard family appeared to be living beyond their means, she hadn't learnt anything that aided her investigation. *Back to the drawing board.*

$$\left(\textbf{62}\right)$$

Macquarie Suite

It was early afternoon and Li Qiang was relaxing on his sofa, again with his obligatory Glenlivet and Monte Christo in hand, when the doorbell rang. He walked over to the door and checked the peephole to see who his visitor was. A solidly built, well-dressed Asian man with a military style haircut was waiting. Li opened the door and welcomed him into the suite.

'Were you noticed by anyone on your way up here?'

'No, I used the swipe card you gave me to access the service entrance and freight elevator like you told me, Mr Li.'

'Good, that was necessary; take a seat and tell me what has transpired since you received your instructions from the Consul General.'

'I followed the targets as instructed and they went to a bar in Surry Hills. I managed to get a seat in a corner of the bar where I could observe them without being too obvious. Later in the evening, they engaged in some kissing. Luckily for me, the bartender turned his back at that moment. I quickly rested my phone on the bar behind my drink, zoomed in and took the photos.'

'Are you certain you weren't observed by anyone?'

'Yes, very sure, Mr Li.'

'And have the photos been delivered?' Li asked, eagerly.

'Yes, to both women this morning.'

'Good, well done, Chen. What else do you have for me?'

'The reporter visited Miss Wu at her house last evening. She stayed the night.'

This wasn't what Li wanted to hear. 'How do you know such a thing?'

'I watched over Miss Wu's house all night and saw them leave together this morning.'

'Lā shǐ,' blurted Li.

'I followed them for some time. The reporter dropped Miss Wu at her office, and I stopped following after that.'

'Did they notice you?'

'No, I've done this before, Mr Li.'

'Okay, I have a couple of things I would like you to do for me. Now that they have received the photos, they will want to discuss the possible repercussions. The women will realise the implications now and won't discuss them over the phone. They will be upset, so will want to meet again very soon, probably tonight, so I want to know where and when they meet. Miss Wu will be the most nervous as she has the most to lose, so I would follow her. If we're fortunate, we'll find out where Ms Granger lives as well and that will be very interesting to know for future reference. If you discover Ms Granger's address maybe you could leave her a calling card, as the Westerners like to say. Now, how is the Consul General lately, Chen?'

'I think he is troubled about our activities with Miss Wu and the reporter woman, Mr Li.'

'He will be more concerned about the future of our candidate if we can't separate them, permanently.'

'If there is nothing else, I will wait for Miss Wu's next move.'

'I don't think the Consul General realises the repercussions of those two women becoming friends, so you will take your directions from me from now on; is that clear?'

'Yes, Mr Li.'

'And, well done, Chen.'

Li wasn't unduly concerned about the Consul General as he could be marginalised easily enough. He only needed him to provide human resources and administrative support for his potential political candidate anyway. Given Miss Wu's recent activities though, it was becoming increasingly clear to him that she may not be that candidate.

For the first time since his arrival back in Sydney, he had no commitments for the rest of the afternoon or that evening and he knew exactly how he would spend that time. He went into the bedroom, undressed and then put on his favourite bathrobe. He returned to the living room, made his way to the liquor cabinet where he poured himself another whiskey and then retreated to the sofa. Li clipped and primed another Monte Christo and then took a long draw, savouring the flavour. Now momentarily content he dialled the number for Kaili Wang.

An hour later, Sophie strode across the hotel's foyer and into a waiting elevator. As she depressed the button for the thirty-eighth floor, she was feeling anything but confident. Even though she was well rewarded by this vile little man, she would extricate herself from this situation in a heartbeat, if she could. As the elevator rose towards the penthouse, she was reminded of the promise she had made to herself many visits ago. Somehow, no matter what, she promised herself this would be the last time she visited the penthouse.

Sophie rang the doorbell to announce her arrival and then let herself into the suite with her swipe card. She wasn't surprised at all to see Li lounging on the sofa in his favourite bathrobe, whiskey and cigar in hand. She was disgusted at what lay ahead of her, but she would compartmentalise as usual and get on with it. Sophie drew strength from the commitment she reminded herself of in the elevator.

'Kaili Wang, good to see you again.'

Stay calm, he's goading you, she willed herself. 'You, too, Mr Li. How are you?' Sophie wasn't staying a minute longer than she needed to, so she placed her handbag on the coffee table, lifted her faux leather black mini dress over her head and stood before him in her Christian Louboutin black patent leather pumps. He rose from the sofa, unlooped the belt of his bathrobe and allowed it to fall loosely to the carpet.

'Come over here, Kaili?' Sophie started to walk towards the opposite end of the vast sofa. 'No, not over there, here,' he said as he patted the sofa next to himself. She hesitantly walked towards his end of the sofa and stood in front of him.

'You have wonderfully full breasts; most unusual for a woman of Asian descent. Surprisingly, that's the second time I have witnessed that little phenomena this week.' Li chuckled as he stood and placed his hands on them.

Sophie wasn't sure which was the more repugnant. The racist implication or his inappropriate behaviour. 'No touching, Li,' she said firmly, taking a step backwards.

'It's Mr Li to you and I'll do whatever I want with you, Kaili Wang.' Sophie had never been touched like that by him and with her current resolute mindset, she wasn't about to let it happen now. She couldn't believe her good fortune when the ringtone of a mobile phone broke the impasse.

'Stay there, I'll be back,' he barked as he walked to the kitchen bench to retrieve his phone. Sophie wasn't about to stand there naked for however long, so she put her dress back on and sat down on the sofa.

'Hello.' Sophie could only hear one side of the conversation, but she was listening intently for anything she might be able use against him or tell the lady journalist. She was surprised that Li hadn't left the room to take the call.

'Yes, everything is on track with the current consignment.'

'Yes, the next instalment should be available in a few days to further finance our cause.'

'The usual, about one million dollars.'

'I don't know.'

Sophie could hear the voice on the other end of the call now yelling. 'I have tried everything to locate Captain Han,' Li responded defensively as he paced up and down the suite.

'Of course it's my business. That will bring unwanted attention upon us.'

Li sighed in resignation. 'Certainly master.' He disconnected the call and turned to Sophie. 'You can go, Kaili Wang; I now have more important things to attend to. Take the envelope on the table. Now go.'

Sophie exited the suite and was thinking hard about the memory training she undertook to help her with her university studies. She needed to apply the principles now, so she could accurately recall the one-sided conversation.

Li picked up his burner phone. 'Wie, it seems we still can't locate Captain Han and I am concerned if he falls into the wrong hands that could be dangerous for us.'

'You should not concern yourself with that matter any longer.'

Li frowned. 'Well, I am concerned.'

'I said, you shouldn't be,' Wie replied threateningly. 'After being detained a second time ,he was eventually released and that's where you and Xiao lost him. I imagine he was prevented from leaving the country. It seems the authorities weren't clever enough to place him in protective custody; rather he was staying at the Seafarer's Mission at the Port of Brisbane. My associates told me he was found dead two days ago.'

'How do you know this, Wie?'

'Unlike someone else I know, I don't leave things to chance,' he responded.

'Are you saying what I think you are?'

'I'm not saying anything and better you don't ask again,' he warned.

63

Julie-Anne's Apartment Newtown

The shock of receiving the compromising photo had dissipated after her meeting with Jack and following her research earlier this afternoon. Julie-Anne didn't ascertain anything new, but what she learnt about the attention seeking Bree Woodard's expensive tastes certainly confirmed Jack's suspicions about why her husband would be conducting illicit activities. She made herself a Sapphire and Tonic, sat outside on her own little balcony and reflected on the day's roller coaster of events. Primarily, she was thinking about how much of what she learned she should tell Melissa. If she told her the truth as she suspected it, then that will be the end of her political ambitions, certainly for now anyway. If she didn't tell her, then she might continue to pursue a career in state politics, completely unaware of the unscrupulous nature of the people who would fund and support her campaign. And, depending how deeply she got involved, she may not be able to extricate herself. And probably not without exposing herself to danger either. Her thoughts were interrupted by a knock on the front door. *Decision time, Julie-Anne.*

'Hi Melissa, you look spectacular as always.' She was wearing a light blue floral printed sleeveless flowing dress that highlighted her complexion. The women hugged, air kissed and then made their way into the small living area.

'Don't mind me. After the day I've had, I wanted my gin and tonic before I thought about anything else. Julie-Anne was still dressed from work. She had worn jeans, a striped #metoo tee shirt under a navy linen jacket and half boots.

'Would you like one of these? I'm having another.'

'Yes, please, I could do with one too.'

The women sat out on the balcony and chatted aimlessly for a few minutes, both obviously avoiding the elephant in the room. 'Beautiful photo, Melissa.' Julie-Anne burst into laughter as she said it.

'In any other circumstance, I would have loved it.'

'Sorry, I was just making light of it for the moment.'

'Yeah, I know,' Melissa replied soberly.

Earlier, while processing her thoughts out on the balcony, Julie-Anne had decided she was going to reveal to Melissa everything that she had learned in her investigation that related directly to her. She wouldn't mention Ironside or Woodard by name at this stage as that could compromise Jack's investigation if Melissa somehow used that information. 'Melissa, I have been thinking long and hard about what to tell you and how it might impact you.'

Melissa's eyes widened. 'What do you mean by that?'

'I've been worried about you in light of what I have discovered these past few hours.'

'The photo was bad enough; what else do you have?'

Julie-Anne leaned forward, laid her hands on Melissa's and spoke softly. 'Let me lay out what I know and then you can ask anything you like, okay?'

'Sorry, go on.' Julie-Anne told her about Fan Chen, his Consular role and what the title Cultural Attaché usually implied, the obvious link to the Consul General, the Asian courier and what that might suggest, Li's link to a casino employee and finally her thoughts on the money laundering. And for the first time she mentioned her suspicions about Wie Ping Lie. Julie-Anne was careful not to mention the Oceanic by name, but there were only two casinos in Sydney, so Melissa could discern that for herself.

'Okay, that's it, everything I can tell you.'

'Geez, Julie-Anne, don't water it down will you!'

'Let's take this inside if you're going to yell and scream.'

'And what do you mean, "everything I can tell you"? What else do you know that you're holding back?' Melissa ranted as she rose and stormed back inside to the living area. The women sat side by side on the sofa half facing each other.

'Look, Melissa, this is not easy for me either you know. I care about you and I am balancing that against my responsibilities to a wider investigation that I'm a part of.'

'What wider investigation?' Melissa asked with suspicion.

'There's an AFP detective I have worked a couple of cases with that is conducting an official investigation parallel to mine. We agreed to share information, join forces if you will, so hopefully he can make a case for prosecution and I will get my exclusive story.'

'You have history with this detective, don't you?'

Where did that come from? Julie-Anne pondered. But she opted for honesty. 'Yes, we do.'

'I don't know much about investigations, but I am a lawyer and I've never known a detective to share information with an investigative journalist. That's a no-go zone for him. Unless he had ulterior motives, or maybe you do for that matter.'

'Stop it, Melissa. Look, let's just park that for now and I'll come back to it later, I promise.'

Melissa's nostrils flared. 'Why not? You seem to have parked everything else up to now.'

'This investigation has only gathered pace in the past twenty-four hours, so most of this is new for me too, Melissa. One day ago, we didn't conclusively know about Li's money laundering and the involvement of casino staff. That came from Jack today,' she clarified.

'Okay, now I have a name for your suitor.'

'Give it a rest, please?' Julie-Anne pleaded, sighing with exasperation. 'And if you and I weren't tailed this morning, we wouldn't have found out about the potential involvement of the Consul General, as tenuous as his connection might seem at the moment. And Li obviously has a relationship with Wie Ping Lie, judging by the intense nature of their interaction at lunch the other day. Jack also told me that Wie is the head of a Chinatown based Triad group. They are not people to be messed with.'

'Geez, Julie-Anne. It seems my career in state politics has disappeared before I have even accepted their invitation. Even with the potential uncertainty surrounding Li and his cronies, I still remained hopeful, and a little excited, that a suitable deal could be reached, and my candidacy could progress. That's gone out the window given your revelations just now. I hadn't given Li a definitive answer anyway, but it's a no-brainer now. My candidacy and funding arrangements would never survive scrutiny or probity checks. It's over.'

Julie-Anne noticed Melissa's eyes starting to water, so she leaned forward and pulled her into a hug. Melissa nestled into Julie-Anne's chest and sniffled. It was some time until Melissa spoke again. Once composed, she lifted her head and sat upright against the back of the sofa. 'So, what are they trying to achieve with their intimidation, Julie-Anne?'

'I'm not absolutely certain it's me they're targeting directly, but I am sure they want me out of the picture. Given their illicit activities, those same ones that were going to fund your campaign, you wouldn't have to be Einstein, or Confucius for that matter, to realise they don't want you being involved with an investigative journalist. I'm fairly confident the photo sent to you was just to coerce you into ending our friendship. Not so subtle blackmail really.'

'Are we involved, Julie-Anne?'

'I have become fond of you very quickly, I loved our time together last night and this morning, wow, but it's a little early to be labelling anything, Melissa. We need to have this investigation resolved ASAP and get some clear air before we can consider anything else.' Julie-Anne then realised she had said the same thing to Jack earlier today. Was she hedging her bets? She didn't think so, but subconsciously, maybe she was. 'In the meantime, we need to make every effort to ensure our personal safety and security and devise a plan.'

'So, tell me about Jack.'

'Oh God, where to start? Essentially, we have been dating for about six months.' Julie-Anne looked at Melissa for a reaction to her use of the present tense. 'I first noticed him at a crime scene and was taken by his charm, good looks and how he carried himself, until I realised he was a cop. I have encountered quite a few policemen through my investigative work, and as a result, I decided long ago to avoid them like the plague. Anyway, one night I was in a bar near work and there were a few policemen there, both state and federal, including the guy I had seen at the crime scene. Then surprisingly, he came up to me, introduced himself and said he remembered me from that particular crime scene I mentioned. He then proceeded to make a mockery of everything I thought policemen were. He was a funny, entertaining and an interesting guy, anything but stereotypical. So, fast forward six months, we are still dating, but our contact is intermittent and there's no commitment on the horizon. We have our highs and lows as does any couple but I guess what goes up must come down.' She paused waiting for Melissa's reaction.

When there wasn't one, she continued.

'Look, Jack is a good guy, but like many men, he craves validation from their careers. Even in this day and age, and I think that's even more prevalent with law enforcement officers. That being the case, there's not a lot of wriggle room for a girlfriend. I don't think Jack rates high on the emotional intelligence scale, or if he does, I see very little evidence of it. He's just a fun guy, when I get to spend time with him, of course. But if a relationship doesn't help you grow, then don't water it. Anyway, I call myself his STG.'

Melissa shrugged. 'Some Time Girlfriend.'

'Do you love him, Julie-Anne?' Melissa felt a twinge of insecurity kicking in.

'Yes, in a way. But what manner of love it is, I have no idea. I think it's more like *"I love you dearly"* than *"I'm in love"*, if that makes sense.'

'Yeah, I think I get it. So, where to for you and Jack now?'

'I have no idea. But I did mention you in a round-about way when we met earlier today.'

'What did you say?' *This will be interesting,* Melissa thought.

'I told him we were followed from your place this morning and he was smart enough to connect the dots.'

'So, I'm guessing having a detective for a boyfriend is the reason you knew we were being followed this morning.'

'Yeah, that and having spent many years as an investigative journalist. Anyway, it's quite bizarre how things changed so quickly. One minute Jack and I were together and then seemingly, we weren't. And while we're discussing partners, you're quite the catch. So, what's your story?'

'I guess I'm a little like Jack, really. Only in that I've been quite vocationally focused for most of my adult life. Like many Asian fathers, mine wanted me to have a professional career and inevitably pushed me to do a law degree, which I dutifully completed.'

Julie-Anne realised they had never discussed Melissa's career. 'What do you specialise in as a lawyer?'

'Social justice. I like advocating for the rights of the less fortunate who are on the wrong side of society and suffer disadvantage. I think that legal action that supports social justice and human rights makes for a better society.'

'It's a wonderful pursuit, Melissa, but there aren't too many wealthy social justice warriors out there.'

'Yes, I know, but I championed a class action a few years ago and that helped considerably, especially in allowing me to purchase the townhouse.'

'Any relationships worth talking about?'

'A couple. One guy in particular was sweet and we dated for a few weeks but eventually my career lessened the amount of time I had available to devote to our friendship. The timing was just so unfortunate, Julie-Anne. I met him about the time I became a Burwood Councillor, so between that new undertaking and my social justice lawyering, there wasn't much spare time to dedicate to him.'

'So, why the flirting?' Julie-Anne was smiling now.

'I'm not certain, actually. I love my home and the sanctuary it provides, I am no longer a councillor, so have more time for me, and the excitement of a potential career in state politics was great for my ego, so, I guess I was in a wonderful headspace for the first time in ages. And, of course, I walked into the Consul General's cocktail party and spied this tall, glamourous, outrageously sexy woman standing out from the B-List not-so luminaries.'

'And then you looked around and saw me.'

'That's very funny.'

'I just crack myself up sometimes. And, of course, you knew all along what the DFAT acronym was, didn't you?'

'Guilty as charged.'

Once the laughter had dissipated, Melissa's expression turned reflective. 'Look, just so you know, I have never flirted with a woman and I have certainly never considered the idea of being intimate with a woman. It was just never on the radar. Having said that, the minute I walked into the cocktail party and noticed you, I was instantly attracted to you.'

'Ditto, Melissa, my heart skipped a little beat, too. And just so you also know, the reason I was dressed seductively that night was to ensure I garnered Li's attention, nothing else. I would never normally dress like that for a formal cocktail party. And, if I was in a serious, committed relationship, I would never have allowed you to flirt with me either. But I'm glad I did.'

Melissa leant forward and rested her hands on Julie-Anne's. 'You don't have to explain anything to me; we're both grown women and I'm sure we know what we're doing.'

'Speaking of which, did you like me leading you into your little flirt with my foreign affairs reference? And, with comedic timing, you ran with it.'

'Guilty as charged again, your honour.' Melissa picked up a dessert spoon and pretended to bang a gavel on the table.

'That sounds hilarious coming from a lawyer.'

Melissa gazed into Julie-Anne's eyes. 'Are you going to invite me to stay?'

'Where have I heard that before? It would be better if you stayed here anyway. I doubt if Li or Fan Chen know where I live, so you should be safe here. Let's go to bed and discuss foreign affairs, shall we?'

Sydney Daily News
Sunday 8th March

'Are you okay to get a cab, Melissa? I'm going in the other direction and after yesterday's episode you might be safer without me driving you anyway,' Julie-Anne said light heartedly.

'Yeah, I'm all good and thanks for the informative chat last night and for allowing me to stay. It was lovely.'

'Yes, it was. Let me see you to your cab, Erin.'

'Erin. Who's Erin?'

'Haven't you seen the film Erin Brockovich? You know, the one about the Californian social justice warrior.'

'Oh, my God yes, that's hilarious.' Melissa opened the front door.

Julie-Anne was just grabbing her handbag and keys off the kitchen bench when she heard Melissa gasp. 'What is it?' she called out as she rushed to the front door.

Melissa was standing with her back pressed against the opposite wall, one hand over her mouth, and the other pointing at the door. An evocative photo showing the two women naked from the waist up and in an enthusiastic embrace in Melissa's pool was pinned to the front of the door. 'Oh, shit,' said Julie-Anne. If she thought the previous intimidatory photo was the money shot, then this would be a cash bonanza.

'That would be an understatement,' said Melissa now regaining her composure. 'What did I say about my private little sanctuary? So much for that,' she lamented.

'Unless Li and his cronies knew where I live you must have been followed here last night, Melissa.'

'I don't have your detective mindset and I was so distracted by what had occurred that I didn't even think to check and see if the cab was being followed. I'm so sorry.'

'I doubt it would have made any difference anyway.' Julie-Anne said, trying to avoid any blame game. 'They're obviously going to continue the intimidation, but as long as it doesn't escalate we should be fine.'

'I'm not going to wait for it to *escalate*. I'm going to do something about it myself. It's time to confront Li.'

'And what, pray tell, are you going to tell him? Stop following me, stop taking pictures of me, stop intimidating me, stop what, Melissa? You don't even know for certain if it's him behind any of this.'

'Well, I can't just sit back and do nothing, now can I?' she seethed.

'Yes, you can. I'll be damned if I'm going to allow them to intimidate me in my own home though. I have some ammunition of my own and it's time to return fire,' Julie-Anne said with a steely resolve. 'You should stay here at my place for a while. They know where I live anyway, so what does it matter, and we can keep an eye out for each other. I intend to speak to my editor today about some security precautions anyway.'

'Thanks, I would feel safer with company too, Julie-Anne.'

'Let me show you a little trick I do. Julie-Anne pulled out a strand of her hair, wedged it between the door and the jamb and pulled the door firmly. 'Always do this when you leave and of course check that it's still in place each time you return. If by some chance it's not, then don't open the door, leave the building and call me straight away.'

'You're good at this detective stuff.'

'Not good enough it seems. Here, take the spare key and I'll see you tonight.'

Julie-Anne drove along King Street and then took the back way via Cleveland and Crown Streets to her office in Surry Hills. She hadn't been to the gym for a few days, so she used her long legs to bound up the fire stairs three at a time to her third-floor office. 'What are you doing here on a Sunday, boss?' Her editor, Chris Russell was seated at a bench overlooking Crown Street reading his own paper.

'I could ask you the same thing, JA. As a matter of fact, I will. I've missed you the past few days, so I could do with an update.'

'Where to start, Chris?' she replied, sighing while walking across to him.

'Well, the last time you came to the editorial meeting you didn't have a whole lot to share, so something's obviously changed.'

Julie-Anne spent the next half an hour walking Russell through the timeline of events that had occurred since their last meeting. He was on her team, so there wasn't much point leaving anything out. She gave him the warts and all version as she knew it thus far. 'There you have it, Chris. That's everything I know. So, what do we do now?' she asked, showing her exasperation.

'We're in the newspaper business, so I would like nothing more than to authorise you to write the first part of your story, but I have a few concerns. Firstly, and most importantly, in light of what's transpired in the past twenty-four hours, we need to consider your personal safety.

Next, the story won't hold up to the inevitable scrutiny unless we publish the names of those involved. And finally, I am concerned if we publish what we have now that could force the players to head underground. If that were to happen, the official investigation will inevitably stall, as will ours. We would then have no follow-up story, which would be embarrassing for the Daily News. And, also importantly, we would put ourselves offside with the official investigation, resulting in the federal and state police forces avoiding any future cooperation with us.'

'I agree entirely and I don't think anyone else has the story anyway, so we can afford to hold off until we have something more conclusive.'

'So, where to next, Julie-Anne?'

'Well, I can't do much until Jack has more information, so I'm in a holding pattern really.' She wasn't about to tell her boss about the little piece of subtle intimidation of her own that she was planning. 'I'll update Jack on what I have and see if he's made anymore headway. Other than that, we can't move forward at the moment, as frustrating as that is.'

'We need to provide you with some protection, JA. I'll talk to security and get back to you with a plan. Anyway, isn't your boyfriend a detective; can't he help?'

'Did I leave out the part about my sleepover in Canada Bay or are you choosing to ignore that, boss?'

'Good point. I'll talk to security.'

Julie-Anne went back to her office and stared at her whiteboard. *Okay, what have we got now?*

(**65**)

Oceanic Security Control

Jack had just arrived at his desk and was pondering the next step in his investigation. It had ground to a halt while he awaited a response to his request from the Oceanic. He really was at a loss what to do next when his mobile rang. Jim Brennan. Jack was hopeful that Brennan was going to say what he wanted to hear, but he wouldn't get ahead of himself just yet.

'You requested access to CCTV footage from the Bennelong Room.'

'Yes, I did.'

'Well, apparently the CEO has run your request past our legal team, and while no-one's ever happy about releasing CCTV footage to external parties, they have agreed that we should support your request on this particular occasion.'

'That's great news.'

'Okay, hold up for a minute buddy; there's a few things you need to know.'

Here come the qualifications, Jack mused.

'Firstly, an authorised officer within the AFP will have to sign a disclaimer confirming that the information provided will not be made available for public consumption without prior approval of the Oceanic. They have agreed that, should legal proceedings be instigated as a direct result of the evidence provided by the footage in question, they will not unreasonably withhold their approval.'

'I'll have to get our own in-house legal team to approve that clause prior to signing, but it sounds fair to me. What else do I need to know?'

'There will be a delay of a day or so while we isolate the footage by the date parameters you identified. It would be impossible for you to undertake that doozy of a task yourself buddy.'

Jack was nodding at the phone. 'Yeah, I can live with that; what's the next condition? I assume there's more than two.'

'You will need to review the footage on-site here at the casino.'

'Why?'

'The casino values the privacy of their clients and won't allow the entire catalogue of footage to be removed from the security of this site.'

'Oh shit, come on—'

Brennan interrupted Jack. 'Hold your horses. If you identify footage that is specific to your investigation we will load that selection onto a USB for you to take with you.'

'That'll work for me. Can you call me when the footage is available for viewing?'

'Will do.'

There was nothing else Jack could accomplish until he had reviewed the Bennelong Room's CCTV footage. He was hopeful he would be able to start that process sometime tomorrow. In the meantime, with no other active investigations pending, he now had the rest of the day to himself. He thought about ringing JA and asking her for lunch, but after her revelations about her new friend Melissa, he dismissed that idea. Suddenly, while thinking about the Bennelong Room activities of a few nights ago, he remembered Danielle, his sexy, flirtatious dance partner. Should he ring her? *'Shit, did I even get her number?'* he mumbled, reaching for his mobile. He scrolled through his contacts and was delighted to see her name listed. He laughed as he saw her name, Danielle Clone. While the phone was ringing Jack was thinking, *do I really want to do this?* Then he thought about JA and her new friend and thought, *oh why not?*

'Hi, Danielle, this is Jack. How are you?'

'Jack?'

'Yes, from a few nights ago. We met in the Bennelong Room and then you took me dancing.'

'Is that what you were doing, dancing?' she mocked playfully.

'They were some of my best moves.'

'I was just teasing you. Hello, Mr Rare Breed, how are you?'

'Yeah, I'm all good, thanks. Look, I know this is short notice, but I now have the rest of the day to myself and wondered what you're up to.'

'Not much really. I've been working a lot lately, so I was just chilling and enjoying a rare day off. What did you have in mind, Mr Rare Breed?'

'Maybe a nice long lunch by the water somewhere. Do you like seafood?'

'I love it, can you hear me drooling?'

'Okay, what about North Bondi Fish at two o'clock. They serve an impressive fish curry and the views across Bondi Beach are superb.'

'Sounds fabulous.'

'See you there.'

Danielle had been hoping to hear from Jack but she thought calling him would have been too brazen. She was looking forward to seeing him again too. This should be fun, she thought, and interesting.

(66)

Chinese Consulate General

'Yes, Mei?'

'Mr Xiao, a letter has arrived for you by courier. Would you like me to bring it in to you?'

'No, you deal with it.'

'Of course, thank you.'

The intercom rang again. 'Yes, Mei?' Xiao said more tersely this time.

'Mr Xiao, can I see you please?'

'Yes, come in now.' Mei Kwong knocked on Xiao's door, entered and made her way across the vast office to his desk. 'What is it, Mei?'

'This was what the envelope contained, Mr Xiao. I don't know what to do with them.' Xiao placed the papers he was studying down on the desk.

'Do with what, Mei?'

'These photos, Mr Xiao.' His assistant handed over the photos and watched as the colour drained from the Consul General's face. 'Are you okay, Mr Xiao?'

'Yes, I'm fine, that will be all, Mei. Leave,' he ordered.

Xiao was staring at the collection of photos. One was a photo of him and Li Qiang, obviously taken at the recent cocktail party he hosted.

The second was Li and Xiao dining at the Golden Phoenix and the third one was a photo of Li Qiang and another man. Li was seated at a table also in the Golden Phoenix talking to a man standing across from him. The man standing was Wie Ping Lie and he appeared to be menacing Li. Each photo viewed independently didn't amount to anything controversial. But, when viewed together, the inference would quickly be drawn that the Consul General was one degree of separation away from the head of the Chinatown based Triad. Now that would definitely amount to something, and not something that would be at all beneficial to himself or his cherished diplomatic career. The final photo was the clincher. It depicted Xiao, Li and Wie Ping Lie standing together, also taken in the Golden Phoenix. There was no accompanying message sent with the photos, but to Xiao it was clear what the inherent intent of the message was. And he didn't need to be Confucius to work that out. Someone was linking him directly to Wie Ping Lie, and that couldn't be allowed to continue.

He rang Li on his burner phone.

'Why are you calling me, Xiao? You know this phone is to be used only in an emergency.'

'Well, I think this qualifies.' Xiao told Li about the photos that were delivered a few minutes ago and the potential implications for the three of them if they were released publicly. 'Yes, I clearly understand the implications.'

'What have you got me involved in? This could have a disastrous effect and ruin my diplomatic career.'

'Don't be so melodramatic. You know very well what we are involved in, Xiao. You have chosen to ignore the obvious as long as you got a candidate elected to the New South Wales parliament. Where did you think the financing for her candidacy was coming from? And it is no matter to our masters in China if you lose your career. That would be a small price to pay to have Chinese interests fairly represented in the state parliament. I am certain you would agree.'

'Of course, and I assume you know the origin of these photos, Li.'

'I will have another conversation with the Granger woman.'

'Yes, because that worked out *so well* for us last time.' Xiao said, not bothering to conceal the sarcasm.

'Goodbye, Xiao.' Li picked up his personal mobile and dialled Granger's number.

'Julie-Anne Granger speaking.'

'Ms Granger, we speak again.'

Ha, gotcha, she thought. 'It seems we do, Mr Li. What a surprise; I was just thinking about you,' she replied cheekily.

'I've no doubt you were. I wish it was under different circumstances.'

'That will *never* happen.' Julie-Anne replied. 'What do you want, Li?' She was being deliberately impolite to draw him out.

'I think we should have a coffee. What about we meet at that cute café around the corner from your office that you seem to prefer? Let's say in half an hour.'

'I'll see you there.' Julie-Anne would need to be more vigilant. Li had obviously had her followed when she walked from work to the café to meet Jack. If Fan Chen was following her, then that told her that he must be working directly for Li. She wondered whether the Consul General was aware of Fan Chen's extracurricular activities.

Julie-Anne had learnt some detective tricks of the trade from Jack, so she arrived at Rogue Café early and took Jack's preferred seat in the courtyard. She had her back to the wall and could see all the comings and goings of the place. She was looking out for Fan Chen. Instead, she saw Li walk in the side gate and make his way to her table.

'Good morning, Ms Granger, a lovely sanctuary indeed. I can see why you like it so much.'

'Yes, I like it a lot and I come here often, but you knew that already, didn't you, Li?'

'Just a lucky guess. It's right around the corner from your office, so it's an obvious choice, Ms Granger.'

'I'm sure Fan Chen agrees with you in that regard,' said Julie-Anne as she stared him down.

'I won't insult you by asking who Fan Chen is, Ms Granger. I know you're too clever for that.' They ordered coffees and made stilted small talk about the café and what a vibrant area Surry Hills was until the coffees arrived.

'Now, what can I do for you, Li? I'm sure you didn't come here to discuss the vibrancy of Surry Hills and the merits of inner city living.'

'You know why I am here, Ms Granger.'

Julie-Anne feigned ignorance. 'I have no idea, so why don't you enlighten me?'

'The photos you sent to the Consul General.'

'What photos?'

'You are a clever woman, but if you want to play spy games then you need to get better at playing the mind games, Ms Granger.'

'Thanks for the advice. I'll keep that in mind.'

'I want the originals of the photos destroyed.'

'They're digital, Mr Li, so they aren't easily destroyed. There will always be a copy somewhere, even in a deleted documents file on someone's hard drive or in the cloud. I could ask the same of you and you would undoubtedly provide me with the exact same response. I think they call that a stalemate.'

Li looked up from his coffee and gave her a half smile. 'Anyway, the photo which depicts the three of us together is obviously photoshopped, so that won't withstand forensic scrutiny. There goes your stalemate, Ms Granger.'

'On the contrary, Li. In this day and age where the populace seems all too eager to believe everything they read and hear, perception becomes reality and cancel culture abounds. And your little triumvirate *will* be cancelled. Check,' she said with a wry smile.

'Look, end your friendship with Miss Wu and all will be forgiven and forgotten, Ms Granger. Surely that's not too much to ask. After all, you've only known her for a short amount of time, so what's to lose? Go back one week and she didn't exist for you at all.'

'Well, she does now, and I'm certainly not going to allow you to pick my friends for me. You don't seem to be very adept at picking friends for yourself, judging by the company you keep. You and Wie Ping Lie seem to be awfully close, and he has a dubious reputation at best.'

'A word of warning, Ms Granger. You do not want to, how do you westerners say it? "Piss him off." He is not as understanding as I. You yourself mentioned his reputation, so I know you are aware of his capabilities.'

'I don't scare easily.'

'You have a reputation for being a fearless investigator, but he is in another league altogether.'

'I'll keep that in mind.'

'Has your boyfriend seen the photo? I imagine the situation must be very confusing for the three of you, but especially for him.' Julie-Anne was fuming at the reference to Jack and wondered how Li had known about him. She maintained her composure and allowed the remark to wash over her.

'Now, Mr Li, just so we understand each other. Don't even think about releasing the photos you have of Melissa and I, even anonymously. If for some reason those photos do make their way into the public domain, the consequences will be dire for your own little threesome.'

Julie-Anne noticed that Li's hands were now clenched into fists. 'Don't threaten me, Ms Granger, you have no idea who you are messing with,' he said through barred teeth.

'Oh, but I do, Li. Shall I continue?'

'Please do, I'm certain this will make for riveting listening.'

'I will send the photos I have to the Department of Foreign Affairs and Trade listing each subject in the photos, and I will provide a little resume on each of you and your activities. I'll let DFAT draw their own conclusions from there. Then I will send both photos to the Chinese Ambassador in Canberra. I'm sure he will be delighted to know that his Consul General keeps such esteemed company. With all the negative media hype surrounding China at the moment you know how that will play out. And finally, I will send my highlights package to the Federal Minister of Home Affairs. My guess is he will take quite an interest, particularly in the immigration status of you and Wie.'

'Ms Granger, DFAT has just overseen a trade deal of significant value between your state government and China, so they wouldn't allow themselves to be embarrassed; the timing would be terrible for them. As for the Consul General, my country will simply replace him and he will find himself being the new Consul General for Angola, Liberia or some such remote outposts far away from the scrutiny of your state and federal governments. Mr Wie and I have every legal right to be in this country, so involving Home Affairs would be a waste of your time.'

'I doubt that's true. It is well known that the Minister for Home Affairs is a right-wing hard arse and he relishes the opportunity to use his discretionary powers. I am certain that he will find you and Wie to be worthy case studies, wouldn't you agree?' Julie-Anne implied smugly. 'Oh, I almost forgot. The Daily News corporate lawyers have copies of the photos and accompanying commentary, with instructions to distribute them to the aforementioned organisations, just in case anything should happen to me. But I'm sure they won't need to act on that.' Julie-Anne said firmly as she fixed a stare into Li's eyes.

Li Qiang meant strong in his native language, and he would need to be every bit of that with this woman. 'You are a worthy adversary, Ms Granger. In another time, we might have enjoyed a different relationship.'

'As I said on the phone, that would *never* happen Li.' She rose from the table, lifted her head high and strode confidently across the courtyard and out through the exit.

Later that afternoon, Julie-Anne's desk phone rang. It was her editor

Chris Russell calling. 'I need to see you in my office immediately. I have a security company representative with me, JA.'

'On my way, Chris.'

Julie-Anne walked into her editor's office and her boss introduced her to David Bedford from MPS Security Services. Bedford, she guessed, was mid-fifties, thick set with close cropped salt and pepper hair and wearing a navy blue suit.

'Hello, David.'

Russell continued. 'I have discussed your circumstances with David and provided him with an overview of your activities, our concerns and the desire to mitigate any risks to your personal safety and security. David has several initiatives he wishes to deploy to ensure we meet our objectives. He will explain these to you now.'

Bedford spoke, his voice soft yet authoritative, 'Firstly, Julie-Anne we will need access to your home. The purpose is to enable us to conduct a daily sweep of your apartment for bugs, hidden cameras and listening devices.'

'I assume all your staff are industry accredited and have the appropriate probity checks if they are going into my private domain,' she enquired.

'Yes, they do, and they will provide the same service here in your office. They will also conduct a check of any letters, packages or parcels that are delivered to you, both at your home and office. Don't open anything that doesn't bear our company stamp.'

'So we know where you are at all times, we will install a GPS tracker in your car and also add a dashboard mounted camera to record any incidents. The GPS tracker will be monitored twenty-four hours a day by our control room so we know where you are at all times. Don't go for walks, take the car, and only use major thoroughfares, no side streets or shortcuts please. You are less likely to be run off the road on a major highway or busy through road. And always go straight to your destination; no stops along the way.'

'This all sounds very professional, but is it really necessary?'

Bedford nodded. 'Yes, it is. You would be surprised how many people we provide this level of coverage for.'

'Okay, then, it sounds great.'

'There's more, JA,' Russell informed her.

'We would like you to wear a body-mounted camera.'

'What? On my head, really?' Julie-Anne laughed incredulously.

'No, we will discreetly install one in a brooch, which you must wear on your upper body clothing at all times. I will show you how to activate it later when we give it to you. And finally, we will provide close personal protection in case you need to attend any functions or public events. We would suggest you avoid them, but if you can't, please advise your Security Department of the details and they will make the arrangements with us.'

'And you're sure this is all really necessary?' asked Julie-Anne with astonishment. 'I mean, really, this is secret agent stuff, David,' she said, bemused.

'Chris has advised me of some of the targets of your investigation and we have had experience with them previously. So, yes, it is very necessary, Julie-Anne.'

'Okay then, well, thank you, David. I'm now going back to my office and hide under my desk. That seems much simpler.'

Back at her desk, Julie-Anne thought she should ring Jack first. The call went through to voicemail, so she left a detailed message regarding Li's awareness of him and for him to be careful himself. Then she called Melissa, told her that security measures were being put in place and she would see her at home.

$$\textbf{67}$$

North Bondi Fish

Jack saw Danielle enter the upstairs restaurant and his eyes followed her as she breezed across the room to the balcony, seemingly without a care in the world.

'You look ravishing, Danielle,' he said as he rose, gently grasped her hand and kissed her cheek.

'Thank you. It's great to be out of that dowdy uniform and it's a beautiful warm afternoon, so I dressed accordingly.'

'You've certainly done that. What do you call the dress?'

'Well, it's obviously white with a floral print. It has an asymmetric hem; a deep vee neck and they call these spaghetti straps.' Danielle said as she flicked the straps on her shoulders. 'There you go. Now you're an expert on summer dresses.' Jack was listening intently, but his eyes were drifting between the split in the hem and her cleavage. 'I can see that you particularly like the deep vee neck, Jack. You're such a boy,' she chuckled. 'And considerably south of where your eyes are, you might even notice my strappy blush sandals.'

'Oh, you're wearing sandals, too. And the tan, Miss Summer?'

'There's this cute, private little bay north of here near South Head. I go there sometimes and just spread myself out, read my book and enjoy the warmth of the sun on my body. You look pretty good yourself, old man.' Danielle said with a sassy smile. 'So, what are you wearing, Mr Rare Breed?'

'Well this is a white, tapered fit, linen shirt with the sleeves folded back, navy dress shorts, tan loafers and my world-famous smile.' Jack tried to demonstrate with all the flourish of a male model. 'What do you think?'

'I think you're funny, but you look very smart.'

'Well, aren't we just the pair then. What would you like to drink?' Jack asked, signalling a nearby waiter.

'I would love a Bellini please.'

'Okay, a Bellini it is. I'm having my usual bright sunny day drink, a Sapphire and Tonic with lots of squeezed lime.' Jack ordered the drinks and the waiter handed them menus.

'Okay, I'm ready. I know what I'm having.'

'That was quick. What'll it be, Danielle?'

'The dish you recommended on the phone, the Turmeric Fish Curry with Zucchini, Mint, Lime and Basmati Rice,' she said, reading aloud from the menu. 'Oh look, my favourite. Can I have glass of the Pierro please?' she asked the waiter.

'Well, my golden rule is, that whenever I'm in a restaurant near the ocean, I always have the Beer Battered Fish.'

'You're such a boy, Jack.'

'That's twice now; is it three strikes and I'm out?' he asked with an impish grin on his face.

Halfway through their lunch, Jack's mobile vibrated. 'Excuse me while I take this call; no doubt you'll be surrounded by handsome young men when I get back. I'll be quick, I promise.' Looking as dazzling as she did, Jack was loath to leave Danielle alone at the table, but he had to take this particular call.

'Hi Jim, I'm at lunch so can we do this quickly?'

'Well okay then, maybe I should call back at a more convenient time,' Brennan retorted.

'Sorry, Jim, continue, please.'

'Jack, it's a quick call anyway. It's not going to take us as long as we thought to isolate the footage you want. You should aim to be in my office at nine o'clock in the morning and we'll have what you need. Now, go back to your lunch, hotshot.'

'Thanks, I appreciate it.'

'My apologies, Danielle.'

'How do you know Jim Brennan, Jack?' she asked directly.

He was bowled over by the question. 'Where did that come from?'

'He just rang you; your mobile was face up on the table and I read his name, even though it was upside down.'

'Very clever, Miss Summer. We've been friends for a long time and he was just calling for a chat.' Jack said dismissively, hoping Danielle would let it go at that. Much to his chagrin, she didn't.

'So, what do you do, Jack?'

'Aaahh, that old chestnut.' Jack thought about inventing a role, but quickly dismissed the idea. He liked Danielle. She was bright and breezy, good fun and refreshingly honest, so he thought he should reciprocate. 'I'm a detective.'

She had already made him for a detective when he walked into the Bennelong Room earlier in the week. 'So, that's how you know Jim, and I'm guessing, also the reason you were in the Bennelong Room earlier in the week. Is that why I'm here too, Jack?' He was stung by her question and paused momentarily before responding.

Looking directly into her eyes he said, 'Danielle, I invited you here for a number of reasons. It was quiet at the office, I saw it was a beautiful day outside, I haven't had a long lazy lunch for ages, and I felt bad for leaving you on the dancefloor the other night. And, if you need even more convincing, I wanted to see you again.' Jack's phone vibrated again, but he let the call go through to voicemail.

'So, what sort of detective are you? One of those snoopy private eyes like Magnum?'

'You're too young to know about Magnum PI.'

'You ever heard of Netflix, Stan or Amazon Prime, Mr PI? Anyway, answer my question, Magnum.'

'I work for the Australian Federal Police.'

'Given I met you in the Bennelong Room and you are talking to Jim Brennan, our head of security, your investigation must have something to do with the casino, am I correct?'

'I can't discuss any ongoing investigations with you.'

'Aaahh, so there is an investigation. See, that wasn't so hard, now was it, Magnum?

He had slipped up. 'I didn't confirm or deny anything.'

'Yes, you did. It's all in the phrasing. Anyway, Magnum, I pegged you for a detective when you first walked up to the bar.'

Jack wanted to make light of the conversation. 'Bugger, and I thought I was anonymous and blending in. You should be a detective yourself, Danielle.'

'Lunch was divine, as was the wine. Can we go for a walk along the sea wall and soak up the atmosphere of Bondi, Jack? It will be lovely.' *Thank God we're back to Jack,* he thought. They walked hand in hand along the Bondi promenade, soaking up the autumn sun.

'Oh, look there's Icebergs. I've never been there so can we check it out and have a drink, even just one, Jack? Pleeeease?' They made their way out onto the balcony of the new Terrace Café at Icebergs and were delighted to be able to secure a table. The balcony faced north and provided uninterrupted views across the entire length of Bondi Beach.

'This is just breathtaking and look, there's North Bondi Fish where we had lunch.' Danielle was so excited she turned to face Jack and pulled him into a firm embrace.

'Thank you, thank you, thank you.' Danielle lifted her arms, looped them around Jack's neck and kissed him firmly. 'Thank you, I love this,' she said. 'Let's have a drink and celebrate.'

'Let me guess, you want a Bellini.'

'A girl's gotta have her bubbles, Jack.'

'Okay then, I'll join you and have one too, back in a moment,' he said as he made his way along the terrace to the bar.

'Thank you, cheers, Magnum.' They clinked glasses.

'Are we back to Magnum again?'

'Yep, I want to talk more about your investigation.'

'I never said there was an investigation.' Jack replied.

'I did though. I remembered something while you were getting the drinks. You asked me about Mr Woodard, our Vice President of Client Services, and I wondered why you would be interested in him. Then it came to me. Do you want to know about my theory?'

Jack splayed his hands for effect. 'You're telling this story.'

'I see a lot of curious goings on from my vantage point in the bar. In particular, I have become aware that Mr Woodard seems to spend an inordinate amount of time with Mr Li, one of our high rollers. I'm sure he's expected to fuss over the high rollers as part of his role, but he seems to always be hanging around when Mr Li is in the Bennelong Room. I find that strange. And I'm guessing so do you, otherwise why would you have asked me who he was and why would you be in the Bennelong Room yourself. You certainly weren't gambling.'

'I have nothing to add about your theories, Danielle.'

'Aaahh, see Jack. You said, "nothing to add," which means my theory is correct, doesn't it?' Jack had had enough of her theories.

'If that's your interpretation of the conversation, then you believe what you want,' he said, a little too sharply.

'Oh, okay then,' she replied as she flopped back in her chair. Wanting to change the subject, he asked, 'would you like another drink?'

'No, thank you.'

Things had gone a little frosty, so Danielle thought she should get the atmosphere back on track. 'I've got an idea. I'm going to order an Uber and take you for a drive.'

'Where to?'

'It's a surprise, but I think you'll love it.' Half an hour later the Uber pulled over at the end of Cliff Street in Watsons Bay and they alighted the car.

'Okay, let's go have some fun, Jack.'

'Where are we, there's nothing here.'

'Yes there is, come on.' She grabbed him by the hand and led him north along the South Head Heritage Trail.

'Are you sure? This is more liked a goat track than a trail.'

Following a short stroll they arrived at a set of stairs that led down to a small, picturesque beach. 'Here we are, my favourite little hideaway.'

'Is this a nudist beach?'

'Yeah genius. Where did you think the tan came from?'

'You must have conveniently forgotten to mention the *all over* bit.'

'I've never seen this place so quiet, especially on a beautiful evening such as this. There's just one couple and they are at the other end of the beach, so let's stay up this end and we'll have it all to ourselves, Jack.'

The sun dipped below the horizon, but Danielle figured there was still at least an hour of dusk left. 'It's still lovely and warm and the water's nice and calm, so let's go for a swim before it gets dark.'

'And what do you suggest I wear?'

'Your birthday suit, silly.' And with that, she lifted her dress up over her head, kicked off her sandals and stepped out of her lacy underwear. *Yep, definitely an all over tan and just look at that body,* Jack mused. She turned to face Jack and began undoing the buttons of his shirt. Danielle leant her leg into Jack's groin and gave him a playful smile. She could feel him hardening against her leg. As she started to undo the belt in his shorts, Jack removed her hands.

'What's wrong?'

'You go for a swim and I'll be along in a few minutes.' Jack wasn't about to undress for a couple of minutes until he regained his composure. He had also never been skinny dipping, well, certainly never on a public beach, so he first needed to pluck up some courage. And if he went for a swim with a naked Danielle, there would be no turning back.

Jack watched as Danielle frolicked around, did tumble turns and duck-dived at will. She seemed to be in her element, and he admired her free-spirited attitude. 'Come on, what's keeping you, Magnum? It's beautiful in here,' she called out. *Okay, here goes nothing,* Jack said to himself. He had regained his self-control, so was feeling marginally more comfortable about undressing now.

'Okay, okay, in a minute.' He had one last look up and down the beach. Comfortable that he was alone, Jack unzipped his shorts and lowered them and his boxers to the   sand. He stepped out of his clothes, slipped off his loafers and stood there naked. He thought of the French expression "in flagrante".

'Wow, check out the naked detective,' she called out to no-one in particular. Jack was quickly overcome with embarrassment and cupped his hands over his manhood. *She is watching the detective, oh he's so cute.* Danielle had started singing the line to a well-known Elvis Costello song and was laughing uncontrollably. He was still feeling self-conscious, but couldn't help laughing at her choice of song and sense of humour.

There was no stopping her now as she launched into another song. *'He's so shy, that sweet little boy who caught my eye'.*

Jack chuckled to himself. She didn't realise it, but she was playing him at his own game. 'Yeah, yeah, you're so funny. I bet you crack yourself up,' he called out.

Jack, now finally composed, walked down to the water's edge and waded out to Danielle. He relaxed somewhat when the water level reached his hips. She was right; the water was a beautiful temperature, so he swam out about fifty metres and frolicked around himself.

'This is a lovely spot,' he said as he swam back towards her.

'Yes, and we have it all to ourselves.' She moved close to him, looped her arms around his neck and wrapped her legs around his naked torso. She leaned forward and kissed him passionately. 'I want you, Jack. I want you inside me, now,' she whispered into his ear.

Jack was suitably aroused, but mentally he was in a world of confusion. If this went to the next level whatever he had with JA was dead in the water. Decision time Jack. *Well, JA seemed to have moved on, so why shouldn't he?*

'Ah… ah… ahh… aaagh…. oh yeah, Jack.' Danielle thrusted and gyrated on Jack as the warm water blended with her own moistness. She released her hands, leant backwards, allowing her upper body to float on the water, gazing up into the dusky sky. Jack, holding her by the hips, thrust back and forth while she bobbed rhythmically in time with him. He tickled her firm nipples and kissed her on the stomach. 'You look mesmerising floating like that.'

She grasped his hands, pulled herself back up and looped her arms around his neck again. 'Aaahh ….. aaahh,' moaned Jack as she pushed down on him.

'Now where's my shy guy gone?' she whispered again. 'I want to come with you, Jack.' She pushed down on him again and began gently gyrated her hips, gradually driving him closer to his peak.

'Now, Danielle.' He was consumed by his desire and moaned with pleasure. She flexed her pelvic muscle and constricted around him, gripped tightly and kissed him passionately.

'Yes, yes, yes, oh Jack, yes,' she said as her body spasmed and she slammed up against him. 'Oh, Jack, you really are a rare breed,' she sighed, then giggled at her pun.

She spread her dress out on the sand and they lay down together. She put her arm across his body and rested her head on his chest. 'Wow, that was wonderful. I'm so chilled. It's almost dark and we still have the beach to ourselves.'

'Yeah, and I'm still naked.'

'Yes, you are, I like that.' Danielle slowly began walking her fingers down his stomach, tickling his skin as she went. Then she grasped him and whispered into his ear. 'I'll be back in a while, Jack.'

Dolphins Point
Monday 9th March

Julie-Anne was at her desk early and thinking about the next steps in her investigation. She was making little progress again, even though she knew full well what was occurring and what the eventual story would be, she had no hard evidence to support either at this point. She considered ringing Jack again, but had already left a voicemail message the previous afternoon. Maybe she could ring the Consul General and ask for his comments about being only one degree of separation away from Chinatown's Triad leader. She doubted the Consul General would even accept the call, let alone address her questions, so that was a no-go.

She was starting to despair, not knowing where the next titbit of information would come from. The ringtone of her mobile brought to a halt the negative thoughts that were pervading her mind. The screen showed No Caller ID. Normally, like everyone these days, she would usually bump the anonymous call, but as a journalist you never knew where your next lead was coming from, so she swiped right.

'Julie-Anne Granger.'

'Hello, Ms Granger, it's me again.'

'Who exactly is me again?'

'I rang you anonymously a week ago and you gave me your number. I would like to talk to you again.' Julie-Anne, knowing her investigation had stalled, thought she should at least hear whatever this woman was offering, but she resolved not to let it happen over the phone. She needed to screen this woman in person if she was going to make a tangible contribution to her investigation and then to her story.

'Okay, Ms Anonymous, let's start with a name, shall we?'

'I'd rather remain anonymous.'

'I'm sure you would, but it's too late in my investigation for that. It's been nearly a week since you first called, so if you have something concrete to offer, then I want to know who you are.'

The woman hesitated, and Julie-Anne wondered if she'd been spooked. 'Sophie,' the woman eventually said.

'Okay, thank you, Sophie, call me Julie-Anne.' She would have to take baby steps with this woman, but she also needed to progress her investigation, and fast.

'I'm not interested in talking on the phone, so what say we meet up?' Julie-Anne didn't give her time to respond. 'Where are you and when would you like to meet, Sophie?' There was silence on the other end of the call and Julie-Anne wasn't about to break it this time. The woman had been given the ultimatum, so she would wait her out.

'I'm in Coogee Beach.'

'Okay, I'm in Surry Hills, so I can meet you at Coogee in half an hour, if that works for you.' Julie-Anne needed to press the point while she had the initiative. 'There's a kiosk on the beach near the bus terminus; we can grab a coffee, take a stroll along the coastal walk and have a quiet chat.' There was another pause in the conversation. Julie-Anne realised she was holding her breath as she eagerly awaited the woman's response, but she wasn't going to push the point any further. This woman had to feel comfortable about the arrangement and make a decision in her own time.

'Okay, I'll see you there.'

'How will I recognise you, Sophie?'

'I'll find you.'

Julie-Anne ordered her usual latte from the Chish 'n Fips kiosk and waited under the bus shelter. She had no idea what Sophie looked like, so she was glancing up, down and across Arden Street hoping for a tell-tale sign. To her left she couldn't help but notice a tall woman of Eurasian appearance waiting to cross the road at the Coogee Bay Road traffic lights. She was wearing dark navy athletic tights and matching crop top, with her black hair pulled back in a ponytail and looped through the back of a Yankees baseball cap. Of course, like many women, she was wearing orange fluoro joggers. Judging by her figure, she was very fit indeed. '*Wow, that could almost be Melissa,*' Julie-Anne murmured. She was looking northward along the Arden Street footpath when she felt a tap on her shoulder. Momentarily startled, she turned, surprised to see the athletic woman she had noticed a few moments earlier, standing next to her. 'Julie-Anne?'

'Oh, hello, yes. You must be Sophie. Nice to meet you.'

'You too, Julie-Anne,' she replied in a quiet voice. Julie-Anne picked up on the tone and knew that she would have to gain Sophie's confidence before they could get into the detail of why she was here.

'Why don't we get you a coffee and then go for a walk? What would you like?'

'A skinny latte please.'

The two women walked in silence towards the beach and then continued north along the promenade. Wanting to get the conversation going, Julie-Anne asked, 'so, do you live in this lovely part of the world?'

'Yes, I have an apartment a few blocks up Coogee Bay Road.'

'Why Coogee, Sophie?'

'Well, I love swimming in the ocean and even try my hand at a little bodysurfing. So, I usually come down here after the gym. Sometimes, I will just grab a coffee and sit on one of these park benches and read my book. Where do you live, Julie-Anne?'

'In an apartment in Newtown. It doesn't have the beautiful beach you have here, but it's a very eclectic area and has some wonderful cafes and lively bars.'

'Sounds nice. I like Newtown too, but I would miss my beach.'

The promenade made way for a pathway and the women followed it up to Dolphins Point, where they sat on the grass not far from the Bali Memorial. Their chosen spot faced south and provided a stunning vista all the way across Coogee Bay to the surf club in the south and out to Wedding Cake Island. The location and the view calmed Julie-Anne and she hoped it would relax Sophie enough to encourage her to open up.

'I was very nervous about meeting you, but having done so, I feel more relaxed.. Especially after the lovely walk up here.'

'That's nice, so do I, Sophie.' Julie-Anne was going to let her introduce the topic of conversation, and if she didn't soon, then she would dive in and raise it herself.

'So, you probably want to know why I rang you in the first place, and why I'm here today.'

'The thought had occurred to me, yes,' she replied with irony as she turned her head towards Sophie and laughed.

'Aaahh, where to begin,' she sighed. 'To help with my university expenses, assisting the family back in China, and I guess, the general cost of living in Sydney, I started doing some escort work. All above board; it's important you know that.'

'I'm not here to judge you, Sophie.' Julie-Anne replied.

'Anyway, I had a client who became a regular whenever he was in Sydney. He was an unattractive, portly, little Chinese man, but you get that in the escort business sometimes and the money was excellent. He treated me well and we would always go out, mostly to his favourite restaurant in Chinatown, where I met some interesting people.' Julie-Anne thought she had probably been to the same restaurant. 'A couple of times we took in a harbour cruise, went to upmarket bars and on a few occasions I accompanied him to the high rollers room at the Oceanic. It was the usual harmless fun you would have as an escort.'

'And then something changed, I'm guessing,' suggested Julie-Anne.

'Yes, it did, and it came out of nowhere, completely blindsiding, or I should say, horrifying me.'

'We're talking about the Li Qiang you mentioned on the phone, aren't we?'

'Yes, we are.'

Julie-Anne noticed the woman's eyes watering; no doubt due to the experiences she was recalling. 'Are you comfortable telling me what happened?'

'Yeah, just give me a minute.' Julie-Anne took the unexpected opportunity to soak up the view. 'One evening out of nowhere, he addressed me as Kaili Wang. That was my birth name before I changed it to Sophie Zhao.'

'Why did you change your name, if you don't mind me asking?'

'For my own personal reasons.' Sophie didn't want to get into that now, so she carried on. 'Anyway, I was quite shocked that somehow he had managed to ascertain my real name and that made me feel uneasy. It was obvious that he must have been researching me and seeking out my true identity for some reason, but I had no idea why. It suddenly became crystal clear.' She paused and Julie-Anne saw her eyes misting over again.

'Take your time, Sophie.'

'We were in his suite one night having a celebratory champagne after he had won a large amount of money in the Bennelong Room. It wasn't much fun, but I didn't care; it was all part of the job for me. Then he suddenly turned to me with this wicked smile on his face and told me to undress. Just like that, out of nowhere. "Get undressed," he demanded. As you can imagine I was quite shocked. I composed myself, and told him that wasn't going to happen. "Oh yes it will, Kaili Wang," he said. Then he stunned me again. He said, and I quote, Julie-Anne, "I'm sure your family back in Tong-Li would be pleased to know how well you are doing in your new life in this wonderful country." In the space of one minute, this supposedly respected businessman had turned into a sleazy, dishonest monster. He knew my birth name, where I had grown up and that I still had family back in Tong-Li.'

'What did you do?'

Sophie paused momentarily. 'I did what any obedient Chinese woman would do when being blackmailed. I lifted my cocktail dress over my head, dropped it to the floor, and stood there naked.'

'That must have been so demeaning.'

'You can't imagine just how much.'

'Was he preying on something in your history?'

'No, the obvious inference was that he knew where my family lived and if I valued my family's safety, then I would comply with his request. China can be a corrupt society and I couldn't risk putting my family in danger.' Sophie paused and dabbed at her eyes. 'You may have seen an article last year about a Hong Kong pro-democracy demonstrator who attended a protest rally at the University of Queensland. He was identified by Chinese agents and his family back in China were visited and warned by agents of the government as a result of his actions. As a high roller, I assumed Li would have similar connections back in China.'

'That's so horrible. You don't have to tell me anymore; I can work it out for myself.'

'No, I want to tell you, it's important. I never, never had sexual intercourse with that vile little man, but I did please him and give him massages. On that first occasion I made a commitment to myself, that I would find an escape route somehow, and from then on I just compartmentalised everything when I was with him and thought of nothing but my family's welfare. And, here we are, Julie-Anne.'

'That's such a heart-wrenching story, Sophie. Why didn't you contact me sooner?'

'I needed time to process what was happening to me and why.'

'And was there a specific reason you called me today?'

'The underlying reason I called you in the first instance was because I want to extricate myself from this horrible situation and I needed help. As I mentioned earlier, I couldn't go to the police without any solid evidence. I thought Li might change his habits if he realised he was under investigation, even from a journalist. Ideally, I was hoping he would flee back to China and forget about me and my family.'

'After you called me the first time, Sophie, I started doing some digging of my own. It was frustrating at first, but then things started to open up quickly. I have a friend who is an AFP detective.'

'What does AFP stand for?'

'Australian Federal Police. Anyway, he heard me mention Li's name and he started his own investigation. Strictly between the two of us, and I mean *strictly*, we've established that Li is laundering money, we suspect from the sale of drugs, at Oceanic Casino. The intended use of some of the laundered money is to fund a political campaign for a carefully chosen candidate.

The rationale behind the whole process is to get their candidate; a Chinese Australian, into the state parliament with the aim of promoting better cooperation with China, amongst other more subversive activities, as you can imagine.'

'Okay, that's very interesting and it relates to why I called you this morning, Julie-Anne.' The conversation was now flowing easily and Sophie obviously felt more comfortable as the day progressed.

'I was in his suite again two days ago when he answered a call; it sounded like it was from China. I couldn't believe he was talking business in my presence. He never did that previously.

The conversation was in Chinese but surely he would realise I speak the language.'

'What was the topic?'

'I could obviously only hear one side of the conversation, but I think I have remembered most of it. They were talking about a consignment being on track. I don't know what of, but after listening to what you just told me, I can imagine. Then Li confirmed to the caller that there should be another one million dollars available to finance their cause. I'm now guessing that cause is the political candidate you mentioned before, Julie-Anne.'

'Wow, that pretty much backs-up what Jack and I think this is all about.'

'Who's Jack?'

'He's the AFP detective I mentioned.'

'Oh, okay. Continuing on, I could hear the voice on the other end of the call now yelling. Li seemed to become very defensive and then blurted out something about a captain; I think he said a Captain Han. And then Li said something like; "what do you mean: it's taken care of?" He then became angry and said, "of course it's my business. That will bring unwanted attention." The caller must have said something threatening to Li as his tone softened suddenly and his final response was, "I will." The call was disconnected and Li shouted for me to leave.'

'I have no idea what the reference to a Captain Han is all about, but I will pass it onto Jack; he may know more.' Julie-Anne said.

'One more thing, Julie-Anne. Li has a wall safe in his suite where I now know he keeps his vast amounts of cash. One day, he opened it in my presence. Because I was dressing, he thought I wouldn't notice. I've seen the size of the cash stacks in that safe and I would think the one million dollars I mentioned previously might be exactly what I saw.'

'Given what you've said, Sophie, I think this whole scenario; the drug smuggling, money laundering and political infiltration is potentially being coordinated directly from China.'

'It certainly seems that way doesn't it, especially given what I overheard.'

'Would you feel comfortable talking to Jack about all of this?'

'I just want Li out of my life, my dignity back and my family safe, so if talking to him helps, then yes, of course I will.' Julie-Anne thought Sophie even sounded excited by the prospect.

'Wow, that's quite a story. But it's getting cool, so why don't we start walking back?'

'In a minute, if you don't mind. I've been so busy talking I haven't really taken in this beautiful scenery. I don't get up here enough.' The two women sat on the grass in silence and admired the view across the bay. The wind direction had shifted and the sea green waves were now rolling in from the southeast in a metronomic rhythm which had now attracted even more surfers into the sparkling ocean.

As they walked back down the pathway towards Coogee neither woman noticed the black-haired, dark-skinned man wearing the large sunglasses and baseball cap. He was holding a bird guide and binoculars and cast a subtle glance at them as they passed.

（69）

Oceanic Security Control

Jack woke at six o'clock and was in a buoyant mood after his afternoon of wining and dining and a free-spirited evening with Danielle. He allowed himself a little reminiscing while preparing for the day ahead. He liked Danielle a lot. She was funny, charming company, smart, although she liked to play the bubblehead occasionally, and she was drop-dead gorgeous with a body from heaven. But, so was JA and look what happened there. Although they didn't see each other regularly, Jack had assumed he was in a relationship with JA. Maybe the *assume* acronym is correct, he chuckled. He wasn't that astute when it came to matters of the heart. Perhaps it wasn't a relationship as such, given the commitment to their respective careers, which ultimately limited them to intermittent and spontaneous catch-ups. That was all in his emotional rear vision mirror now.

He wasn't certain which straw broke the camel's back, but he guessed that using JA's information for his own benefit had probably been the deal breaker. In hindsight he knew that he had crossed an invisible line between them and he should have asked her permission first. And now it was too late. In the space of a week, JA had a new *friend* and Jack was looking forward to seeing Danielle again. 'Enough of the what ifs, back to work, Jack,' he mumbled, chastising himself for letting his mind wander.

He was eager to review the Oceanic's CCTV footage and finally move the investigation forward again. His mood was dampened slightly when it struck him that he hadn't checked his voicemail since yesterday morning. *Not very professional Jack: work first, play second.*

JA had left a detailed message warning him of Li Qiang's awareness of who Jack was and the circumstances of her conversation with Li. He felt terribly guilty all of a sudden. His ex- girlfriend was concerned for his safety, all the while he was making love to another woman. He needed to meet with Jim Brennan first, so he would have to call her back later.

Brennan was waiting in the foyer of the Oceanic Hotel and Casino when Jack walked through the revolving doors just before nine o'clock. 'Hello, Jack, welcome back.'

'Thanks, Jim. I appreciate the prompt response.'

'That's fine, now let's get you signed in and we can go downstairs and get to work.'

They sat alongside each other at Brennan's desk facing two large desktop monitors.

Brennan took a USB device from his desk drawer and plugged it into the port. There were eight video files on the device with each labelled by date, recent to oldest.

'Can I view the most recent first please?' Brennan double clicked on the file from a week ago and the video began playing. The video footage was from the camera strategically placed outside the vault in the Bennelong Room and directed at the vault entrance. 'I've watched video footage many times, so you can speed it up to three or four times normal speed if you like, Jim.'

'Okay, stop there and wind back a few seconds if you would please. Right, play it at normal speed. Who is that entering the vault, Jim?'

'That's Mr Woodard, the Vice President of Client Services.'

'And what's that he is carrying under his arm?'

'It looks like a briefcase of some sort to me.'

'Yes, it does.' Jack thought back to his latest conversation with

Michelle Ironside. What reason would he have to be in the Treasury Room, let alone enter the vault? 'And where is the Treasury Manager, Jim?' Jack knew all the answers, of course, but he wanted Brennan to reach his own conclusions.

'I'll have to look into this, thanks for the head's up, Jack.' Brennan made a couple of entries in his notebook, including the time of the video at the crucial point highlighted by Jack.

Jack's phone vibrated, displaying the number for Chris Coleman. Jack thought it better to play nice with the Canberra bureaucrats, so he walked outside the office and accepted the call.

'Jack, I've got some information for you. I've just noticed the Oceanic's TTR Report for the date you required has been uploaded into the Austrac database.'

'That's great news what do you have for me?'

Well, there is a transaction listing for our friend.'

'There should be two transactions listed Chris, one for buying the chips and another for when he exchanged them back for cash or an EFT.'

'Nope, there's only one transaction listed and it's for an EFT of one point seven one five million dollars.'

'Sheeesh.' Jack exclaimed. 'Can you send me a copy of the TTR?'

'Only if it's officially requested in writing by your Commissioner or his deputy.'

'Okay, thanks. I'll get onto it.'

'What was that all about, Jackie boy?'

'I'll tell you later.' Jack was hoping Jim would forget about the phone call as he wasn't ready to reveal what he knew just yet and didn't want to be dishonest with his old friend.

'Alright, can we go back to the second most recent video file please, Jim?' Brennan closed the file and double clicked on the next file in the sequence.

'Let's see if we have anything useful on this piece of footage,' Jack stated hopefully. Moments later he noticed movement at the very edge of the screen, but it was only a partial image. 'Stop there please.' A tall blond woman was walking towards the vault and had half turned towards the camera at the point Jack asked Brennan to pause the video. Jack thought his heart had stopped for a moment and he was suddenly short of breath. *Am I seeing things?*

Brennan looked at Jack. 'Are you okay, buddy? Your face has gone very pale.' Jack was stunned by what he was seeing. He took a deep breath and quickly tried to regain his composure.

'I can see why you went pale. She's a stunner that one.' Jack couldn't believe he was looking at footage of Danielle entering the vault, and with a navy blue briefcase under one arm no less.

Having regained his composure and his focus quickly, Jack feigning naivety, asked Brennan who the woman was.

'That's Danielle Mortimer. She works in the Treasury Department. I think she is part time in the role as she also covers some shifts in the Bennelong Room bar. Jack wasn't sure where to go next, but he didn't want Brennan becoming suspicious of Danielle until he could make sense of this latest revelation himself.

'So, Ms Mortimer is entitled to be inside the Treasury Department, Jim?'

'Yes, and she has a high-level security clearance just so she can work in Treasury.' *Not for much longer,* thought Jack.

The time of day was very similar on the remaining six videos and Jack guessed that each coincided with Danielle's roster. He needed to work out how he was going to handle this scenario. It could come back to bite him in the proverbial and ruin his career if he wasn't careful. And how was he going to keep this from Julie-Anne, given the spirit of their supposed joint investigation? She would do backflips over this revelation.

'What do you propose to do about Woodard, Jim?'

'I'll subtly make some enquiries and see where it leads. There may be an innocent explanation for his actions.'

'Can you please talk to me before you discuss your findings with anyone else?'

'Why, Jack? I'm obligated to take any findings involving suspicious matters directly to the CEO.' Jack was thinking about both Michelle Ironside and Danielle.

'I know, but it could compromise my investigation and destroy any potential for prosecution, if it comes to that.'

'I'll think about it.'

'Thanks for everything, you've been a big help, Jim.'

Jack left the casino and walked to his car. He was furious, both with himself and Danielle. All those questions she had asked and theories she espoused yesterday, and he didn't pick up on anything untoward. His radar must be off, but more likely he was consumed by something else. He rang Danielle.

'You want to go for another swim? It was very stimulating, Jack,' she said. He picked up on her play on words and any other time he would have found her hilarious.

'I thought we might catch up this afternoon if you have some spare time, Danielle.' Jack was being as unassuming as possible even though he was fuming internally.

'I have a few hours until I start work, so why not? That would be nice.'

'I'll meet you at Sappho Café in Glebe Point Road in half an hour if you like. It's close to your apartment and not far from your work. Does that work for you?'

'See you soon, Jack.'

Before he went to meet up with Danielle he quickly typed an email to the Deputy Commissioner outlining the reasons he wanted a copy of a particular TTR from Austrac. He asked the DC to submit the request directly so as to expedite the process. He added a PostScript to the email: *Can you also request the TTR for the previous two days as well?* Jack wanted to be certain that Li hadn't exchanged his cash for gaming chips in the days prior.

(70)

Jack and Danielle Sappho Cafe

Jack arrived early and sat at a table in the courtyard. Danielle sashayed in a few minutes later and garnered the attention of most of the men. Jack loved her confidence and that she always appeared so bright and breezy. He had quickly become fond of her and she looked gorgeous again in another little summer dress. This is going to be difficult, he thought.

'Hi Danielle, how are you?'

'I'm fabulous thanks to you and our wonderful adventure yesterday.' She kissed him on the lips and held onto the kiss until Jack pulled away. She sat down and they ordered coffees. There was a long pause between them.

'Is everything okay, Jack? You seem preoccupied.'

'No, everything's not okay. After yesterday I thought, wow, how good is my life?

It's been all downhill this morning though.'

'Why, what's happened?' Oh, so sweet, Danielle had a look of genuine concern on her face and Jack felt sorry for her. She was a good kid. He thought about how much he should divulge to her given the direction his investigation was now heading. He was torn between his affection for this gorgeous young woman and his duties as a federal law enforcement officer. He paused again and took a deep breath.

'Danielle, yesterday you theorised about me conducting an investigation that had something to do with the Bennelong Room.'

'Yes, and you didn't acknowledge anything, so I eventually let it go.'

'So, tell me, what have you got yourself involved in?'

'What do you mean?'

'You know exactly what I'm referring to.' He noticed her face draining of colour and her eyes were watering. 'I have spent the morning with the Director of Security for the casino reviewing CCTV footage from Treasury Department in the Bennelong Room. You know what we saw, don't you?'

'I just knew that's why you asked me to lunch. You were spying on me,' she said, feigning disappointment.

'Don't be ridiculous, I didn't ask you one question about your work, what you do in the Bennelong Room or its clients. I just wanted to see you again and I've now been made to feel absolutely stupid. I didn't know about your involvement until this morning.' She was now upset, tears sparkled in her eyes and she dropped her head. Jack felt sorry for her. You couldn't make love with someone one day and not care about them the next, even if you are a detective. He waited for her to regain her composure.

'How did it start, Danielle?'

She remained quiet for a moment and then lifted her head and looked at him. 'I was in the staff restaurant one day on my break having a coffee when Mr Woodard came and joined me. We were just talking about our families and I must have mentioned something about my little brother, Ollie, who has a heart condition.'

'What sort of heart condition?'

'A congenital heart defect and unfortunately, surgery might be necessary to repair it and that would be very expensive. He's currently taking medication, which, hopefully, will help his heart's pump function to improve.' She paused, thinking about her brother.

'Continue.'

'Mr Woodard said there might be a way to help my family with the costs of Ollie's medication and treatment, if it's required.

'How did he suggest you would achieve that?'

'He explained that there was a high roller that needed to get rid of some cash and I might be able to help with that. I knew what *get rid of some cash* meant, but I didn't know who the high roller was at that stage. Having seen how much time Mr Woodard spends with Mr Li, I guess I know now.'

'So, how did the process work?'

'There was never any formal structure if you like. Mr Woodard asked for a key to my staff locker and every so often I would find a briefcase in there containing substantial amounts of money.'

'How substantial?'

'Usually around one million dollars, give or take.'

'Go on,' Jack prodded.

'I would take the briefcase with me to the Treasury Department, pretending it contained my lunch and some personal effects, and when I was alone I would enter the vault and swap the cash for pumpkins. Then, on my break or at the end of my shift, I would take the briefcase full of chips and place it in my locker. The next time I opened my locker, the briefcase would be gone.'

'When was the last time you performed your little magic trick?'

'Don't say it like that. It sounds so terrible.'

'It is. When was the last time?'

'About six weeks ago.' That jelled with the date for the second to last transaction in the TTR extract Coleman had sent him.

'How many times have you undertaken this transaction?'

'Seven.' That was consistent with Jack's number, so at least she was telling him the truth.

'And how much did you receive each time?'

'Five thousand dollars.'

'How does the saying go? "Nice work if you can get it." What did you do with the money?'

'I spent some on the expensive medications which aren't covered under the PBS and the rest is tucked away for Ollie's operation, if he requires one.'

Jack was quite sympathetic towards Danielle's plight, but he had to separate his personal feelings and sympathy for her situation from his responsibilities to the job.

'Did you know that the penalties for money laundering range between ten and fifteen years in prison? Especially given the value and number of your transactions.'

'No. All I was thinking about was helping my brother.'

'Have you spoken to Woodard recently?'

'No, not for ages, probably months. I see him all the time in the Bennelong Room, but we don't make contact. Although, the sleaze actually asked me out on a date once. He's married.

Can you believe it?'

'Did you go?'

'God no, I don't go out with work colleagues and he's too old.' 'What even older than me?'

Danielle offered a subdued smile. 'You're still funny, Jack.'

'I don't feel very humorous at the moment.'

'Jack, I want to be honest with you. I didn't make any connection between my activities and whatever you were doing in the Bennelong Room until yesterday. Once I saw Jim Brennan's call register on your phone at the restaurant, I knew something was happening. While you took the call away from the table, I made a decision. I would try to get you to open up about your investigation and I thought you might even discuss it with me, without revealing any secrets or proprietary information, of course. It was my intention to confess about my involvement in the money laundering, if that's what you were investigating, and ask for your help. I even tried to raise the issue again at the Terrace Café, if you remember.'

'And you accused *me* of subterfuge by asking you to lunch. Not half bad, Danielle. There's a saying "keep your friends close and your enemies closer," is that what you were doing yesterday?'

'What, before, during, after we had sex or all of the above?' Danielle adopted a melancholy tone. 'I had sex with you because I am attracted to you, detective. You are a funny, intelligent, interesting and handsome man and I enjoy your company. I don't have sex with someone just for the sake of having sex.' After a lengthy pause, she asked. 'So, where to from here, Jack?'

'What, personally or professionally?'

'Both, I guess.'

'I have no idea about either. I need to evaluate the information I have and formulate a plan.'

'Can I help? I want to make it up to you,' she begged.

'I don't know. I should formally arrest you and take you to the AFP offices for questioning, that's what I do know. But I'm not going to do that. I'll see you later.' He stood up and walked out. A moment later, he came back into the café and she was still seated at the table. She had her head in her hands and was weeping softly. It hurt him to see her like that, but for the moment, he needed to keep his detective head on; he had an investigation to progress.

'Two things; speak to no-one, and I mean no-one, about this until you hear from me again. And, if by chance, you find the briefcase in your locker, leave it there and make up any excuse why you couldn't complete your part of the transaction. Then call me.'

71

Oceanic Security Control

'Jim, it's Jack here. Can I come over and steal a few minutes of your time? I'm just across Darling Harbour, so I can be there in fifteen.'

'Sure, you're lucky I'm still here, see you soon.'

Brennan met Jack at reception, signed him in and escorted him to the Security Office. 'Let me guess what you're going to ask me, Jack. You want to know about my follow-up on Mr Woodard, am I correct?'

'You're on the money as usual.'

'Well, first you need to know that company policy prohibits one-on-one interviews, primarily to ensure there is a witness present and to avoid unsubstantiated claims of bullying and harassment. I decided to inform the CEO of my inquiry, so he and the HR Manager joined me in the interview. You also need to know that I have kept your involvement out of this for now, with the blessing of the CEO.'

'I arranged for Mr Woodard to come to this office and he was obviously surprised to see the CEO and HR Manager in attendance. "What's this all about" he asked? I told him it was a routine security review of CCTV footage and we had some questions for him.'

'What was his demeanour like?'

'His face paled somewhat at first and he seemed uncomfortable, on edge, but he recovered after a few anxious moments. I showed Mr

Woodard the footage of him entering and leaving the vault on the day in question. I even halted the video at the crucial points, so he could clearly see it was him in the frame. The CEO then assumed the questioning.'

'That's interesting. Why would he do that?'

'I think to ensure Woodard realised the potential seriousness of his actions, to show support for my inquiries and avoid any inference of a witch hunt by my office; to show independence, if you like.'

'Okay, I get that now,' said Jack.

'The CEO got straight to the point and asked Mr Woodard what he was doing in the vault. He took some time to respond. Then he offered this answer. He said, "there was no-one in attendance in the Treasury Department and he had an anxious client who wanted to purchase some gaming chips." 'Then he said, "it was less than the ten thousand dollar reporting threshold, so I saw no reason why I shouldn't accommodate my client". The CEO wasn't letting it go at that, so he asked for the name of the client. Mr Woodard said, "he couldn't recall." The CEO persisted. "Tony, you're the Vice President of Client Services and you're telling me you can't recall the name of your own client?" Mr Woodard once again said he couldn't recall.'

'What happened next?'

'In front of Mr Woodard, the CEO instructed me to provide him with the CCTV footage for the period of one hour either side of the time Mr Woodard entered the vault.'

'What was Woodard's reaction?'

'Surprisingly, he was quite calm.'

'The CEO then asked the HR Manager to contact his office and make an appointment for the Treasury Manager to meet with him ASAP.' Jack knew this would be problematic for Woodard and he couldn't allow Michelle Ironside to meet with the CEO.

'How was Woodard's reaction to that?'

'To my suspicious eye, he didn't seem to like that idea at all. And finally, the CEO reminded Mr Woodard that he didn't have authorisation or a security clearance to be in the Treasury Department in the first instance and that he would be issued with an official written warning as a result. Woodard tried to argue the point but the CEO shut him down. He's a good CEO this one, you'd like him Jack.'

'Jim, I'm going to tell you something, but you can't ask me any questions at this point. Can you do that for me?'

'Shit. What's going on here?'

'I promise to tell you everything I know when the time is right. In the meantime, you need to provide Michelle Ironside with close personal protection. No questions, remember. Can you do that, for her sake, Jim? She could be in imminent danger. And you should keep this strictly between the three of us. If you need to advise the CEO, then by all means do so, but no-one else.'

'It's just as well that I trust you, Jack. Alright, I'll get onto it.'

Macquarie Suite

'Client Services, this is Sage.'

'I would like to speak to the Vice President.'

'Unfortunately, Mr Woodard is unavailable at this time, Mr Li, can someone else assist?'

'This happened the last two times I have called, Miss. Does he still work here or not?' Li demanded.

'Yes, he certainly does, Mr Li. I'll do my very best to locate him for you now.'

'Good and when you do locate him will you tell him to come to my suite.'

'Absolutely, Mr Li, will there be anything else?' Sage replied in her obliging, corporate voice.

'No.' With that, Li disconnected the call, poured himself a Glenlivet and waited for Woodard.

While he waited he picked up his burner phone again and rang Wie Ping Lie. 'We need to meet.'

'Yes, we do.'

'Would you like some Pipis on my account?'

'Yes, say six o'clock.'

'See you there.' Both Li and Wie knew to keep their phone conversations brief now.

Li was taking a sip of his whiskey when he heard the doorbell chime. He walked across, looked through the peephole and then let Woodard into the suite. 'Hello, Tony, how are you today?'

'I've had better days. I spent an hour earlier this afternoon being questioned by Oceanic's Director of Security, the CEO and HR Manager.'

Li's face darkened. 'What about?'

'Their enquiry was very specific. The CEO himself wanted to know what I was doing in the Treasury Department vault at a particular time last week.'

'What particular time, and what did you tell him?' Li asked suspiciously.

'You know which time we are talking about here, Li.'

'Mr Li to you, as I have reminded you numerous times.' He continued. 'I thought you had someone else to conduct the exchanges, so you weren't directly implicated. How did you allow yourself to be in that compromising situation? You were supposed to keep yourself one step removed from the exchanges, which kept me two steps away, Tony.'

'The person who has been conducting the exchanges on our behalf wasn't available and you were quite forceful in demanding the exchange was handled expeditiously, if I remember correctly. You said something like, "I should think one hour would be sufficient time for a man in your executive position." That's how it happened,' Woodard said folding his arms over his chest.

'Okay, that changes things. The impending exchange will be the last in our arrangement. What was the outcome of your interrogation?'

'I will be issued with a written warning for entering the vault and breaching the Treasury Department security protocols.'

'Is that all?' Asked Li, still concerned.

'No, the CEO has asked for the Treasury Manager to attend a meeting with him where she will no doubt be quizzed about her own activities on the day in question.'

'And what will she tell him?'

'She realises I can argue that she was a key participant in the arrangement and, as such, was well rewarded for her assistance. Whether it's true or not won't matter, given it's her word against mine, and that in itself should create enough doubt. I'm hoping she will simply feign ignorance, as I did, and be satisfied to receive an official warning.'

'That's leaving too much to chance and you know it. We need to deal with her, and soon.'

'What are you suggesting?'

'Something stronger than a cup of coffee this time, Mr Vice President. I will take care of it. In the meantime, we have business to transact.'

'How much is in the briefcase this time?'

'There is no briefcase, yet. I am just giving you sufficient notice in case you have arrangements to make. I will have it in my possession tomorrow and I will call you when it is available for collection.' Woodard knew it was pointless having another argument as he was in far too deep already to extract himself. He was keenly aware the arrangement was close to expiring, so he would go with the flow.

'How much this time?'

'Tony, it's about the same amount as last time which you managed with such ease.'

'Okay, I'll do it.'

'Of course, you will.' Li said with a wry smile. 'I'll see you tomorrow.'

Prior leaving for his dinner engagement, Li made a phone call. 'I have another task for you that requires urgent handling and it needs to be undertaken tonight. He explained the task and then disconnected the call. He then once again rang the VIP Guest Relations number and ordered a limousine to take him to his dinner meeting. Shortly thereafter, the Mercedes Benz S Class deposited him at the Golden Phoenix Restaurant.

'Huang, I see my guest is already here, so I'll see myself to the table. Can you get me my usual please?' As Li walked to the table, he noticed the familiar navy blue briefcase under the table next to Wie's leg.

'Wie, how are you?' Li asked as he shook his guest's outstretched hand.

'I am very well.'

'Good, we have a number of things that we need to discuss. '

'First let us talk about that lady reporter that seems to have the better of you, Li.'

'What about her?'

'I hear she has some photos that the Consul General does not wish to become public. What have you done about that messy state of affairs?'

'She won't release them; they're just a retaliation for our own intimidation.'

'The fact that she has used them at all is a big concern to me. She should never have been allowed to become so close to your candidate. That it was allowed to happen in the first place shows me you selected the wrong candidate and her priorities are misplaced.'

'She was the perfect candidate; it was just circumstances that put her and the Granger woman together,' Li said defensively.

'Rubbish, Li, there are over two hundred thousand ethnic Chinese citizens living in Sydney and you chose the disloyal, feisty one with less than appropriate tendencies. And that Granger woman cannot be allowed to get any closer to me, you or our operation. I will take care of her,' he promised. Li didn't dare tell Wie about Granger having a detective for an ex- boyfriend; he could find that out for himself.

'I listened to you last week when you were warning me against becoming complacent. Since then I have given it some thought, Li. Maybe we *have* become somewhat complacent, but you yourself have also potentially exposed our business arrangement to scrutiny by the authorities with your extracurricular activities.'

'And finally, I saw you look at the briefcase under the table as you walked in. You can take it with you, but this will be our last transaction. The shipment that is on the water now, I will handle myself. I won't need your involvement.'

'That is not your decision to make, Wie.'

'If you don't like it, call your master in China.' Wie pushed the briefcase across to Li with his foot. 'Enjoy your precious Pipis,' he said with a curled lip, as he rose from the table and strode purposefully towards the exit.

(73)

Treasury Department

Michelle Ironside was finishing her end of shift reconciliation before handing over to the incoming supervisor. For some reason she was unusually tired tonight, but put it down to the stress of the Woodard scenario, which still remained unresolved. She hadn't heard from the detective since their second meeting a few days ago, so she therefore assumed that he was still collecting evidence. She had been ordered to meet with the CEO tomorrow afternoon and while she was oblivious as to the agenda, she could take an educated guess. She badly needed a good night's sleep if she was going to be alert for that. The incoming supervisor verified and signed for the Treasury holdings and Michelle made her way to the staff room to collect her belongings.

She noticed a missed call and saw whoever the caller was had left a voicemail message. It was from the hotel's Director of Security asking her to contact him urgently, but it was now too late in the evening, so she would ring him in the morning. Michelle booked her Uber, collected her handbag and jacket from her locker and made her way outside to the rideshare collection point. *Thank heavens my ride is already here*, she thought, as she opened the SUV's door and sat in the rear seat behind the driver. She was so fatigued that she rested her head against the seat back and closed her eyes.

Michelle awoke with a start. She looked at her phone to check the time and was aghast that she had been in the Uber for over half an hour. The ride home at this time of night should only take fifteen minutes, tops. She started to worry when she looked out the window, only to see that the car was pulling into the driveway of a warehouse.

'What are you doing? Where are we?' she called out to the driver. There was no response. Michelle leaned around the driver's seat and fear set in as she saw the driver's head was covered with one of those knitted headpieces she had seen on TV police shows, but could never remember the name of.

Telling herself to remain calm, she grabbed her phone again, only for the driver's large hand to reach around his seat and snatch it. As the driver exited the SUV, he took the back cover off of her old Nokia, removed the battery, threw the phone on the ground and stomped on it numerous times. Michelle burst into tears as he opened the rear door, grabbed her by the arm and dragged her out onto the concrete tarmac. He then extracted another of the knitted headpieces out of his jacket pocket and pulled it down over her head. Only this one had no eye cut-outs. A chill ran down her spine. She was now completely in the dark.

"Help! Help!' she screamed. 'Who are you? Why are you doing this to me?' she struggled against her attacker as best she could, bucking her shoulders.

'If you don't want to get hurt, shut up, lady.'

'Who are you, what are you doing, why are—' Michelle felt a hard thump to the back of her head. Flashes of light invaded her vision and then everything faded.

She had no idea of the time when she woke. What she did know though was, her head was pounding and she had a large bump on the back of her skull. Her hands were tied behind her back, but she knew the bump was there without having to touch it. Her mouth felt like it was full of cotton balls and tasted of bile. She was lying on a doona or a thick blanket of some sort.

At least she was still alive. She guessed if they, whomever they were, wanted her dead, she would be. Her body shuddered at the thought though.

'Is anyone here? Help me please,' she cried out. There was no echo, so she deduced she must be in a small room. She was feeling slightly dizzy and felt a wave of nausea pass over her, so it was likely she had a mild concussion. 'Help! Help! Help!' she cried out again and again.

Her head throbbed with every shout, but she continued on. 'Help… Help…' After receiving no response and with tiredness kicking in again, she lay down on her side and drifted away.

The sound of heavy metal banging jolted her awake. The door to wherever she was, was being unbolted and her thoughts were confirmed by the squeaking of hinges. Next, she heard the sound of footsteps approaching her and she began to fear the worst. She had no idea how long she had been asleep, but she knew it must have been more than a catnap. She quickly gathered her composure and moved into the foetal position to protect herself. 'Who's there? What do you want with me?' she croaked.

'I'm not going to hurt you,' was all she heard in a thick, accented voice. Then she felt a hand on the knitted headpiece and she recoiled in horror, but her movement was restricted by her bound hands and feet. She felt like a retreating crab.'

'I told you, I'm not going to hurt you. Sit still,' was all she heard in the accented voice.

From behind, the headpiece was lifted above her mouth and the opening of a bottle was pushed against her lips. 'Drink,' demanded the voice.

An indignant Michelle wanted to tell the man to fuck off and to demand he let her go, but her mouth was so parched, that she sipped slowly and quenched her thirst. She strained to turn her head, hoping to see the man, but it was quickly jolted back. 'What do you want with me?' she asked in a more conciliatory tone this time. Silence.

'What do you want?' She felt the headpiece being pulled down over her jaw and moments later heard the squeak of the hinges and for the second time, the sound of heavy metal banging against heavy metal. The man had left and she was alone again.

AFP Headquarters
Tuesday 10th March

Jack arrived at his desk on the tenth floor of the AFP Building and began planning for the tasks he needed to complete during the day. His priority was to meet with Danielle and explain his plans for her, plans which if successfully implemented, might just be enough to mitigate any serious charges that would inevitably be levelled against her. He had called her from his car on the drive into the office and she had agreed to meet him for coffee at Sappho again later that morning. After compiling his notes, he hit the phone.

He checked in on Sanderson and Romano, which he hadn't done since ten o'clock last night. They had grabbed a few hours' sleep and then headed out very early this morning looking for Ling Jun and Wang Wei, so far to no avail.

He then called Jim Brennan. 'I'm just checking in on Michelle Ironside, Jim. Have you been able to arrange the personal protection for her yet?'

'Yeah, it's all taken care of. It starts this afternoon when she finishes with the CEO. He has kindly given her a few days leave from that point onwards and she will have someone with her at all times.'

'That's great. Her safety is paramount,' he reminded Brennan again.

Brennan pushed him for an explanation, but Jack said, 'In good time, Jim, just trust me for now.'

Jack was a stickler for accurately documenting all aspects of his investigations, primarily so any evidence he was to provide during future legal proceedings couldn't be successfully challenged and also to cover his arse. He had just begun to write-up his latest report for submission to the DC when his mobile phone rang. He saw JA's name on the display and realised he hadn't provided her with an update since their catch-up at the Rogue Café three days ago.

'Hi, JA, how are you?'

'Jack, it's not Julie-Anne. My name is Melissa Wu.'

'Why are you calling on JA's mobile? What's happened, where is she?' Melissa could hear the concern in Jack's voice.

'Do you know who I am, Jack?'

'Yes, now answer my questions,' he demanded.

'The reason I have her mobile is that she asked me to call you. She *is* okay, but there's been a terrible incident—'

Jack interrupted her. 'What sort of terrible incident?'

'Her car was shot at while she was on her way to work this morning.'

'What, where, why?' Jack blurted out even though he probably knew the why.

'I can tell you more when I see you. At the moment, she is undergoing tests at Royal Prince Alfred. They should be finished soon, then we'll be able to see her and find out more. I'll wait for you at reception.'

For the first time, Melissa felt insecure about her relationship with Julie-Anne. Even though Julie-Anne had asked the hospital staff to contact her first, she was caught off guard by Jack's response. He obviously still cared deeply for her, and this scenario might provide him with a wake-up call. That might not bode well for Melissa in the future. She quickly dismissed the thought as selfish. Julie-Anne needed her undivided attention and committed support at the moment.

Twenty minutes later, Melissa noticed a tall, athletic looking man striding into the RPA's reception. From Julie-Anne's description this had to be Jack. She stood up, ready to attract his attention, but he was already making his way straight towards her.

'How is she?'

'Hi, I'm Melissa,' she said, offering her hand in greeting.

Jack recognised her from the Daily News photo taken at the consular cocktail party. 'I know who you are. How is she?' Jack asked sharply without returning the greeting.

Melissa understood his anxiety, so she maintained her calm demeanour despite his rudeness. 'As far as I know, she's fine. They're running some more tests as we speak.'

'What sort of tests? What happened?'

'Jack, the doctor will come out and provide an update on her condition when they are finished with the tests. In the meantime, why don't we grab a coffee and I will tell you what I know.'

They rode the elevator in silence to Alfredo's Café on level five, where they found a table in a quiet corner and waited for their coffees to arrive. Melissa couldn't fathom why Jack had gone from being overtly abrupt to very quiet in only a few minutes. She would maintain her own silence until he was ready to talk, or listen, for that matter.

'I'm sorry for being snappy earlier, Melissa. I'm sure you're just trying to help. Can you tell me what happened?' he asked in a more conciliatory tone.

'Firstly, you need to know that she is reasonably okay. And all I know is what Julie-Anne told me in the Emergency Department before they took her off for testing. She said that she was driving down Raglan Street in Waterloo near the public housing estate basketball courts. All of a sudden, a black SUV with tinted windows came up alongside her, as if it was overtaking.

The SUV suddenly slowed, matching her speed and it was at that moment that she knew something was seriously wrong. Luckily, she had her wits about her, because the SUV's passenger side window then lowered and she saw a gun. She'd slowed sufficiently that she was now in the shooter's peripheral vision. I guess he couldn't see Julie-Anne clearly, so he fired two shots into her front driver's side tyre instead, hoping to disable her car.'

'What the hell was she doing on Raglan Street? That's not her usual route to the office and I warned her to be careful.'

'I don't know; you'll have to ask her. Anyway, apparently her tyre shredded pretty much instantly, causing the steering wheel to violently jerk to the right. Her car careered across the road, narrowly missing the SUV, jumped the kerb and ploughed into a fence upright. That's all I know at the moment.'

'I'm going downstairs to the ED waiting room,' Jack said brusquely. 'Well, I guess I'll come too then,' Melissa replied.

As they entered the waiting room an older, homely looking woman in a knee-length white laboratory coat with a stethoscope dangling around her neck was walking towards them. 'Here comes the doctor.'

'Yeah, I can see that.' *Okay, we're back to being rude,* Melissa thought. The doctor's lanyard said her name was June Mellor and she began addressing Melissa, much to Jack's obvious annoyance.

'You need to know that she is as well as can be expected.'

Before she could continue, Jack interrupted. 'That's not saying much.' The doctor gave him an indignant look. 'And you are, sir?'

'I'm her…boyfriend.'

'Really, Jack?' Melissa said, looking at him, dumbfounded.

The doctor looked back and forth between them. 'May I continue? She has quite a lot of bruising, predominantly around her chest, and some abdominal pain, both caused by the seatbelt tightening on impact. There is also minor bruising on her face due to the airbag deploying. And finally, she has a mild concussion, once again caused by the airbag.

'Is she going to be okay?' The doctor ignored Jack and addressed Melissa again.

'We're going to keep her for observation until later this afternoon.

All being well, you'll be able to take her home then. You can go and see her now if you so wish.'

'That's wonderful news. Thank you very much, doctor,' rejoiced Melissa.

$$\boxed{75}$$

RPA Emergency Ward

Melissa and Jack walked down the sterile corridor, replete with its competing odours of disinfectant and floor polish, to the emergency ward. The ward was a largish, windowless room with eight beds all partitioned into cubicles by drab grey plastic drapes hanging from wraparound curtain rods. Julie-Anne's curtain was pulled back and she saw them enter the ward. 'Over here, guys.' She watched Melissa's face light up when she spied her, but she also noticed Jack's uncomfortable expression.

Jack leant forward and went to kiss Julie-Anne on the lips. She turned her head and offered her cheek, feigning pain, so as not to hurt his feelings. Melissa picked up on this immediately, and when she approached Julie-Anne, she leant in and kissed her on the cheek. 'How are you feeling?'

'I'm a bit on the stiff and sore side, but otherwise I reckon I'm okay. They think I might have a mild concussion, but I feel reasonably alert.'

There was an awkward silence in the room, which was eventually broken by Jack. 'What were you doing on Raglan Street, JA?'

That was Melissa's signal. 'I might leave you two to talk about that. I'm going to grab another coffee, Julie-Anne.' Melissa beamed a smile and blew her a kiss. *Is that really necessary?* thought Jack.

'Where were we, Jack? Oh yeah, Raglan Street. The traffic on Regent Street was a nightmare, so I thought I would cut across Raglan to Elizabeth Street. The security company told me to avoid using side streets, but I wouldn't class Raglan as a side street, so I took it,' she explained.

'What security company, JA?'

'I don't remember their name, but the Daily News engaged them for my protection.'

'Protection,' he blurted out. What's changed since we caught up three days ago that you now need a security company protecting you?'

'Have you checked your voicemail messages this week? I left one two days ago.' Jack remembered the call he had bumped to voicemail while having lunch with Danielle. It definitely seemed appropriate at the time, but he regretted it now. Julie-Anne continued and told him about the photo left on her apartment door and Li's threats at the Rogue Café. She thought it might not be wise to mention her own piece of retaliation.

'Did you notice the shooter by any chance?'

'Vaguely. I was more focused on the gun and trying to avoid being shot, Jack. I'm glad I didn't panic and had the foresight to slow down when I did, otherwise the gun would have been pointed straight at me. The shooter had on large dark sunglasses, wore a black shirt and I'm pretty sure he was of Asian appearance.'

'Was it Fan Chen?'

'I don't think so. From the glimpse I got, the shooter looked smaller, leaner.' Jack had warned her before about Wie Ping Lie, so if it wasn't Li Qiang's man, then it would probably be one of Wie's.

'Are you up for looking at a few photos, JA?'

'Yeah, sure.' Jack texted Sanderson and asked him to send through photos of Ling Jun and Wang Wei. Just then, Melissa walked back into the cubicle. Jack was already feeling uneasy with her presence around JA. Maybe it was his own insecurity he was sensing. 'I might grab a coffee myself while I wait for the photos; I'll be back soon.'

Once Jack had departed, Melissa tilted forward and brushed back the errant strands of hair from Julie-Anne's face. Then she leaned in and gave Julie-Anne a long, gentle kiss. 'That's better,' gushed Julie-Anne.

'I didn't want Jack to feel uncomfortable, hence the cheek kiss.'

'That was very considerate, thank you.'

'Jack has been quite abrupt with me, but I guess that's understandable, given the circumstances.'

'Yes, he is aware of who you are, but I'm sure it's still awkward for him. Anyway, he'll be okay now. He's always better when he's got his policeman's head on and he has already started investigating the attack on me. He wants me to look at some photos and see if I recognise the shooter.'

Two men in suits entered the Emergency Ward and made their way to Julie-Anne's cubicle.

'What the hell happened, JA? Are you okay?' Chris Russell had been a mentor of Julie-Anne's and had always looked out for her, almost like a surrogate father, and he wore a concerned expression.

'I'm fine, Chris, just a little knocked about.' 'Melissa, this is my editor, Chris Russell.'

'A pleasure to meet you, Melissa, although under different circumstances would have been preferable. This is David Bedford.' Melissa greeted both men with a smile and firm handshake. 'Nice to meet you both.'

'JA, David's team noticed on their tracking software that your car was stationary on Raglan Street, Waterloo. That made no sense to them as you shouldn't be making unscheduled stops. David sent a team to the site, but by then you were already being transported here in an ambulance. Can you tell us, for David's benefit in particular, what occurred?'

Julie-Anne began reiterating the events of that morning when Jack walked back into the ward. She introduced him to the two men. Jack knew who Chris Russell was, but not the other suit.

'Who's David and what's his involvement here, JA?' he asked curtly.

'David's the head of the security company appointed to look out for me, Jack.'

'That's worked out well so far.' Like most policemen, Jack didn't regard private security companies very highly and he had no intention of letting them inside his investigation.

'Jack, enough.' admonished Julie-Anne. She finished providing Russell and Bedford with her best recollection of the events that occurred a few hours earlier. As she concluded her account, two more men in suits walk into the ward. With their inexpensive, off the rack suits, scuffed shoes and loosened ties, they couldn't be anything but detectives. As they walked across to her cubicle she sighed, 'aaahh, I'm getting to be a popular girl today.'

'Have you eaten, Julie-Anne?' asked Melissa.

'No, I haven't actually and I'm starving.'

'Let me reduce the assembled throng by one and I'll go get you something. I'll take my time and maybe the crowd will have thinned by the time I return.'

Just as the two detectives reached the cubicle, Jack put out his arm and halted their progress. He quickly introduced himself and ushered them aside to a nearby vacant cubicle.

'I'm Jack Wagner and I'm with the Australian Federal Police,' he said as he extracted his ID card from his wallet. The two detectives introduced themselves as Peter Crawford and Harry Newman. Jack guessed through the obvious age difference that Crawford must be the senior of the two.

'So, what interest does the AFP have in this woman's incident?' enquired Crawford.

'She's a friend of mine.'

'What sort of friend, Jack?'

'A close friend is all you need to know.'

'Okay then. We've had a thorough look at the incident site and the

Major Collision Investigation Unit are conducting a re-enactment as we speak. Now we'd like to talk to your *close friend* if that's okay with you,' Crawford stated with intended sarcasm.

'Before you do, there're some things you need to be made aware of.'

'Here we go,' said Crawford. 'Are we going to get into a pissing match, Wagner?'

'Not at all, but let me continue. The incident, as you described it, is related to a cooperative investigation being carried out by Maritime Border Command, New South Wales Police and the AFP. This investigation is at a sensitive stage and I don't want it disrupted, or worse, compromised by over enthusiastic state police.'

'Maybe you could put in a good word with the hierarchy about our *over enthusiasm*,' Crawford said with no desire to hide his sarcasm. 'I'm sure they'd be delighted to hear that, especially from one of the AFP's finest.'

Jack took a deep breath. 'How about we go upstairs, grab a coffee and I'll give you an overview of the investigation? Then you can decide how you want to proceed,' he said in a conciliatory tone. The three men made their way along the corridor to the elevator.

Julie-Anne had finished recounting the events of that morning for Russell and Bedford. Bedford was horrified that it had happened on his company's watch. 'I really wished you had listened to me and not taken a diversion though; I specifically warned you about that,' he said by way of mild admonishment.

'I don't suppose it would do any good if I told you I have taken Raglan Street many times before, David,' she replied, trying to justify her actions.

'No, it wouldn't. You need to follow our security plan to the letter. It's for your own benefit, Julie-Anne. If you slowed down sufficiently, then the SUV may just have ended up far enough ahead of you that it was picked-up on your dashcam. I will contact my techs and see what's on there. In the meantime, I will place a guard at your door for the interim until your release.'

'I'm surrounded by detectives, David; I think I'll be okay in here.'

'Needless to say, don't concern yourself with the investigation for the moment. Just take whatever sick leave you need and focus on your recovery,' offered Russell.

'Well, Julie-Anne, how are you feeling?' asked Doctor Mellor as she breezed into the ward.

'Other than a bit battered and bruised, not bad, all things considered, Doctor.'

'That's good to hear. What you have is a mild concussion and with sufficient rest and plenty of fluids you should be fully recovered in a few days. You may experience mild headaches, so I suggest taking a paracetamol such as Tylenol if you do. Now, there's no specific cure for concussion. You need to rest and allow your brain time to recover. That also includes limiting activities that require thinking and mental concentration. More specifically, you should reduce screen time, limit your exposure to bright lights and loud sounds, avoid unnecessary movement of your head and neck and stay hydrated. Your brain needs complete rest. Do you understand? Julie-Anne?'

'Yes, thank you for everything, Doctor.'

'Give me half an hour to complete your paperwork and then you can be out of here.'

'No hurry, Doctor, I think I am about to be interviewed by a couple of detectives anyway.'

(76)

Macquarie Suite

'Sage, I would like to speak to the Vice President again.'

'Unfortunately, Mr Woodard is unavailable at this time, Mr Li, can someone else assist you?'

'This is the fourth time in a row that I have called and he has been unavailable. Have him come to my suite when he is available,' Li demanded.

'Mr Li, Mr Woodard is not at work today, apparently he is unwell and he has called in sick. I'm sure he will be back tomorrow.'

Li slammed the handset down. This was most unusual and he doubted the timing was a coincidence. This was supposed to be transaction day and he could not countenance the fact that Woodard was absent from his duty. He rang Woodard's mobile. The call went straight to voicemail, as Li suspected it would. 'Call me as soon as you get this message, Tony.' Ten minutes later his mobile rang.

'You asked me to call you, Mr Li.'

'Of course I asked you to call me; today we are supposed to be conducting our transaction. I've got a million dollars sitting idly in my safe and you're not at work because you've got a common cold. What is it you Australians say? "You need to toughen up, princess."'

'I'm sure I will be back at work in the next day or so, Mr Li.'

'Well, you had better make certain you are, Mr Vice President, or else.'

'Are you threatening me again?'

'No, Tony, I am making a promise. I want the transaction completed on your first day back at work, that being tomorrow. Is that clear?'

'Yes.'

'Aaahh, Mr Consul General, how are you?' Li hadn't spoken to Xiao for a couple of days and thought he would give him the courtesy of a phone call.

'I am well, thank you, Li. I would be even better if I would see more positive media coverage about China. The Australian media have been running propaganda stories about the protests in Hong Kong for months with no sign of letting up. And things won't improve now they are accusing China of giving the world COVID-19. Even Chinese restaurants in this country are being abandoned by their customers who think they will catch the virus while indulging in their sweet and sour pork. We urgently need the capacity to influence the anti-China sentiment and conversation in this country, Li. Speaking of which, how is your candidate coming along?'

'We might have to find another candidate, Xiao. I have contacted Miss Wu's office twice to arrange another meeting and her staff say she is taking some personal leave. I have also rung her mobile numerous times and it is obviously turned off as it's going straight to voicemail. I can only assume she is spending more time with the journalist.'

'Have you heard anymore from the Granger woman, Li?'

'No, but I think we reached a mutual understanding at our meeting a couple of days ago, so she shouldn't be a problem, Xiao.'

'Li, read the tea leaves. She is obviously spending time with your preferred candidate. I think it's time you made a swift decision about Miss Wu's candidacy and moved on to another option. Do we still have the financial support to run a candidate at the state election?'

'Yes, money is not the problem. I already have a substantial fund set up for a robust political campaign and we have one more transaction to be completed which will add to our war chest.'

'For everyone's sake, I hope so. We can't bring funds in directly from China to support our election campaign.'

'I don't need a lecture from you, Xiao, I know what I am doing.'

'I also hear you have conscripted Mr Chen to conduct some errands for you.'

'He has just been looking after my best interests, which of course, are also your best interests, Xiao. That's all you need to know.'

'Well, if things get out of hand and he comes to the attention of the authorities, we can try and claim diplomatic immunity for him.'

'Let us hope it doesn't come to that.'

'You might want to consider availing yourself of a similar safeguard, Li,' offered Xiao.

'I'm sure that will be unnecessary.'

Next Li would call Fan Chen. Even though they were both now using burner phones, the conversation would be clipped, just in case the authorities were listening in.

'How is everything, my friend?'

'Just as you requested.'

'Is the package in good condition?'

'Yes, it arrived safely and in good order.'

'That is good. And how are you?'

'Very well, thank you.'

'Okay, I'll talk to you soon.'

(**77**)

Central Station Sydney

Melissa walked back into the Emergency Ward carrying a leafy salad and an orange juice for Julie-Anne. 'Thanks, I'm starving now.'

'Where is the cast of thousands, Julie-Anne?'

'The doctor's been and gone and the trio of detectives are upstairs having coffee. It's nice having just the two of us sharing these salubrious surroundings, for the moment at least.' Julie-Anne chuckled as she tucked into her salad.

'What did the doctor say?' asked a concerned Melissa.

'She is just completing my paperwork and then I can go home.'

'That's wonderful news.'

'I'm not so sure. For the first time in my career, I'm quite anxious. I've never been shot at before. Maybe this investigative stuff's just not for me.'

'You need to give yourself a few days to recover, then start thinking about your future. You know what they say, Julie-Anne, never make an important life-changing decision when you are upset.'

'Yeah, I know,' Julie-Anne replied, absentmindedly fiddling with a loose sheet thread. 'If whoever they are, can attack me that easily, then when and where will I ever be safe while in this job? They know my mobile number, place of work and where I live. I've been the subject of their intimidation three times now, and it escalates each time. I'm not keen to give them another shot, no pun intended.'

Melissa could plainly see the concern written all over Julie-Anne's face. 'You could stay at my place, but they will surely be expecting that, so that's not an option. I'm sure Jack will know the right thing to do. After all, he is a detective. He'll work something out.'

Jack was next to walk into the ward in company with the two detectives and they made their way across to Julie-Anne's cubicle.

'This place is busier than Pitt St Mall in peak hour,' she joked. 'Back for the interview I'm guessing, detectives.'

Crawford addressed Julie-Anne. 'Actually, Ms Granger, after speaking with Detective Wagner, we won't need to speak to you at this stage. The detective has provided us with all the information we require for now.'

She breathed a heavy sigh. 'Well, that's a relief. I'm all talked out anyway.'

'We will need to speak with you in the future, however. Can we contact you through Detective Wagner?'

'I'm sure that will be fine, detective.' Melissa picked-up on Julie-Anne's response and wondered if she was missing something.

'And here comes Doctor June with my paperwork. I'm outta here,' whooped Julie-Anne. 'Ouch, that hurt, I shouldn't have done that.'

'And where exactly are you going to go, JA?' Jack asked.

'I hadn't decided yet. Obviously I can't go home as I'm guessing they followed me from there this morning.'

'I have a plan, JA.' *Here it comes*, thought Melissa. Jack must have noticed the slight look of disappointment on her face. 'No, not my place. Melissa, do you have your car here?'

'Yes, Mercy's outside. Why?'

'Do you have any bags or cases in your car?'

'Yes, again. I always keep a packed overnight bag in the boot of the car, just in case.' Melissa smiled bashfully at Julie-Anne.

'Okay, I have a plan,' Jack said.

'Whoever these guys are, I'm not certain that they know of my involvement at this stage, or even who I am, hence why we're in your car, Melissa.' Jack had bought a baseball cap at the hospital gift shop and now had it pulled low down over his forehead as he drove east along Cleveland Street. 'Just as I thought, we're being tailed girls. There's a black SUV a few cars back. It's been there since we left the hospital.'

Melissa thought back to Julie-Anne picking up their own tail a few days ago. 'You and Julie-Anne are good at this detection stuff.'

'Comes with the territory, I guess.'

'Jack, why not just pull over, and confront them?'

'JA, I don't know if they're armed, but I have to assume they are, and secondly, if they are, I don't want to risk a peak hour shootout in the middle of the city. Finally, I don't want to put your lives at risk either. We need to lose them. So, let's put this plan into action, shall we?'

'Okay, what's the plan?'

'JA, I'm going to drop you off at the Eastern Stairs of Central Station on Elizabeth Street. Melissa, you need to get out as well and make an exaggerated farewell gesture as if JA's going on a train journey to the country to recuperate. Then, with the overnight bag in hand, JA, you need to walk down the stairs, as briskly as you are able, and continue straight through the underground concourse. Then take the escalator, cross the Northern and Grand Concourses and exit onto the Western Forecourt. There's a kiss and ride bay right near the exit and we'll meet you there. Are you up for this?'

'I'm a bit sore and I don't know about brisk, but I should be okay.'

'Good, and hopefully they'll follow you,' Jack said calmly.

She looked at him in disbelief. '*What.* Jesus, Jack, you actually want them to follow me!' she exclaimed.

'Yes. These guys will want to find out which train you are supposed to be catching, and what your destination is, so they should follow you. Don't worry, they won't try anything with thousands of commuters around. If they don't follow you, then they must have assumed that you're leaving the city and they don't see you as a threat any longer. If they do follow you, then we'll lose them when you reach us on the Western Forecourt. It's a win, win.'

'That's easy for you to say.' She was apprehensive, but she would have to stare down her fears if this plan was going to work.

'Whatever you do, don't look back, otherwise they will realise we're onto them. You will hopefully lose them on the crowded concourses, but if not, they won't be able to follow us, not by car anyway. You need to be strong. Just keep walking with your head held high like you know precisely where you are heading. You can do this.'

Jack turned into the Light Rail lane. 'Jesus, where are you going now? We'll get rundown by one of those rhinoceros on roller skates,' Julie-Anne said, looking out the rear window.

'Let's see if they have enough balls to follow.' He continued along the tracks until he was adjacent to the Eastern Stairs on Elizabeth Street. 'Okay, JA, you're up.' She picked up the overnight bag and gingerly exited the car along with Melissa. The women hugged gently and then Melissa kissed Julie-Anne passionately.

'Was that exaggerated enough do you think? I think I like this plan,' Melissa said, hoping to relax Julie-Anne. 'You can do this; I'll be waiting for you on the other side.' Then she gave an extravagant wave as Julie-Anne made her way down the stairs to the lower concourse. Melissa lowered herself into the passenger's seat and Jack slowly pulled away from the kerb. As he did so, in the rear vision mirror he noticed the SUV had come to a halt thirty metres behind him on the Light Rail tracks. He watched two men alight, leave their vehicle behind and hurriedly make their way towards the stairs to the lower concourse. Jack laughed. 'I'd love to be around when seventy-two tonnes of tram meets a one tonne SUV. Okay, now let's get around to the Western Forecourt.'

Julie-Anne walked as hurriedly as her bruised chest would allow her. She passed through the lower concourse and took the escalator up to the Northern Concourse and the entry to the suburban train platforms. She reached the eastern edge of the Grand Concourse. If she was being followed, her pursuers would think she was heading for the regional train platforms. Now halfway across the station near Platforms 10 and 11, she risked a look in her peripheral vision. She was horrified at what she saw. Two scruffily dressed, unkempt men of Asian appearance were about forty metres adrift and their attention was clearly fixed on her. She thought she recognised a face from this morning and was overcome with dread. Fortunately for her though, they appeared to be caught amongst the large peak hour crowd pushing towards the two platforms. Emboldened by this, she tried to quicken her pace through the concourse, but the chest pain was restricting her breathing and slowing her down. She slowed momentarily and gulped in two deep breaths, which caused a sharp pain to shoot across her chest.

She couldn't have paused for more than two seconds, but having risked another glance as she passed the station office, she saw the men jump the crowd barriers. They were now only thirty metres from her and gaining. She wouldn't be stupid enough to dare risk another look behind her. Melissa's travel bag was slowing her down, so she threw it towards the station office. *I'll buy her another one.* The effect of her concussion was rearing its ugly head, her bruised chest was screaming and her stomach was churning. Ignoring the pain and nerves, she used her freed arms to drive her through the crowded concourse towards the exit. She stretched her long legs out and strode out as fast as her body would allow. Julie-Anne could now see the sign for the Western Forecourt about thirty metres ahead of her. Disregarding the butterflies in her stomach and the feeling of trepidation bearing down on her she maintained her faster pace towards the exit. The glare of the setting sun stinging her eyes told her that she must be close. Putting in half a dozen long strides, she burst out of the exit, onto the Western Forecourt and gingerly slid into the backseat of Melissa's Mercedes. 'Ouch, that hurt.'

'Are you okay, Julie-Anne?'

'Far out, what an adrenalin rush. My heart is pounding, my chest is raging now and my hands are shaking, but yeah, I think I'm okay, Melissa.' Jack saw the two trailing men hurriedly emerge from the station exit and sprint towards the car. But they were too late and judging by their dark expressions and angry gesturing, they were as furious as all hell at being played.

Melissa was looking out the rear window. 'They look livid, Jack.'

'Not as angry as they will be when they see their SUV.' Jack floored the accelerator pedal and the car charged forward and out into the traffic on Railway Colonnade Drive. He could still see their pursuers' angry glares in the rear vision mirror as he and the women made their getaway. He couldn't resist extending his arm out the window and flipping them the bird, while allowing himself a satisfied smile.

After regaining her breath and composing herself, Julie-Anne looked at Jack in the rear vision mirror and asked. 'Was that really necessary, Jack?'

'I was just rubbing it in.'

'No, I meant that elaborate stunt I just put my body through.'

'Yes, it was. We needed to lose them, permanently.'

'Okay, so what's the rest of the plan?'

'Now we're clear of those two, I'm going to take you to an AFP safe house in Randwick, hence why we had to lose those guys.' Jack, remembered the enthusiastic kiss outside the station. 'There's room for both of you to stay there.'

Now it was Melissa's turn to smile.

'Can you both turn off the GPS on your phone while we're still a few kilometres from our destination? We're about twenty minutes out.'

(**78**)

Randwick Safe House

Jack turned off Avoca Street and into the sloping driveway of an underground carpark which serviced a modern-looking apartment building. He retrieved a remote control unit from his jacket pocket, pressed the green button and waited while the roller shutter clanged upwards into its recess.

'This place is fully secured, including swipe card access to the building and elevators. There is an intercom system and the entry door release and lift access for your guests is operated remotely from your apartment. Rest assured the lift will not operate manually. Access via the stairwells is also restricted to swipe card access only.' Jack leaned across and extracted two swipe cards from his breast pocket, giving one to each of the women.

They exited Melissa's Merc and walked across to the elevator foyer. Julie-Anne tried to use the lift without the swipe card and was pleased when there was no response. 'What did you tell those two detectives at the hospital, Jack?'

'I just told them that there was a bigger, multi-agency investigation underway and that their colleagues at Day Street would keep them in the loop when necessary. Michael Sanderson, a state detective who is a part of this investigation, is based there, so in return, they will provide the findings from your incident this morning to him. He will keep me updated.' Upon exiting the elevator Jack led them along the corridor to their apartment. 'Make yourselves at home girls. You could be here for a few days,' he said, ushering them into the expansive living area.

'This is lovely,' Melissa said as she surveyed the open plan layout. 'It's nice and bright with all this light flooding in from the floor to ceiling windows. And just look at this kitchen with its huge benchtop. I'll be cooking up a storm in here.'

Jack noticed Julie-Anne eyeing off the sun-filled balcony. 'JA, I know you love your sunshine, but the balcony's been locked off for obvious reasons.'

'Damn.'

'Now ladies, with the Prince of Wales Hospital across the road, the shopping centre on the corner, and the Randwick Police Station only a block away, this is quite a busy area twenty-four- seven. Hopefully, that will deter anyone from snooping around, should they happen to learn of your whereabouts, which I seriously doubt. You should be safe here.'

'I hope you're right,' said Julie-Anne.

'And you should restrict any excursions to the supermarket within the shopping centre, and nowhere else. Buy some magazines to keep yourselves amused. JA, before I go, can you have a look at these photos that Sanderson has sent me?' Jack handed his mobile across to her. 'Just swipe across for the second photo.'

'Oh, shit,' she blurted out.

'What?'

'I think that's him, Jack, the guy who shot at me this morning. I'm fairly sure he was also one of the guys at Central Station too.'

'Have a look at the second photo, please.'

'I'm not certain. He could have been the second guy at the station, but I don't know.'

'The guy you identified, JA is Ling Jun and we're pretty certain he is an associate of Wie Ping Lie and the second guy is Wang Wei, another associate.'

'How did you find them so quick, Jack?'

'They are linked to a suspected drug importation and are known associates of Wie Ping Lie. I did warn you about that guy.'

Melissa was seated on the lava-coloured sofa listening intently. 'Should we be scared?'

'They're not nice people, Melissa, so you need to keep your wits about you. Having said that, you should be safe here. I've also asked the state police not to release any details about your incident to the media for a couple of days.'

'While we're on the subject, Jack, I had another call from Ms Anonymous yesterday.'

'What did she have to say, JA?'

'Quite a lot really, but nothing particularly new. We actually met up at Coogee Beach, went for a walk and had a long chat. Her name is Sophie Zhao and she works as an escort, which is how she met Li Qiang.' Julie-Anne gave Jack an overview of how the woman found herself in her precarious situation and why she rang Julie-Anne in the first instance. 'What was particularly interesting though was her recounting of a phone conversation she overheard between Li and another Chinese man who Sophie thinks resides in China.' Julie-Anne gave Jack Sophie's version of the one-sided conversation. 'There was a consignment mentioned and a figure of one million dollars available to finance their cause.'

Melissa picked up on that. 'I'm pretty sure I'm the cause he referred to,' she offered disconsolately.

Julie-Anne continued. 'Sophie also said she noticed large amounts of cash in his wall safe one day, which I guess we would expect. She also heard a Captain Han mentioned. That name didn't mean anything to either of us, but it may do to you, Jack.'

'It sure does. I was on a conference call yesterday with the Maritime Border Command and other agencies discussing a drug smuggling investigation. I'm fairly certain that investigation has direct links to mine. Anyway, Shane Williamson, the head of MBC, advised the meeting that a Captain Han was found dead at the Seafarer's Mission in Brisbane. He was captain of the cargo ship suspected of bringing in the drugs I mentioned earlier. They must be getting nervous if they're cleaning house.'

'Jesus, the pieces of the puzzle are starting to come together,' said Julie-Anne. 'Sophie also said that at one stage the Li phone conversation she overheard became very heated, so I'm guessing you're right, they're feeling the pressure.'

'That makes sense and it appears this whole scenario is being orchestrated from China.' Jack suggested. 'At some point I'll need to interview Sophie Zhao, but, as she is your source, I'll let you make the arrangements when the time comes.'

'Is it okay to use my mobile? I need to contact my editor and David Bedford and tell them I'm okay.'

'Is your phone clean?'

'Yes, David Bedford's guys had it checked for bugs yesterday.'

'Okay, but do not divulge your location. The less people who know your exact location, the better. That means just the three of us, ladies. Now, I'm going to hail a taxi down by the shopping centre and go fetch my car at the hospital. I'll be in touch.'

'Thanks for everything Jack, you were great this afternoon,' said Julie-Anne.

'No, you were the star, JA. That was gutsy stuff back at the station. Wait until I'm gone before you head down to the shopping centre. I don't want the three of us to be seen together.'

'Okay, let's go get something for dinner; you up for a short walk?' Melissa asked.

'Yeah, after my terrifying dash through the station this afternoon anything else will seem like the proverbial walk in the park.' Aware that they might be holed-up in the apartment for some time, the women returned with enough food and drink supplies to last them for a few days. They also bought some casual clothes and underwear. Half an hour later they were sitting on the sofa eating dinner and watching the news on the TV. 'Oh shit, there's my car,' blurted Julie-Anne.

'I thought the police wanted to keep this quiet for now, hence why they haven't released any information about your incident,' proffered Melissa.

'And Jack wonders why I don't trust police officers. I heard through my contacts in the police force that they are moving to digitally encrypted radios, which will stop people, in particular the media, listening to their communications through the police scanner apps. Judging by what we are seeing, I'm guessing that hasn't happened yet.'

Melissa nodded. 'Alternatively, someone's leaked the story and that someone must be from within the police force.'

'That was a lovely dinner, particularly given the circumstances. Thank you, I feel much better now.' Melissa had made an Asian prawn and rice noodle salad and they had washed it down with a glass of sauvignon blanc. 'It's been a long day, so I might head off to bed, Melissa.' Julie-Anne noticed Melissa looking a little forlorn standing by herself in the middle of the sparsely furnished living room. 'Come on, there's plenty of room for both of us.'

Melissa smiled. 'I'm just going to double check all the door and window locks first. The doctor said you have to keep up your fluids, so I'll bring you a bottle of water as well.'

The two women lay in bed, ruminating over the day's events. Melissa was lying on her left side with her head on Julie-Anne's shoulder and her right arm across her stomach.

'You were simply amazing today. After everything you went through with the shooting this morning you still managed to pull off that ruse at the station this evening. You're one gutsy chick. I don't know where you got the courage or the strength from. I couldn't have done it.'

'Nor do I, but I trusted Jack's detective's instincts.'

'Speaking of Jack, that must have been one hell of an interesting time for him too, especially having me around all day.'

'He's a detective, so he can roll with most stuff, well once he gets his head around it anyway, Melissa.'

'I know I'm a strong person and very comfortable in my skin, but there were a couple of moments today when I just found myself feeling ever so slightly insecure around him.' Melissa shrugged. 'He is quite a handsome and dynamic guy.'

Julie-Anne tilted her head and kissed Melissa on the forehead. 'With everyone coming in and out all day, my tests, the detectives, the questioning, the doctor, you were my constant, my rock.' Melissa looked up at Julie-Anne and they gazed into one another's eyes. Then she adjusted the angle of her body, leaned in and kissed her tenderly.

'I love the way you kiss. You make me feel like I'm in a warm, safe place, especially now,' Julie-Anne whispered. Melissa let her right hand drift downward, her fingertips dancing across Julie-Anne's stomach. Her body was involuntarily twitching at the sensation and she started giggling uncontrollably. 'Please be gentle; I'm still sore.' Melissa's fingers continued tickling down past Julie-Anne's navel. She softly kissed her left breast, then her right, and alternated back and forth, becoming aware of her hardening nipples. At the same time, she was gently massaging her. 'Oooooohhhhhh, ohhhhhhhhhhhh,' she heard her sigh. 'Aaahhhh, yes, right there.' Melissa was aroused herself as she felt Julie-Anne slowly writhing and contorting on the bed. 'Oh yes… Yes… Yes… Kiss me, Melissa, now.'

Julie-Anne lay there panting. 'Wow, just wow, that was just amazing. After my ordeal today, that was such a wonderful release, thank you.'

'Look at the colour of you, with these bruises there's every shade of the rainbow on your chest.'

'Maybe there's a pot of gold at the end of it,' she replied, trying to stifle a laugh. Melissa couldn't help herself.

'Well if there is, I think I just found it.'

'Oh, yes, you surely did.' Julie-Anne slowly twisted her body, rested her head on Melissa's chest and snuggled in. 'How about we get some sleep?'

'Sweet dreams.'

(79)

AFP Headquarters

Jack collected his car from the RPA and drove along Broadway then up George Street before turning into Goulburn St and entering the AFP's Headquarters. It was now almost dark and with the events of the day he had lost a valuable twenty-four hours from his investigation. And he still had to finish writing up his report for the DC. 'Bugger,' he muttered as he exited the elevator.

It had been his intention to meet with Danielle earlier today and workshop her role in snaring Woodard, and hopefully Li. That plan had evaporated with the events earlier this morning and again later this afternoon. Jack needed to regroup, and quickly. He was dog-tired, but he was also determined to complete a few simple tasks on his to-do list, even if just to give himself a head-start tomorrow.

He rang Danielle, apologised for missing her today, told her there had been another change of plans and that he would contact her again tomorrow. She asked if he would like to come over for a late supper, but as much as he loved the idea, he politely declined. 'There's too much going on at the moment, but perhaps another time when this is all over,' he had said.

Then he rang Sanderson. 'Hey, Michael, how are you guys?'

'Yeah, good, but there's been no sign of our two targets unfortunately.'

'Well, I have some news on that front.' Jack told him the whole story about the attack on JA this morning.

'Shit. That's your ex-girlfriend, isn't it?'

'Where did you hear that?'

'No idea. Maybe Billingsley mentioned it.' Jack mulled that over for a minute.

'Anyway, Michael, Ms Granger has tentatively identified the shooter as Ling Jun, so I'm guessing the driver was probably Wang Wei. We need to find these guys and drag them in for questioning. Given what occurred this morning, it would be great if we can hold them for a while and keep them off the streets. That should make Wie Ping Lie decidedly nervous. Are you any closer to locating and arresting them?'

'No, Jack, they're obviously staying away from their known addresses, so I have a couple of CIs keeping an eye out for them. We'll find them soon enough, don't worry.'

'Okay, stay in touch. It's important.'

David Bedford was sitting at home with a Furphy in one hand, the television remote in the other, and was contemplating whether to hit the sack when his mobile rang. He didn't recognise the number listed on the mobile's display, so he let the call go through to voicemail. He heard the phone beep to signal a message had been left, so he picked it up, tapped on voicemail and then hit the little triangular play icon. He was surprised to hear that the message was from Jack Wagner. Wagner hadn't been very civil this afternoon, so Bedford momentarily thought, *bugger him,* and went back to his beer and TV. Eventually his curiosity got the better of him and he called Wagner's number.

'Hi, David, this is Jack Wagner.'

'Yeah, I know who you are. It's late. What do you want, Wagner?' Bedford asked bluntly.

'I suppose I deserved that.'

'Yes, you did. Now what's up?'

'Something odd has come to my attention and I need someone to have a close look at it for me.'

'Go on, Wagner.'

'I can't authorise it from within the AFP without stirring up a hornet's nest, so I thought you might be interested in helping. There's no money in it for MPS, but there may be a link to my investigation and also to your close protection job. Are you interested?'

'Give me some details and I'll give you an answer in the morning.' Jack gave Bedford an overview of his suspicions and what he wanted Bedford to do on his behalf.

'Okay, I'll call you tomorrow, Jack.'

Jack, that's an encouraging sign, the detective thought as he hung up the phone.

Jack let his mind wander to JA and Melissa. He thought about calling JA to check on her, but she would be asleep at this hour after her mentally exhausting and physically distressing day. His mind drifted to Melissa. He could see what JA liked about her. She had been very supportive of JA all day and was obviously a strong woman in her own right, particularly given the way she maintained her sense of calm at the railway station. She had made it clear by her affectionate actions that she was very fond of JA, too. *And of course, being a tall, gorgeous, assertively self-confident woman with a body to die for doesn't hurt either.* 'Mmmm,' he mumbled.

He regained his focus and recommenced writing his report for the Deputy Commissioner. Well, at least by being delayed in submitting the report, he now had more information to share with the DC. He included notes from the conference call, even though the DC was on the call, a summary of Jim Brennan's observations from the Oceanic's interview with Tony Woodard, mentioned Michelle Ironside's protection and described the events of today involving JA. He covered Ling Jun and Wang Wei's suspected involvement, Sanderson's failed efforts to locate them and JA's tentative identification of Ling Jun as the shooter. He included a note about the unauthorised use of the safe house, just to cover himself. Then he made a note about a suspicion he had that was nagging away at him. And finally, he advised the DC of his meeting with Danielle Mortimer tomorrow to workshop his plan to snare Woodard.

When Jack picked up his mobile again to check his notes, he saw a red number 4 overlaid on the green call button. How had he not noticed that? 'Bugger.' He was so busy focused on his report and the calls he needed to make, that his ability to concentrate was fading. He quickly pressed the call button, which revealed two missed calls and two voicemail messages, all from Jim Brennan's mobile. He didn't check the messages, but realising something must be wrong, he simply called Brennan back.

'Jim, I'm sorry about the missed calls. What's happened?'

'Michelle Ironside didn't arrive for her meeting with the CEO this afternoon.'

'That's not good at all. I'm on my way.'

(80)

Oceanic Security Control

Jack arrived at the Oceanic for the third time in two days and once again Jim Brennan was waiting to sign him in. Jack collected his pass and walked with Brennan down to the Security Office. 'How come the security offices are always in the basement, Jim? You'd think they would be located upstairs on the main casino floor where all the action is.'

'You'll have to ask the suits that.' Brennan didn't look to be in a good mood as the men sat on opposite sides of the desk. 'Ok, Jack, I think it's high time you told me what is going on here.'

'I will, but first tell me about Michelle Ironside.'

'As you know, she was due to meet with the CEO this afternoon. She didn't arrive at the appointed time. The CEO's secretary waited half an hour and then rang the Human Resources Manager to see if Michelle had contacted them for any reason. Having got a response in the negative, she advised the CEO and he contacted me. I have rung her mobile several times, but the calls are going straight to her voicemail. I then despatched a member of my team to her apartment in Drummoyne. Just in case, I gave him a set of lock picks. There was no answer, so he let himself in as I had instructed. Ominously, there was no-one home except her hungry cat, Jack. According to HR this is extremely unlike her as she is known to be creature of habit, so something is seriously amiss here. Now, your turn buddy, and no holding anything back this time,' Brennan said, offering Jack a determined look that said, I'm serious.

Jack provided Brennan with all the facts as he knew them. He also reiterated details of the conversations he had with Michelle at the Bayside Café in Pyrmont. 'The key issue here, and the cause of all the angst, Jim, is that she has proof that your Vice President of Client Services, Tony Woodard laundered one million dollars on behalf of one of your high rollers. And the high roller in question is Li Qiang, who has links to the Triads. That's the primary reason that I strongly suggested you arrange a personal protection detail for Michelle. Secondly, also because she was being threatened by Woodard.'

Brennan projected a bemused look. 'I suppose I should be surprised, but after viewing that footage yesterday, I'm not.'

'He also threatened Michelle with ruining her career.'

'How? She's as straight-up as they come.'

'I know that now. If she reported his illegal behaviour, he threatened to name her as a co-conspirator and offload some of the blame onto her. And, with her knowing about his money laundering activities for Li, Woodard certainly couldn't have her meeting with the CEO. And now you know why Woodard was in the Treasury Office and who his mystery client was.'

'Oh shit, Jack.'

'What?'

'Woodard called in sick today.'

'You know us detectives: We don't believe in coincidences. What action have you taken about Michelle?'

'I've reported her missing to the local police, but you know better than anyone they won't take it too seriously for a few days. In most cases, missing persons just turn up out of the blue after unexplained absences. I also have one of my guys stationed outside her apartment in case she returns.'

'Jim, you need to update the police. Tell them we suspect foul play and they need to get proactive. Michelle told me she usually catches an Uber home as she doesn't drive. Have you checked the CCTV cameras around the rideshare pick up?'

'Not yet. I'll get one of my guys onto it now.'

'And be sure to tell the local police about her Uber booking. Uber will have a record of Michelle's booking and they will be able to identify the driver easily. In the meantime, I'm going to contact a local detective I know from Day Street and get him to follow-up as well. I'm specifically going to ask if he can have her mobile phone checked and see where it pinged most recently. And now the matter of your Vice President. What are we going to do about him?' Jack asked pointedly.

'At this late hour, there's probably not much we can do.'

'Yes, there is. When you provide an update to the police, you should tell them of our concerns surrounding Woodard as well. That might just pique their interest and get them to become more proactive. Do me another favour if you will. Don't go into specifics with them, for now anyway until we tie this up tighter.'

'I'll need to run that past the CEO first. He won't want the police involved in, what is still at this stage, an internal investigation.'

'I think we're past the point of internal investigations, don't you, Jim? I'm pretty certain, one way or another, there's a link between the two absences.'

Jack called Michael Sanderson while walking to his car.

'Do you know what time it is, Jack?'

'Yes, I sure do, and we have an urgent issue that I need your help with.'

A groggy Sanderson sat up in bed. 'Okay, what's up?'

'There is a woman who is key to my money laundering investigation who has gone missing. And, before you say anything Michael, she is not the type to simply disappear. Her name is Michelle Ironside and she is the Treasury Manager for the Bennelong Room at the casino.'

'That can't be a coincidence, surely,' exclaimed Sanderson, now wide awake.

'I would like you to see if you can track her movements through her mobile phone.'

'Can't you AFP guys do that?'

'It's a state-based crime, and even though I'm certain her disappearance is linked to our wider investigation, no, not at this stage. You'll need to get a warrant from a justice, too.'

'Okay, I'll get onto it first thing in the morning; text me her mobile number.'

'Will do, and thanks, Michael.'

AFP Headquarters
Wednesday 11th March

Jack was feeling decidedly foggy as he drove over the Anzac Bridge. His eyes were stinging in the bright morning sunlight and from the reflections off of the waters of Jones Bay. His wish for an overcast day had been ignored. He and Brennan had finished up after midnight, finally realising there wasn't much else they could do to aid the search for Michelle Ironside themselves; it was up to the New South Wales Police now. Brennan had given them the basic information related to Tony Woodard and they assured him they would aggressively interview the man about Michelle's disappearance. Jack knew full-well Woodard would now remain a person of interest to them until she was located. He rang JA as he descended the bridge and drove past the Sydney Fish Market.

'How are you girls going, JA?'

'We're just wonderful, thanks,' she said, still buoyant from her interlude with Melissa last night. 'And you, Jack?'

'I'm quite knackered actually. I was at the office for hours last night and then with Jim Brennan at the casino until midnight at least. Michelle Ironside has gone missing.'

'Oh no, what happened?'

'We don't know as yet, but the state police are interviewing Tony Woodard and Michael Sanderson is trying to track Michelle's mobile phone movements, once he gets a warrant from a justice. Jim Brennan's guys are reviewing the CCTV footage around the casino's exit points as well. Woodard didn't show-up for work yesterday, so no doubt he will be the primary focus in their search for her.'

'This whole thing is just getting worse by the day. What with Captain Han's death, shots being fired at me and now Michelle Ironside missing, this whole sorry state of affairs has escalated very quickly.'

'I know, and the key players are obviously getting nervous. They're feeling the pressure and they are acting desperately as a result. They will make a mistake; the bad guys always do, JA. With Sophie's comments about the China phone conversation and the Chinese guy yelling down the phone, Wie's men going after you and Michelle missing, which I'm sure will come back to Li Qiang eventually; these guys are obviously panicking and have become quite brazen. Their activities at the Seafarer's Mission in Brisbane, against you in broad daylight on Raglan Street yesterday and abducting Michelle from the casino doorstep are testament to that. They've upped the ante, so whatever this is really about has to be vitally important to them.'

Jack then gave her a redacted version of his activities at the office last night. Even though she was obviously outside the investigation now, out of respect, he wanted to keep her in the loop. He was still withholding Danielle's involvement from her though.

'Any news on Ling Jun yet, Jack?'

'No, the state detectives haven't located him, but they will soon, I'm sure. Do you girls feel safe where you are?'

'Yeah, we're fine and are all stocked up with provisions, so we don't need to go anywhere for a few days. I know I don't need your permission, but just so you know, I am going to start writing my first article about this whole investigation. I have sufficient information that I can start drafting the first part of the story. I won't publish though, not without speaking to you first. I don't want to put your investigation at risk.'

'Okay, thanks, I'll check in later.'

Jack's mobile rang just as he pulled into the underground carpark at AFP Headquarters, but he didn't recognise the landline number. 'Jack Wagner.'

'Jack, it's Graeme Dawson here from Electronic Monitoring.' Jack had arranged for the AFP's tech guys to instal listening devices in Li Qiang's sumptuous suite on Monday night while he was indulging himself at his favourite restaurant. 'We have had some activity transmitted from the devices we installed in the Macquarie Suite at the Oceanic. I won't go into the details now, but we have truncated the tapes down to the key pieces we think you'll be interested in. It's now all contained in one audio file and we have time-stamped the key moments in case you need to build a timeline.'

'That's good news, Graeme. Where is the file now?'

'In your inbox.'

'That's excellent work. I'm almost at my desk. Thanks for the call.'

Once at his desk, he logged in to his desktop and went straight to his emails. He was surprised to have received one from the Deputy Commissioner. Jack double clicked on the email heading, quickly read the email and then clicked on the attachment. It was a copy of the TTR Report he had the DC request from Austrac. Just as Coleman had said on the phone, there was only one transaction listed for Li Qiang on the day in question and no recorded transactions for the two previous days. That confirmed to him that Woodard's presence in the Treasury Office was how Li received his gaming chips in the first place.

Jack scrolled down his inbox until he saw Graeme Dawson's email and double clicked on the message. He put on his noise cancelling headphones and double clicked on the audio file attachment. There was nothing worse than having to listen to hours, or even days, of audio files, so he was grateful to Dawson for trimming the files. Jack would still have to be extremely alert, as he would only be hearing one side of every conversation. He moved the desktop's cursor to the first cue point on the file.

That took him to what he realised was a conversation between Li and Woodard. Li was angry that Woodard wasn't at work and that he still had a million dollars sitting in his safe. Jack sighed with relief at that. He had been too preoccupied with the disappearance of Michelle Ironside and hadn't had time to implement his plan yet. And Li had confirmed Jack's suspicions that the next transaction would happen tomorrow. Li then threatened Woodard again and disconnected the call.

Jack moved the cursor to the next cue point in the audio file. Li was talking to someone named Xiao. While listening to the file, Jack texted JA. *Do we know someone called Xiao, JA?* Jack laughed out aloud as he listened to the next piece. Apparently, Melissa had been giving Li the run around, as he had been unable to contact her, and he was concerned about losing his precious candidate. Melissa's phone was obviously switched off. *Good girl.* Li guessed correctly that she was spending time with JA, but that wouldn't help him at the moment; given that she was safely secreted away. Jack couldn't hear the question, but the next response from Li was interesting.

Jack's phone buzzed with an incoming text message. *He's the Chinese Consul General I mentioned. Why?* Jack paused the audio file. *I'll tell you later.* He texted back and then pressed play again.

Li had said "money is not a problem, Xiao." Jack guessed that the money referred to was to fund Melissa's candidacy. What he was quite sure of though was the source of those funds. Jack noticed by the timeline he had missed a piece of the conversation somehow. Jack listened and the replayed the piece again. "No, but I think we reached a mutual understanding at our meeting a few days ago, so she shouldn't be a problem, Xiao." The "she" mentioned by Li could only be JA, given Melissa was incommunicado and the comment was raised as part of the Melissa candidacy conversation. *What had JA been up to now?* Jack wondered.

The final piece of the audio file for this conversation was of particular interest to Jack. "He has just been looking after my best interests, which of course, are also your best interests, Xiao." Who was the "he" referred to in this segment? Jack pondered.

Jack once again moved the cursor to the next file. The conversation initially made no sense to Jack, so he listened again.

'How is everything, my friend?'

'Is the package in good condition?' 'That is good. And how are you?' 'Okay, I'll talk to you soon.'

Jack was wondering what the package referred to by Li could be? 'Oh shit, it couldn't be,' he cried out. Were they referring to Michelle Ironside as the "package"? Jack had access to all the modern technology, equipment and intelligence resources of the AFP, but like all good detectives he still listened to his gut instinct and now his was rumbling like an awakening volcano. Li and Woodard certainly wouldn't want Michelle talking to the CEO. Jack couldn't confront Li without any evidence, neither for Michelle's disappearance nor for money laundering. He had nothing to directly link Li to either at this point. He rang Jim Brennan's mobile.

'Did you get anything from your CCTV cameras regarding Michelle Ironside and her Uber ride?'

'Hello to you too, Jack. Yes, we did, but all we know is that she was picked up by a black SUV. The driver had parked with the back of the vehicle facing the cameras, so we have no vision of him.'

'What about a number plate?'

'No rear plate; this guy's smart, Jack. We're still waiting to hear back from Uber.'

'Fuck,' Jack blurted out. 'Sorry, that wasn't aimed at you. I've got a call coming in, so I'll talk to you later.'

'Jack, it's Peter Crawford here. We met yesterday at the RPA. I have some good news for you.'

'Yeah, hi Peter, go on.'

'We have obtained some local CCTV footage not far from the site of the shooting.'

'That's great, what have you got?'

'We were very fortunate that there was a CCTV camera positioned in a convenience store at the corner of Raglan and Cope Streets. Given we knew the precise time of the incident, it was very easy to loop the footage to that exact time. It clearly shows a black SUV following Ms Granger down Raglan.' Jack wondered whether it was the same SUV that had taken Michelle Ironside.

'They must have followed her from her home and were waiting for a quieter area before opening fire. Raglan Street provided just that opportunity for them, Jack.'

'Yeah, I know Peter and Ms Granger was warned about that.'

'Anyway, Jack, the dumb bastards didn't have enough sense to cover the SUV's license plates, and it was clearly visible on the CCTV footage. You'll be delighted to know the SUV is registered to a Ling Jun, who I believe you mentioned in your briefing to my partner and I at the hospital yesterday.'

'Yes, I did, and I showed Ms Granger a photo of him and she confirmed him as the shooter, so now we have corroborating evidence. If only we could find him and his partner in crime though.'

'There's more, Jack.'

'Really? What else have you got?'

'We dug out the two bullets from Ms Granger's car and I sent them to the Forensic Services Group for analysis. We also got lucky and found a shell casing down a run-off drain close to the scene of the incident. The shooter must have held the gun outside his vehicle window for one of the shots and the ejected casing rolled into the drain.'

'Wow, what a stroke of luck.'

'The FSG guys have analysed both the slugs and the casing and they are convinced we are looking for a Beretta 9mm and that it fired 9 x 19mm Parabellum rounds. Both the gun and the rounds are quite common, but you find the Beretta and the FSG guys will match it to the slug and the shell, Jack.'

'That was quick work.'

'Yeah, I was impressed too. I think the FSG guys figured it must be important if the Feds are involved.'

'Either way, I'm very grateful. And I think I know exactly where the Beretta is, if only the Day Street boys could locate the owner.'

'Good luck, Jack.'

He felt like he had been on the phone all morning when his mobile rang once more. *What now?* It was David Bedford calling as promised.

'I've had a think about what you asked me last night and I reckon my guys will enjoy that little exercise, Jack. It's always nice to turn the tables, so to speak. We have already commenced the operation.'

'Thanks, David, I appreciate it and if it leads where I think it will, that will answer a few questions.'

'Give me your email address and I will have an activity summary sent to you daily. Jack recited his email address for Bedford. 'Before you go, Jack, we've downloaded the footage from Ms Granger's dashcam and body mounted cameras.'

'What? She was wearing a body mounted camera as well?' Jack blurted out.

'Jack, we take our close protection duties very seriously at MPS. Moving on, both cameras operated as they should, but unfortunately there was nothing definitive to identify either the shooter or the vehicle.'

'That's okay. I have CCTV footage of the vehicle and Ms Granger's tentative identification of the shooter.'

'Well done, that's good news.'

'Yeah, it would be if the state cops could bloody well locate him.'
'Good luck and check your email at the end of the day.'

Jack once again picked up his mobile and rang Sanderson. Michael, I had a call from the local detectives earlier regarding the attack on Ms Granger.' Jack told Sanderson that Ling Jun is the probable shooter and Wang Wei is his likely accomplice. 'Why can't we find these guys? It can't be that hard, surely,' he asked, his frustration obvious.

'They always seem to be a step ahead of us, Jack. Our CIs provide confirmation of a sighting and when we follow it up, our targets have moved on and then we're back to square one.' Jack thought he knew why. 'Okay, have your guys keep at it please, Michael.'

'How did you go getting a warrant to track Michelle Ironside's phone?'

'Billingsley's working on it.'

'Michael, we need to expedite that warrant. She's been missing for at least twenty-four hours now, and you know as well as I do, the longer she's missing the less chance we'll have of finding her alive.'

'I know, I know, we're onto it, Jack.'

$$\left(\textbf{82}\right)$$

Tong-Li – Wujiang District China

Deming Pan guided his gondola under the Taiping Bridge and toward the stone wall that served as the quay where he would dock his vessel. As his body had yielded to the ravages of a life of backbreaking work, he had been forced to cease his long held occupation of cormorant fishing. He had then modified, painted and decorated his gondola and established his little water taxi business. His was a modest operation, but he derived much pleasure in taking visitors through the one thousand year old water town on tours of the numerous bridges and canals of the Venice of the East. As he searched for a space along the busy quayside, he noticed two men wearing the green uniform of the Public Security Bureau standing nearby. 'Taiping' meant peace and tranquility, but he was feeling anything but at the sight of the stern-looking men whose gaze was clearly fixed on him. He tied off his gondola and scrambled over the limestone wall, all the while pretending he hadn't seen the uniformed men.

'Mr Pan,' the taller of the two officers called out.

His worst fears were confirmed, so he slowly tilted his head towards the officers. 'Yes, can I help you, officer?' he asked fearfully.

'We have a matter of some importance to discuss with you. You will come with us,' the officer demanded.

Li walked across to the officers. 'I am just a humble water taxi driver. What could you possibly want from me?'

'You will come with us,' the officer repeated.

'But I have done nothing wrong,' he protested.

The grim-faced officers clutched his arms and escorted him along the walkway that skirted the canal until they reached a nondescript building with a narrow centre doorway. He was ushered through the door, down a dimly lit hallway and into a tiny, windowless room that only contained a cheap, square metal table and three matching chairs. Pan took the single seat on the opposite side to where the officers would sit.

'We believe you have a niece, Kaili Wang, who has been working in Australia for some time.'

Fearing the worst, Pan's heart began to race and he felt faint. 'What has happened? Is she okay?' he asked, clasping his hands together to stop them from shaking.

'Your niece is more than okay; she has been actively working to bring the reputation of the great People's Republic of China into disrepute.'

Pan knew his niece to be intelligent, globally aware and strong willed, but he couldn't imagine her being involved in such an activity, whatever it was. 'No, she would do no such thing.' Like most people in his country, he was deeply suspicious of the motives and secretive operations of the security services. 'What are you implying?'

'You are naïve, old man. She has been witnessed having secret meetings with a reporter who has a vendetta against the People's Republic. This reporter woman continues to impugn the good name of our beloved country and undermine the noble ambitions of our masters in the Party. Kaili Wang is obviously engaged in subversive activities with this reporter and that cannot, and will not be tolerated.'

Pan began to protest when the officer slammed his fist down on the table. 'You know nothing of what she does and your objections will not be tolerated,' the officer raged, forcing Pan to push back on his chair. 'Furthermore, she has also been engaged in a less than noble profession that brings further shame to our country. I'm certain I don't need to paint a picture for you.'

Deming Pan had often wondered how his niece had managed to provide support to him and his wife while being a humble student. They had funded her travel to Australia and had wondered how Kaili Wang had managed to repay them so quickly. Now, she had been sending them money regularly to supplement the modest income they derived from their water taxi business. *Surely not.* 'No, she is just a humble student at university; that is all.'

'You obviously know little of your niece's activities and professional choices, Pan. You need to speak to your zhínǚ and remind her of her obligations to the People's Republic of China and to the welfare of her family.'

The threat was as plain as day. 'Yes, of course.'-

'We would not like to have reason to visit you again. That will not bode well for you or your family. Is that understood?'

Pan stood and bowed respectfully. 'Wǒ xiāngxìn nà jiāng shì méiyǒu bìyào de,' he replied obligingly.

The two officers stood and escorted him out of the building from where he walked back along the ancient waterfront to his gondola. He had heard many stories about expatriates and exiles whose Chinese-based relatives were used as leverage to try and control the country's image abroad. With his hard-working, simple lifestyle, he never thought he would be in that situation. What had his beloved niece done that could lead to this intimidation and threats against his family. Deming meant strong in his native language and he would need to be now.

(**83**)

Danielle's Apartment

'Bugger, I haven't rung Danielle,' Jack mumbled to himself. 'Another bloody phone call,' he grumbled again as he speed dialled her number.

'Hi, Jack, how are you?'

'I'm exhausted if you want to know the truth, Danielle.'

'Aaahh, my poor Jack. Why don't you come over and I'll make you a nice dinner?' With everything that was happening, Jack knew he shouldn't go to her apartment, but he couldn't be bothered going somewhere public and the last thing he felt like doing was cooking dinner for himself.

'I've missed you; it's been two whole days.' Danielle looped her arms around Jack's neck, leaned in and kissed him enthusiastically. It had been such a long and exhausting thirty-six hours for him that he was too tired to even contemplate resistance. And, as wrong as it might be under the circumstances, he wasn't about to deny himself this little pleasure. A *guilty* pleasure.

'Would you like a beer, Jack?'

'I could kill for a nice cold beer.'

'Well, you won't have to as I went to the liquor store and bought you some,' she replied sassily.

'You are always so cheerful, Danielle, which can't be easy under the prevailing circumstances.'

'Can't we just enjoy this little moment together, Jack? We can talk about the serious stuff later.'

'Yeah, why not. Cheers.'

'I have made something slightly different for dinner, which I hope you will like.'

'Are you going to tell me what it is, or do I have to guess?'

'Okay, I walked into the Fish Market and bought some lovely, juicy, fresh tiger prawns. So, we're going to have my latest culinary creation, a light and tasty Prawn Caesar Salad with my special sauce.' Jack remembered the last time he had a Caesar Salad and that evening didn't end so well for him.

'That sounds fabulous. I'll just pop out and get some wine then.'

'All sorted too, Jack. I bought a Margaret River Semillon Sauvignon Blanc on my way home. It's a Pierro LTC, my favourite.'

'What does LTC stand for?'

'You'll have to work it out, aren't you a detective?' *What is it with these women and their acronyms?* he thought to himself.

'That was a lovely meal; I've never had a Prawn Caesar and your homemade sauce was mouth-watering. And the wine went really well with the whole thing; good choice.' They were sitting side-on on the sofa sipping the remainder of the wine.

'Danielle, we need to discuss your situation.' She was dressed for chilling at home, only wearing a tight-fitting white tank top that he was trying hard not to stare at, a short, tropical patterned wraparound sarong and her blonde locks tied up into a bun. Danielle's legs and bare feet were tucked up under her body as she listened intently to Jack. He thought she looked so young and innocent; vulnerable even. He looked down at his dowdy suit, removed his jacket and rolled up his sleeves. 'I have a plan, which hopefully will lead to us apprehending your Vice President and then, all things being equal, he should give us Li Qiang. And, hopefully, if it leads to arrests and convictions then my Deputy Commissioner will seek to reduce your culpability in their crimes. I assume you are working tomorrow.'

'Yes, I am, at two o'clock.'

'I thought so. Okay, this is what I would like you to do.' Jack explained his plan to Danielle, verbally walked her through it again and then asked her to detail it back to him. 'There's one other thing you need to know. The Treasury Manager has been missing for over twenty-four hours now.'

'Oh, no, Michelle is a lovely woman; she's almost like a mother to me. What happened?'

'We don't know yet, but every effort is being made to locate her.'

'I bet this is because of the money laundering; is this all my fault?' she asked through misty eyes.

'No, it's not your fault. We think it's related to another scenario that was unfolding.'

'I'm scared now.' Danielle leaned against Jack, rested her head on his shoulder and drifted away.

She awoke a while later, feeling slightly disorientated. She sat upright on the sofa to gain her composure and heard Jack snoring away. *The poor guy must be so tired.* She gently woke him, took him by the arm, helped him stand up, and then lead him to the bedroom.

Jack woke with a start and momentarily wondered where he was. He turned over to face Danielle. He was naked and trying to recall when and how he came to be in her bed.

'What time is it? Is it daylight yet?' Danielle asked with her eyes firmly closed.

'Yes,' Jack mumbled as he pulled the pillow over his head.

She slowly rolled over, rested her head on Jack's chest, laid her right arm across his body and snuggled in. He loved the feel of her full, firm breasts against his chest, her naked body entwined with his and he became slightly aroused. He felt Danielle's hand slowly moving down below the sheet until it found what it was looking for. Slightly didn't last long, as she grasped him firmly.

Danielle tilted her head and whispered into his ear. 'That's my Jack, I'll be back in a while.'

'I think I've heard that somewhere before,' he said softly as she was disappearing beneath the linen.

They were in the open-plan kitchen and living area, having their first coffee of the day. Danielle once again, at Jack's insistence, was talking him through her responsibilities for the implementation of his plan.

'Okay, I think you've got it down pat. Now, just to be on the safe side, Danielle, don't leave the apartment until I return. I will come back later and drive you to work today.'

'Thanks, I feel better for that, Jack.'

Randwick Safe House
Thursday 12th March

'Wow, what have we got here?' Julie-Anne said as Melissa walked into the bedroom with a wooden tray covered with a linen napkin.

'Hey presto,' Melissa said as she removed the napkin with the flourish of a magician pulling a white dove from a handkerchief.

'Oh my god, what's all this?'

'Okay, we have strawberry and banana yoghurt, diced fresh mango, these cute little pastry things, poached eggs on sourdough and of course, a strong coffee.'

'Where did all these treats come from?'

'Jack won't be happy, but I snuck out and went back to the shopping centre where I found this great little bakery.'

'You're a star, this looks amazing, now come here.' Melissa placed the tray on the bedside chest and sat on the bed. Julie-Anne reached up, placed her hand on the back of Melissa's neck, and pulled her into a kiss. 'Thank you for taking such good care of me.'

'After what you went through yesterday, you're entitled to be fussed over.' Melissa adjusted Julie-Anne's pillows and helped her sit upright. 'How is your body feeling this morning?'

'Better, I think, but my chest is still sore and it's difficult to breathe deeply. Other than that, I feel okay. Can you grab my phone for me, please?'

'Oh dear, that can't be good news,' Melissa said as she retrieved the phone from the living room.

'What can't be good news?'

'You have five missed calls from a Sophie. Is that the woman you were talking to Jack about?'

'Yes, she is the anonymous caller I told you about over dinner at your place.' Julie-Anne grasped her phone and perused the home screen. 'Shit, she's left five voicemail messages too.' She unlocked her phone, tapped on the green call icon, the clicked on the voicemail tab and played the first message. *Julie-Anne, I need to talk to you urgently. Please call me as soon as you can.* She didn't bother listening to the remaining messages. Presuming they would be a carbon copy of the first, she called Sophie.

'What's wrong, Sophie?' she blurted out before the other woman could speak.

Julie-Anne could hear her new friend take a deep breath amid a couple of sniffles. She stayed silent while Sophie regained her composure. 'My uncle called me from Tong-Li yesterday evening. Two officers from the Public Security Bureau visited him yesterday. The PSB has a deliberately vague remit, but essentially they use a range of excuses to involve themselves in anything and everything that takes their fancy. State security is at the top of their list.'

Julie-Anne was listening intently, and given what she had gleaned through her research on Chinese interference, she guessed where this conversation was heading.

'Essentially, they told my uncle that there would be serious repercussions for him and his family if I didn't stop associating with you.'

'They said what?' Julie-Anne blurted out as she lurched up from her pillows. 'Ouch,' she said as her chest heaved with pain.

'What's wrong, Julie-Anne?'

'I've had an interesting day or two. Carry on, Sophie.'

'Well, apparently they know who you are and about your interest in China's affairs in Australia. They think you have a vendetta against China and that we are both involved in subversive activities against the People's Republic, to use my uncle's terminology. Basically, they have demanded that I have no further association with you.'

'Oh, that's just terrible. Are you okay?'

'Not really. My uncle and aunt raised me for much of my life and they are the reason I am studying in Australia. I owe them a lot and I can't bear the thought that they are being threatened because of something that's out of their control. They are lovely people who live a humble existence and it's just not fair.'

'I'm really sorry.' Neither woman spoke for a moment and Julie-Anne was working her investigative brain to understand how this scenario came about. 'Sophie, the only time we have been together was at Coogee on Monday. Before that, our friendship didn't exist, so someone must have followed me there. And I think I now know who it was. There was a guy supposedly birdwatching, but I noticed him look up at us a couple of times when we were sitting on the grass near the memorial. I didn't think anything of it at the time. Bugger.'

'There's more, Julie-Anne. My uncle said the security officers also made insinuations as to my profession. If they think they know what my profession is then that information could only have come from Li.'

'I agree and he would be someone who would definitely have the appropriate contacts in China, especially given his relationship with the Consul General.'

'What do we do now?'

'I'm sorry you've gotten tangled up in this, Soph. This is nothing but emotional blackmail aimed squarely at me.'

'It's not your fault, Julie-Anne. I contacted you remember.'

$$\textbf{85}$$

Macquarie Suite

Tony Woodard arrived back at work earlier than usual after his sick leave. He now had a backlog of tasks to complete and he still had to arrange for Li's one million dollars to be transacted. The primary reason he was early was to escape from his nagging wife. Bree had been badgering him for days to book another holiday in Fiji, and if he didn't, she would go without him anyway. Which is exactly what he suggested she should do.

By lunchtime he had worked through half of the items on his to do list. He knew Danielle Mortimer was starting her shift at two o'clock, so he had to have the briefcase full of money in her locker well before then. He took the elevator up to the thirty-eighth floor and rang the doorbell. Judging by the darkened peephole Li was obviously checking who the visitor was. 'Aaahh, Mr Vice President, welcome back,' Li said, making no effort to hide his sarcasm as he ushered Woodard into the suite.

'Where's the briefcase, Li?'

'It's still Mr Li to you,' he demanded.

'This is our last transaction, so how about we forget the semantics. Where's the briefcase?' demanded Woodard.

'You should find this transaction easier to complete this time Tony, especially given the Treasury Manager is apparently still missing.'

'I don't suppose you know anything about that, do you, Li?' challenged Woodard, offering up his own dose of sarcasm. He continued. 'I was interviewed by the local police for two hours about her disappearance. They came to my house for Christssake. I had to lie to my wife about the reason for their visit.'

'Tony, she will forget all about it when you take her on another holiday. Apparently, she's quite fond of the lifeguards in Fiji.'

'Is there anything you don't know about my family, Li?' Woodard had dropped the mister again, but Li couldn't care less now. He just wanted this final transaction completed and then he would focus his attention on finding another more suitable candidate to serve his master's political agenda. He went to the wall safe and entered the combination. He opened it, withdrew the bulging navy blue briefcase and walked it back to Woodard. 'There you go, Mr Vice President, one million dollars. I expect to see you again before the end of the evening. I am looking forward to another round of blackjack.'

Woodard stepped into the elevator and pressed B for basement, where the staff lockers were located. He exited the elevator, walked along the soulless corridor and into the staff room. So as not to arouse any suspicion, he walked purposefully and confidently over to the area containing the lockers. Without pausing, he inserted the key into the lock and opened the locker, whereby he placed the briefcase inside and then closed and locked the door.

He was relieved to be rid of the cash. That was his part completed for now, and all Danielle had to do was play her role as she had many times previously. Then, he would be free of Li and his intimidation forever, although he would miss the extra money. *Not as much as the wife though,* he thought, allowing himself a chuckle.

Li was relaxing on his sofa with a cup of Green Leaf and thinking about everything that had occurred during the past two weeks since his arrival in Sydney. He enjoyed spending time in Sydney; he loved the harbour city and had arrived with such high hopes. The XO Pipis at the Golden Phoenix and Kaili Wang's services were always high on his agenda, but it was the task of securing a political candidate sympathetic to China's cause that excited him the most. Li thought he had identified the ideal candidate; the early signs were promising and his CCP masters in China were pleased. Melissa Wu's energetic pursuit of her relationship with the Granger woman had compromised her candidacy and cast considerable doubt over his initial plan. He took another sip of his tea. Maybe his latest persuasive attempt to encourage Granger to end the relationship would prove successful. In his mind though, he had already cast Wu adrift and he would now need to source a new, more amenable candidate. His masters in the Chinese Communist Party would not be pleased with the delay. Luckily, there was still six months until the New South Wales election, so he had ample time to source the most appropriate candidate, assuming of course he wasn't recalled to China, and to an uncertain fate. His ruminations were interrupted by the ringtone of his burner phone. He hated it when the burner phone rang as it usually brought unwelcome news.

'Hello.'

'Li, it is me.'

He wondered if his master's ears had been burning. 'What can I do for you?' he asked apprehensively.

'This whole operation has qù lā shǐ, Li. The product importation has been compromised, which hampers our political ambitions and your choice of political candidate turned out to be less than ideal. I know there are over two hundred thousand Chinese born citizens living in Sydney, so how did you get it so wrong? We are less than pleased with how you are dealing with this important issue in Australia,' the master reiterated.

'My responsibility in the operation hasn't gone to shit at all; I just need to re-evaluate my candidate profile. The importation isn't my responsibility, as you well know. Anyway, we have sufficient funding for a political campaign already and I am about to complete another transaction.' Li knew he shouldn't speak so freely over the phone, but he was frustrated at the continual micro-management by his masters in the party.

'And what about the Captain Han situation? All you had to do was get him on a plane to Shanghai and you couldn't even manage that. You caused me to become involved and resort to less than desirable means to resolve that little problem.'

'How was I to know that he would be picked up by the authorities again?' Li said doggedly.

'Li, now that we have sufficient funding for a candidate you will no longer be a part of the importation process and the financial contributions will now cease. You will concentrate on sourcing a suitable candidate for the New South Wales election. Do you think you can manage that simple task the second time around? If not, I am certain we can keep you busy back here in the people's republic. Goodbye.'

That would be the least of Li's concerns.

(**86**)

Oceanic Security Operations Room

Jack had developed a strategy to snare Tony Woodard and had enlisted the support of the Deputy Commissioner, primarily to obtain legal clearance and to request warrants from Federal Court Justices for the placement of listening devices and arranging phone taps, if required. And with his DC's approval, he had also recruited Danielle Mortimer to the team. Jack had provided the DC with an unadulterated version of her involvement in the money laundering scheme. John Robertson had made no promises in relation to lessening her culpability, even given the motivation brought on by her brother's circumstances. Nor had he offered any inducements or reduced charges or penalties, which were outside his authority anyway.

At one o'clock in the afternoon, Jack arrived back at Danielle's apartment. So he wouldn't unduly scare her with a knock on the door, he rang her mobile from outside her apartment.

'Hi Jack, where are you?'

'I'm outside your front door.' Danielle opened the door and Jack walked in carrying a small black box.

'You brought me a present; you shouldn't have,' she said, giggling away.

'Funny girl. You need to wear this for your entire shift today. This is what we talked about last night.' With that, Danielle took off her work jacket, undid the buttons of her blouse and neatly placed it over a chair.

'Would you like me to remove my bra?' she asked, giving him a cheeky wink.

'You know the answer to that, but for now, be serious. Do you want to put this on or shall I?'

'No, I think it's your turn, Jack,' she teased. He reached around Danielle and clipped the small pack to her work skirt and then taped the wires to her chest and stomach, while trying to ignore her breasts.

'Okay, let's have one more run-through just to be safe.'

'It's okay, I'm comfortable with the plan. It's not rocket science. Let's go, shall we?' She clasped his hand and led him out the apartment door.

After dropping Danielle at the Oceanic's staff entrance, Jack parked his car and walked around the vast building to reception, where he was again met by Jim Brennan. Once Jack had signed in they took the stairs down to the basement and the Security Operations Room. Graeme Dawson was already set up with a radio receiver on the desk and a headset in place. Jack tapped him on the shoulder to get his attention and Dawson lifted one side of his headset.

'Any action yet, Graeme?'

'Oh yeah, Jack. We have Woodard on audio tape collecting the briefcase, which I assume contains the cash you mentioned. And my good friend here has Woodard on CCTV depositing the bulging briefcase in one of the staff lockers.' Seated next to Dawson in front of a bank of CCTV monitors was one of Jim Brennan's security staff. His name badge read Cam Peterson.

'Play it again please, Cam, so Mr Wagner and I can view it,' Brennan requested. He and Jack watched as Woodard deposited the briefcase into the locker.

'Do we know whose locker it was?'

'I can answer that.'

Brennan's eyes widened. 'And just how would you know that, Jack?'

'That is a long story Jim and we don't have time for chapter and verse now. It's Danielle Mortimer's locker.' Jack had briefed Brennan on his plan that morning and confirmed the assistance he would require from him. He had omitted any reference to Danielle until now.

'Jesus Jack, are you ever going to tell me the whole bloody story?' Brennan hollered as his face turned red. 'What does she have to do with this?'

'Later, please. Let's focus on the monitors for now,' Jack said firmly.

'There's Ms Mortimer now.' Brennan grumbled. She was clearly visible on the video feed as she walked into the staff room with a takeaway coffee in her hand. Jack had told her to go to the café and grab a coffee, to allow him sufficient time to get down to the Operation's Room. 'Wow,' exclaimed Peterson. Danielle was clearly having some fun of her own as she sashayed across the staff room with an exaggerated swing of her shapely body.

'You're a funny girl.'

'What did you say, Jack?'

'Just mumbling to myself, Jim.'

Jack plucked an earpiece out of his pocket and firmly inserted it into his outer ear. Then he turned on the electronic device in his hand, to which the earpiece was connected. Finally, he pressed the push-to-talk button. 'Can you hear me, Pierro?' Jack wanted to avoid using Danielle's name during communications, just in case someone had hacked into their radio frequency. She had suggested using the name of her favourite wine.

'Who are you talking to, Jack?' Just then Brennan watched as Danielle waved her arm above her head in a circular flourishing motion before she extravagantly pulled opened the locker door. Clearly visible on the monitors was the navy blue briefcase resting against the inside of the locker.

'Okay, that confirms the briefcase is still in place.' They continued to watch as Danielle pulled the briefcase towards her and unzipped the top. She then held the two sides apart and angled the opening towards the CCTV camera to confirm the cash was in place. 'Okay, that's all good, Pierro,' Jack said into his push-to-talk microphone. She zipped up the briefcase and placed it back into the locker.

Jack tapped Dawson on the shoulder again. 'Graeme, can you set up the audio file, so I can listen to the piece involving Woodard please?'

'Here you go,' Dawson said as he handed the headset to Jack. Most of the Woodard and Li conversation was about the briefcase and the money. What was particularly of interest to Jack was the reference to Michelle Ironside by Li. His gut instinct was kicking in again, but he was also questioning himself now. He assumed the black SUV mentioned by Brennan was the same one involved in the attempted shooting of JA by Wie's men. But, maybe the two incidents weren't directly related at all.

'Okay, now we wait, gents,' said Jack, stating the obvious. 'Woodard won't be expecting the exchange to be made and the briefcase full of gaming chips returned to the locker until Ms Mortimer has her tea break, at the earliest.'

'Jack, got a minute while it's quiet?' He guessed what was coming, but he knew Brennan was owed an explanation. 'Yeah, sure.'

The two men moved to the rear of the Operations Room. Jack spoke quietly. 'Jim, Danielle Mortimer is involved in the money laundering.'

'Oh, no, you're joking. She's a great kid.'

'There are extenuating circumstances surrounding her involvement, but she has agreed to assist us today. It's important you know that we haven't promised her anything to reduce her level of culpability and whatever subsequent action the casino decides to take is entirely up to them. She just wants to make amends for what she's been involved in.'

'So, when we saw her on the CCTV footage the other day, she was actually laundering the money then?'

'Yes, Jim, she was. I haven't told anyone about her involvement to ensure her safety, especially after what we fear has happened to Michelle Ironside.'

'So, what is she going to do to assist us, Jack?'

'What she does best.'

'You should know that I have informed the CEO of our activities today, so don't be alarmed if we get a visit.'

'Did you tell him we suspect one of his high rollers is involved?'

'No, that might be a bridge too far at the moment. He is very nervous about the casino gaining a reputation for money laundering. I spoke to him at length about the Vice President and he's happy to let that play out for now. He won't be so comfortable though when he finds out one of his treasury staff and a high roller are also involved.'

'I can provide you both with some background information at the appropriate time, Jim.'

'Jack, I also heard from the local police this morning about Michelle's Uber booking.'

'That's great.'

'Not so fast. Uber have no record of a booking in Michelle's name.'

'How can that possibly be? She uses them every night after she finishes work.' Jack asked, perplexed.

'I have no idea unless she utilised another rideshare company.'

'Jim, can you ring them back and get them to check with Uber again and see if that includes cancelled bookings? It's at least forty-eight hours since she went missing and we have nothing. You know the longer this goes on the more remote—'

Brennan interrupted him. 'Yes, I know all too well and I don't want to think about it.'

(87)

Treasury Department

It was now seven o'clock in the evening and there had been no activity since Danielle's little performance at the locker over five hours ago. The tension was building, so to fill in his time, Jack had called Sanderson to get an update on the search for Ling Jun and his partner. He was appalled that two well-connected state police officers couldn't locate a couple of Chinatown's finest. The conversation didn't end well. Then he rang JA and checked in with her. Both women were in good spirits despite being housebound, and JA was well into writing the first part of her story. Late in the afternoon, he had received a call from David Bedford. He had something he wanted to show Jack. 'I'm at the Oceanic at the moment, David.'

'I can be there in an hour if you like and I don't require much of your time.'

'Alright then, I'll meet you in the foyer.' Jack was reluctant to leave the Operations Room, but he was directly connected to Danielle via the technology beneath her blouse, as was Dawson, so they could both monitor her conversations. So far, they had all been directly related to her treasury role. Jack excused himself and went upstairs to the casino's grand foyer where he found Bedford sitting in the rear of the foyer's café.

'I can't stay long, David. I'm in the middle of something at the moment.'

'This won't take long; I just need you to look at some photos.' Jack scrolled through the photos as requested. The photos he was scanning through confirmed his suspicions and validated his decision to involve Bedford. 'Do you have video as well?'

'Yep, these are stills taken from the video.'

'Can you get the original videos onto a laptop, with the stills and be available around eleven o'clock tomorrow morning?'

'Yeah, okay.'

'And are the videos date and time-stamped?'

'Yes, there is a running date and time clock at the foot of each video, Jack.'

'Okay, great, I'll call you with a location tomorrow morning, but it will be in the CBD somewhere. I've gotta get back downstairs. Thanks a lot. I appreciate you expediting this for me.'

'Jack, you need to see this.' Dawson called out as Jack entered the Operations Room. 'Cam, can you rewind that and play it for Jack?' Peterson skipped back to the section of video where he had added a marker.

'Okay, here you go, gents.' They were watching Woodard open the locker and slowly pull the soft leather briefcase towards himself, careful not to expose the contents within. Woodard's facial expression became contorted, but Jack couldn't decide if he looked angry, frustrated, worried or just plain confused. Maybe all of the above.

'Okay, Pierro, you should expect a phone call or a visit shortly.' Jack said into his dangling microphone. The occupants of the Operations Room all laughed as Danielle looked up and gave a wink of acknowledgement to the CCTV camera positioned in the corner ceiling of the Treasury Office. A few minutes later Jack heard the Treasury landline phone ringtone. 'Have you got this, Graeme? Here we go.' Jack had decided it was too complicated to place a listening device in the Treasury office phone, given the level of judicial approvals that would be required. Instead, he asked Danielle to put the phone on speaker, which would enable Dawson to record both sides of the conversation.

'Treasury, Danielle speaking,' she said in her usual bouncy tone. 'What the hell's going on, Danielle?' came the gruff voice.

'Oh, hello, Mr Woodard,' she replied calmly.

'We had a deal, Danielle, what happened?'

'Yes, I know we did, but I'm by myself this evening and haven't been able to leave the office.'

'Why not? You always have before.' Woodard asked angrily.

'It's just not possible, that's why, especially with Ms Ironside away.'

'Have you got me on speaker for God's sake?'

She had to think quickly. 'Yes, I'm in the middle of counting cash and chips and I can't do that one-handed.' Danielle looked up at the CCTV camera and gave another wink at her comeback to Woodard's comment.

'She's enjoying this, Jack,' snorted Brennan.

'Yes, she appears to be, but she has to be as nervous as anything beneath her brassy exterior.' Jack was reminded of just how fond he was of Danielle while watching her on the screen.

'Well, if you know what's good for your brother, you'll find a way to do your job,' Woodard yelled. Jack could see Danielle taking a deep breath to help maintain her outwardly calm and professional demeanour.

'I simply can't leave here; I haven't even had my dinner break. You'll have to conduct the transaction yourself.' Danielle looked up at the CCTV camera and held up her crossed fingers.

There was a pause in the conversation and the team in the Operations Room were nervously waiting for Woodard's response. The tension was thick, palpable even.

Jack looked around at each of the men in the small room. 'Crunch time, gents.'

Woodard was deep in concentration, contemplating what to do.

This wasn't how it was supposed to transpire. He should stay one step removed from the process, but delaying it wasn't an option as Li wanted his money tonight. And, after all, this was to be his final involvement with Li and his money laundering scheme. Including his share of tonight's transaction, his compensation would total two hundred thousand dollars. This had contributed significantly to the mortgage, school fees, the deposit on the wife's BMW and, of course, her holidays with the lifeguards. From hereon in, on his executive salary, he should be able to manage the family's financial commitments. And if the self-absorbed wife wants her holidays in the sun, then she can get a job. In an hour, this would all be behind him.

'Alright, I'll be there shortly.' Danielle gave the thumbs-up sign to the camera and the team in the Operations Room chorused a muted cheer.

'That didn't take long at all,' commented Dawson.

'Check out screen one.' Woodard was already entering the staff room again and making his way directly to the locker. He unlocked the door, lifted the briefcase out of the locker, not even bothering to lock it again, and headed for the exit.

'Pierro, he's on his way. He should be with you in three or four minutes.' Danielle gave the universal thumbs-up sign to the camera again.

'Okay, gents, checkout screen two. He's exiting the elevator and making for the Bennelong Room entry doors,' Dawson said, pointing at the screen. They all watched as Woodard pulled open one of the heavy mahogany doors that led into the Bennelong Room. The moment of silence was broken by Brennan making a call on his two-way radio. Jack knew who he was giving instructions to.

'He's in the room, Pierro,' Jack said into his mike. Danielle looked up at the camera but there was no cheekiness this time. The realisation had obviously descended on her, judging by the serious expression she now wore. Jack felt for her, but he was helpless now. It was all up to her. The four men were watching screen three and could see Woodard making his way across the Bennelong Room towards the Treasury Department.

Danielle heard a knock on the Treasury Department door. She inhaled as deeply as she could and then exhaled slowly and then repeated the process. That afforded her the time to compose herself sufficiently and after checking the peephole, she opened the door and ushered Woodard into the office.

'I can't believe you're doing this to me, Danielle, especially with everything I've done for you and your brother.'

'I'm not doing anything to you. Look around, I'm by myself. What was I supposed to do? Just lock the door, ignore the clients and go collect your precious briefcase?' she snapped. 'The vault's unlocked.'

Don't push it Danielle. Jack was saying to himself. 'Are you guys getting all this?' Neither Dawson nor Peterson looked away from their controls, merely nodding their assent. After five minutes, Woodard exited the vault. 'Open the briefcase and let me check it,' Danielle demanded. Woodard paused halfway across the office and gave her an incredulous look.

'What?'

'You heard me. Open the briefcase, Mr Woodard,' she reiterated.

'What the hell is she doing?' Jack blurted out, not believing what he was hearing and seeing. Following an awkward stand-off, and much to Jack's surprise, Woodard held open the briefcase and showed it to Danielle. She glanced inside and conducted a quick mental calculation of the value of the sleeves of pumpkins. 'Okay, you're all good,' she said in a calm voice.

The team watched as Woodard exited the office and made his way across the Bennelong Room. 'Switch to screen two please, Cam,' asked Brennan. Jack was watching screen four, which showed the Treasury Office, still concerned about Danielle's welfare. He turned back to screen two and watched as the heavy door of the Bennelong Room opened again and Woodard exited, straight into the waiting arms of two burly, uniformed security men.

'What's the meaning of this? Don't you know who I am? I'm the Vice President of Client Services? I'll have your jobs for this,' Woodard bellowed. The taller of the two security guards tugged the briefcase away from Woodard, unzipped it and checked the contents. He then gave his own thumbs-up to the CCTV camera.

'What are you doing? Give me that back. I was just conducting a transaction for a valued client,' Woodard pleaded.

'I'm sure you were, Mr Woodard. Now come with us, please,' insisted the older of the two guards as they grasped him firmly by the arms, turned him around and marched him away backwards.

$$\textbf{(88)}$$

Oceanic Security Operations Room

'Tony, I am quite troubled to see you in this terrible situation in which you now find yourself. You have worked here for many years and have been a well-respected member of the executive team. In many ways, you have been my right-hand man. How did it come to this?' asked Adam Benedict, the CEO.

'You've met Bree, so that should give you an idea why. Or have you forgotten the night I found the two of you in your pool together.'

'You're blaming this mess on Bree? Do you know how pathetic you sound?' insisted the CEO.

Jack approached Woodard and interrupted the conversation. 'There's no undoing what you have done here, Mr Woodard, including the irreparable damage to your reputation and the inevitable blight you have cast upon your family. That will be the least of your concerns though when you're spending the next decade of your life in prison.'

'I remember you now,' said Woodard, with narrowed eyes. 'You were in the Bennelong Room last week. I noticed you because you spent an inordinate amount of time at the bar. People come to the Bennelong Room to gamble, not drink. And then, later in the evening you were hovering around the blackjack table, even though you weren't playing.'

'Your suspicions were well-founded, and you should have acted upon them. That's the night you should have applied your best judgement and walked away from this, Mr Woodard. Why don't you tell your CEO why you spent such a disproportionate amount of time at that particular table that night?'

'I'm not saying anything more,' Woodard said with defiance.

Jack addressed the CEO. 'Put simply, Adam, Mr Woodard was accompanying one of the Oceanic's high rollers while he successfully laundered one million dollars.'

'Damn, which high roller, Tony?' Woodard now had his head bowed and remained silent. 'You're entitled to know, so I'll tell you Adam. His name is Li Qiang and I strongly suspect he has links to a Chinatown based Triad. I would think that Liquor and Gaming NSW wouldn't look too kindly on that association,' Jack suggested.

'Li Qiang, really? Oh Tony, what have you done?' lamented the CEO.

Jack continued. 'Mr Woodard, let's go back to what I was about to say earlier. There's nothing you can do about your past actions, the impending loss of your job, your devastated reputation and the collateral damage you have caused to your family. I am prepared to give you an opportunity to regain a morsel of your integrity and maybe even a shred of dignity.'

'What are you offering, detective?'

'I just told you.'

'That's not much of an offer.'

'I imagine your dignity and integrity might have mattered to you once. I'm giving you an opportunity to regain some of that which you have lost through your indiscretions. Nothing more, Mr Woodard.'

Woodard's mobile rang. 'I'm pretty sure I know who that will be,' Jack said, probably too smugly, he thought. 'My guess is someone is enquiring as to your whereabouts, and more importantly, that of the briefcase and its contents.' Jack received no response and the unanswered call was left to go through to voicemail. Woodard's mobile pinged with the voicemail alert. 'Enter your pin number and play the voicemail message,' ordered Jack.

"Mr Vice President, I have been waiting patiently for you to return with my belongings, but my patience is fast evaporating. Call me straight away if you know what is good for you."

'Well, there you have it, Mr Woodard, that was quite unambiguous I thought; the choice is yours. Your friend Mr Li has direct links to the Triads in Chinatown, and they don't play nice, so I doubt very much that was an empty threat. You need to think of your family at a time like this.'

'For heaven's sake, Tony, man-up will you,' yelled the CEO.

'Alright, alright, what do you want me to do?' asked a besieged Woodard.

'Graeme, did you bring the video camera?' Jack asked.

'Yes, but I could've just used my mobile phone.'

'No, that wouldn't do. In a court of law, it's too easy for defence counsel to dispute the efficacy and integrity of videos or photos taken on a mobile. I'm going to discreetly place a mark on both ends of each sleeve of gaming chips and I want you to video the whole process from start to finish as I do it, including me placing them back in the briefcase.'

'Alright, Jack, give me a minute please.'

'Mr Woodard, it's getting late in the evening and I imagine Mr Li is very keen to visit his favourite blackjack table tonight, so let's get this done, shall we?'

Woodard looked puzzled. 'Exactly how would you know that?'

'I'm a detective, Mr Woodard, that's what I do; I detect.' Jack certainly wasn't going to tell him about the listening device in Li's suite.

'Detective Wagner, have you got a minute?' asked the CEO. Jack and Adam walked to the rear of the Operations Room. 'I don't want to sound insensitive to your investigation, but is there any way we can keep this quiet? If details of this sorry state of affairs are leaked, the authorities could unreasonably crack down on our high roller operations because of one rogue executive; it could crucify our business.

'I'm sorry, Adam, but it might be too late for that. I know the Sydney Daily News has been conducting their own investigation, so you can expect to be very popular, sooner rather than later.'

'Do you know who the journalist is, detective?'

Jack wasn't about to divulge JA's name and put her under undue pressure, especially while she was recovering, so he danced around the question. 'No, I don't, but I'm sure you know the editor, Chris Russell. To him, I imagine this will be viewed as a huge public interest story and he will milk it for all it's worth.' Jack turned back to his technician. 'Are we ready to go, Graeme?'

'As I will ever be,' confirmed a smiling Dawson, obviously enjoying his part in the sting.

'Okay, you're going with Woodard. I want you to video me marking the sleeves and then you and Mr Woodard are going to take the freight elevator to the thirty-eighth floor. Your camera must keep filming for the entire duration until you exit on Li's floor and are in sight of his suite.

So you are not put in harm's way, the in-house cameras can pick up Woodard from then onwards, and you can return here. Cam, can you check that the CCTV cameras on the thirty eighth floor are functioning correctly please? We need to ensure the chain of custody of the marked gaming chips isn't broken at any point in this process,' Jack declared.

'Mr Vice President, and about time,' said Li, as he ushered Woodard into the Macquarie Suite. 'What was the hold-up?'

'With the Treasury Manager being absent, they were short staffed, so my contact wasn't available. I had to conduct the transaction myself. And before you start threatening me again; there was no other option.'

'Okay, okay, Tony. Let's go play some blackjack, shall we?'

Woodard walked to the door, followed by Li carrying the soft leather case under his arm. 'What the hell is this?' shouted Woodard, feigning ignorance. He had opened the Macquarie Suite door and was confronted by two suited men with weapons drawn and aimed at him.

The men ignored Woodard and focused on Li. 'Mr Li, we are Australian Federal Policemen, step out into the hallway.'

Li was momentarily stunned, but quickly regained his composure. 'What's the meaning of all this? Do you know who I am?' he demanded.

'Mr Li, I asked you once already, step out into the hallway. Now.' The taller man ordered.

'Okay, okay.'

'Now, lean against the wall, place your hands above your head and spread your feet, please. I will relieve you of that briefcase if you don't mind,' said the taller man.

'This is ridiculous. Do you know who I am? I demand you call the CEO, now. And I want to call my consulate immediately,' bellowed Li indignantly. The shorter of the two men ignored the outburst, placed his weapon in its holster and searched and patted Li down.

'You can turn around now.'

The senior of the two officers addressed him. 'I am Officer Paul Jamieson, and this is Officer Rocco Scerri, and we are from the Australian Federal Police Serious Financial Crime Taskforce. Mr Li, you are under arrest for breaching Division 400 of the Criminal Code Act and Proceeds of Crime Act 2002, that being the principal criminal offence of money laundering in Australia,' recited Jamieson.

'That's a load of rubbish. I haven't laundered anything. It was all him,' yelled Li while pointing at Woodard.

Jamieson overlooked the latest outburst and continued. 'Mr Li, the law requires me to inform you that you do not have to say or do anything in response to questioning and that anything you say or do may be used in court. Do you understand?' Li glared at Jamieson but didn't speak. 'We are now going to take you into custody and escort you to Australian Federal Police Headquarters.'

Scerri turned to Woodard. 'You will need to accompany us also, Mr Woodard.' Scerri repeated the caution notice Jamieson had given Li, took Woodard into custody as well and the four men proceeded to the elevator.

The team in the Operations Room let out a louder cheer this time. 'Well done guys, that's an excellent result for the team. Adam, do you have a room master keycard?'

'Yes.'

'Could you provide me with access to Li's room, please? I need to retrieve his mobile phones. He wouldn't have been allowed to have them in the Bennelong Room, as you would know.' Jack also wanted Dawson to remove the listening devices before they were discovered; just in case the DC hadn't received the judicial warrant.

Jack had just finished searching Li's room when his mobile phone rang. He saw Danielle's picture displayed on the screen. 'Hi Danielle, are you okay?'

'I'm fairly nonplussed by the whole episode, but I think I'm okay. I've just finished work and wondered if you'd like to give me a ride home, Jack.' There wasn't much more that Jack could achieve tonight. It had been another long day and Jamieson and Scerri would take care of Li and Woodard until the morning. He needed to discuss Danielle's circumstances again with the DC, and pending the outcome, this might be her final night of freedom for a while.

'I've got a couple of things to do, so give me twenty minutes and I'll pick you up at the staff entrance.'

Danielle flopped into the passenger seat and leaned across to kiss Jack on the cheek. 'Are you sure you're okay?' he asked.

'I know I looked like I was having fun, but in reality, I was probably just covering up for my nervousness.'

'Well, it's all over now,' he replied.

$$\textbf{89}$$

Danielle's Apartment

It was one o'clock in the morning and Danielle and Jack sat on the sofa sipping a glass of her favourite white wine. 'What's going to happen to me, Jack?' She had changed into her chilling at home clothes and was sitting sideways on the sofa with her legs and bare feet once again tucked up under her body. Jack detected a note of hopefulness in her question.

'I have no idea. My Deputy Commissioner is fully aware of your involvement in Li and Woodard's activities. Although, I have also told him about the circumstances which caused you to become involved. It will be up to him and the DPP to decide your fate. There's too much going on with other investigations, so I don't imagine it's high on his agenda at the moment. He will at some stage want to interview you himself, if for no other reason than maintaining transparency over the whole operation.

'What do you really think will happen to me, Jack? Tell me the truth.'

He detected a slight quiver in her voice, so he took Danielle's hands in his and looked into her eyes. Jack didn't want to get her hopes up by sugar coating the situation. 'I really have no idea, but you can't expect to walk away from this without charges of some sort being levelled against you. It's just not how the system works. Money laundering, particularly in relation to casinos, is a hot-button issue for law enforcement around the country, and primarily because it is usually related to other more violent crimes. Middle Eastern crime gangs, various European mafia, Triads, motorcycle gangs, drug syndicates and the like are all trying to source ways of legitimising their ill-gotten gains.' He paused. 'Sorry, that sounded too much like cop speak.'

Jack noticed her eyes watering and he pulled her in closer and she rested her head on his shoulder. 'It took some courage and strength of character to do what you did tonight and I'm sure that will be taken into consideration.'

They were quiet for some time, no doubt both were reflecting on the events of earlier this evening. Jack broke the silence. 'And, what the hell were you doing demanding Woodard open the briefcase?' he asked with a chuckle, endeavouring to lighten the mood.

'I just wanted to make sure it only contained the pumpkins and that he wasn't stealing anything else.'

'You crack me up sometimes.'

They lounged on the sofa a while longer and Jack thought she may have drifted off to sleep. He gently kissed her on the top of her head, and she stirred. 'Take me to bed.'

Jack was laying back against the bedhead and Danielle had nestled into his chest. 'Thank you for trusting me and putting yourself out there like you did tonight, Danielle. I won't forget it.'

'I hope your DC doesn't forget it either. I could never have played my part in your plan tonight if you hadn't been there. I never once felt unsafe because I knew you would look out for me. Thank you. Now, do you mind if I just lay here and drift away?'

'No, not at all. Good night, Pierro.'

AFP Headquarters
Friday 13th March

Jack had called Sanderson from his car earlier and requested that he and Billingsley attend a meeting at AFP Headquarters at eleven o'clock this morning, under the premise of workshopping the drug importation case. "The DC wants to be involved, hence meeting at the AFP, Michael." Jack had told him. In the meantime, he would join Jamieson and Scerri in their interview of Li Qiang.

'Where have the large amounts of cash you have been laundering originated, Mr Li?' asked Paul Jamieson. What began as a simple investigation into cocaine distribution had morphed into one of money laundering which was not part of Jack's responsibilities. Jamieson and Scerri were deployed to the AFP's Serious Financial Crime Taskforce, so Jack had passed Li onto them. 'You may as well tell us as we will ascertain the source eventually.'

'Then you don't need me to answer your question, do you?' Li responded smugly.

'Do you think if we asked Wie Ping Lie that he might know the answer?' Jamieson suggested.

'I don't know who that is,' Li replied. 'I want to speak to the Chinese Consul General.'

'Yes, I'm sure you do, all in good time, Mr Li.'

Jamieson continued? 'Mr Li, we can detain you without charge for twenty-four hours, and if we so desire, we can get a Detention Order from a court for another twenty-four hours. We will continue to do that until you provide the answers we know you have. It's entirely up to you. Is that clear?'. Li didn't reply.

'One thing I do know though, is that I will go home to my family every night, have a lovely home-cooked meal, watch my favourite TV show and then sleep like a baby, all while you languish in your holding cell for days at a time,' said Jamieson, smiling. He heard the door open and turned to see Jack Wagner walking in.

'Do you mind if I ask Mr Li a couple of questions, Paul?'

'Knock yourself out, Jack. We need to go and talk to Woodard anyway.'

'Hello, Mr Li. Why did you need to get rid of Michelle Ironside?' Jack asked, coming straight to the point. Li was trying to remain composed, but Jack noticed a subtle twitch in his facial expression.

'I don't know what you are talking about.'

'I'm talking about the mysterious and timely disappearance of the casino's Treasury Manager right before she was about to be interviewed by her CEO.'

'I have no knowledge of any of that.'

'Yes, you do. You and Woodard knew she would be compelled to reveal to the CEO her knowledge of your illegal activities, and you simply couldn't allow that to happen,' Jack said. 'Could you?'

Li smiled at Jack. 'Maybe you should ask the Vice President about that.'

'We have you on tape confirming your knowledge of her being missing. How did you know she was missing, Li?'

'Oh come on, detective, I'm sure the entire casino staff knew she was missing,' Li replied, knowing it to be true.

'What would prompt Woodard to ask you if you knew anything about her disappearance then?'

'Maybe you should ask the Vice President about that too,' Li repeated.

Jack removed his phone from his jacket pocket and swiped across until he found the app he wanted. He pressed the play button. *"Is the package in good condition?"* Graeme Dawson had downloaded the audio file capturing Li's in-room conversations to Jack's mobile phone. 'You are asking about Michelle Ironside there, aren't you?' Jack detected the subtle facial twitch again.

Li sighed. 'If you must know detective, I was enquiring about a valuable figurine I was having sent home to China, that's all.'

'That's rubbish and we both know it,' roared Jack. He was no closer to proving a link between Li and Michelle Ironside's abduction, so he moved on for now. 'Let me play you something else which you might find interesting.' Jack picked up his mobile, opened the app again and pressed play. Li looked up at the ceiling, feigning disinterest.

"My responsibility in the operation hasn't gone to shit at all; I just need to re-evaluate my candidate profile. The importation isn't my responsibility, as you well know. Anyway, we have sufficient funding for a political campaign already and I am about to complete another transaction."

'Aaahh, Mr Li, where to start,' Jack said. 'Let's start with the operation, shall we? Would that be Wie Ping Lie's drug importation operation by any chance?'

'Well detective, you said yourself, it was Wie Ping Lie's operation, so it couldn't be mine then, could it?' Li leant back in his chair with a self-satisfied look on his face.

'Oh, so you do know Wie Ping Lie then.' Jack teased. 'Okay, what about the importation, or are you going to tell me you were actually bringing *in* a valuable figurine this time?' Jack asked, not trying to hide the sarcasm.

'Detective, detective, you can mock me all you like, but I haven't committed any crime, and once again you have nothing to suggest that I have,' Li said, calmly.

'I'm not mocking you, I'm actually enjoying this little tête-à-tête. You see, you admitted on the tape that you were about to complete another transaction, and low and behold, we caught you doing just that, the very same day. How dumb are you?'

'You've got nothing, nothing at all,' Li raged as he banged the table with his fist. He wasn't going to tolerate some snotty nosed detective calling him dumb. 'Charge me or release me.'

Jack remained composed. 'Oh, Mr Li, my guess is that when Detective Jamieson returns, he will charge you with federal money laundering offences, so you will get your wish. I imagine Mr Woodard is also singing a lovely tune right about now.'

'You've got nothing, detective,' Li replied belligerently. 'Get me the Consul General.'

'All in good time. Let me play you something else. Tell me about this quote of yours.' Jack pressed play again on his app.

"That wasn't my responsibility and you know it."

'What are you referring to there? I would suggest to you that you were talking about the unfortunate demise of Captain Han. My guess is that it was the handiwork of your friend Wie Ping Lie, but that won't prevent me or the boys from Maritime Border Command and Queensland Police linking you to the captain's death, however tenuous that link may appear. This whole scenario is unravelling at a feverish pace, and you're right in the middle of it.'

'I'm not in the middle of anything, detective,' Li said, composed again.

'Deny, deny, deny, just like that line from that well-known sixties film. My best guess would be that your conversation was with a senior party or government figure from China. I don't know who that person is just yet, but I imagine they will be very displeased with your less than successful activities.'

'I'm not in the habit of failing, detective,' Li uttered, with false pride.

'You lost your political candidate—Jack halted as he noticed a reaction from Li. Yes, Mr Li, I am well aware of your attempts to recruit Miss Wu; how did that work out for you? I believe you lost her, in more ways than one. How am I doing?' Li was shifting uncomfortably from side to side in his chair now and his expression had darkened.

'Anyway, continuing on. You certainly got into the habit of failing with Miss Wu. And, apparently, you weren't much better at dealing with Ms Granger.' Jack was baiting Li now, waiting for him to explode and hopefully reveal information out of an uncontrolled anger. 'And you and Woodard couldn't deal with Michelle Ironside either, so you arranged for her kidnapping.' Jack let that sink in.

'And, a little birdie tells me you think you're something of a ladies' man…' Jack let that hang in the air as well. Even though he hadn't met her yet, he was thinking about Sophie Zhao and the demeaning tales JA had regaled.

'But, given all the evidence, it seems to me you're not very good with women at all, Li,' tormented Jack. 'I bet you can't even get it up anymore, fatboy.' Li's face turned bright red and Jack thought he was about to burst. He was correct.

'Cāo nǐ de zhū,' raged Li as he launched out of his seat at Jack. 'Wǒ huì shāle nǐ.' Jack lurched backwards reflexively, even though he knew Li wouldn't be able to reach him.

Unfortunately for Li, his legs were secured to his chair, which was in turn bolted to the floor, so he ended up face planting on the hard metal table. Jack thought of JA, Melissa and Sophie and the pleasure they would get when he told them of Li's reaction.

'I assume you said something debauched about my mother or sister in all that waffle. You think you're the first, little man. Okay, where were we? Oh, that's right, we were listing your litany of failures. Well, you've had one million dollars of someone else's money confiscated, you're also involved in kidnapping and a ship's captain was killed. I imagine these failures will be reverberating around the halls of some ancient palace belonging to some powerful people back in Beijing or Shanghai. But, don't worry Mr Li, I'm sure you'll be much safer here in Long Bay Prison. Surely, no harm could possibly befall you in there.' Jack chuckled as he stood and collected his files.

'Oh, and one more thing Li, if you or your so-called state security cronies go anywhere near Sophie Zhao or her family back in Tong-Li again—' Li endeavoured to remain indifferent to Jack's comment, but Jack noticed another little tic. 'Yes, that's right, I know about that too and rest assured, I will personally come after you, wherever you are, with the full force of the AFP behind me. Are we clear?'

'Don't threaten me, Detective. You can't touch me. Maybe you should be thinking about your ex-girlfriend's welfare.' The rhythmic, nervous twitching of Li's cheek betrayed his bravado.

'Where you're going, she no longer has anything to be concerned about. Unlike your confiscated money, you can take that to the bank.' Jack said as he stared Li down.

(**91**)

AFP HQ Conference Room

Jack had achieved little on his first go-round with Li, so he left it to Jamieson and Scerri to continue their own line of questioning related to the money laundering. He had to meet David Bedford at reception. 'Have you got everything on your laptop, David?' Bedford tapped the laptop bag hanging over his shoulder to signal all was as requested. Jack signed him in and they made their way to the elevator that would take them up to the twelfth floor conference room.

In the centre of the conference room was a highly polished cherry mahogany table that was accompanied by twelve evenly spaced leather chairs. He and Bedford took a seat in the centre of the long side of the boardroom table. In the centre of the table was one of those modern cordless voice stations; it had obviously replaced the cumbersome octopus like contraption. What garnered his attention, as it always did, was the photos of the eight men who had held the position as Commissioner of the Australian Federal Police since the agency's formation in 1979. The Commissioner of the AFP was a universally respected role and Jack had worked under four of them during his tenure. In his experience, he had found their respect to be well-earned and he had a particular high regard for the previous Commissioner.

The DC had already arranged for Sanderson and Billingsley to be escorted to the same room and the three of them were chatting, seemingly amiably, when Jack and Bedford had walked in. Jack didn't introduce Bedford, but just indicated where he could connect his laptop to the video screen.

'Okay gents, let's get straight down to business, shall we?' Jack suggested as he eyed the two state detectives. 'Firstly, I can advise you that we have arrested Li Qiang and Tony Woodard and they are currently assisting us with our money laundering enquiries.' Jack paused as he watched the faces of the two detectives for a reaction. Sanderson smiled and Billingsley remained impassive. 'We have enough evidence against both men and I anticipate charges will be laid later today.'

'That's great news. Well done, Jack,' congratulated Sanderson.

'Unfortunately, another component of the investigation isn't going as well. We still haven't found Michelle Ironside. She seems to have disappeared into thin air, so to speak. Which brings me to the primary reason you are both here. Why are you having so much trouble locating Ling Jun and Wang Wei?'

Sanderson started to respond defensively. 'Save it, Michael,' Jack said as he held up his hand.

'We know they were in Raglan Street three days ago and at Central Station that same evening, so it's not like they've been trying to be inconspicuous. We also know they'll probably be hanging out in Chinatown somewhere and the area's not that big either. How hard can it be to locate these guys?' Jack asked, ensuring he looked appropriately frustrated.

'It's like they've been a step ahead of us ever since we started this investigation. I'm as frustrated as you are,' moaned Sanderson.

'Let me play you something that will help you understand your frustration, Michael.

David, whenever you're ready,' Jack indicated towards the screen.

The video screen hanging from the ceiling at the end of the conference room came to life.

Judging by all the symbols and characters on the building signs the first video was shot in Chinatown. 'Gents, this was filmed two days ago outside the Golden Phoenix restaurant,' advised Bedford, as he let the video tell its own story. Jack was closely watching the two detectives for their reaction.

'You're kidding me,' exclaimed Sanderson, as he watched the video showing Detective Nathan Billingsley in conversation with Wie Ping Lie.

'I can explain,' said Billingsley calmly.

'Let's hear it then,' Sanderson said sharply as he stared down his younger partner.

'I was simply asking him about the whereabouts of our two suspects, that's all.' Bedford had paused the video. Billingsley remained outwardly calm, but his forehead was now shining with beads of sweat.

'What, and you thought Wie was going to give them up, just like that? That's crap Nathan, and you know it,' yelled Sanderson.

'Continue please, David,' Jack prompted. Bedford clicked on the next video file and leant back in his chair.

'What the hell?' Sanderson blurted out as he turned to face Billingsley.

'I assume you know the identities of the two men on the screen, gents,' Jack said. Bedford had paused the video and the men in the room were looking at a still of Ling Jun and Wang Wei. Also pictured on the screen was an attractive woman of Eurasian extraction and New South Wales police detective Nathan Billingsley. In the drama of the moment, no-one seemed to notice the two uniformed AFP officers who had stepped quietly into the room and were now standing behind Billingsley.

'What the hell's going on, Nathan? What the hell have you done?' roared Sanderson. Billingsley sat there silent, knowing that there was no point in explaining anything. It wouldn't diminish his guilt one iota, so why bother.

'Well, I can tell you a few things, Michael. Now we know why you couldn't get the warrant to track Michelle Ironside's mobile phone. Billingsley hadn't submitted the application. And, he obviously also told Ling Jun and company where Ms Granger lived. They then tracked her from her apartment and tried to take her out in Raglan Street. Billingsley, do you realise you would have been an accessory to murder if Ms Granger had been killed in that stunt?'

Billingsley was staring down at the table, hands clasped on his lap and remained silent.

Jack was furious at that possibility, but kept his cool. 'And of course, he's been feeding Ling Jun and Wang Wei information in relation to your search, Michael, allowing them to avoid your every effort to capture them. Does that pretty much cover it?' Jack asked as he glared at Billingsley.

Sanderson's face was flushed from embarrassment. 'I can't believe this, Jack. How could I not have noticed or suspected anything?'

'Don't be so hard on yourself. I only became suspicious when you referred to Ms Granger as my ex-girlfriend. Neither you nor Billingsley should have known that, at that stage anyway, so I got David Bedford here, from MPS to do some investigating on my behalf.

The DC stood. 'We can discuss the recriminations and what-ifs later gents.' He turned to address Billingsley. 'Detective Billingsley, you will be charged with perverting the course of justice under the Criminal Code Act of 1995. Section 319 General offence of perverting the course of justice reads: A person who does any act, or makes any omission, intending in any way to pervert the course of justice, is liable to imprisonment for fourteen years.' He looked directly at Billingsley. 'I think that categorisation could comfortably be applied to you. Get him out of my sight, gentlemen.' The two uniformed officers dragged him to his feet. The older one relieved him of his weapon, handcuffed him and the two officers frogmarched him out of the conference room.

As Jack stood to leave the room, his mobile phone rang, and he saw

Jim Brennan's name on the digital display. 'Hi, Jim. How are you?'

'Much better now, Jackie boy. I've finally heard back from the state police regarding the Uber booking for Michelle Ironside.'

'Did they come up with anything positive?' Jack asked hopefully.

'Yes, they sure did. Uber eventually got around to doing what you asked and checked their cancelled bookings. And, low and behold, they had a record of a cancelled booking for Michelle Ironside.'

'Why would she cancel the booking Jim? She always catches an Uber home after work.'

'She never cancelled the booking Jack, the driver did. I don't know exactly how Uber's software system works, but the driver must have cancelled the booking at the precise time Michelle entered his vehicle. Any earlier and it would have shown up as cancelled on the Uber App on Michelle's phone and she would have ordered a different Uber.'

'Did the state police manage to get the details of the driver from Uber's records?'

'Yes, and you're going to love this, Jack. The driver's name is Fan Chen. I seem to remember you mentioning him in passing a while back.'

'Wow. Assuming it's the same Fan Chen, he supposedly works as an attaché for the Chinese Consul General here in Sydney, who in turn has links to our Mr Li Qiang. What are the state guys doing about it, did they say?'

'They have issued a state-wide "Keep A Lookout For" notice for the vehicle. Apparently, kidnapping falls under the jurisdiction of the Robbery and Serious Crime Squad, so they will be heavily involved as well. Given the potential political sensitivities surrounding the Consul General, the Assistant Commissioner himself is going to meet with the CG this afternoon. That's as much as I know, Jack.'

'Well, at least the state cops know who they're looking for now, which will make it a whole lot easier for them to locate him. Then, we will no doubt be forced to sit back and watch the politics kick in. Thanks for the head's up, Jim.'

'Pleasure. Bye, Jack.'

AFP Headquarters

Sanderson was sitting with Jack at his desk while they were both eating a sandwich. 'I still can't believe I could be so blind about my partner, Jack. We were together for over two years and I never suspected a thing. I feel so stupid,' he grumbled.

'We detectives are required to be ever vigilant and suspicious by nature, but that suspicion rarely extends to our partners; that just goes against the grain of mutual trust. We rely on our partners to watch our back at all times, so we have to trust them, Michael.'

'Yeah, I get that, but it doesn't make me feel any better.'

'We'll let Billingsley sweat down in holding for a while and then I'll interview him and see if he'll give up Ling Jun and Wang Wei's location,' Jack said. 'If he does, the DC has said he will consider downgrading his charges to that of hindering police instead of perverting the course of justice. That should be sufficient incentive for Billingsley to cooperate, Michael and it will potentially reduce his sentence from fourteen years down to seven.'

Jack was checking his emails while they ate lunch and chatted. 'Bingo,' he exclaimed.

'What have you got, Jack, two fat ladies?' Sanderson laughed at his own joke.

Jack fleetingly thought about JA and Danielle's figures. *Definitely not.* 'On the contrary, Michael. Anyway, I have received an email from Shane Williamson, you remember him from the conference call a few days ago. Maritime Border Command have finally received CCTV footage from the Seafarer's Mission in Brisbane. And, guess what it shows?'

'I can guess, our elusive boys up to mischief,' responded Sanderson. 'Dumb bastards. They leave their fingerprints on the yacht, don't strip the SUV's numberplates when attacking Julie-Anne and get caught on CCTV at the Mission.'

'They're just drug dealers, not master criminals. That's why we always apprehend them eventually,' Jack said dismissively. 'I will send Ling Jun and Wang Wei's information to Williamson and he can pass it along to the Queensland state police. I will have to discuss this with the DC as well, because we don't want to get into a jurisdictional pissing match over who's charging these guys when we do catch them.'

Jack and Sanderson were discussing Billingsley's predicament when a mobile phone on Jack's desk rang. They looked at the three mobile phones on his desk and Jack was surprised to see that it was Li's burner phone that was ringing. 'Michael, check this out,' Jack said as he pointed to the ringing mobile phone. He swiped right on the burner. 'Hello.' There was a moment of silence and Jack was worried that the caller had disconnected the call. 'Hello, don't hang up please,' he said.

'Where is Mr Li?' The voice asked.

Jack quickly gathered his thoughts. 'He has been arrested. I am Detective Wagner, don't hang up,' he repeated. There was silence, and Jack wasn't sure if the caller had disconnected the call. Remembering the text from the audio tapes taken from Li Qiang's room, Jack started talking again. 'I assume you are calling about the package.' Through the listening devices in Li's room, Jack knew there had been no further contact regarding *the package*. There was more silence from the caller, so Jack kept talking. He had to keep this guy on the phone until he had said what he needed to. 'If you have Ms Ironside, you should take her somewhere safe and release her. At the moment I don't care about you, I just want her returned safely.' The caller was obviously thinking about the ramifications. 'That's the best offer you'll get today.' Jack waited for a response, but none was forthcoming. 'Bugger, he hung up.' He told Michael. 'I have to go downstairs and have a quick chat to Billingsley. If you want to join me, Michael you'll need to keep your thoughts and comments to yourself. Can you do that? I don't want you losing your cool.'

'Yeah, that's a fair trade-off,' Sanderson conceded.

'Detective Billingsley, for the record, it is two o'clock on the afternoon of Friday 13th March 2020 and I am Senior Detective Jack Wagner from the AFP. You don't have to confirm anything as this whole interview is being recorded on a video camera.' Sanderson took a seat at the rear of the room and leant back against the wall with his arms folded across his chest.

'Detective Billingsley, I don't intend to spend hours down here in holding wasting my time with you and your sorry arse. All I want to know is the location of your associates, Mr Ling Jun and a Mr Wang Wei.' Jack noticed a puzzled expression materialise on Billingsley's face.

'Aaahh, you picked up on that.' Jack heard Sanderson shift in his chair and he guessed he had also detected the subtle distinction. 'That's right I used the word *associates*. So whatever we eventually charge them with, you will be charged as an accessory to their crimes, in addition to your perverting the course of justice charge. At this stage, we have them implicated in drug importation, the murder of a seaman and the attempted murder of a journalist.'

Billingsley squirmed in his chair. 'I don't know anything about any of that.'

'Whether you do or you don't matters little to me, detective, as I can, and will, implicate you in all of them,' Jack said forcefully.

'You know how this works. Now, as I said earlier, all I want to know is the location of your associates, Ling Jun and Wang Wei. Provide me with that information and I will leave you in peace in these salubrious surroundings.'

'What's in it for me, Wagner?' Billingsley asked.

'I tell you what I will do for you, Nathan. I'll put my "good cop" hat on for a minute.' Jack made the universal quotation mark symbol with his fingers. 'You tell me where I can find Ling Jun and Wang Wei and I will forget about the accessory charges I mentioned earlier, and we will just stick with your perverting the course of justice indictment.' Jack wasn't going to tell him just yet about the DC's offer of further reducing the charges down to that of hindering instead of perverting the course of justice. 'I have no interest in spending days down here in this shithole talking to a corrupt cop. And, just so we're very clear on this, it is a one-time offer. How does that sound, detective?' The three detectives sat there in silence. Jack had no intention of saying any more. It was up to Billingsley to determine his own fate.

'Alright. I'm not doing this for you, Wagner or the feds. Michael has been a good, hard- working, honest cop for years and I have realised my actions have cast a pall over his reputation, career and future prospects. I'm sorry, Michael,' Billingsley said regretfully, as he looked directly at Sanderson. 'Write this down, Wagner.'

Jack wrote the address down in his notebook. 'Who was the woman in the video, Nathan?'

Billingsley sighed. 'Haven't I given you enough already?' Jack folded his arms, leaned back in his chair and didn't respond. 'Okay, her name's Lucie Chan and she's a dealer for Wie. I've never had any dealings with her.' That confirmed what Jack's CI had told him about the "chink chick". He went back upstairs to his desk and rang the DC with the news of their suspect's whereabouts. The Deputy Commissioner then convened a planning meeting for five o'clock the same evening. Jack rang downstairs to the Watch Commander and instructed him that Billingsley was to have no physical or phone contact with anyone until further notice.

It was four o'clock in the afternoon and Jack was working away at his desk, writing another report for the DC, this time his summary of the events at the Oceanic last night. He was surprised when the DC walked into the room and approached his desk. He was wearing a beaming smile. 'You look happy, boss.'

'And so will you be once you've heard my news. Michelle Ironside has been found.'

'Oh, wow, that is great news. Is she okay?'

'Yes, it is and yes, she is okay. She was found wandering aimlessly around Wilson Park, near the banks of the Parramatta River in Silverwater. A couple of footballers arriving for training found her.

Apparently, she seemed disorientated and was rambling to herself. They were obviously very concerned, so they asked her name and called Crime Stoppers straight away. They gave her some water and then waited with her until the uniformed boys from Auburn Station arrived.'

'That's wonderful news. Where have they taken her?'

'She's at Auburn Hospital.'

'I'll go and pay her a visit after the SRG meeting, boss.'

'I'm sure she would appreciate that. Also, could you call Danielle Mortimer and arrange for her to meet with me at nine o'clock tomorrow morning? I'll greet her at reception.'

'Okay, will do boss.' Uh oh, D Day for Danielle, he thought.

$$\textbf{(93)}$$

AFP Headquarters

At a quarter to five in the evening, Jack and Sanderson arrived at the same conference room on the twelfth floor where Billingsley had been outed a few hours earlier. Given Sanderson's frustratingly fruitless attempts to locate the suspects in the case, the DC had invited him to attend. Jack and Sanderson took their seats at the large conference table and were soon joined by the DC and Oliver Campbell, the head of the AFP's Specialist Response Group. Jack introduced Sanderson to Campbell. He was tall and tanned, athletically built, with close cropped greying hair and he was wearing SRG's fatigues.

'Oliver, Detective Sanderson is attached to Day Street Police Station and has an enduring involvement in this case, so I have invited him to join us this evening. As you are the head of the SRG, his future involvement is at your discretion,' the DC confirmed.

'Thanks, John. Firstly, Jack, are these guys likely to be armed?' asked Campbell.

'Oliver, we suspect them of being involved in the murder of a ship's captain in Brisbane last Saturday and the shooting attack on a journalist here in Sydney a few days ago, so we should be prepared for them to be armed. Also, a Eurasian woman who I suspect is part of Wie's crew and has been dealing coke in the eastern suburbs might be living at the address. She was threatened at gunpoint by the local gang in Bondi a couple of weeks ago, so that would be another reason for them to be armed.'

'Okay, thanks. Secondly, I need to know all the details on their location.'

'They are holed-up in Apartment 1417 in the Darling Harbour Apartment Building at 362 Sussex Street. We haven't been able to verify the apartment number, so we are relying on the accuracy of Billingsley's information, Oliver. Having said that, the nominated apartment is owned by a company that lists only one director. That director is Than Ping Lie, who I imagine is Wie Ping Lie's mother, wife or sister, so I think we can be relatively certain it's the correct apartment,' Jack confirmed.

Campbell continued discussing the raid with the DC while Jack was working on his tablet. 'Here we go,' he interrupted. 'I have just found the layout of the apartment from a previous online real estate advertisement. I'll send it to you now, Oliver.'

'Okay, we need someone in civilian dress to engage the Night Manager and provide us with access cards to the elevator and the building's upper floors, just in case he is sympathetic to our targets.

'I can do that for you,' offered Sanderson.

'It will be five o'clock in the morning, so you need to dress casually like you are arriving back from a night out, Michael. We don't want to tip our hand to the Night Manager until you have the access cards.'

'That's right up my alley, Oliver.'

'Alright, the target building is only seven hundred metres from where we are sitting now. I suggest we meet here at four fifteen tomorrow morning for a final briefing and then head directly to our target. I have some planning to undertake with my guys, so I'll bid you good night and see you at oh four fifteen tomorrow.' Campbell then promptly left the room.

Jack was keen to get to the Auburn Hospital and see how Michelle Ironside was bearing up after her ordeal. As he was driving west along Parramatta Road, having finally cleared the CBD peak hour traffic, he rang JA.

'Hi Jack, how are you?'

'I'm great and I have news galore. So much so, that I don't know where to start,' he answered eagerly.

'At the beginning, as always,' she said with a smile in her voice.

'Okay, we caught Li and Woodard in a sting operation last night and they're now both in the AFP's holding cells as we speak.'

'Wow, that's great news. How did you pull it off?' she enquired excitedly.

'It was a team effort with our electronic people, the security guys at the casino and Danielle from Treasury. It went without a hitch.'

'I don't suppose that would be the same Danielle that you went dancing with, by any chance, would it, Jack?' Julie-Anne teased.

'JA, we've had this conversation. With Michelle Ironside being absent from her Treasury role, we couldn't have achieved the successful outcome without Danielle. She was the conduit in the operation and handled Woodard with aplomb,' Jack stated, probably too proudly.

Julie-Anne felt a twinge of jealously. While she had been holed-up in the safe house another woman had joined with Jack in the investigation and they had successfully snared Li and Woodard. *That should have been me*, she lamented.

'That's great,' Julie-Anne said reticently.

'I also found out why the Day Street detectives were having so much difficulty in locating Ling Jun and his partner.' Given Julie-Anne had been shot at by Ling, she was particularly invested in their capture.

'Go on,' she said.

'Billingsley, that's Sanderson's partner, had let something slip that he had no right to be aware of, so I engaged David Bedford's company and had him tailed. On separate occasions, David's guys caught Billingsley meeting with Wie Ping Lie and your two assailants.'

'You're kidding. How did that play out?'

'He has been arrested and is being held in custody pending further interrogation.' Jack wouldn't tell JA about the proposed raid tomorrow morning.

'That's fantastic news. Hopefully, he will lead you to my attackers and Melissa and I can get our lives back,' Julie-Anne said.

'And, I have even better news.'

'What could possibly be better than that?'

'Michelle Ironside was found alive this afternoon,' Jack said buoyantly.

'Oh, Jack, I am just so relieved to hear that. That's wonderful news.'

'That's all I know about her disappearance at the moment. I don't think she has any close family, so I am just driving to the hospital to check in on her and provide her with some support. Then, I will need to ask her some important questions.'

'I hope she's okay.'

'Me, too. How are you and Melissa coping with being cooped up?'

'Yeah, we're fine. Melissa's been doing a lot of reading and cooking and is quite relaxed. I'm nearly finished writing the first instalment of my story but, I might need you to fill in some blanks for me. Now you have nabbed Li, Woodard and Billingsley, I can start drafting my follow-up. When do you think you will have some time, Jack?'

He bristled at the apparent selfishness. 'Jesus, JA, have you even been listening? The investigation has been blown wide open with these major developments, and all of them occurring in the past twenty-four hours. We still have an active investigation to follow through as well,' he sighed.

'Sorry, that was a little self-seeking of me, but I really do need to get the whole story written and published as soon as possible. I'm just doing my job, like you.'

'Look, I've just arrived at the hospital, so I'll talk to you later,' Jack said. He parked his car in Hargrave Road and made his way along the footpath and entered the reception area. He explained who he was and why he wanted to see Michelle Ironside. The receptionist asked him to take a seat and she would contact the Nurse Unit Manager. A short while later, a tall, red- headed woman wearing a dark blue tunic over matching slacks and with a hospital ID Card pinned to her tunic walked into reception and called Jack's name. He stood up, raised his hand in the air to signify he was the person in question, and walked over to the nurse.

'Mr Wagner, I'm Nurse Unit Manager, Daisy Threadgold.'

'Thanks for coming out to see me, Daisy. How is Ms Ironside?'

'I don't know the details of her ordeal Mr Wagner, but whatever it was, she is in reasonably good health, other than being quite dehydrated. We are intravenously giving her fluids to treat the dehydration. We have also taken blood samples to check for the levels of electrolytes in her system and her kidney function. Ms Ironside also has a mild concussion from a blow to her head, but she appears to be quite lucid now. We will keep her in our Close Observation Unit for twenty-four hours to maintain a watch over her, just in case. I can take you to see her if you would like, detective.'

'Thank you, that would be great.'

Jack walked into the COU and across to Michelle's bed. 'Oh, hello, Detective Wagner,' she said, sounding surprisingly cheery.

'Hi Michelle, how are you feeling?'

'I feel quite weak and a tad tired, but other than that, not too bad really, all things considered.'

'I am pleased to hear it. You look quite good, too.'

'Thank you, but I'm sure that couldn't be true,' she said, forcing a modest smile. 'Do you want me to tell you what happened, detective?'

'That's not why I came here. I just wanted to check in with you and see how you were doing.'

'That's very kind of you, but I'm okay. I've already told the uniformed police and local detectives what happened, but I'm happy to repeat it for you, if you would like.'

'If you're certain it wouldn't cause you too much anguish,' Jack said gently.

'Okay, I finished my shift, and as I always do, I walked outside and got into the back seat of my Uber. I was quite tired and stressed, most probably due to Mr Woodard's threats. Anyway, I must have drifted off to sleep. When I awoke half an hour later, it was clear I wasn't anywhere near my home. It looked like an industrial area. I was dragged out of the car and one of those knitted headpieces was placed over my head.'

'A balaclava, Michelle.'

'That's it, a balaclava, but with no holes. Anyway, I was screaming and yelling at the man, then something hit me on the back of my head, and everything went dark after that. I woke up some time later in a small room with my hands bound behind my back, legs bound together and with a throbbing headache.'

'Did you notice anything distinctive about the man?'

'He was quite a thickset man with big strong arms. His skin was darker than average, maybe swarthy, but other than that, nothing notable really. Oh, and he had a slight accent, possibly Asian, but I'm not certain, Detective Wagner.'

'That's quite okay,' Jack said.

'I feel quite silly about it in a way detective. You told me to be careful and have someone walk me to my cab every night. And, I didn't do that,' she lamented.

'Don't be too hard on yourself. Anyway, I have some news that will brighten your evening.'

'Oh, really? Do tell detective; some positive news would be nice.'

'We have arrested Li Qiang and your Vice President and we will inevitably charge them both with money laundering offences.'

'Wow, that is excellent news, just wonderful news really.' Michelle's face lit up and she was beaming.

'What happened? How did you do it? What did they say?' she blurted out.

'I will tell you the whole sorry story over another coffee when you have recovered fully. In the meantime, I have a very early start tomorrow, and I really just wanted to make sure you were okay.'

'Thank you, detective, I really appreciate your thoughtfulness.'

Jack was thinking about the pre-dawn raid he would participate in a few hours from now as he drove back eastwards along the M4 Motorway towards his apartment in Balmain. He badly wanted to capture Ling Jun and Wang Wei for what they had done to JA. It was also important to him, as the MBC guys from Brisbane were obviously saddened by the needless killing of Captain Han. He hoped he would be able to call Harvey and Benson later tomorrow and give them the good news that the two suspects were in custody. 'Oh heck.' Jack hadn't spoken to Danielle and she wouldn't be aware that Michelle Ironside had been found.

'Hi Jack, how are you?'

'Yeah, I'm all good, Pierro, and yourself?' 'You're a funny man, Jack Wagner.'

'I'm sorry, but I can't talk for long as I'm nearly home and I have a four o'clock start tomorrow morning, Danielle.'

'Why, what's happening at that ungodly hour, Jack?' she asked, aghast at the thought of getting up that early.

'I can't tell you about it now, but what I can tell you, is that Michelle Ironside has turned up safe and well.'

'Woohoo, that's wonderful news; I'm soooo excited. I've got a million questions. What happened?'

'Once again, you'll have to wait until I have some time. She is in the COU at Auburn Hospital if you want to try and call her.'

'I'll call her as soon as we hang-up. I'm so relieved.'

'Now, I have more news for you. The Deputy Commissioner would like to interview you at nine o'clock in the morning.'

'Damn, I guess I knew this was coming, but I'm not sure I'm prepared for it.' Danielle replied pensively, having quickly come down from her momentary high.

'Just talk him through the process of how you were recruited, your brother's illness and tell him exactly what you told me. You'll be fine.'

'Should I take a lawyer with me?'

'I think the DC will try and be as accommodating as possible, under the circumstances anyway, and the presence of a lawyer might be counterproductive to that. It's your call though, Danielle. Now, I'm sorry, but I really have to go. I will call you tomorrow afternoon and I will hopefully have even more to tell you then.'

'Okay, mystery man, I'll talk to you tomorrow. Mwah.'

$$\textbf{(94)}$$

362 Sussex Street Sydney
Saturday 14th March

Jack walked into the conference room that he had left only a few hours earlier. 'Good morning, Jack,' greeted a cheery Oliver Campbell.

'It's almost still good evening, Oliver.' The DC entered immediately after Jack and took his customary chair at the head of the table. Sanderson next arrived, wearing his best non-detective outfit of jeans and a loose hanging Hawaiian shirt and carrying a steaming cup of coffee.

'Where'd you get that at this hour, Michael?'

'After John let me into the building, he kindly showed me the lunchroom down the corridor, and I made a brew with one of those drip things, Jack. You Feds must be higher up the law enforcement food chain as we only have instant down the hill. There's plenty more where this came from.'

'No time now,' Jack grumbled. Although he could do with a coffee having only had three hours sleep.

The DC lowered the projection screen, to which Campbell connected his laptop and immediately displayed the layout of the subject's fourteenth floor apartment.

Precisely at fifteen minutes past four, four members of the AFP's

Specialist Response Group walked into the room, fully dressed in their tactical assault gear. They were clad in their iconic black coveralls, ballistic vests, black gloves and boots. Jack could see they were fully equipped with their belts and vests bulging with gadgetry. The four men carried their ballistic helmets and black balaclavas under their arms. Each man looked to have a taser, expandable baton, pepper spray, handcuffs, torch, ammunition magazines and of course, body cameras. They each had a holstered sidearm, which he knew was a Glock 22 pistol. They were obviously taking no chances and were equipped for any eventuality. Once the team was seated, Campbell went immediately to their tactical deployment strategy. He reiterated that there was every possibility they would encounter early morning workers and early rising hotel guests, so discretion and caution were paramount.

'Okay, we will park around the corner in Liverpool Street's left turn lane. We will exit the vehicles less than forty metres from the entry to the target building. Michael, from the time we pull up, you will have thirty seconds to obtain the master access swipe cards from the Night Manager. Any longer than that, and we'll be coming in the front door regardless. Make sure you obtain two swipe cards just in case and ensure they both also have lift access.'

'This is important, Michael. Do not, under any circumstances, leave the Night Manager, or any other staff member for that matter, unattended at any time and he or she is not to access a phone. Take their mobiles off of them if you have to. As soon as we enter the building, hand me the swipe cards and then take him or her and any others into the back office,' Campbell instructed. 'It is entirely possible that our targets may have accomplices living on the same floor, so one of my men will be stationed at the apartment door. Jack, remain in the hallway and usher any wandering guests back to their rooms. Are you armed and do you have a vest?'

'Yes, I'm all good, Oliver.'

'Okay, my guys know the rest of the drill, so let's go get these guys, shall we?' Campbell said with steely resolve and determination.

The two specially equipped Toyota V8 Land Cruisers headed down the one-way street and parked exactly where Campbell had said. 'Off you go, Michael, remember, you've only got thirty seconds' head start.' The rest of the team exited the vehicles and retrieved their silencer fitted Heckler & Koch G36 5.56mm rifles from the rear compartment. The team were holding their rifles diagonally in the eleven o'clock to five o'clock position across their body as they jogged in formation around the Liverpool Street corner into Sussex Street. Jack had his own Glock out and pointed down at a forty-five degree angle in a two-fisted grip.

As they entered the apartment building foyer, Jack was relieved to see Sanderson already waiting for them with two swipe cards in his hand and the Night Manager's arm firmly gripped with the other. 'Good job, Michael, now get him out of here.' Campbell ordered as he led his SRG team to the elevators.

The assault team exited the elevator on the fourteenth floor and made their way stealthily along the carpeted corridor to room 1417. Campbell led the way with the four SRG officers in double Indian file behind him and Jack bringing up the rear. One of the SRG officers positioned himself to the right of the target's door, so Jack quickly identified that he needed to be on the left. He watched as the remaining officers, including Campbell, lowered their visors, turned on their rifle mounted torches and body worn cameras, butted their assault rifles into their shoulders and then raised them into the horizontal position in front of their eyes. Jack had worked with the SRG team numerous times before, but he never ceased to be amazed at their level of discipline.

'Okay, go,' ordered Campbell, quietly but firmly. The lead officer swiped the access card and Campbell led the officers through the open doorway and into the apartment's large living area. 'Armed police, stay where you are, do not move,' he called out clearly. He remained in the living area while two officers made their way briskly, but surely, to their designated bedrooms.

'Armed police, stay where you are, do not move,' yelled the two officers as they kicked open the bedroom doors.

Two neighbouring residents had ventured to open their apartment doors, but Jack flashed his AFP ID card, and yelled 'back inside,' and they quickly withdrew into their respective apartments. 'Shit,' Jack mumbled to himself as he heard a gunshot. That wasn't what he wanted to hear as all of the officers all had silencers affixed to their weapons. One of the target occupants must have heard the initial entry and had quickly accessed a weapon. It was immediately followed by a series of rapid fire thwacks, which Jack assumed was the officer returning fire. He hoped the loud gunshot hadn't hit its target and the silenced weapon had.

'All clear,' Jack heard one of the SRG operatives yell which was closely followed by a second 'all clear,' albeit in a less than firm voice. Even though it was a weakened confirmation, Jack was comforted that the second operative was alive at least.

'We're all clear,' boomed Campbell.

'I need an ambulance.' Jack heard Campbell call into his radio. 'Wagner, I need a hand in here.' Jack got the nod of confirmation from the SRG operative guarding the doorway and hurried into the apartment.

Once in the living area, Jack was immediately hit by the smell of the G36's propellant gases. 'Is everyone okay, Oliver?'

'Stephenson's been hit in the shoulder, but he'll be okay. One of the targets is deceased.' Jack quietly hoped it was Ling Jun.

'Sanderson, come in,' Campbell calmly called over the radio. 'Go for Sanderson.'

'Release the Night Manager and bring the paramedics up here as soon as they arrive.'

'Wagner, take this gauze pad and press it into Stephenson's wound and hold it there until the paramedics get here.'

'Stephenson, how are you feeling?' asked Jack, peeling off the operatives vest and undoing the zipper of his coveralls.

'I think I'm okay, just bloody sore. It feels like someone has smashed my shoulder with an axe.'

'Hold tight, the paramedics are on their way,' Jack said as he pressed the gauze pad into the wound to stem the bleeding.

'Jack, which one of our targets is this, do you know?' Campbell asked, pointing at the handcuffed man sitting on the floor in the doorway of the second bedroom.

Jack looked down the hallway. 'That's Wang Wei, which means the deceased in there should be Ling Jun. He was the shooter in Ms Granger's attack, so no loss as far as I'm concerned.'

'Maybe not for you, but I don't like people dying on my watch, Wagner, criminals or not,' Campbell replied gruffly. 'Forrester, you and Brannigan take Wang Wei back to Head Office and put him in holding until the DC decides what to do with him,' he ordered. Campbell could see his man sitting upright with his back propped against the bedroom's outer wall. 'How's he doing, Wagner?'

'The bleeding has slowed a little and he's conscious. He'll be okay.'

'Good job. Here are the paramedics now.' Jack stood back to allow the paramedics to go to work on Stephenson. They inserted a drip into his arm, checked his vital signs, taped a pad onto the wound and with Jack's help, were now lifting him across onto their gurney. They raised it to normal height and wheeled Stephenson out of the room.

'Anything I can do?' asked Sanderson, who had arrived with the team of paramedics. 'Can you grab a crime scene kit out of one of the vehicles and place markers around the deceased's body? Then we'll seal the room.'

'Okay, I'm on it,' replied Sanderson.

Jack rang the DC and requested a Crime Scene Investigation team be sent to their location immediately and asked him to contact the coroner. Sanderson returned with the crime scene kit, and together, he and Jack sealed off the bedroom.

'Leave the shell casings and the victims pistol exactly where they are guys,' ordered Campbell. 'There will be an internal investigation into Stephenson firing his weapon and I want the CSI's to accurately document and photograph the scene, so we can prove beyond any doubt it was a clean shooting.' He then asked the SRG officer guarding the entry to remain on the door until the CSI team arrived and the uniformed police could take over the crime scene's security. 'Now let's get back to Head Office and debrief with the DC, Jack.'

(95)

AFP Headquarters

Oliver Campbell, Jack, Sanderson and the remaining members of the SRG team assembled in the twelfth floor conference room again. 'Congratulations on a job well done, gents. It's never easy entering an unfamiliar and potentially hostile environment, so you are all to be commended on the success of the operation. Well done,' lauded the DC. 'I realise we are all concerned about Stephenson, but I am led to believe that his wound was a through and through and he will make a full recovery. Oliver, I know it's been a stressful morning for your guys, but I will need your written reports ASAP. No doubt the media will be all over the story by lunchtime, so I need to be able to provide a definitive response to their questions if we're forced to hold a press conference.'

'You'll have them all in a couple of hours,' promised Campbell.

'Good, thanks. Now, we all have a busy day ahead of us, so here's the plan as it stands.' 'Jamieson and Scerri can continue their interrogation of Li Qiang. Notwithstanding your good work, Jack, the case against Li is essentially one for the Serious Financial Crime Taskforce, so let them do their job. They can then move onto Woodard and see what he gives up. Given your knowledge of the drug importation case and the Granger shooting, you are best placed to interview Wang Wei, but I would suggest you let him sweat for a while, particularly given the death of his accomplice. Talk to Charlie Romano from Maritime Border Command if you need support and take Sanderson with you if you like. We've got a full house today. Li Qiang is in Interview 1, Woodard in IV2 and Wang Wei will be in IV3.'

The DC paused momentarily and then turned back to Campbell. 'Oliver, I know this is primarily Jack's case, but he has his hands full with the Wang Wei interview and collating information from the others today. Can you please liaise with the forensic guys and ensure they expedite their analysis of Ling Jun's weapon, discarded shells and slugs from the crime scene please? Can you also ask them to conduct a comparison with the slugs and bullet casings found by the state Forensic Services Group at the Raglan Street crime scene? I'm sure we're all hoping for a match to Ling Jun's Beretta he used at the apartment this morning,' the DC said, hopefully.

'I'll make it a priority, sir.'

'I don't suppose you found Lucie Chan by any chance?'

'No, she wasn't there, sir.'

'Never mind. Now, I need to go downstairs and conduct an interview myself, so I will leave the rest of you to write up your respective reports. I want the SRG's reports by midday. By the way, I will be using IV4.' Jack knew very well who the subject of the DC's interview was, and he glanced across as the DC left the room. The DC didn't acknowledge him.

Moments later, the DC walked out of the elevator and into the ground floor foyer. He looked around and saw a young blond woman wearing a stylish navy jacket, cream blouse and navy skirt seated in the waiting area. 'You must be Danielle Mortimer, I'm John Robertson, Deputy Commissioner of the AFP.'

She stood and shook the DC's hand firmly. 'Hello, Mr Robertson.'

'Miss Mortimer, I'm going to escort you to an interview room where we can formally discuss your involvement in the money laundering scheme involving Mr Woodard and Mr Li Qiang. Would you like a female officer present?'

Danielle thought the Deputy Commissioner seemed like a nice enough man. 'No, thank you, but can I request one later if I feel uncomfortable, Mr Robertson?'

'Yes, of course you can.'

The DC escorted Danielle from the elevator and down the corridor to Interview Room 4. 'Please take a seat. Miss Mortimer, it's important that you know you are not being placed under arrest at this time. That may change depending on your responses to my questions. Do you understand?'

'Yes, Mr Robertson.' Danielle had been awake for most of the night after Jack's phone call. She had no experience in criminal or legal matters and had been in a state of dread all night. Mr Robertson seemed like a decent guy, so she decided right there and then that she would tell her story openly and honestly. *Well, mostly.*

Danielle told the DC that she was initially courted by Woodard and how he even invited her on a date. She then went into detail about her brother's congenital heart condition and the possibility that he would require expensive surgery to repair his heart.

'When I told Mr Woodard about Ollie's heart condition, he said he might be able to help.' Danielle was holding a small pack of tissues in her hand just in case this moment arrived. She paused to dab at her moist eyes. 'My family doesn't have the kind of money needed to pay for Ollie's heart surgery, Mr Robertson.'

'Do you want to take a moment, Miss Mortimer?'

'No, let's keep going, she replied, sniffling. 'That's why I accepted Mr Woodard's offer of help.'

'You did realise, of course, what you were doing was illegal?' The DC stated, more than asked.

'I guess so, but I had no idea it was actually something as serious as money laundering. I presumed that Mr Woodard just didn't want his transactions recorded in the TTR Report for his own reasons. He is the Vice President after all, so I just did what I was asked.' She detailed to the DC how the laundering process had worked throughout the seven times she had conducted transactions for Woodard.

'Was anyone else involved?'

'No, just Mr Woodard.'

'What about the Treasury Manager?'

Danielle had to stifle a laugh. 'Good God, no, Michelle would never be involved in anything illegal.'

'How were the transactions handled?'

Danielle walked the Deputy Commissioner through the process from the time she found the briefcase full of cash in her locker until she returned it loaded with gaming chips.

'Did you have contact with Mr Woodard at any stage throughout the exchanges?'

'No.'

'What was your payment for the services rendered?'

'Five thousand dollars was deposited into my back account on the day following each transaction.'

'Was the deposit accompanied by a description or the remitter's details?'

'No, it was always detailed as cash.'

'Were you aware of the involvement of a Mr Li Qiang?'

'I sort of guessed, given the amount of time Mr Woodard spent with him in the Bennelong Room, but it was only confirmed to me two nights ago when he was arrested.'

'Is there anything else you would like to say in your defence, Miss Mortimer?'

Danielle straightened in her chair. 'Do I have to pay back the money, Mr Robertson? That would be just devastating for Ollie's chances of having surgery.'

The DC was impressed that her first response was related to her brother's welfare, not herself. 'If we prove that the monies are the proceeds of crime, then you could conceivably be charged with being a recipient of those same criminally sourced funds.'

'I hadn't thought of that.' There was a moment of quiet while Danielle absorbed the new revelation. 'Mr Robertson, I am glad though, that I could help Detective Wagner with his plan to capture Mr Li and Mr Woodard. That makes me feel better about the whole sorry episode.'

'That was very brave of you and the AFP are grateful for your assistance.'

'Miss Mortimer, I will now consider what you have told me this morning and then I am obliged to speak to a representative of the Commonwealth Director of Public Prosecutions Office about your case. Subsequent to that, I will be in touch with you again.' In the meantime, you are free to leave.'

'Thank you for your time, Mr Robertson,' Danielle said politely as she rose and shook his hand.

Jamieson was further down the corridor in IV1 interviewing Li Qiang for the second day when his mobile phone rang. He listened to the voice on the other end of the phone. 'Okay, I'll be right up.'

'Li Qiang interview suspended at ten thirty a.m. Mr Li, I have something to attend to, but I will return shortly.'

Jamieson locked the door from the outside, instructed the guarding officer not to leave, took the stairs up to the ground floor and walked across to reception. The receptionist pointed to a woman leaning against the glass wall. Jamieson turned around to face the waiting area and saw an attractive blond woman wearing a crop top, leggings and joggers. She was tanned and toned and obviously spent significant time working out. Jamieson found it hard to ignore the woman's assets, as they were being given plenty of airtime. 'I'm Detective Jamieson, can I help you?' he asked as he walked up to the woman.

'I am Mrs. Bree Woodard and I want to see my husband; now detective,' the woman demanded.

'Your husband isn't being interviewed at the moment, so I will have you signed in as a visitor and then take you to his location.'

'I should think so, detective,' she replied presumptuously.

Jamieson ignored the attitude and escorted her into IV2 and then instructed the officer guarding the door to stay alert.

'What the hell have you done to us, Tony?' Bree Woodard demanded as she entered the interview room.

'Whatever happened to "hi Tony, how are you, are you okay?" he asked, making no effort to hide his sarcasm.

'How did we end up in this ungodly mess?' she demanded.

'Who is the *we* you mentioned? I only see one of us in custody for Chrissakes, Bree.'

'Alright, how did you end up here, Tony? I heard you were stealing money at work. Why would you do such a thing?'

'Oh fuck off, Bree. Where did you think all the money came from that funded your gym habit, lunches with the girls every day, holidays with the lifeguards, the deposit on the townhouse and the private school fees? Oh, and let's not forget the new boobs you just had to have,' he raged.

'You always were given to exaggeration, Tony,' she said dismissively.

Woodard looked her up and down. 'You were so worried about my welfare that you obviously still managed a gym workout this morning. Weren't you even remotely concerned about my absence when I didn't come home last night? What sort of person did I marry?' He lamented.

'You know very well who you married and why you married me, Mr Vice President.' Bree said, accentuating his title. 'You got the attractive trophy wife that you could show off at all those boring casino functions and gala dinners you forced me to attend.'

Woodard scoffed at his wife. 'You didn't seem so bored when you were fucking my CEO in his own pool, Bree.'

She immediately rebounded. 'How do you think you got your promotions? For heaven's sake, you're not that smart, Tony,' she seethed.

The reality of her remark hit him like a freight train, and he realised for the first time, that his wife was probably right. 'This arguing and name calling isn't getting us anywhere, Bree.'

'So, what's going to happen to us?' she asked again.

'You're back to *us* again. I'm the one in custody, not you, so there's no *us* here.' Woodard noticed Bree's eyes watering. 'Oh, let me guess what comes next?' he said with intended disdain. 'Will it be the pouty look, the fluttering of the eyelashes or, wait for it, maybe the fake sniffles?

'What about the children? How am I going to be able to look after them now?'

'Well, I'm guessing you might just have to find yourself a job. Imagine that, Bree Woodard working in the real world, I like the sound of that.' For the first time since his arrest he allowed himself a chuckle.

'You're not funny. I have no idea what to do about any of this,' she said as she dabbed at her eyes again.

'Here's a thought, Bree. Why don't you and your lunch gals start up your own reality TV program.' He was on a roll now. 'You could call it the Real Housewives of Chiswick.'

'You've ruined my life,' she sobbed.

Woodard wasn't falling for that trick. 'It's my life that's in ruins, Bree, not yours. You'll still be able to walk the streets as a free person while your ex-husband rots in a prison cell.'

'What do you mean, ex-husband?' she asked.

'Bree, let's face it, we were only together because of the lifestyle and the kids. Now, the lifestyle's gone and I probably won't spend quality time with my children for a long time. So, the only two reasons we were together will be gone from my life as I know it. And, so will you. Goodbye Bree.' Woodard called for the guard to show his ex-wife out.

96

AFP Headquarters

Jamieson returned to IV1 and, for the benefit of the recording, restated his name, date and time. 'Let's continue, shall we, Mr Li. How did you enjoy your salubrious accommodation? I would be sleeping with one eye open and my back to the wall if I were you.'

'I have nothing to say, detective, about anything, including your ridiculous attempt at humour.'

'Just so you are aware, Mr Li, we have obtained a court ordered extension to the Detention Order and we will be holding you for another twenty-four hours.'

Scerri had now returned to the interview room. 'Mr Li, we have evidence that you were the beneficiary of money laundered through the Bennelong Room at the Oceanic Casino.'

Li afforded the younger detective a smug look. 'You have nothing of the kind.' Scerri was undeterred. 'Mr Li, we have audio of you confirming that you handed Mr Woodard one million dollars in your hotel suite.'

'That was just a hypothetical conversation. There was never any money,' Li said, dismissively.

'Well then, how did you come to be in possession of one million dollars in Oceanic Casino gaming chips?'

Li sighed. 'Mr Woodard handed me a stylish briefcase and said it was a bonus from the casino to reward me for my loyalty.'

'What, the casino simply hands out one million dollars to anyone, just like that,' Scerri suggested, incredulous.

'I am not just anyone detective, I am what is known as a high roller and being appropriately rewarded for my loyalty is not uncommon.'

Scerri continued. 'The gaming chips found in your possession were the result of one million dollars in cash being illegally exchanged.'

'I have no knowledge of that,' Li said calmly.

'We have a chain of custody for both the cash and the gaming chips for the complete duration of the transaction.' Scerri was hoping Li would slip up.

'Detective, I don't see how that can be the case. I never had the cash in the first instance, as I told you previously.'

'Yes, you did.'

'No, no, that is incorrect, detective. Why don't you show me where I had the cash?' Li demanded.

'Later, Mr Li.'

'I am pleased though, that you seem to have evidence of Mr Woodard being in possession of the so-called one million dollars that you keep mentioning as that should exonerate myself,' Li said calmly.

'Who said we had proof of anything against Mr Woodard?' Interrupted Jamieson.

'Come, come now gentlemen, feigning ignorance isn't your strong point,' Li said, as he projected a self-satisfied look.

Jamieson and Scerri knew the case against Li was circumstantial at best. Yes, they had him in possession of the million dollars in gaming chips, but Li's explanation could conceivably hold up in court. And they had him on audio claiming to give Woodard the one million dollars in cash, but no visual proof of that. So, if Li indeed did give Woodard the million dollars cash, there was a crucial break in the chain of custody, as no money was actually sighted until Miss Mortimer opened the briefcase just before two o'clock on the afternoon in question. And that break in the chain would be a gift for Li's lawyer.

'I have decided I have had enough of this charade, detectives. I would like to make a phone call please.'

'Do you want to call your lawyer?'

'No, I would like to call the Chinese Consul General for New South Wales and have him get me out of here.'

'I will get you a phone, Mr Li,' offered Jamieson. 'But you're not going anywhere for another twenty-four hours. Detective Scerri and I will leave you to your phone call while we interview Mr Woodard now. I'm certain he will have plenty to say about the matter,' Jamieson smarted.

Detectives Jamieson and Scerri walked next door and entered Interview Room 2. 'Good morning, Mr Woodard. How was your wife's visit?' Jamieson asked innocently.

'That would be my ex-wife, detective.'

'Why doesn't that comment surprise me,' Jamieson said. 'She obviously prioritised her gym session over your predicament. Nice girl.' For the benefit of the recording, Jamieson stated his and Scerri's names and the date and time the interview would commence. 'Mr Woodard, we have just finished our second interview with Mr Li. Qiang and he had some very interesting things to say about you.'

'It's taken you guys forever to get here. I've been stuck in that holding cell wearing these ridiculous overalls for over twenty-four hours now. Aren't I entitled to an expeditious process or something?'

'No, not at all. Just so you are fully informed, we obtained a court ordered extension to your Detention Order that authorises us to hold you in custody for a further twenty-four hours. And, we can do it again if we so require. Is that clear, Mr Woodard?' He didn't reply. 'Mr Woodard, the law requires me to inform you that you do not have to say or do anything in response to questioning and that anything you say or do may be used in court. Do you understand?'

'Yeah, sure. Let's get to the point, shall we? What did Li drop me in for?'

'Well, he is very confident that the AFP can't prove anything criminal that will lead to him being charged with a crime. So, indirectly, he is leaving you to carry the bag, so to speak. How's that for openers, Mr Woodard?' Jamieson asked. 'Now, let's cut to the chase, shall we?'

'After a twenty-four hour wait, that would make for a nice change, detective.' Woodard replied sarcastically.

'We have you on camera depositing the cash into the staff locker, extracting the cash later in the evening, you then conducting the cash for chips swap yourself, and finally, delivering the gaming chips to Mr Li. That's a comprehensive chain of custody that directly implicates you in the entire process and will stand up under examination in a court of law. How's that, for starters?'

'I was only doing what I thought was in the best interests of the casino and accommodating one of our high rollers. I'm not a money launderer,' Woodard asserted, defiantly.

'Oh, but yes you are, Mr Woodard. There is no dressing this up as anything other than wholesale, large-scale money laundering. Maybe it makes you feel better trying to justify it to yourself.'

Woodard's handcuffs rattled as he banged the metal table with his fist. 'I'll say it again: I'm not a money launderer.'

'There is overwhelming evidence of your guilt and we have irrefutable proof of the crime of money laundering that will withstand any scrutiny in the Federal Court,' explained Jamieson. 'And that, Mr Woodard, will earn you ten to fifteen years behind bars.' Woodard slumped forward in his chair, dropped his head down and stared at the table. The officers allowed him some thinking time.

'Okay, if I'm guilty of anything, it's being naïve in thinking I was doing the right thing by a valued client and the casino itself. That's all,' Woodard said.

'How much were you paid to do the right thing?' asked Scerri.

'It wasn't much at all, more of a bonus, really.'

'Come on, Mr Woodard, I wasn't born yesterday. Who paid you the bonus? The casino or Mr Li?'

'Both, the casino paid me a bonus and Li offered me a gratuity.'

'What, he only gave you a lousy tip for laundering millions of dollars? Don't insult me please,' pleaded Scerri. 'So, if I call Adam Benedict, your CEO, he will confirm the bonus payment issued to you?'

Woodard breathed deeply, leant back and stared at the ceiling.

'I didn't think so, Tony.' Scerri tried to soften the mood by using his first name. He continued. 'We will forensically analyse your bank and credit card accounts. Then, if we don't find what we're looking for, we will contact the kids' school, travel agents, your wife's gym and favourite fashion houses, real estate agents, restaurants and anyone else you or her might have spent money with. Why do I think they might tell us that many of your accounts with them were settled in cash?'

'That would be a universal breach of my privacy,' replied Woodard indignantly.

'We have full investigative powers under the Australian Federal Police Act 1979 and we will deploy them as necessary. It is not our intention to embarrass your family, heaven knows, you've already brought enough shame upon them already. So, how about we start again from the top. What do you say, Tony?'

Woodard breathed a deep sigh, a wave of reality sweeping over him. 'Where do you want to start?'

Jamieson was pleased Woodard had finally seen the light and understood the predicament he was now in. 'Tell us how you got involved with Mr Li.'

Woodard was resigned to his fate and walked them through the beginnings of his relationship with Li. His family's expenditure was outstripping his income and he was particularly struggling to maintain the living standards expected by his wife. 'The mortgage, school fees and household expenses I could manage, but Bree's personal expenditure on lunches, gym membership, salons, holidays and clothes were beyond my financial capacity. One night I was entertaining Li in the Bennelong Room when he surprised me by alluding to my financial struggles. I had no idea how he became aware of them, but he had obviously conducted his own research. It's patently clear now why. Anyway, on this particular night he said he had an opportunity for me that could, over time, mitigate my financial problems. And, the rest as they say, is history.' Woodard sighed, seemingly pleased to have that off his conscience.

'Can you walk us through the mechanics of the operation?' Woodard explained the collection of cash from Li, transporting it to the staff room and storing it in Danielle Mortimer's locker, her part in the transaction, his collection of the gaming chips, and finally, Li gambling the ill-gotten chips in the Bennelong Room, which effectively laundered the money.

Jamieson was unaware of Danielle Mortimer's actual involvement up until this point. 'How did Miss Mortimer become involved?'

'I wanted to stay one step removed from the transaction itself and she has a brother with a heart condition. Her family couldn't afford any expensive operations if they were required, so I offered to help. To kill two birds with one stone if you like.'

Scerri jumped in. 'How very generous of you, Tony,' his remark dripping with sarcasm. 'Where did Li get the cash in the first place?'

'I have no idea where the cash originated, detectives. I asked myself the same question numerous times and the only thing I could put my finger on was that he usually called upon my services on days that coincided with him having lunch at the Golden Phoenix in Chinatown.'

'How do you know that?'

'Client Services provides a limousine service for our high rollers, and that's where he mostly went.'

'Are you willing to make a formal statement confirming what you have just told us?' Jamieson watched as Woodard crossed his arms in front of his chest and leaned back in his chair.

'What's in it for me, detectives?' Woodard asked, looking from Jamieson to Scerri.

'As far as we are aware, it's actually Li's money that's being laundered and there would be a high probability that it's illicitly gained. Give us Li and we might be able to downgrade your charges to one applicable under Section 400.9 of the Criminal Code, which attracts a lesser penalty. I promise you we'll do what we can, Tony,' confirmed Jamieson. 'But just so you know, at this stage we still can't prove that the laundered money is actually from the proceeds of crime, so it is quite possible that Mr Li may also face the lesser charge. You also need to know that under the Anti-Money Laundering and Counter-Terrorism Financing Act of 2006, the casino could be charged,' Scerri added. 'Shall we commence?'

Woodard paused, more to collect his thoughts than anything else. He was thinking about his family, principally his children and how they would navigate their formative years without him. By cooperating, his time incarcerated could be reduced, and he could resume his life earlier than otherwise would be expected. Then he could return to his family, minus the wife, and hopefully rebuild his relationship with his boys.

Woodard gulped a deep breath. 'Yeah, let's do this.'

(**97**)

Chinese Consulate General

The Consul General was seated at his desk reading the Australian national broadsheet. He was focused on yet another article about the so-called China virus and his country's attempts to suppress the flow of information rather than suppress the virus itself. Did they really think China would endanger its own citizens just to cover-up its country's medical inefficiencies? Xiao knew the answer to that. He was interrupted by the ringtone of his desk phone.

'Yes, Mei.'

'Mr Xiao, Mr Li is on the phone for you. Would you like me to connect him.?' Why would Li call on the landline and not the burner phone, he wondered.

'Yes, of course, thank you, Mei.'

'Li, how are you?'

'I am at the Australian Federal Police headquarters, so how do you think I am?' Fan Chen, after unexpectedly speaking with the detective yesterday, had alerted Xiao to the fact that Li had been arrested. Xiao had never countenanced Li's superior attitude, so he thought the humiliation of spending some extended time in custody would be a well-deserved and humbling experience for him.

Feigning ignorance, Xiao replied. 'What are you doing there, Li?'

'I was arrested and have spent the past thirty-six hours in custody. You need to get me out of here, now.'

This was Xiao's opportunity to redress the imbalance in their relationship. 'Li, you know we can't interfere in another country's law enforcement matters; that could potentially be counterproductive to the relationship between our two countries.'

'Don't give me one of your bureaucratic speeches, Xiao, just get me out of here.'

'Why have the Federal Police arrested you and have you been charged with any offence as yet?'

'No, and they seem insistent on implicating me in some sort of money laundering activity.'

'Where would they get that idea from?'

Li didn't pick up on the sarcasm. 'That is beside the point; I want you to arrange for my immediate release. Do you hear me, Xiao?'

'I'm not certain that I can be of any assistance with this delicate matter. The western world isn't looking favourably towards China at the moment, given they think we exported COVID-19 across the globe and are in bed with the WHO.' Xiao was enjoying this exchange now.

'Xiao, hear me clearly. Get me out of here, otherwise I will bring the wrath of the party down on you, and you will find yourself being an attaché in Uzbekistan or some such remote shithole, as westerners like to say. Do you hear me?'

'Ah, Li, you haven't been reading the tea leaves have you? The party has grown tired of your western influenced excesses. Did you really think those in power back in China weren't aware of your unhealthy appetite for Scotch whiskey, Cuban cigars, expensive restaurants and glamorous call girls visiting you in your luxury hotel suite.'

'Shut up, Xiao, you don't know what you are saying. That was all a part of creating the persona of a wealthy businessman, so I could successfully conduct the transactions necessary to fund your political candidate. You know that. And need I remind you where the funding for that candidate was coming from.' Li then calmed himself.

'Anyway, can't you arrange for me to be provided with diplomatic immunity from whatever charges might be brought against me.'

Xiao detected a softening of Li's tone. 'Come, come, now, Li. You know full-well that you have to be granted a classification by the host country according to your position within the consulate. In your case, you have no official position, and as such, were never issued with a classification. I can't be of any assistance with that.'

'You have no idea what you are doing to your career, Xiao; it is finished.'

'Aaahh, but I do, Li. You see, as usual, your decisions were influenced by your fondness of beautiful women. This led you to select the most inappropriate candidate to drive our political agenda. The simplest of tasks was afforded to you by the party and your inability to complete it satisfactorily has led to your untimely demise. Li, your actions remind me of one of our proverbs. *"The person attempting to travel two roads at once, will get nowhere."'*

'My candidate's suitability changed after she met that Granger woman, the cause of which you created yourself by allowing her to attend your cocktail party. That was out of my control, Xiao, and you know that.'

'Excuses, excuses. I am sorry, but neither myself nor the party are in a position to assist you in this matter. Goodbye, Li.'

Xiao replaced the handset and then removed the burner phone from his desk drawer. He pressed one on the speed dial. 'It is done.' He then depressed the red button, placed the phone back in his drawer and allowed himself a smile.

98

AFP Headquarters

Jack was seated in Interview Room 3 across from Wang Wei, whose legs were chained to the metal chair, which in turn, was bolted to the floor. Jack recited his name, date and time for the video record, read him his rights and advised him that the man standing in the corner was Charlie Romano from Maritime Border Command.

'Mr Wang, do you know why you are here?'

'No, I not know.' Jack knew from the scene of this morning's shooting that Wang had a limited command of English, so he had arranged for an interpreter to be available.

'Mr Wang, do you understand English?'

'Little bit.'

'Charlie, would you bring the interpreter in please?'

Romano re-entered the room with a smartly dressed woman. She wore a two piece navy woman's business suit over a white blouse and a pearl necklace. The smart look was completed with cream coloured pumps and she had her jet black hair tied back in a high ponytail. 'Jack Wagner meet Paula Chen.'

'Hi Paula. Can you explain to Wang Wei who you are and what your role will be today ,please?'

She spoke to him in his own language and then turned back to Jack.

'Mr Wang says he understands, and I am ready to commence when you are.'

'Thanks, Paula. Can you start by asking him if he understands why he is here in custody?'

'Nín kěyǐ xiān wèn tā shìfǒu lǐjiě tā wèishéme zài zhèlǐ ma?'

'Wǒ bù zhīdào chén xiǎojiě.'

'He says he has no idea, Detective Wagner.'

'It looks like this is going to be a long day for both of us then, Paula.' Jack said with a sigh.

'Okay, tell him this for openers. We are going to question him in relation to three separate crimes. Firstly, Mr Romano will interview him about his role in importing illicit narcotics into Australia. Then I am going to ask him some questions about the murder of a ship's captain in Brisbane. And finally, I am going to ask him about his involvement in the attempted shooting of a journalist in Waterloo a few days ago. Is that too much to translate at once?'

'No, I've been doing this for a while,' she replied confidently.

It seemed to Jack that it was taking forever for Paula to explain to Wang why he was in custody, but Jack knew nothing about the nuances of the Chinese language. The expression "as patient as the ox" from an old movie came to mind.

'Detective Wagner, Mr Wang says he knows nothing about any of the things you mention,' Paula translated.

'Charlie, you're up.' Jack stood and Romano sat down across from Wang.

'Mr Wang. I am Charlie Romano from Maritime Border Command and I have some questions for you about the Midnight Express.'

'Wáng xiānshēng wǒ shì hǎishì biānfáng sīlìng bù de bǎoluó·luómàn nuò Charlie Romano, duìyú "wǔyè kuàichē" Midnight Express, wǒ yǒu yīxiē wèntí yào wèn.'

'He says he doesn't know what you are talking about.'

'Mr Wang, we found traces of the drug cocaine on the Midnight Express and we also found your fingerprints on board, so please don't insult my intelligence by denying your involvement in the drug smuggling activity.' Paula translated Romano's accusation to Wang, who sat staring blankly down at the table.

'Mr Wang,' yelled Romano. Wang jerked upright in his chair and looked Romano in the eye. 'That's better now. Furthermore, we have a signed statement from Captain Han which clearly states that twenty packages were handed over to the crew of the Midnight Express. That crew consisted of you and Ling Jun, who is now deceased.' Paula translated again.

'Mr Ling, he boss, not me. I no carry drugs.' Wang stated in his broken English. Romano picked up on Wang's use of English, so he sidestepped Paula and asked Wang.

'Who did Mr Ling provide the drugs to?'

'I not no, I not see when we get to Sydney, no more.'

'Where you go in Sydney, Mr Wang?' Romano tried his own shorthand speech.

'I go to hotel in Chinatown.' Wang stammered.

'And where did Ling Jun take the drugs?'

'He say he take to restaurant.'

'What name of restaurant?' Wang remained quiet. Romano turned to Paula again. She nodded.

'Cāntīng de míngzì shì shénme.' 'Jīn Fènghuáng.'

'Wang says the name of the restaurant is the Golden Phoenix.' Paula advised.

'One more question please, Paula. Ask him who Ling Jun gave the drugs to.'

'Lǐ xiānshēng bǎ dúpǐn gěile shuí?'

'He says he doesn't know.'

Jack interjected from the back of the room. 'Charlie, sorry to interrupt. Paula, ask him if he knows Wie Ping Lie?' As he spoke, Jack saw Wang vigorously shaking his head.

'Nǐ zhīdào wèipíngliè shì shuí ma?' she asked. 'He didn't seem to like that question, detective.'

'No he didn't; tell him I want an answer,' Jack demanded in a raised voice.

'I not no.' Wang said in a soft, shaky voice before she could ask the question.

'Charlie, show him the video still, please.' Romano opened his investigation folder and withdrew the still shot of Billingsley, Ling Jun and Wang Wei that Jack had given him earlier. He lifted the photo up and held it in front of Wang's eyes.

'Judging by the worried look on his face, I think he now realises we're a step ahead of him, Jack.'

'That not me.' Wang offered feebly.

'Now the other photo please Charlie.' Romano lifted out the photo of Billingsley and Wie Ping Lie standing outside the Golden Phoenix. The photos linked the three Chinese nationals with Billingsley, the restaurant, and through Wang's earlier response, the cocaine.

Romano resumed. 'Mr Wang, we now have the detective, you, Ling Jun, Wie Ping Lie, the cocaine and the Golden Phoenix restaurant all linked together. 'Can you tell him that please, Paula?'

'Wáng xiānshēng xiànzài, wǒmen jiāng zhēntàn, nín, lǐ jūn,Wie Ping Lie, kěkǎyīn hé Golden Phoenix cāntīng liánxì zài yīqǐ.' Wang shook his head but offered no reply.

Jack leaned back in his chair and sighed. 'Unfortunately, it's all circumstantial, Charlie. We have nothing definitive that will stand up in court that links Wang directly to the drug trafficking. Let me try something else.' Jack took Romano's chair at the table and opened his own file.

'Mr Wang, this is a photo from CCTV footage that shows you and Ling Jun entering the Seafarer's Mission at the Port of Brisbane last week. Jack held up the photo. Shortly after this photo was taken, Captain Han was stabbed to death by you.' He glanced at the translator. Jack waited patiently while she translated.

'Me no kill Han, was Ling,' Wang blurted out.

'The Queensland Police recovered the knife from a drain at the

Caltex Truck Stop less than two kilometres away. They matched the prints on the knife to Ling Jun's file prints and also those taken from the Midnight Express. Paula, if you please.'

'Me no kill Han, was Ling.' Wang repeated angrily.

'I know that, Mr Wang. I also know you were in the car when Ling Jun fired upon the journalist in Raglan Street.' Jack pulled another CCTV still from his folder and passed it to Wang. This one was from the convenience store camera that showed the SUV, allegedly being driven by Wang, at the corner of Raglan and Cope Streets moments before Ling Jun fired upon JA. Both Jack and Paula noticed the look of recognition in Wang's eyes.

'Me no in car.' Wang pleaded. 'Yes, you were.'

'Unfortunately, Charlie, once again, we have nothing concrete to link Wang to the attempted murder of Ms Granger either. I had hoped that we could at least charge him with firearms offences, but we didn't find one at the Sussex Street apartment that we could connect him to.'

'I know, it's extremely frustrating, Jack.' Jack closed his folder and accepted the inevitable. 'Mr Wang, we are not going to charge you with any crime today.' Paula Chen translated and all could see the relief on Wang's face. 'Thank you, thank you.' Wang said, his hands pressed together as he nodded his head in gratitude.

'You will, however, be extradited back to Queensland where you will be charged with being an accessory to the murder of Captain Hsin Han.' Paula, again, if you wouldn't mind.'

'I no do anything, was Ling.' Wang declared.

'Charlie, do you want to call Damian de Vries and bring him up to speed? He and his boys, Benson and Harvey, will be disappointed about the lack of stronger evidence against Wang Wei, but I am sure they'll be pleased to hear about Ling Jun's demise.'

'Sure, the boys were keen to avenge the good captain's unnecessary death, so I think they'll be somewhat happy with the outcome.'

(**99**)

AFP Headquarters

Jack limped along in peak hour traffic across the Anzac Bridge on his way home to his apartment. He was looking forward to putting his feet up out on his balcony, having a cold beer and enjoying the joyous sounds of the bird life from the adjacent bushland. It had been another long and exhausting day at work and the last thing he needed was the glare of the setting sun burning into his eyes again. He looked left over the bridge's railing and spied the Boathouse Restaurant. *I'm definitely going there one day.* For now though, he wasn't going anywhere in a hurry, so may as well use the time to make some calls.

'Hi, Jack, how are you?' Came JA's bright, bubbly voice through the car's Bluetooth speaker.

'You sound very cheery. What's going on?' he asked her, not feeling the least bit bright and bubbly himself.

'I saw on the news that there was an AFP assault on an apartment in Chinatown and I guessed it might have been Ling Jun's. Am I correct, Jack?'

'As always, ever the clever investigative journalist.'

'What happened? Were you involved? Are you okay? Did you catch him?' Julie-Anne's questions came at rapid fire.

'A lot, yes, yes, and no, JA.'

'You're still funny, Jack. Okay, one question at a time.'

Jack was too tired to get into chapter and verse, so he just gave her a snapshot of the events of that morning. 'Billingsley eventually gave up Ling Jun's address, so we organised the raid this morning. We gained quick access to the target's apartment, but Ling Jun must have heard the front door opened and managed to get to his pistol. He wounded one of the SRG guys before being shot and killed himself.'

'I don't know if I'm pleased about that or not, Jack. It's a weird feeling. I'm happy that he's out of business, but I would also have liked some court justice for his attack on me. Is it okay to feel that way?'

'It's a natural reaction. Anyway, we captured Wang Wei and I have interviewed him this afternoon. Unfortunately, we don't have sufficient evidence to charge him for the drug importation or your attempted murder.'

'Bugger, that's not good at all, Jack.'

'No, not for the AFP, but the Queensland Police will be seeking his extradition and I imagine he will be charged with being an accessory to the murder of Captain Han.'

Julie-Anne sighed with disappointment. 'I suppose that's some consolation.'

'We don't know what Wie Ping Lie's reaction to losing both of his lieutenants will be, so you and Melissa will need to stay in the safe house for another day or so, just in case.'

'Really, Jack, are you sure that's necessary?' She asked, sounding exasperated.

'One more day won't matter, JA.'

'Jack, just so you know, I have finished the first instalment of my story and it's going to press in tomorrow's edition of the Daily News.'

'Now that we've arrested the majority of our suspects, that's fine, JA. I would have preferred that you waited until our investigation is complete, but I understand you have deadlines too.' Jack had enough of talking for one day. 'You girls enjoy your vacation and I'll check-in again soon.'

'Thanks for calling, Jack.'

AFP Headquarters
Sunday 15th March

'Good morning, Jack.' A cheery Jamieson walked into the office and made his way to his temporary desk.

'Why are you so chirpy this morning?'

'Well, Woodard has made a statement implicating Li Qiang and we will be charging them both with money laundering offences. It will inevitably be Woodard's word against Li's but the audio recording should corroborate Woodard's version of events. Unfortunately, both their charges will be at the lower end of the scale as we can't prove that the money laundered was actually the proceeds of crime.'

'That's a bummer, Paul.'

'Yeah, I know, and there's more. Li contacted the Chinese Consul General, and as a result of their phone conversation, Li is claiming diplomatic immunity. I think he's bluffing though.'

Jack didn't like the sound of that. 'Will that be recognised, Paul?'

'I don't think so, foreign representatives of embassies and consulates are allocated colour codes depending on their level of seniority. I have checked with DFAT and they don't have any record of Li ever being allocated a classification. Therefore, he isn't entitled to diplomatic immunity, but no doubt he will challenge that in the Federal Court at some stage.'

'Yeah, good luck with that,' said Jack.

'Anyway, Rocco and I are going down to holding shortly and we will officially charge him with money laundering under Section 400.9 of the Criminal Code. Then we will move onto Woodard and charge him with exactly the same lesser offence, and for precisely the same reason. I have no doubt the laundered money is linked to Wie Ping Lie's cocaine trade but proving it is another thing altogether.'

'That's the big pity in all this, Paul. That was the initial focus of my investigation, so I don't feel like I've achieved much at all,' Jack bemoaned.

'While we're chatting when were you going to tell me about you and Danielle Mortimer?' Jack felt the colour drain from his face at Jamieson's assertion.

'What about her, Paul?'

'Come on, Jack, I have watched the video of the Woodard sting and she was swanning and shimmying around and seemed to be playing up to the cameras at times. I can't imagine that was for old Jim Brennan's benefit, can you?' Jamieson laughed.

'I have no idea what you're talking about.' Jack said, keeping his head down and beginning to type an email.

'Well, she's a looker for sure, but I hope for your sake you don't get any blowback. And, be sure to let me know if she's got a sister. See you later, Jack.'

Jack's desk phone rang. It was the DC's personal assistant requesting Jack meet with the boss as soon as possible. Jack logged off from his desktop and made his way to the elevator for the short ride up to the DC's twelfth floor office.

'Come in, please,' the DC said as he motioned Jack into his spacious office. As well as the formal office desk, ergonomic chairs, desktop and bookcase, the DC's office also contained a casual seating area consisting of a beige-coloured sofa, two matching lounge chairs and an oblong glass coffee table topped with the day's newspapers. The DC gestured to the seating area and Jack sat in one of the lounge chairs.

'You've had a busy few days, Jack. How are you feeling?'

'I'm okay, just a bit disappointed with some of the outcomes, boss.'

'Sometimes we just have to accept that we can only prove what we can and then we move on, Jack.'

'After everything the team went through, we are no closer to proving any illicit activities against Wie Ping Lie, and that's the disappointment in all this. It would also have been nice to nail Li Qiang for the more serious money laundering charges. And now he's seeking diplomatic immunity.' Jack sighed.

The DC sympathised with Jack. 'That won't be recognised, so don't let that be a concern to you.'

'Now on a more positive note,' the DC continued. 'We have the forensic results back from the FSG and they have matched Ling Jun's Beretta to the bullet casings and slugs found at the scene of Ms Granger's shooting incident. I know it's small consolation to you now, and I assume, for Ms Granger too, but at least everyone has closure on that case now.'

'That's true enough,' Jack said half-heartedly.

The DC looked directly at Jack. 'Tell me about Danielle Mortimer.'

'What would you like to know, boss?'

'You know precisely what I am asking, Jack. I didn't get to be the Deputy Commissioner by chance; I pride myself on knowing what's going on with my people.'

Jack wasn't going to admit he was dating Danielle.

'There's not a lot to say, really. We met through the investigation and I convinced her to assist us with our plan to entrap Woodard and then Li Qiang,' Jack replied, without offering anything further.

The DC offered a wry smile. 'Well, whatever your relationship is, it wasn't taken into consideration by myself or the Commonwealth Director of Public Prosecutions when considering what to charge her with.'

'I wouldn't expect anything less, boss.'

'The DPP agrees with me though, that we should take into

consideration Miss Mortimer's invaluable assistance in supporting the investigation into the money laundering scheme. As such, she will only be charged under Section 400.8 of the Criminal Code, which stipulates a lesser charge relating to negligence. The code specifies ten penalty units be levied against the perpetrator. Penalty units are defined in section 4AA of the Crimes Act as $210 each. I can't see any benefit in pursuing her for more serious charges. I have also spoken to Jamieson and Scerri and they are in agreement.'

'I'm sure she will be very appreciative of that outcome,' Jack said.

'I will call her myself and advise her of the decision,' the DC affirmed.

'She will appreciate that, especially coming directly from you, boss.'

As he arrived back at his desk, Jack realised he hadn't spoken to his contacts in Canberra since very early in the investigation. It was occasionally useful to be able to call upon the federal bureaucrats from time-to-time, so he needed to ingratiate them. He called up Lucas Bourne from Home Affairs.

'Hi Lucas, it's Jack Wagner, how are you?'

'Good thanks, Jack, how did you get on with our Mr Li Qiang?'

Jack gave Bourne a condensed version of the events surrounding Li. Like Jack, Bourne was disappointed at Li being charged with the lesser money laundering offences. 'The good news though, Lucas, is that the state police are hoping to be able to link Li Qiang to a kidnapping case they're working on. The Robbery and Serious Crime Squad are now involved as well, so fingers crossed they get a result.'

'Either way, the whole unsavoury saga should bring Li to the attention of Home Affairs senior bureaucrats here in Canberra and potentially, the minister. I imagine Li will be on a one- way ticket back to China after he completes his sentence here in Australia, Jack.'

Jack's next call was to Chris Coleman from Austrac. Once again, Jack gave Coleman an abbreviated version of events surrounding the money laundering and expressed his disappointment at not being able to lay more serious charges.

'I hear you, Jack, but sometimes we just have to be satisfied with whatever charges we can lay. We get that type of situation quite a lot here in Canberra, particularly when the politicians get involved in our cases.'

'Anyway, Chris, thanks for all your assistance, it was greatly appreciated.'

'Anytime. Bye'

Then Jack suddenly remembered JA and Melissa were still locked away in the safe house. 'Hello, Jack.' said Julie-Anne, sounding bored.

'How are you girls getting on?' Jack asked, feeling guilty for ignoring them.

'Well, if you must know, we're going a tad stir crazy after being locked up in here nearly a week. It would be lovely just to do something normal like go for a walk, a swim or even to the pub,' she griped.

'Okay, we've pretty much wrapped up the investigations, so you should be safe from now on. Let me finish my reports. You girls start packing up, and I will come and collect you later this evening. I will call your mobile when I'm outside your door, so don't open it for any reason until I call, just in case, JA.'

'Yeehaa, that's great news, thanks, Jack.'

Jack spent the remainder of the day writing up reports for submission to the DC. He particularly enjoyed writing the report on Nathan Billingsley's case. Jack couldn't abide corrupt cops, so he recommended that Billingsley still be charged with the higher penalty offence of perverting the course of justice. That decision would be the DCs and Jack was happy to leave that consideration to him. *That's why he gets the big bucks.* He sent his investigation notes to Jamieson relating to Li Qiang and Tony Woodard's cases and then wrote an official thank you to Oliver Campbell and his SRG team for their invaluable support. Finally, he wrote another thank you email, this time to Damian de Vries at MBC. If it hadn't been for the information supplied by him and his team, Jack would never have become aware of the actions of Ling Jun and Wang Wei. As for their boss, Jack would be keeping a close eye on Wie Ping Lie and his activities from now on.

'You're still here, Jack,' said the DC as he walked into the Detective's Office.

'It's been a hectic few days, so I'm using today's downtime to catch up on paperwork and phone calls. What's up, boss?'

'I just wanted to share a couple of things with you, and to be honest, I needed to stretch my legs, hence why I'm down here.'

'I know how you feel; I've been sitting at this desk and in interviews rooms for the past two days. I need a good long run around the harbour to work up a sweat and get the blood flowing.'

'Anyway, Jack, the KALOF worked and the state police have located Fan Chen and passed him onto their Robbery and Serious Crime guys. Apparently he's claiming diplomatic immunity too, but the state's Assistant Commissioner who oversees the RSC squad had already anticipated that move. As he promised the other day, he met with the Chinese Consul General and made it abundantly clear that the New South Wales Police will not entertain the claim for diplomatic immunity.'

'That's good news, boss.'

'Yeah, at least until the politicians get involved. The other piece of good news is they have located a black SUV, and sure enough, it's registered to Fan Chen. The RSC guys think it's most likely the one depicted on the CCTV footage outside the Oceanic at the time Michelle Ironside was kidnapped. Their FSG guys will thoroughly examine the vehicle, looking for proof of Ms Ironside's abduction. She has already given them a sample of her DNA, so with any luck they will be able to match it with samples from the vehicle. And if they do, then they will be one step closer to charging Fan Chen with kidnapping. That hopefully will take diplomatic immunity off the table forever, Jack.'

'Okay, fingers crossed they can do just that. I'm still angry about her abduction and Li Qiang getting away with it. Maybe Fan Chen will wise up and give them Li. Now, that would be a great outcome,' Jack said, wishing it to be true.

'Let's hope so. Did we obtain anything from either Li Qiang or Wang Wei that could incriminate Wie Ping Lie, Jack?'

'Plenty of circumstantial information, but nothing that would give us cause to charge him with a crime. After speaking to Ms Granger about Li Qiang's luncheon visitor, comments from both Wang Wei and Tony Woodard in their interviews and with Billingsley's incriminating photo, it seems clear to me that the Golden Phoenix is epicentre of all the criminal activity we have been investigating. And, we know Wie Ping Lie is a habitual guest there, so the restaurant will be a focus in the future as well. In the meantime, he'll have to keep for another day, but we'll be all over him from now on, boss,' Jack stated with conviction. 'And, at some stage, we need to dig deeper into the Chinese connection.'

'That will be some sort of challenge, Jack, and I'll guarantee you the politics will definitely kick in when we do. That's for another day though. Okay, that's all great, but for now enjoy your couple of days off; you've earned them,' the DC said as he made his way towards the elevator.

Jack was driving his ten-year-old Holden Commodore over the Anzac Bridge for the umpteenth time in his detective career and was once again staring into the glare of the setting sun. He realised he hadn't spoken to Danielle for a couple of days, even though she had been in his thoughts. One of the traits that he liked about Danielle was that she wasn't needy, didn't place demands on his time and seemed very comfortable in her own skin.

'Hi, Jack, how's my favourite detective?'

'I'm sorry I haven't called earlier, but I had some deliveries to make.' He wasn't about to go into details about JA and Melissa's enforced holiday. 'How was your interview with the DC?'

'Well, at the end of the interview, I wasn't any the wiser as to what my fate might be. Your Deputy Commissioner is a lovely man and he was very fair with me.' Jack knew the DC would have already spoken to her today, but he would let her get to the point in her own time.

'Understandably, he didn't give anything away in the interview, but he called me earlier this afternoon. He said that I would still be charged with a money laundering offence, but the DPP kindly agreed to reduce my charge to a lesser offence, which would only attract a manageable fine.'

'That's wonderful news; I'm pleased for you, Danielle.'

'Thanks, I really appreciate that. Where are you, Jack?'

'Just driving home after a long day and the last thing I need is this bloody sun glare burning into my eyes.'

'Aaahh, poor, Jack. Why don't you come over? I'll cook you a late dinner and if you're really lucky, I'll give you a massage and relieve some of that tension that I'm sensing in your voice.'

'I need a shower and a freshen up first, Danielle.'

'Well, you could do that at my place and maybe, just maybe, if you're really lucky, you'll get your massage in the shower.'

'Okay, I'm not far away, so I'll see you shortly.'

'I've missed you, detective,' Danielle said as she threw her arms around his neck and pulled him into a passionate embrace.

'The DC has given me a couple of days' leave, so it will be nice just to chill out and clear my head.

'Well, that was very generous of him, Jack. Would you like a nice cold beer?'

'That would be wonderful; I could kill for a beer.'

Danielle laughed. 'I think I've heard that somewhere before, detective. Cheers, and here's to your successful investigation.'

'Cheers to you too and thank you again for all your assistance, Danielle. I've been thinking. Everyone has been so deeply immersed in these overlapping investigations, I thought it might be nice to have a long lunch one day next week. The weather forecast for Wednesday is warm and sunny, so I have booked a table at The Boathouse on Blackwattle Bay.'

'That sounds like a wonderful idea.'

'I should tell you that my ex-girlfriend will probably be in attendance. She's a journalist for the Daily News and has been conducting an investigation parallel to mine. Are you going to be okay with that?'

'I appreciate you telling me, but I'll need to sleep on it. We haven't known each other very long and that might be a bridge too far at this early stage. I'm not big on meeting exes, Jack.'

'I think I understand. Will you at least think about it? I would like you to be there.'

'Okay, now why don't you have your shower while I start dinner, otherwise we'll be eating at midnight.'

Mmmm, no massage in the shower. Even though he thought he was doing the right thing, it dawned on Jack that he had probably complicated things, yet again.

The Boathouse
Wednesday 18th March

'Most evenings on my way home from the office, I cross the Anzac Bridge and I always look down at this restaurant jutting out into the shimmering waters of Blackwattle Bay. And, I've said to myself, one day I will have something special to celebrate and I'm going to do it right down there. And with COVID-19 now being declared a pandemic, and a nationwide lockdown imminent, we might not get the opportunity again for some time. So, here we are.'

Julie-Anne was facing the interior of the restaurant and she noticed a tall, tanned, attractive, young blonde woman swanning across the room in their direction. Her lustrous locks were bouncing off her bare shoulders in time with her walk. She was wearing a white floral patterned sleeveless and backless mini dress. *Surely not*, she mused. 'Take one guess who is walking towards us, Jack,' she said with mild cynicism, having recognised the young woman from the newspaper photo.

'Who, JA?' He asked over the noise of the restaurant.

'You're about to find out.'

Jack turned his head to see what JA was talking about and he found himself suddenly locking lips with Danielle. 'Sorry, Jack, but I'm really nervous,' she whispered as she withdrew from the kiss.

'This is a lovely surprise.'

'Well, it was kind of you to invite me and it's a beautiful day, so I thought, why not? And I get to meet your ex-girlfriend,' she said playfully.

Jack stood and wrapped his arm around Danielle before realising his rudeness and turning back to the group. 'Sorry, this is Danielle Mortimer. Danielle this is Julie-Anne Granger, Melissa Wu and Paul Jamieson.'

'Hi, Danielle, I've seen you on TV,' Paul said offering his hand to a bemused Danielle. 'Well, CCTV anyway.'

'Oh, of course, my screen debut,' she said, bursting into laughter. 'That's too funny; it's a pleasure to meet you.' Danielle walked around the table and greeted Julie-Anne and Melissa with a handshake and an air kiss. 'It's really nice to meet you both.'

'Lovely to meet you, too,' said Melissa. 'Hello, Danielle,' said Julie-Anne coolly.

As Danielle walked around to Jack Melissa turned to Julie-Anne. 'What was that all about?

That's most unlike you to be so cold.'

'I don't know, Melissa; it just feels kind of weird. It's only been a couple of weeks and Jack's moved on already. She's so damn bubbly and gorgeous too,' Julie-Anne lamented.

'So are you, Julie-Anne, inside and out. And, as far as moving on quickly goes, do I need to get you a mirror?' Melissa asked with an ironic smile.

'I know, I know, you're right, and after all, I have you. Oh, look who's here,' gushed Julie-Anne. The guests all turned to face the centre of the restaurant and spied a tall, gaily dressed woman walking towards their table.

'Wow,' Paul said far too loudly.

'Easy tiger.' Jack said in a placatory manner. 'Don't get your ambitions mixed up with your capabilities, buddy.' The woman walking towards their table was wearing a cream and navy, floral, boho sleeveless, summer dress that accentuated her sleek figure and she had completed the look with navy pumps. She had a chin-length classic bob hairstyle that highlighted her eyes.

Julie-Anne leapt out of her chair and greeted the woman warmly. 'You look drop-dead gorgeous, and you've cut your hair, wow.'

'Thank you,' Sophie replied shyly.

Julie-Anne turned back to the table. 'Everyone, can I introduce you to Sophie Zhao.'

'Hi, I'm Paul, it's lovely to meet you, Sophie,' he said as he stood up, leant forward and kissed the back of her hand, triggering a bout of laughter around the table.

'Okay, leave her alone, Paul. Let me introduce you to the rest of the group, Sophie,' said Julie-Anne as she gestured to the others.

'Here you go, Sophie, there's a spare seat right here,' Paul said predictably, as he pulled back the chair immediately next to his own.

'Here we go everyone, now we're getting serious.' Jack said excitedly. The waiter had arrived at the table with a bottle of Veuve Clicquot and six frosted glasses. 'I thought we were entitled to celebrate in style after the tumultuous few weeks we've all had. In your own way, you have all played a part in a successful investigation and the arrest of numerous dangerous criminals, so you should feel proud of what we have all achieved.' Once the waiter had finished pouring the champagne Jack proposed a toast. 'If life brings you troubles drink some Champagne, then your troubles will just become bubbles. Here's to us everyone, cheers.'

'To us,' they chorused.

'Do you mind if I propose a toast to an absent friend?' Danielle asked the group. 'Not at all. It's a day for celebration, go ahead,' replied Paul.

'I would like to propose a toast to Michelle Ironside, my lovely boss and mentor. I'm just so thankful for her safe return.' Danielle raised her glass. 'To Michelle.'

The waiter returned to the table, presented everyone with a menu and announced the specials of the day. He then held up the wine list. 'Who would like to choose the wine?' he asked. Jack reached out, accepted the wine list and handed it to Danielle. *Of course,* thought Julie-Anne.

Inevitably, the conversation turned to the recently completed investigation, with each of them discussing their respective involvement. Eventually, the discussion turned to Danielle and her involvement. 'Well, I got myself into something illegal, but to my mind, for all the right reasons. My brother Ollie has a congenital heart condition which could conceivably require surgery one day, an operation my family simply won't be able to afford. Anyway, long story short, that horrible Mr Woodard offered me a way to financially assist the family in exchange for me aiding his criminal activities, and I fell for it.'

'Oh, no, that's a horrible scenario, Danielle,' said Melissa sympathetically. 'Really, Melissa,' said Julie-Anne, glaring at her.

Danielle picked-up on the tension between the two women, so she quickly continued her story. 'At the time, naïve me didn't realise his activities were criminal. Anyway, thanks to Jack, I was given an opportunity to redeem myself and I grabbed the lifeline with both hands. I was still charged with a money laundering offence, but my charges were downgraded to a manageable fine. As far as the casino goes, I have been demoted back to hospitality and placed on three months' probation. I am grateful I was able to keep my job, though.'

'How is your brother's health?' asked Melissa.

'He's on medication which seems to be working at the moment, but really it's a wait and see. Thank you for asking.'

The waiter returned and moved around the table, collecting everyone's food orders. 'Would anyone like oysters for a starter? We have lovely plump oysters from twelve different regions around Australia and you can have them either mignonette or simply drizzle them with lemon.'

'I would love some, you decide which region and just with lemon please,' gushed Danielle.

'I wouldn't have thought she would have needed them,' grumbled Julie-Anne.

'*Julie-Anne*,' Melissa said sternly.

'Has the young lady decided on the wine?' The waiter asked, addressing Danielle. 'Can we have a bottle of the Pierro LTC and a bottle of the Leeuwin Estate Art Series

'Shiraz please?'

'Excellent choices, if I may say so.'

'Oh puh-lease.' Julie-Anne mumbled with exasperation.

Melissa turned to face Julie-Anne and spoke quietly, 'I've never seen you behave like this before, what's got into you?'

'Everything seems to be about her today,' sighed Julie-Anne.

'Don't exaggerate. We've been here for less than an hour. The waiter was playing up to her, not vice versa. This is not the time or place to start developing insecurities, Julie-Anne. Anyway, she's appears slightly nervous to me so maybe she's just overcompensating.'

Sophie spoke for the first time, but she didn't really want to discuss her interactions with Li Qiang or Tony Woodard for that matter, so she deftly deflected the attention away from herself. 'Did anyone have the opportunity to read Julie-Anne's piece in the Daily News about the investigations and the links between the two? And Julie-Anne, you must have been delighted that it was the lead story on the front page, and above the fold, no less. I found it fascinating.'

Jack had filled JA in on all the details she needed to know to complete her story while on the drive from the safe house to her apartment in Newtown a week ago. She had recorded the conversation on her mobile phone to ensure she didn't miss any relevant information.

'I particularly liked the part where Julie-Anne subtly linked Michelle Ironside's abduction to the Chinese Consul General; that was very interesting,' Melissa offered.

Sophie politely waited for a pause in the conversation. 'Jack, do you mind if I ask you something please?'

'Of course. What would you like to know?'

'I am still concerned about my family back in Tong-Li. What will happen to Li?' she asked quietly.

'I have spoken to Li about your family in China, Sophie. I made it crystal clear to him, that if I find out he or anyone else threatens them, there will be serious consequences for him.' The other guests at the table were listening intently to Jack now. 'Li has been charged with money laundering offences, but unfortunately, that incurs a sentence at the lower end of the penalty scale. He tried to claim diplomatic immunity, but that was immediately rejected as an option by the Deputy Commissioner and the DPP. For now though, Li should be spending the best part of the next three years incarcerated. His visa has been cancelled and upon his release, he will be deported back to China.'

Sophie sighed with relief. 'That's wonderful to hear. Thank you, Jack.'

The waiter arrived with their lunch order.

'Okay, a little trivia for you while we eat. Who here can tell me what LTC stands for in the name of the white wine?' asked Jack addressing the table. Danielle knew the answer, but politely remained quiet.

'Come on, someone must know,' he implored.

'No idea, Jack,' said Paul, completely bemused.

'Anyone else? Julie-Anne, any ideas?' The words had hardly left his mouth when he realised his mistake.

'What about Long Term Commitment, Jack? That sounds appropriate to me.'

'Good try, JA.'

'Well, at least I tried, Jack,' she responded sarcastically. He knew exactly what she meant by her pointed and nuanced comeback, but he let it pass.

An uncomfortable silence had engulfed the table. 'It's quite straightforward really. Danielle?'

'A Little Touch of Chardonnay.' Danielle paused while blushing. 'It's added to the Semillon Sauvignon Blanc to give the wine a little more body,' she explained, self-consciously.

'Slightly nervous, did you say, Melissa? Hey Jack, you're good with acronyms,' Julie-Anne teased.

Uh oh, here we go, thought Melissa.

'I've got one for you. What does STG stand for?' Jack knew exactly where JA was going with this and he wasn't going to accommodate her again.

'I've got it already; STG is an acronym used in currency markets to designate Pounds Sterling,' Paul replied proudly. Julie-Anne ignored him and continued to glare across the table at Jack.

'Jack, any ideas?'

'That's an easy one JA: Swear To God.'

'You're just too clever, Jack,' said Melissa, knowing full-well that wasn't the answer Julie-Anne was mischievously searching for. She turned to Julie-Anne and gave her a dead stare. 'Don't you dare go there, girl,' she whispered.

Julie-Anne reluctantly heeded Melissa's advice. 'Sydney Theatre Group. See that wasn't hard at all, now was it?'

'How's your Snapper Pie, Paul?' Jack asked in an endeavour to change the topic of conversation.

'What, Jack?'

'How's your Snapper Pie?'

'Sorry, I got side-tracked; you're not going to believe what distracted me.'

'You're a copper, Paul, you'd notice everything within a hundred miles,' Jack laughed.

'Oh my God. The blonde woman with the tall guy walking through the restaurant towards us.'

'What about them, Paul?' Jack asked, wondering where this conversation was going. 'That's Bree Woodard, Tony Woodard's wife.'

'You're kidding.' Jack looked across and studied the woman.

Bree Woodard was wearing a short, floral patterned, sleeveless, pink summer dress with a plunging vee neck, which left little to the imagination. The man accompanying her was younger, with a tanned complexion and an athletic build. He was wearing a hot pink polo shirt, white tailored slacks and tan loafers. 'Look at her swanning through the restaurant and gushing at her young beau, Jack. What is he, her kid's tennis coach or something?' Paul snorted.

'Who are you guys looking at?' Julie-Anne asked, having noticed the dumbfounded expression on the men's faces.

Paul turned back to face the table. 'That woman is Tony Woodard's wife.'

Danielle and Sophie both knew Tony Woodard, but for vastly different reasons. 'You're kidding,' they said unconsciously in unison.

Bree Woodard appeared to be living up to Julie-Anne's impression of her. An impression formed from what she had seen on the woman's Facebook and Instagram pages when she was researching her husband. She had swapped the lifeguards for a tennis coach, but nothing else appeared to have changed. With her heavily manufactured appearance, attention-seeking flamboyance, and of course, having the puppies on parade, Bree Woodard was hard to miss.

'I love the killer heels,' Danielle gushed. 'I guess we now know how they were paid for too,' she offered.

'Ladies, if I may interrupt your very interesting fashion commentary.' Paul gently cajoled. 'Her husband is on remand, awaiting formal charges from the DPP and will inevitably be incarcerated for a number of years. All the while she's swanning round town with her toy boy,' he said with disgust. 'I won't spoil everyone's lunch now, but I'm going to say something to her later.'

Jack gave him a curious look. 'And what exactly are you going to say?'

'Oh, I don't know, maybe I'll start with, how's your husband doing?' replied Paul, grinning roguishly.

'Melissa, we haven't talked much about you. Do you have a tall, tanned, athletic type in your life?'

'Don't put Melissa on the spot, Paul,' Jack said, endeavouring to avoid the impending awkwardness.

'No, it's okay, Jack. It was an innocent question,' she said as she gave him a cheeky smile. 'As a matter of fact, I do, Paul,' she said with a twinkle in her eye. *This will be very interesting,* Jack thought. 'My partner is exactly as you described, tall, tanned and athletic. And, drop-dead gorgeous, too.' Julie-Anne slowly moved her hand onto Melissa's thigh in acknowledgement.

Melissa continued. 'Anyway, Paul, my partner is also the intelligent, thoughtful and knowledgeable type. Pretty sexy too, if I may say so.' Jack was becoming more uncomfortable with every word from Melissa and he knew she was having fun with this.

'He sounds like an interesting guy; I'd love to meet him sometime,' said Paul genuinely.

Julie-Anne was stirring inside again while listening to Melissa's flattery. Not bothering to compose herself, she turned her head, leaned into Melissa and kissed her on the lips.

'Have another glass of wine, Paul,' suggested Jack, changing the subject.

'It's a bit difficult when my foot's in my mouth, buddy,'

'Some detective you are.'

The four women at the table burst into laughter. 'Oh, Paul, if you could have seen your face then. It was like watching a human eclipse,' Sophie said as she leaned across and gave him a consoling pat on the back of his hand. 'It was an innocent enough comment, but we live in different times now, so you have to be careful with what you assume. Anyway, the girls took it in the right spirit, which says a lot about them. They're both great girls and I like them a lot. I like you as well, Paul. You're an interesting, funny guy and decidedly normal, which has been a rarity in my life lately. Are you sure you're really a detective?'

'Yeah, I'm a detective,' he said, laughing along with Sophie. 'You can imagine the things I experience in my job, so when I'm socialising I like to switch off, enjoy myself and I tend to make the most of it.'

'This is great fun, Jack; I'm really enjoying myself. Julie-Anne has been a bit cool, but everyone else is lovely.'

'In what way has she been cool, Danielle?'

'She hasn't smiled at me once and has mumbled a couple of comments she didn't think I would pick up on.'

'I haven't noticed anything.'

'You're such a boy, Jack,' she said as she stared at him fondly.

'Where have I heard that before?' he laughed. Jack turned back to the table. 'It looks like the staff want to reset the restaurant for dinner, so we better head off. Why don't we go back to my place and have a couple of drinks on the balcony?' Jack proposed.

'I'll be in that, Jackie boy,' Paul said enthusiastically.

'You're a given; I was asking the ladies.'

Julie-Anne still had fond memories from a couple of weeks earlier in regard to Jack's balcony, but given the changed circumstances, she wasn't keen to return.

'That's kind of you. I've heard about your balcony, Jack.' Melissa said innocently. Jack turned to JA and gave her a curious look, as if to say; *what did you tell her*?

'Jack's balcony backs onto native bushland and it's very private and just so tranquil. You'll love it,' enthused Danielle. Julie-Anne gave Jack a withering return look that said, *surely not, not her as well*.

As they rose from the table, Paul turned to the group, 'I'll meet you at the front door. I've got something to attend to first.'

'Maybe use the other foot this time.' Jack called out. Sophie remembered the earlier conversation, and, also not wanting to be the fifth wheel in the remainder of the group, said, 'I'll keep you company.' She linked her arm inside Paul's and accompanied him toward a table farther along the window.

'Hello, Mrs. Woodard, how are you?' Paul enquired. Sophie eagerly watched on as the colour drained from the woman's face.

'I'm sorry, but do I know you?' she asked, feigning ignorance.

'Yes, we met earlier this week in the city. Paul Jamieson,' he said, as he offered the woman his hand in greeting.

'Oh, yes, of course. This is Todd Leverson,' she said, trying to divert the conversation. 'Hello, Detective Paul Jamieson, pleased to meet you, Todd,' he said, accentuating the word detective as he offered his hand in greeting.

Sophie watched Bree Woodard's face redden from embarrassment at Paul's formal introduction.

'Mrs. Woodard, Todd, this is Sophie Zhao.'

'Pleased to meet you.' Sophie was particularly interested in the woman, the woman who was married to a guy who had been so presumptuous, and crude with her a couple of weeks earlier. She wondered if either of them had really known the other.

'Have you heard from Tony?' Paul asked in a spritely tone.

'Yes, I spoke to him two days ago and he's doing well,' she said, recovering quickly.

'You must be pleased for him then, Mrs. Woodard,' he prodded.

'Yes, I am. He seems to be taking everything in his stride, as always.'

'That's good to hear. It seems you are as well,' he goaded. Bree Woodard glared at him, but remained silent.

'Well, we will leave you two lovebirds to enjoy your day,' said Paul provocatively again. I just wanted to say hello.'

'Nice to meet you both,' said Sophie, as she turned to join Paul. She hooked her arm into his again and they walked away smiling.

'What was that all about, Bree? Why were you meeting with a detective? And who's Tony?'

'Shut up, Todd, just shut up,' she said as she stabbed angrily at a seared scallop.

(102)

Balmain Inner West Sydney

'Hi,' Sophie said as she walked up beside Julie-Anne and leant on the balcony railing. 'You seem to have been out here for a while, so I thought I would keep you company. Are you thinking about Jack?'

Julie-Anne looked at her with surprise. 'Why on earth would you ask that, Sophie?'

'Well, you told me about him that day up at Dolphins Point and I thought then, why would an AFP detective be sharing information with a journalist? And then today, I overheard you make a couple of comments at lunch about Danielle, which I, rightly or wrongly, took for resentment or jealously. And then you were obviously baiting Jack with the acronym question. How'd I do, Julie-Anne?'

'You should be in psychology, Sophie,' she said with a stifled laugh. 'Well, today was the first time I have seen them together and I guess it just came as a bit of a shock.'

'They seem happy together, as do you and Melissa.'

'Yes, they do, and we are too, Sophie. Two weeks ago, I was out here on this very balcony having a wonderful time with Jack, and now we both have new people in our lives. How does that happen, and so quickly?'

Sophie chuckled. 'I'm not sure you should be asking an escort who got tangled up with the likes of Li Qiang for relationship advice.'

'I know, it wasn't meant to be a question; I was just thinking out aloud.'

'So, do you mind if I ask what happened, Julie-Anne?'

'There's not a lot to explain, really. Jack and I were cruising along; no, more drifting aimlessly along for about six months. We were both so focused on our careers; Jack more so than me. We always had fun together, but I seemed to be the one putting the time and effort into the relationship, if that's what it was. Then one night Melissa walked into my life and I was immediately attracted to her. Apart from an innocent kiss, nothing happened that night. The following day Jack did something that greatly disappointed me, and I guess I pulled back somewhat. From then on, I started spending more time with Melissa, as I guess Jack did with Danielle.'

Sophie stirred her drink and then looked up at Julie-Anne. 'I became aware earlier today at lunch that I recognised her from somewhere.'

'Who, Sophie?' enquired Julie-Anne.

'Danielle. The moment I first saw her at The Boathouse this afternoon I thought; where do I know you from? And it finally came to me.'

'Okay, do tell,' Julie-Anne said too eagerly while wondering whether her jealously was getting the better of her emotions again?

'She was walking out of the Golden Phoenix restaurant in Chinatown one day when I was walking in with Li. As you yourself so obviously noticed today, she's hard to miss. She was by herself; I didn't know her then, so I never thought anything of it. Then Li and I walked over to a table where a good looking, smartly dressed Asian man was seated.'

'Wie Ping Lie.'

'How did you know that, Julie-Anne?'

'I've met him too, and given what I now know of him, I don't want to encounter him again.'

'Anyway, when Danielle walked in today I recognised her face from somewhere. It took me a while to remember where from though. Eventually it came to me. And, knowing what I do now about the whole money laundering investigation and its participants, I'm wondering, whether she was Wie Ping Lie's lunch guest.'

'Jesus, Sophie, that would open a whole new can of worms, especially for Jack, both professionally and personally.'

'I know, but unfortunately, or fortunately, I can't definitively say she was actually with Wie Ping Lie.'

'One part of me would really like to tell Jack, probably all for the wrong reasons, but I realise that's not fair,' Julie-Anne lamented. 'My mind is also going at a million miles an hour now over another possible investigation or whether there could be a postscript to the recently completed story we published. And, I'm just like Jack, I don't believe in coincidences either.

Coincidences are God's way of remaining anonymous.' 'Aaahh, quoting Einstein, Julie-Anne?'

'I just knew you would know that, Sophie. Anyway, I have unfinished business with Wie Ping Lie after he had his cronies tried to kill me.' Julie-Anne paused while reflecting on her near-miss in Raglan Street.

Sophie noticed a tear form in the corner of her friend's eye. 'Are you okay, Julie-Anne?' 'Yeah, sure. Sophie, maybe you could talk to Danielle and quietly tell her you remember seeing her at the Golden Phoenix and see how she responds.'

'Yes, I could, but tonight is supposed to be a celebration, so I think it's best left for another day. I don't want to potentially ruin the evening for everyone. Maybe you should raise it with Jack another time.'

'Yes, maybe I will at that.'

'Hi girls, what's happening out here?' asked Melissa, as she breezed out onto the balcony with a glass of champagne in her hand.

'We were just celebrating Sophie and Paul's new friendship,' Julie-Anne teased.

'Oh stop that,' Sophie replied bashfully.

'Oh, you noticed that too,' Melissa kidded.

'Girls, please! I'm going to leave you two comediennes and go mingle.'

Melissa was looking up at the stars shining brightly against the black sky. 'What a beautiful evening.'

'Yes, I know, I love it out here.' Julie-Anne replied without thinking.

'Of course, I forgot you've been here before. If I remember correctly, this is your outdoor tanning salon.'

Julie-Anne realised she had made Melissa feel ill at ease with her reference to Jack's balcony. 'I would prefer to be on your deck with you though, Melissa.'

'Nice recovery and impeccable timing, Julie-Anne.'

'Yeah, I dug myself out of that little hole just in time hey.' The women laughed happily together.

Wanting to change the subject, Melissa asked, 'so how do you feel about the past couple of weeks?'

'What do you mean, regarding you and I or the investigation?'

'Well, both I guess,' said Melissa tentatively.

'As far as the investigation goes, Chris, my editor is happy with what we published and the readership was up significantly, as were the clicks on the paper's website, so that's all good. I will write a follow-up once the court cases begin.' Julie-Anne wasn't going to mention Sophie's revelation about Danielle at this stage for fear of Melissa having misgivings about her motives.

'That's good for you and your career.'

'Yeah, I think so too. Luckily, Chris affords me quite a bit of latitude with my investigations, but in this competitive media landscape, I will need to move onto the next one, and quickly.'

'Do you have anything in particular in mind?'

'As a matter of fact I do. Remember, I told you about Wie Ping Lie at my place last week. Well, he has managed to avoid serious scrutiny this time around, but I'm going to take a closer look at him. And, I owe him for trying to have me killed and I'm sure his cocaine trade is still flourishing, so he's next on my list.' *And Miss Bright and Breezy might just be a good place to start,* she thought. 'And, I can't help but think that the Chinese will keep seeking to influence the political discourse in this country, and as such, they will be on the lookout for another candidate as a priority. And, I just know that candidate will be financed by Wie Ping Lie's drug activities.'

'Good for you, Julie-Anne, but remember what Jack told you. You need to be careful around Wie. He won't be happy at all about losing two of his drug-running lieutenants, he could easily link that to your investigation as well, and if he does, that could place you in danger again.'

'Yeah, I know, you're right, Melissa, but I owe him big time for what he put me through in Raglan Street, so I'm not backing off.'

'And, what about us?'

'We're all good aren't we?' Julie-Anne queried.

'That's not quite the response I was hoping for. We've spent significant time together over the past two weeks, particularly being confined together at the safe house, but now we'll go back to our normal lives. The relationship dynamic might be different as a result. And, your infatuation with Danielle at lunch concerns me. She seems like a fun person, so I can only assume your behaviour towards her was related to your feelings for Jack. How am I doing so far Julie-Anne?'

'I don't know what to say, Melissa. You know I'm very fond of you and we are great together.'

'That's a start, Julie-Anne.' *Here comes the but though.*

'I was as surprised as you were at my conduct towards Danielle at lunch, it's just not who I am.'

'I thought we were discussing *us*, not Danielle,' Melissa said. She guessed where this conversation was leading and began to feel sad.

'Even though I thought there might be something going on between them, I think it just came as a shock to see Jack with another woman, particularly someone so damn gorgeous. And, they seem so darned happy together too,' Julie-Anne said trying to suppress the jealousy bubbling away in her head.

'So, you left Jack because he hurt your feelings and violated your trust, but now he's with a gorgeous young woman, you want him back. And you're thinking; why isn't that me? Does that just about cover it, Julie-Anne?'

'It's not that simple.'

'We've just spent the best part of a week confined together and I got the distinct impression that we really enjoyed each other's company, intellectually, emotionally and physically. And, I also thought, obviously mistakenly, that our relationship was actually blooming and strengthening. So, I think I'm entitled to an explanation as to the reasons behind your sudden misgivings, Julie-Anne,' argued Melissa.

'It's not so much misgivings, Melissa.'

'Then what is it?'

'Maybe I walked away too quickly, maybe I was hurt, maybe I judged him too harshly, maybe I should have given Jack the benefit of the doubt, maybe we were actually going somewhere. I don't know,' she said wistfully.

'Well, Julie-Anne, that's waaaay too many maybes for me. I like who I am, I'm comfortable in my own skin, I'm a very giving person, I think I'm a pretty good catch, I know what I want from a partner and I certainly know what I want out of this wonderful life. No *maybes* in there. You were right in what you said that night at my apartment. This did become complicated,' Melissa said resolutely through misty eyes. 'But not by me.'

Julie-Anne turned to face Melissa, noticed a tear on her cheek and reached for her hand.

Melissa stepped back.

'You really need to decide who or what you want in this life, Julie-Anne. You won't be able to move forward until you do. And *maybe* just won't cut it. In the meantime I'm going to call an Uber.'

'Ladies, how are my two favourite pillow princesses?' Jack asked as he stumbled over the door trim and almost face planted onto the balcony deck.

'Just wonderful, Jack, great timing,' Melissa grumbled. 'Good luck, Julie-Anne. Goodbye Jack. I'll see myself out.'

'What did I say, where's she going, why's she leaving, JA?' Jack slurred.

Julie-Anne was torn between going after Melissa and remaining on the balcony. She knew why. 'Oh, poor naïve Jack. I'll be back in a minute; I'm going to grab another drink and get drunk, too.'

Julie-Anne walked back out onto the balcony and gazed up into the night sky. 'Do you remember the last time we were out here on the balcony?'

Jack placed his thumb and index finger on his face and struck the thinking pose. 'I reckon I'll get this; hang on, it's on the tip of my tongue.'

'You're still a funny man, Jack Wagner.'

They had both consumed considerable quantities of alcohol throughout the afternoon and evening and he was well on his way to cultivating a hangover. They were both quiet for some time, leaning over the railing, staring out into the darkness and enjoying the serenity. Eventually Jack broke the silence. 'I could stay out here forever but it's getting a tad on the chilly side.'

'Where's blondie?'

'She headed home a while ago.' Hmmm, thought Julie-Anne.

'I've had enough to drink for one day, so I'm going to hit the sack, JA. Do you want me to book you an Uber?'

This was the moment. Julie-Anne had become excited at the memory of their last interlude on this very balcony and was wondering if Jack was feeling the same. She knew what lay beneath his fitted linen shirt and dress jeans, memories of his naked, athletic body flooding back. Her insides were stirring again. He had offered to book her an Uber, so his thought process was obviously heading in a different direction, unless of course he was just being a gentleman.

Which was it, she couldn't tell by his expression, or lack of it. Did she risk embarrassment and ask him if she could stay or should she just raincheck herself. She opted for the middle ground and subtly deflected the question. 'Yeah, I suppose you could,' she replied, leaving the comment hanging out there.

Epilogue. AMSA Control Room Canberra
Thursday 14ᵗʰ May

Three hundred kilometres to the south west of Sydney, James Fairweather was once again sitting at his desk in the secure monitoring room of the national headquarters of the Australian Maritime Safety Authority. Two months after having proved his worth as an analyst by alerting his boss and the MBC officers to the illicit activities of the Chinese Horizon, he was still the only operator in attendance on the night shift. He remembered a thought from that time, *Analysts used their brains, monitors used their eyes.* James was hoping that an analyst opportunity would open up within AMSA following his Chinese Horizon success, but he also knew the wheels of government turned slowly. So, here he was again, sitting in front of the seven screens that showed the location and movements of over four hundred commercial vessels operating within Australia's Exclusive Economic Zone.

Given the China Shipping Company was the owner of the Chinese Horizon, all analysts had been instructed to closely monitor all ships owned by the CSC. James had flagged all five CSC vessels in Australian waters from the time they each had entered the EEZ and was now monitoring their progress diligently.

'What is she doing so close to the coastline?' He murmured to himself. Early into his shift he noticed that one of the CSC vessels was positioned a few kilometres off the coast from Townsville, adjacent to Magnetic Island in north Queensland. The Marine Traffic website

had the Chinese Panorama listed as travelling from Qingdao in north-eastern China to Brisbane. If it was heading for Brisbane via the traditional navigational routes, then she should have been about three hundred nautical miles further east.

Surely not again ...

Acknowledgments

Thank you to Jochem Groeneveld, Nat Sikora and Claire Malcolmson for making the time to read and critique the draft version of Uncharted Waters many moons ago and for providing your valuable feedback and encouragement. It was, and is appreciated.

A big shout out to 'my fave neighbour' Loretta Farrelly for listening to my endless ramblings and for continually enquiring about the book's progress and showing her genuine and boundless enthusiasm.

As a first time author this was a steep learning curve, particularly with the key technical aspects of writing and I am grateful to my editor, Steph Huddlestone for her knowledge and guidance. Thanks Steph.

With extremely limited opportunities available in the market for new authors to be considered by the traditional publishing houses I was delighted after days and weeks of extensive research to come across Shawline Publishing. Particularly as a first time author without any publishing industry experience the one stop shop was just what I was seeking, and desperately needed. I will always be grateful for the support and opportunity afforded to me. A big thank you to Brad Shaw and his team.

About the Author

Peter Cruskall has been an avid reader of contemporary fiction for many years. He has read in excess of five hundred books in the past decade particularly from such globally successful authors as James Patterson, Lee Child, David Baldacci, Tara Moss and Stella Rimington. In early 2020, being semi-retired, and with Melbourne plunged into lockdown, Peter needed to discover new activities to occupy his time and maintain his sanity. He decided to challenge himself, put pen to paper and embark on a new journey as an author. Uncharted Waters is his first book along that journey.

Shawline Publishing Group Pty Ltd
www.shawlinepublishing.com.au